BEHIND

the

MASK

THE ASSOCIATES:
BOOK FOUR

Carolyn Crane

To my readers, each and every one of you on your own mad, wild, beautiful journey.

CHAPTER ONE

Miami

Zelda rooted through her twin sister Liza's suitcase; the thing was pink and orange and studded with rhinestones in true Liza style. It squeezed Zelda's heart.

Zelda would carry it now. She'd do whatever it took to save her sister.

Liza brought over a pair of fuck-me heels, looking apologetic. Liza had looked apologetic a lot over the past twelve hours. "They're a little crazy, but it's what I'd wear," Liza said.

Zelda took them and ran her finger over one spiked heel, thankful for the closed toes. She didn't want Liza to see her toes. The men she needed to fool definitely couldn't see them.

"Mikos knows they're my favorites, though," Liza continued. "It's what I'd wear on a day like this. To make myself feel better...*you know.*" This last in an angry whisper.

Zelda nodded, glad Mikos would recognize the shoes. A strong visual cue went a long way toward fooling people, and she'd need all the help she could get during the twenty-minute limo ride to the airport. Even an active field agent would have a hard time fooling a shrewd and paranoid drug dealer like Mikos, and Zelda was six years retired.

Liza insisted that Mikos had no idea she had a twin, but you had to expect the worst.

"You probably can't walk in them."

"Oh, I can walk in them." Zelda had walked in plenty of shoes like that. She put them aside and grabbed the bottle of red nail polish and shook it, feeling like she might actually throw up. When she looked up next, she found her twin watching her, pretty lips parted, eyes sparkling. The look brought her straight back to their childhood.

They hadn't spoken for years, but in some ways, it was as if she'd seen Liza just yesterday. "When you were a *spy*, you mean? You would wear shoes like this when you were a fucking spy? Because, fuck, Zelda!"

"Field agent," Zelda corrected for the umpteenth time.

"Fuck," Liza said. "You were out chasing bad guys in different countries and wearing disguises and stuff, so I'm going with spy. All this time I thought you were a botanist, and instead you're this spy?"

"I was still doing some botany as an agent." Plants could tell you a lot, like whether a body had been moved and how long it had been there. Forensic botany was how she got into the CIA.

"So wild." Liza was impressed. She shouldn't be; a lot of spying, especially for the female agents, was done on your back. She and Liza hadn't turned out so differently after all.

"I'm best behind a desk," Zelda mumbled, although the truth was that she'd loved being in the field, loved being out there making a difference. Until a good agent had been killed because of her.

"You used to say the CIA did bad things. When we were in high school? Remember? You always had so many opinions on everything."

"All the more reason to get involved. If you don't like something, change it, right?" She was shaking the nail polish again, way too vigorously. She forced herself to put it down. "Tell me the limo ride like a movie. How you see it going in your mind."

"I'll show you." Liza sat on the couch, draping a hand over the back and crossing her legs. Her pose was relaxed, cool, and angry all at once. "Because this is how I feel. Pissed. But not beaten. Don't sit up all straight and attentive, like you are right now, or he'll suspect. This kind of sitting says, 'I'm fun. I'm the joy in your life, and you ruined it.' That's how I would be to make him feel bad for handing me over to some creep." Liza shifted, looking relaxed and elegant now. "The way you take up space changes everything."

God, that big attitude. That had always been the beauty of Liza—the wild, fabulous twin.

Again Zelda picked up the bottle of nail polish and shook it, wondering if she could put it on without trembling. She'd need to make up some excuse about why she didn't put it on her toes.

"Or this." Liza shifted into another pose. Liza always had a knack for transforming herself into the picture of leisure fun.

Zelda didn't actually need this lesson. She had Liza down cold—they used to switch places all the time, but Liza needed to feel like she was contributing.

"Mikos will want to fuck in the back of the limo," Liza continued, "but under no circumstances would I fuck him. He feels bad—he won't press it. I loved him. If he tries anything, you tell him, 'I'm not a fucking poker chip to be lost in a card game. Some possession to be gambled away like cattle.'" The tears were starting now. It broke Zelda's heart. Through all the trouble between them, all the hell of Liza's drug addiction, she'd never stopped loving her sister.

"Okay, let me try." Zelda changed her posture and mimicked Liza's smooth tone. "I'm not a fucking poker chip to be lost in a card game like cattle, Mikos. Some possession to gamble away. So fuck you," she added.

"Exactly. Motherfucker." Liza grabbed a tissue and dabbed her eyes.

"Here—help me with this." Zelda held out the nail polish.

Liza tossed the tissue and took the bottle, sniffling as she unscrewed the top. She grabbed hold of Zelda's fingers. "You're shaking."

"Too much caffeine."

Liza smiled uncertainly. Could she tell that Zelda had no business going back into the field? It wasn't just about being out of practice. It was about what happened with Friar Hovde. It was about getting Agent Randall killed. It was about the way guilt operated in the heart of an agent, every bit as lethal as a ticking time bomb.

Liza drew a thick, gleaming swath of red over Zelda's fingernail. "I'm so sorry."

"Stop apologizing."

"I'm done with all that life, I promise," Liza said. "I really promise this time—I won't fuck up on you again. I'm so, so sorry—"

"Stop it. Look at me."

Liza finished a nail and lifted her gaze.

"I'm your sister, okay? And seriously, this is a gift. Do you know how great it is to get inside that cartel right now? Inside Brujos's ugly, stupid palace? We're going to get something we desperately need because of you."

Liza looked dubious, but it was true. The Association had never been able to get on the inside with Brujos and infiltrate his cartel. The timing couldn't be better. A nice, juicy file full of damaging intel on Brujos was a bargaining chip they could use to prevent a serious disaster that was brewing on the other side of the equator.

"Easy in and out," Zelda said. Instantly, she regretted her choice of words. They both knew she might have to fuck a few bad men before the thing was done. "It's so nothing," she added.

"*So nothing.*" Liza frowned and concentrated on the nails. "You are so full of shit."

Zelda used Liza's voice. "You are so full of shit."

"God, you're me." Liza moved on to another nail. "Fucking Mikos. He could've sent a runner to get a million bucks to put in the pot, you know?" She sniffed. "A million is nothing to Mikos. He promised me he'd win the hand. He was so sure. And suddenly all the guys are throwing down their cards, and Mikos goes, 'I'll have her on a plane in twenty-four hours.' Like I'm a kilo or something. On a plane to fucking Mexico. We were going to be married."

Zelda nodded. She hadn't said it, but she didn't believe Mikos would have married Liza. She'd known a lot of guys like Mikos. Guys like that would say anything. You could never let yourself feel warm toward them.

Liza's eyes went to the track marks on Zelda's arm. Temporary tattoos. They'd stay on there at least two weeks. "Fuck," she said.

"Stop it. We're good. Okay?" Zelda stared into her eyes. It was like looking in a mirror—that was how completely she and Zelda had switched appearances.

Liza moved on to the other hand. Just hours ago, they'd colored Liza's crazy bright platinum blonde hair brown, and they'd dyed Zelda's dark brown hair platinum. They'd trimmed Liza's hair to match Zelda's cut, and now they both had shoulder-length hair. Liza had styled Zelda's bright new hair all Marilyn Monroe. "You'll just say you got a cut for your stint as a cartel leader's whore," Liza had said bitterly. "I would totally do something like that."

"Good. Perfect," Zelda said. "Perfect."

Zelda and various IT guys had erased the link between Zelda and her family many years ago—way back when Zelda had joined the CIA. The idea had always been to protect Liza, not to mention their mother and father in their pretty little home in Okinawa. Now the erased link would protect Zelda; nobody could know she was a twin.

"I can't believe you're an agent."

"Retired," Zelda said. "And I can't believe you wouldn't come to me with this."

Silence.

Stupid question. Because why would she come to Zelda after Zelda had ejected her from her life? Zelda had used her connections to bail Liza out of jams over the years, but the last time had jeopardized her CIA career. It was then she'd gone the tough-love route, telling her she couldn't help her as long as she was using drugs. Yeah, it had to happen, but it had never felt much like love.

"Brujos is a horrible man," Liza said. "I've met him."

"I'll just have to be more horrible. If he's not careful, I may have to put soap on his motherfucking toothbrush. See how he likes that."

Liza snorted. Soap on the toothbrush was a mean move from teen days gone by. "You always tried to protect me, Zelda. Remember that time when the kids were squishing poison berries in my hair by the swing? You were like a shining warrior. I should've known you'd fight for right. You always tried to protect everyone. You always had a passion that way—a passion for justice."

Zelda smiled wistfully. Passion for justice wasn't enough, unfortunately. Nobody in their right mind would put her in the field now.

But nobody could stop her. That was one of the advantages of helping to head up the secretive and powerful Association—nobody told them what to do. No officials. No governments. No corporations. She and Dax sent their agents—the Associates—on dangerous missions every day, taking down international criminals and terrorists, preventing flare-ups and massacres. Only fair that she'd be willing to get out there and risk herself.

In and out. It would be easy. Nothing.

Zelda looked longingly at the glasses Liza now wore. *Her* glasses. Zelda hadn't worn contacts since her field agent days, and of course, Liza couldn't have normal contacts. They had to be an insane shade of green—dazzling with the bleached hair. Their mother was Japanese; their father of mostly European ancestry. This mix of genes had allowed

Zelda to pass for different ethnicities in global hot spots in her agent days, though she'd never gone quite so blonde.

"I have something for you." Liza closed up the nail polish and handed her a small paper sack. Zelda took it and looked inside. Blue and yellow Jelly Belly jelly beans.

"Oh, Liza." The blues were blueberry, and the yellows were buttered popcorn. When you put two blueberries with one popcorn, you got a blueberry muffin. It was Zelda's favorite candy, what she always got after doing something successful, a childhood habit. "But I only get to eat these after a mission is accomplished."

"I'm not going on to a plane right now to be prostituted to Brujos," Liza said, "because you're taking my place. Because of your bravery. Because you saved me. Mission accomplished."

Zelda crinkled the small bag, tears heating her eyes. She spoke without looking up. "You'll stay in that safe house, right? Don't listen to anybody outside of my guys. You'll be bored—"

"I know, I know," Liza said. "Don't worry. I'm ready. I want a boring, simple life."

A phone beeped. It was time.

"If anything happens to you..."

"Nothing will." Zelda whispered. "I'll go in there and do my job, and the intelligence I gather will be a gift. And you know what else?"

"What?"

"After this, I'll personally make sure the only job Mikos can get is licking trash cans at a Buck 'n Burger."

Liza smiled, tears shining like diamonds in her deep brown eyes.

CHAPTER TWO

Zelda stood in front of the hotel waiting for Mikos's limo, clutching the handle of Liza's bejeweled suitcase full of her crazy outfits and some cleverly disguised equipment. Business travelers streamed in and out of the hotel, ready for their meetings and presentations, everything perfectly predictable.

She closed her eyes. *Stop it.*

The worst thing an agent could do was to dwell on the possibility of unpredictability, of danger, of failure. But when you were a failed agent, failure was all you thought about.

All you have to do is last, she told herself, scanning the street.

Just last. It had become her mantra over the past few years. *Just get through it.* She kind of hated that she'd developed a phrase like that. Because really, what was *just last?* Gum stuck on the bottom of a table could *just last.*

But she needed it now. She'd use everything to get through this. She'd pull it out for Liza.

A man absorbed in his phone moved into her periphery. He was waiting for a taxi, or so he would have it seem. He spoke without looking up. "Nice day for a limo ride."

"You've got to be kidding," she hissed through her teeth. *Clears the mind* was the response he was looking for: the all-clear signal their organization used. "I'm not saying it. What are you doing here?"

He waited.

"Clears the mind," she grumbled.

"Mikos was detained. There'll just be the driver now."

So. Dax had created an emergency to keep Mikos out of that limo.

Zelda quelled the impulse to react angrily. He was trying to help her—she knew that. But couldn't he see that this last-minute help just showed that he didn't trust her to pull this whole thing off? They'd run the Associates together for years now. He should realize this. She took a breath. "That works," she said, in the way a strong agent would reply.

"We located a body—same age as you and your sister. Car crash—"

"Oh, right, that wouldn't be suspicious," she said sarcastically. "Liza miraculously dies in a car crash the hour before being whored out to some monster. That exposes our contacts and our machinery—and you know it, Dax. You *know* it."

"Putting yourself in harm's way—"

"Stop it," she said. "Seriously. I'm not doing this again,

and especially not out here."

"What is that old saying? Shame splits you into two people deep down; the one who wants to get free of it and feel good again, and the one who believes only death can set you free."

Zelda smiled. If she became reactive, he'd think he was right—that going on this mission was half death wish. "With any other Associate, we'd see that as a plus," she said.

Dax didn't reply. He knew it was true. Look behind the best spies, and you'd find plenty of darkness.

"This solves something big," she continued. "Does this not solve something big?" She paused, letting the rhetorical question hang. "How many lives are we talking about?"

A man in a white suit got out of a white Mercedes. A valet walked up and took his key.

"Is white the favorite color of everyone in Miami?" she asked. "All the fabulous blues around here with the sky and ocean, but they all go for white."

"Zelda—"

"I'm the only one who can do this. I'll have the run of the mansion," she added. "It's a no-brainer."

"I don't like the odds."

"We never like the odds," she said.

Dax was usually the one to sacrifice compassion. He always argued that any Associate was expendable if his death saved lives. Dax worked on numbers like that—one life for the many. And she was taking perverse pleasure in smacking him down with his own arguments. Not a lot of people won an argument with Dax.

"I'll get those files," she said.

The files were key to saving a lot of lives. They would

serve as bargaining chips to defuse a nasty standoff on the South American coast. "Or have you found something else to bargain with? A bargaining chip that's somehow more tantalizing than those files?"

"There's always another bargaining chip."

"Any other Associate, and you'd be 100 percent behind this mission. The only problem we have here is you standing there looking like an amateur PI from an Elmore Leonard novel. You haven't touched your phone in, like, forever. God, swipe or tap already!"

He tapped his phone. Dax had never been an agent. He was the brains behind each mission: the big-picture thinker.

"Everybody is expendable," she said, trying not to smile. Because that's what Dax always said.

"Though some people feel more expendable than others."

That hit. Dax was her best friend, and he could hit a target inside her like nobody else. He had no conscience—not like regular people, anyway. His lack of conscience made him dangerous, unless he was on your team. When he was on your team, his lack of conscience made him effective.

"I don't plan on dying," she said smoothly. "I need to be able to come back to lord this whole thing over your head. Here it is, finally—the day you suggested one *couldn't* be expended for the many. I will never stop giving you shit about it. I will make you so sorry, my friend."

His lips quirked in a half smile. "I look forward to it."

She snorted. A flash of black appeared down the road. "Here we go," she whispered.

The limo pulled up to the curb, gleaming in the sun. Zelda's heart pounded as Bernie, the driver, got out and came around to open the door.

The backseat was empty.

"Where's Mikos?" she demanded in Liza's emotional tone.

"Called away," Bernie grunted.

She gave Dax a quick glance as she slid in, sitting in that Liza style, getting into character. *I'm medium friendly with Bernie the driver, but not at all a pal,* Liza had said.

Bernie shut the door.

She winked at Dax through the window as Bernie went around to the driver's seat. A little private joke. Dax hated winking. His brown Armani suit looked great with his dark hair. He'd head back into that hotel and find a stranger to fuck within ten minutes. Maybe five, looking like that. Hopefully nobody too crazy, though. She wasn't the only one who needed worrying about.

Bernie guided the limo slowly away from the curb.

"A meeting? He couldn't postpone that?" It felt good to vent. She really was pissed off on Liza's behalf. Mikos saw her as a possession to be gambled away, nothing much more than a prostitute, but he'd said he'd see her off. He could've at least done that much.

Bernie drove on, silent and uncomfortable.

"Is this an inconvenient time for him to send his fiancée off to slimy Brujos?" she pressed. Liza would do this—let out a torrent of emotion.

"Something came up with the Baja line. An unexpected accident. I was there when he got the call." Bernie met her gaze, finally, in the rearview mirror. "I swear it, Liza."

She sat back, breathing deeply to calm her nerves.

When they arrived at the airport, Bernie actually parked the limo in short-term parking and walked her to security. Liza had said Bernie wasn't at all a pal, but Liza didn't understand how people took to her. Bernie felt sorry about sending her to Brujos—it was all over his face. He stuck out a hand. "Good luck, Liza."

Zelda took his hand. "Thanks, Bernie."

She watched him walk off. They'd know if she didn't get on the plane, of course. Mikos and Brujos had eyes everywhere.

Just yesterday, right about the time Zelda had been enjoying a late lunch at her favorite Manhattan bistro, Liza had gone to the DEA, begging for protection in exchange for providing information on trafficking routes, trying to get out of being sent to Brujos. Luckily, the right person had recognized her resemblance to Zelda and had gotten Zelda involved, and they'd yanked Liza the hell out of there before anything went further. Liza would be dead by now if they hadn't pulled her out then and there, because it was true—the cartel guys had people everywhere, including the DEA and the US Marshals. Liza wouldn't have been safe even if they'd agreed to give her witness protection, which they likely wouldn't have.

The plane boarded an hour later. Zelda found her seat between two guys with bad cases of macho leg-spread, which she immediately handled by grabbing both their knees and simply relocating them. "Got plans for my space," she said sweetly. Yeah, she was going on a dangerous mission with a blown mind-set, and she damn well wasn't going to tolerate leg- spread. People taking advantage. Guys hardly ever leg-spread her when she was cool, powerful Zelda in an awesome business suit, but they would for blonde Liza in a too-tight metallic gold skirt suit. Thinking they could take advantage because of the way she was dressed? She was fighting for Liza in every way now.

That was one of the great things about being in the CIA—bringing down an asshole or two at the end of most missions. That's really what most criminals were—assholes.

The Association brought down criminals, too, but with more freedom and precision. She sometimes had the idea that if they could take down enough baddies, the balance sheet would finally agree, and she could stop feeling like shit for letting Friar Hovde get Agent Randall's name out of her. Friar Hovde with his little beard, giant eyes, and his end-of-the-world church with all their weapons. If only she'd held out. If only she'd been stronger.

Stop it.

She flipped open the fashion magazine she'd brought and pulled out her slim copy of *Medicinal Wild Plants of the Prairie: An Ethnobotanical Guide,* which she'd hidden inside. Her seatmates were obviously civilians; she didn't have to playact in front of them and nobody else would see. She'd read a brainy book if she wanted.

She'd never set out to be in the CIA; she'd consulted on a case as a turfgrass expert and had fallen in love with forensic botany. And then she got deeper. A lot of agents got in sideways like that.

The time flew by. It seemed like she'd barely begun reading when the tray-tables-in-upright-positions announcement came on. She ditched the magazine with a sigh.

A driver waited at a prearranged spot outside the Cancún airport. It was a bumpy three-hour ride to Brujos's narcotecture palace.

Impossible to get into. Until now.

Zelda's blood raced as they entered his town—his territory. They passed through a checkpoint layered with barbed wire and manned with armed guards, and then another. Finally, they headed up a drive toward a building with candy-colored turrets. She reminded herself how missions always got easier once she was in the flow. Beforehand was always the worst.

The Jeep stopped. She opened her own door and stepped out with her suitcase. A pair of guards came down the steps. One gave her a pat-down while the other rifled through her suitcase, right there on the drive. She and Dax had expected a thorough search.

The guard took her phone. That, too, she expected, though she didn't much like it.

The other guard pulled out a vibrator and sneered. She frowned, giving him Liza's haughty I-don't-give-a-shit look. He put it back without question.

That, too, they'd expected. The thumb drive was hidden there. The suitcase was repacked, and an elderly maid waiting at the door escorted her into a foyer full of lavishly carved wood and stone. She managed to press a parabolic microphone under a table while she waited, a little something that wouldn't register on the most sophisticated equipment. A lot of business was transacted in foyers. Coming-and-going business, they called it.

Another maid appeared and guided her up a winding staircase and into a small bedroom. The maid spoke only

Spanish. Zelda spoke Spanish fluently, but not Liza. She was Liza now, so their conversation consisted of gestures. The maid pointed to a little pile of red and white fabric on the bed and then at her. She was to put that on.

She lifted the top. *Really?* She wanted to say. *Seriously?* But that wasn't the attitude she needed, so she pressed her lips together and pretended to inspect it.

The sexy maid.

Stunning how little men's fantasies changed from one country to the next, from one year to the next.

Brujos wouldn't hurt her—that had been part of the bargain with Mikos. But he'd want to make it hard in order to get the most out of his win—the outfit would be part of that. He'd fuck her and demoralize her, and after that he'd probably let a few of his guys fuck her. He'd allow her to report to Mikos when she was at her lowest.

She sighed. It would happen over the space of a few days, and then it would be over. Things would get back to normal. She'd go back to her cat, her plants, and running spies with Dax.

She changed quickly as soon as the real maid left. The bra plumped up her breasts to a crazy, almost comic-book height, tapering down into a partly see-through bodice. There were thong panties for bottoms, plus garter stockings and a tiny apron that was more like a lacy loincloth.

How many times had she put something like this on? The outfit was designed to expose her and make her feel exposed, but it was truly the best camouflage because it drew attention away from her face, away from her as a human being with intelligence and agency. She could strike like a fucking cobra in this sort of outfit.

Back in the day, anyway.

She'd been a star back in the day. Nobody had expected it of her, coming in as a forensic botanist, but she'd been cool and dependable under fire, and a master at coldfucking. Yeah, she could have sex with truly awful, truly evil men without breaking a sweat. It actually did something for her when they fucked her devoid of passion or even emotion; it made her feel safe in a perverse way.

She tried not to think too hard about that little talent—it was convenient, mostly. Coldfucking was a big part of a female CIA operative's toolbox. Male agents did it too, of course—with women and with men, but not as often as female agents, and it wasn't the same.

She smoothed on the stockings. She clipped the stays into place. She hadn't coldfucked for six years. Well, she hadn't fucked at all for six years.

She and Liza both fucked without love, but in opposite ways. Liza was looking for love. Or really, Liza was looking for their dad, the alcoholic army man who lived at the bottom of a whiskey bottle. Zelda was proving she didn't care. Yeah, she could fuck a guy as easily as she could shake his hand. The colder he was, the better.

She sat at the door, listening to the hall chatter. An hour went by. Then another. One guard sounded sick. He'd be less than alert.

Another sounded disgruntled. His name was Sal, and the more she heard of his conversations and phone calls, the more she suspected he could be turned. His mutterings under his breath after a phone call with Brujos certainly said yes. Interesting. An ally, maybe.

Another hour.

She didn't really dread what she'd have to go through over the next few days. Back when she'd been a spy, she'd at least dread the guys a little bit. That was shame for you—it made your comfort matter less.

She smoothed the apron over her crotch, happy with the pocket. She'd last into the night, wait until most of the mansion slept, and then she'd get to work searching for the files. That would be the dangerous part. The files would not be easy to find. She'd bluff if she got caught. She could sell it in this outfit. Probably. Maybe.

It was an insanely dangerous job, no question. But she hadn't lied to Dax—they'd send any other Associate in a heartbeat. They'd feel shitty about it, but they'd send them anyway. Only right that she should be here.

She wouldn't have volunteered to do this if other agents were involved, but this was a situation where she could only let herself down. No partner, no support. And at the end, they'd get the bargaining chip that would defuse the standoff. Everybody would get something they wanted. No oil tankers would be blown up. Nobody would die.

Totally worth it.

She thought about how Liza had looked at her, as though Zelda was a fucking angel sent from heaven to save her ass. Liza. The one person who still thought Zelda was brave.

She'd find and copy the files tonight. After a few days, security around her would loosen and she'd get away. It would have to be at just the right moment—an escape Brujos could believe from an untrained, unskilled woman like Liza. Something that could be chalked up to guard error.

She'd get away and fake Liza's death. There were cliffs

out there. Rio and another Associate were out in a boat beyond the cliffs as fishermen, ready to report seeing her fling herself off.

Liza would have a fresh start. They'd have their bargaining chip. And maybe Zelda could hate herself a little less.

A sheer white robe went along with the outfit—totally see-through, except for the feathers part. They'd find the robe washed up, and she'd be long gone.

Handle it, she told herself.

Brujos would want to make it shitty. He'd want to upset her and make her feel like hell, but she'd been upset and feeling like hell for six years, ever since getting Agent Randall killed. Brujos couldn't touch her—not in any way that counted.

CHAPTER THREE

Near Buena Vista, Valencia, South America

Hugo Martinez steered the Jeep down the twists and turns of the mountainside trail heading down toward Buena Vista. The tiny farming village was nothing more than a collection of cinder block homes and shabby businesses, a school, an open market, and a *pensión* for the floral wholesalers. And there was a café—Café Moderno, it was called. Hugo and the boy were its best customers. Most days its only customers.

Hugo's stomach growled. He was dreaming of *llapingachos,* thick with potato, stuffed with cheese, topped with fried eggs. The boy was dreaming of connectivity, holding up his cell phone, looking for reception. Their isolated mountaintop home was too far from civilization to get a signal, but the little village had a tower that worked.

Sometimes.

The mountaintop was the first real home Hugo ever had, and its isolation suited him right down to the steel blades he still kept in his boots. The harshness suited him. The windswept barrenness suited him. Even the savinca crop that grew in gnarled rows upon the terraced mountainside suited him. The plants calmed his mind and dulled his pain.

The savinca farmers down in the village never allowed the crop to flower. The *Savinca verde* was only valuable to wholesale florists when the flowers were in bud form, so that they could bloom just before they were sold for exorbitant amounts of money in high-end floral shops. In fact, a tract of open flowers always meant tragedy—no farmer would let the precious flower open unless he was injured or dead. You never wanted to see the blood-red heart of the savinca.

In this way, it was the perfect metaphor for him.

He sometimes wondered if it was in his DNA to feel at home among the savincas. His mother had come from the village, after all. His ancestors would have farmed them for generations.

The villagers didn't know. To them, Hugo was an outsider. It was better that way.

Walking between the ancient rows of plants was the closest Hugo ever came to serenity.

People rarely understood that it was the large, violent animals that most needed serenity.

Hugo and the boy had their own field of savincas. Their land was too high in altitude to be the best growing spot for the rare flower, but some grew. Hugo allowed the boy to sell whatever crop he could harvest. The surly, snarling boy had been kicked out of every school he'd been sent to. Selling the crop was one of few opportunities to interact with people and use math. The boy used the proceeds for spending money. Hugo was rich now; he didn't need money from flowers.

The killing business had been good to him.

Hugo had tried hiring governesses and tutors for the boy, but none had lasted more than a week with them—miles above anything, trapped with a barely civilized boy and a master who was cold and harsh as the devil himself.

And with every new servant came renewed risk of exposure. It was for the best that nobody would tolerate them.

He and the boy passed the stand of scrub trees and the bright blue rubble of the old church and turned onto the main street.

Café Moderno was anything but modern, but it had become crucial to his and the boy's existence. It allowed them to live without a cook, and provided for more interaction and math for the boy. Nobody had to know that Hugo had funded it using the nearby Banco Valencia de Bumcara branch as a kind of front.

Today wasn't a market day, but even so, the main street was eerily quiet.

Instantly, he understood the cause. He tasted the faint scent of destruction on the back of his throat the way a wine connoisseur might take a whiff of Cabernet, identifying its distinct notes. This was a mix of melted plastic and sulfur. Rubber. They'd find burnt-out stores and at least one burnt-out vehicle. A body or two. It took only one more breath to identify the fuel used. They rounded a corner, and he had the user. Like anything else, violence had a signature, right there in the open if you had the eyes to read it.

El Gorrion's people.

He'd always regretted not killing El Gorrion before he'd

left the killing game.

He looked over at the boy, who was still viewing his phone. A furrow in his little brow told Hugo that the consciousness of what he was smelling had gotten at least as far as his instinct.

How long it would take? Would the boy know to feel fear? The boy had been around five when Hugo had lifted him from the bloody, burning battlefield. A child of a child soldier, crying. It had disgusted and moved Hugo, this helpless sobbing boy, surrounded by dead. Utterly unlike him to rescue a child; but that day, he had. Hugo was not a man to question himself. It led nowhere good.

Hugo drove on, feeling eyes peer out from brightly painted cinder block hovels. He knew precisely what they'd find in the village center, but he went on now, needing to see the particulars.

Finally, the boy honed in on the world outside his phone. He looked around, confused, then pointed at the padlock on the door to the school he'd been kicked out of. He'd lasted a mere day.

"*Qué?*" Hugo asked, as if he didn't understand. It was preferable for the boy to feel smart and observant, because feeling smart and observant had the effect of actually making the boy smarter and more observant. The boy was no good to him stupid.

"*La escuela esta cerrada,*" the boy said.

Hugo nodded. "*Sí.*"

"*Debería estar abierta hoy.*"

"*Sí.*" The school was locked, when it should be open. Hugo pulled the vehicle to the side of the dirt street in the village center, waiting for him to spot the burnt-out hulk of a car. He suspected that the boy's body would spot it before his mind would. You learned to trust your instincts when you were a killer, a hunter. He waited, and indeed, the boy stiffened. Hugo watched the fear come over the boy's conscious mind, then the horror. Expressions Hugo knew well, although they were most often directed at him.

The boy's heart would be beating hard now. Hugo sometimes wondered how specific the boy's memories were.

"*Combate,*" the boy said, turning his brown eyes to Hugo for confirmation.

Hugo remained impassive. The boy needed to be able to determine such things for himself.

"*Combate?*"

It was now a question. Hugo scowled. "Don't look at my face for the answer. What do you see?"

Hugo turned off the Jeep and climbed out.

The boy looked surprised that Hugo would treat this as a lesson, but there was no better time for a lesson. The boy cast his gaze around. Movement behind the iron gate of a shop.

"*Miedo,*" the boy whispered, scrambling out from behind Hugo.

"*En inglés,*" Hugo said, strolling into the rubble. "Complete sentence."

The boy's adrenaline was kicking in. Hugo's old Moro teacher had always instructed him to train at the points of high adrenaline in order to best simulate battlefield conditions. Hugo had lived his life under battlefield conditions. He supposed he should be thankful for having been cast into the pits of rabid dogs that went for schools in Germany and America and other foreign lands, a rough-looking brown boy knowing only Spanish.

As rough as the schools had been, they had always been safer than home.

"Fear. The people are frightened."

Hugo nodded. "Why?"

They turned the corner and found the worst of it—*la plaza de mercado* burnt. *La farmacia*. El Café Moderno. Hugo's heart sank.

The boy looked up at him, gauging his reaction.

Hugo kept walking.

The boy followed him to the gate of a shop farther down the way. The shopkeeper came to the gate. Ramona or Renata. She had several children and a husband who was away on the oil rigs. "Get out! Go back! Pack your belongings! El Gorrion. They killed Pedro, Victor..."

Hugo nodded grimly as she related the tale in her rough hills dialect. Hugo had been born in the south, near Valencia's capital city, but his family had been yanked away before his first birthday, so his Spanish sounded foreign to them. The villagers thought he was American. He was content to let them think it.

Some of the eligible women had tried for him when he'd first taken over the crumbling mountaintop villa, but he'd made it clear he was not interested. When he wanted to enjoy a woman, he went into the city and enjoyed one. He liked women, but only in small doses. And he never brought them to the house.

"They've given us twenty-four hours to get out," she continued. "They'll kill anybody who stays—unless they're prepared to cooperate. Like they did in Lapas. They want fields..."

Hugo squinted down the street.

"They're desperate," she said. "Looking for cropland this far up the mountainside..."

He could feel the woman's eyes on him as he followed the direction of her pointing finger. He always knew when people were watching him with any kind of intensity. It was a tickle. Waiting for him to react.

She expected fear. Alarm.

They rarely interacted, he and the villagers, but social order always broke down at a time like this.

"*Ve por ti mismo.*" She pointed across the way.

Another gated storefront. The little repair shop. He knew what he'd find there—he could hear the flies. She bade the boy to stay and help her with something, thinking she was sparing the boy some hell. She had no idea where they came from, Hugo and the boy.

The boy turned his big brown eyes to Hugo.

Hugo nodded, telling the boy to obey. The boy understood Hugo's every gesture and expression.

Hugo walked across the street and peered inside. Pedro had crawled a ways, judging from the marks upon the dusty slab floor. They had shot him far more than they'd needed to for a kill. Bullets were expensive these days, but this was an efficient use of them nevertheless. Death had never been the goal here. Terror had been the goal.

Humans were animals, and it didn't take much to spark terror in them. Terror was something between a taste and a feeling in the blood—when you were on the giving end of it, anyway. When you were on the receiving end, it was a form of madness.

He stood there for an acceptable amount of time staring

at the old man on the ground, but really he was testing the contours of his own darkness. Trying to see if the violence touched him in the way that it touched regular people. He looked at the blood path and imagined Pedro crawling—doomed, but still fighting to get away, trying to work up some sadness or empathy, but it didn't work. The sight of the man's body made him feel like killing somebody. Nothing more.

He turned, watching Ramona guide the boy to some task involving cans. He looked around at the destruction. The villagers had imagined that the remoteness of the village would protect them—that the coca gangs wouldn't bother reaching up the mountain. But the coca gangs were desperate these days—they were being driven out of places like Colombia and Ecuador in favor of tourism, mining, and legitimate farming. Driven into Valencia.

El Gorrion. Expanding up the mountain.

He came back. "*Lo siento,*" he said.

She nodded, stroked the boy's hair. The boy frowned, barely tolerating it.

"Fernando?" he asked. Fernando owned Café Moderno.

"Drove out an hour ago. They can take what they want. They'll want your farm, and they'll take it. Julian is trying to save some of the bushes, but..."

He nodded. This was the only place in the world that the savinca thrived. The farmers would be saving plants.

Again he squinted down the street. He should feel more than a killing anger, but that was what he felt. He felt it strongly. Because this was his goddamn village.

Nobody fucked with his village.

"*No creo que vayan a volver,*" he said simply. *I don't think they'll come back.*

He could feel the excitement shoot through the boy like a fucking arrow. The boy knew not to show it.

"They will come back," Ramona or Renata said. "They'll want your land. You have good land for coca." Cocaine land. Because that was what this was about. Not quite up to the frost line.

"*Ellos no volverán,*" he said. "Tell the others—twenty-four hours will pass, and they will not return." He shouldn't feel happy about returning to the killing.

Hugo started up the Jeep. Fighting and killing was going to be hell on his burns.

The boy got in, face glowing. He spoke in Spanish. "You'll save them. You'll make them sorry for what they did to the old man. El Gorrion has hit the nest of a hornet."

Hugo kept his eyes on the road. The boy was still idealistic. He wanted him to be something more than a cold-blooded killer.

"You think this is about justice?" Hugo growled.

The boy's silence told him yes, he thought it was about justice. At least he hoped it was.

"This isn't about justice." Hugo said icily. "It's about *llapingachos.*

CHAPTER FOUR

Footsteps in the hall. She sucked in a breath. It was night—maybe eleven. She'd wondered when he'd come.

A key in her door.

She spun around. A slim man with a goatee strolled in—Brujos himself—followed by a woman and then two guards.

The woman came up to her with fire in her eyes and slapped her.

Zelda forced herself to cry, to look bewildered. Brujos's girlfriend—it had to be.

Brujos came up to Zelda, now. She braced herself. It was going to be something bad with the two of them, or nothing at all.

But Brujos didn't touch her. "La puta de Mikos," he said—*Mikos's whore*—and he spat in her face.

She wiped it off because Liza would wipe it off. *Just last.*

It was easy to guess what had happened. The girlfriend had learned about Brujos winning her in a card game and had come to stake out her territory. She wanted Brujos all to herself.

She could have him.

"*Ahora. Antes de que se vayan.*" The woman pointed sideways. *Now. Before they leave.*

They? Who?

But she and Brujos were already walking away.

"What about the deal?" she asked.

The two guards came up and took her arms, one on either side.

"Wait!" She twisted away and grabbed the small suitcase. She couldn't leave that equipment behind, dammit. She couldn't leave at all—she hadn't gotten the files.

She was hustled out of the mansion and put in the back of a Jeep. She wanted to scream, thinking about the standoff, about the pirates holding that tanker off Costa Amarrilla. People would die if they blew that thing up. The ecosystem up and down the coast would be destroyed. She had to get back into that mansion.

Two guards with fully automatic weaponry sat up front. There were Jeeps in front and behind her, also full of guards. A convoy of five. The seat covering was rough and warm on her bare ass, which the thong did nothing to cover. At least she had the apron to cover her in front. And the top.

Her blood raced. Why the heavy guard? "Where are we going?" she asked.

Nobody answered, not that she expected it. She really just wanted to remind them that she spoke only English, so that they'd feel free to speak in front of her.

One thing was clear: they weren't guarding her. Something larger was going on.

Headlights were flipped on and the small motorcade rumbled to life in a cloud of diesel. She strained to listen to the chat in the front seat, but got nothing of importance. Deep down, she knew they weren't going back to that mansion, or at least she wasn't.

She eyed the suitcase. Wherever they were going, the stuff in there could give her away. Put Liza in danger. She eased open the lid and pretended to be searching for something, but really she pulled out the vibrator, unscrewing the top and dumping the drive. She quickly crushed it under her heel and shoved it out a rust hole in the bottom of the vehicle, and then she ripped that remaining parabolic mic out of the lining.

"No!" the man in the passenger seat said, tension in his voice.

She held up a shirt. "I'm getting a shirt to wear." She pressed it to her front.

He took it and threw it out onto the shadowy wayside.

"Hey!"

He shook his head, pointing to her barely covered breasts. "No more." He clapped his hands together and pointed to the suitcase. A sign to shut it.

She complied, and once he turned, she got rid of the parabolic mic. Clean now. But where were they going?

She'd done enough time in hot spots around the world to know when soldiers were tense. These men were on high alert. Beyond high alert. It wasn't so evident in their banter with each other, quips and jeers in Spanish over the screaming muffler, putting on brave, macho faces, but you could tell it in the way they held themselves in the silent moments. They expected trouble.

Damn.

She looked down at her feet. She wanted to take the shoes off—she could run and move better in bare feet, yet she still felt protective of them. She always had, ever since Friar Hovde.

The convoy of armed Jeeps turned onto a dark side street and rumbled past barren *cantinas* strung with lights. They parked in front of a dark strip of restaurants. Zelda surveyed the area. She could make a run for it, but her odds of surviving wouldn't be good—running could turn into hunting practice with men who were tense like this. The question was, what would her odds be of surviving where they were going? And what was happening?

Bottom line, the mission had failed.

She thought miserably about the standoff. All the lives threatened. It had begun two weeks back, when South American pirates had seized an oil tanker off the South American coast, demanding the release of certain prisoners, mostly in Valencian prisons. The Valencian delegation had refused to negotiate. The pirates were threatening to let the oil run out into the bay and set it all on fire. It was bad.

It had been Dax's idea to slide the pirates something to trade. Brujos's legendary files would have been perfect—the files would've enabled officials across the region to move on cartel collaborators, taking prisoners far more valuable than the pirates' friends.

Now they were back to square one.

Dax was resourceful. He'd think of something—he always did. He saw things other people didn't.

A man in an apron scurried out with a box full of bags

of fried food of some sort. He was obviously frightened, and apologized for not having enough. *"Esto es lo mejor que tengo. Lo mejor,"* he said. *The best I have.* The food was loaded into the vehicle in front of them.

They headed back out.

"Where are we going?" she asked in English. "Where?"

The driver turned his grizzled face to her and smiled an ugly smile. He understood the question, and the ugly smile was the answer.

They bumped on. Scrubby roadside became walls of thick jungle illuminated by headlights and searchlights wielded by soldiers. They passed small concrete buildings, bright paint still on the parts that hadn't crumbled. Here and there lights flashed on broken-down vehicles slowly being reclaimed by nature.

Zelda looked at the thick walls of foliage. She would've loved to get out and study the leaves. Touch them. Smell them.

She was a leaf person. She loved the ways they formed themselves, the way they smelled and grew. The dendritic patterning of the veins, like tiny river systems.

Flowers were what everybody saw first, what people typically remembered about a plant, but the leaves were just as important. The soldiers around her were the same way. They put on a good show for each other, but it was in the quiet moments, the leaf moments, when the truth in a man emerged.

The jungle grew thicker. The road more rugged.

Nobody knew where she was—nobody who cared, anyway, and it made her feel so alone. Dax wouldn't expect contact for at least twenty-four hours.

An hour later, they entered a clearing. Some of the guards got out and started pulling brush and netting this way and that, and she realized it was a landing strip. Was she being sent back with a shipment north? Returned un-fucked as a macho slap in Mikos's face?

She hated the idea of leaving empty-handed. Yeah, she'd planted the parabolic mic, and she had the name of a dis-gruntled guard still inside Brujos's mansion, but they need-ed those files!

The men lined up the vehicles at the edge of the clear-ing. They made her get out—without her suitcase. It made her nervous.

She was sweating. Even at night, the humidity was sti-fling, and the night bugs droned too loud, and she didn't like any of this.

She could make out white stripes spray-painted onto the scrubby ground, alongside lights and reflectors. Beyond them on the other side of the clearing, were camouflaged hangars and a few outbuildings. The men stood around their Jeeps, smoking, waiting. She read tension in every-body's stance. Judging from the direction of their attention, a plane would be coming in from the south.

A black SUV roared onto the field and parked at the end of the line. Brujos and his woman got out of the back. They ignored Zelda, speaking instead to armed men some dis-tance away. They stopped talking when a low rumble sounded in the distance.

The navigation lights of a small plane came into view—a small, fast plane. Drug-running plane, probably out of Cos-ta Amarrilla, maybe Valencia. The field came to life with rows of lights.

Weapons came into view as well. A few of the men set up in the jungle around the perimeter. Snipers. A full twenty armed men waiting for a plane that couldn't hold more than eight.

Who the fuck was coming?

Zelda didn't like it on a lot of levels, but she was about to witness something, and she liked that. More information was better than less.

The plane bumped neatly onto the field, kicking up the dust and grit. It went right to the edge and circled back. The military-issue plane was a Soviet-era workhorse, an expendable plane. The drug runners probably lost their fair share of them.

A camo-clad guard came down the steps first, assault rifle over his shoulder, followed by a man with dark curly hair and a scar on his neck, obviously the leader. Three more camo-wearing, rifle-toting guards followed him. They all had the walk of battle-hardened guerrillas. The last one pulled along a blonde woman who looked hurt. Dress ripped to hell.

Zelda bit her cheek.

Brujos and his girlfriend went up and spoke with the leader with the curly hair. Two things were instantly obvious. One: they'd never met before. And Two: Brujos, though he was hiding it, was deferential to this curly-haired leader. They both stood like bulls, but Brujos was a bull with something to lose. Too much the bull. Brujos snapped and suitcases were handed over. Money.

The guards began unloading the plane with the help of Brujos's men—square packages about the size of couch pillows with red birds on the front.

El Gorrion cocaine. Shit—these were El Gorrion's people. Brujos was bad, but El Gorrion was worse. This curly-haired man was an El Gorrion lieutenant.

Why was Brujos letting her see this? She shouldn't be seeing this.

It was then Zelda knew: she wasn't going back.

She swore under her breath and looked around. Twenty feet of clearing behind her, and then jungle. Could she make it without getting shot?

No.

The other option was to kick off the heels and grab a weapon. The leader was the only high-value hostage in this scenario. Could she get to him? It would be running into the fire, but it might be the only way to survive this.

Somebody carried the food onto the plane—the three brown cardboard boxes full of white bags of food. Grease stains spread out on the sides.

Decide. Her pulse raced.

What would young Zelda have done? Zelda before Friar Hovde?

Suddenly Brujos gestured in her direction. The curly-haired leader looked over at her, up and down, her in that ridiculous outfit. Brujos's girlfriend smiled at her.

A gun butt was shoved into her back. A voice behind her. *"Vamos!"*

Zelda stiffened. Well, this was one way to get close enough to take a hostage. But she was out of practice. Unarmed. Surrounded by guerrillas used to action. Wearing sexy maid's lingerie.

She felt paralyzed. Options were dwindling too quickly.

The leader looked her over. He reached out and she

jumped back. Wrong answer.

The man smiled. "Okay."

"*Ella no habla español*," Brujos said. *She doesn't speak Spanish.*

"*Bueno*," the leader said. "*Sólo hay una palabra que ella necesitará saber.*" *Only one word she'd need to know.*

Zelda didn't need the word supplied, but she got it anyway, courtesy of Brujos's girlfriend. "*Mamar.*" Suck.

Dammit.

At that point, two things happened at lightning speed. One of the guards moved behind her and zip-tied her hands. She splayed her wrists, but they got them tight enough that she wouldn't be able to work out of them instantly. And then another grabbed the blonde woman, and before the poor woman could even complete her exclamation of surprise, he shot her in the head. Casually, quickly, aiming for the blood and brains to fly away from the group. He guided her to crumple to the ground in a well-practiced motion that chilled Zelda to the core.

Even Brujos and his girlfriend looked surprised.

Another guard counted money out of a suitcase as if nothing had happened. "Okay," he said.

Her heart pounded. She should've gone for the jungle.

Because she'd just been traded to El Gorrion's people. El Gorrion, the Valencian guerrilla. Up-and-coming players. Jungle labs. They purchased crops directly from the farmers, though *purchasing* was a euphemism. El Gorrion's men would kill farmers who didn't produce for them. Even farmers who wanted to plant legit crops.

The food was loaded onto the plane. She'd be next. Favors for the trip.

People averted their eyes from the dead woman, but Zelda didn't. The woman deserved a witness, an ally, if only in spirit. Zelda imagined the woman's soul rising peacefully from her tortured body, even though she wasn't sure if she believed in such things.

She'd seen too many people die horribly, but she always took the time to honor the dead in her mind, and to imagine a kind of peace for them. She used to do it with animals on the roadside as a girl, and even plants.

Zelda honored and fought for all living things.

During her time with the CIA, she'd been to some places where there were too many bodies to honor individually. She'd always felt bad when she couldn't, but she'd do it for the group, imagining them finding peace.

She wondered if anybody would do it for her—witness her death with respect and imagine some sort of peace for her.

Certainly nobody in this group.

A teen with a beaten-down look emerged from the plane and threw a plastic trash bag out onto the field. Brujos would take care of it—that was the message.

The flies had already found the blonde woman. If Zelda were really Liza, she'd have thrown up by now, but there was little point in convincing anybody of anything. She was on that plane. She was the in-flight entertainment. There was no going back.

She looked out at the jungle, so beautiful and dark and cool, wishing she'd tried for it. There were two ways to survive this flight: total submission or total domination.

CHAPTER FIVE

Zelda was pushed up the flip-down ladder into an interior just large enough to fit two compact cars. The sides were lined with fold-out seats—two near the front were down, seat belts dangling. The teen had taken the seat nearest the cockpit, which was closed off by a metal door.

She was shoved down the steel grate walkway that ran between four air mattresses. One of her spiked heels caught in a gap. She barely got her balance back before she was shoved farther back between upended crates that served as makeshift tables, and farther on between messy stacks of wooden pallets to a small bedroll in the back. Next to it lay a pack of tissues. Lip balm. A squeeze tube of lube. The blonde's spot. These were her things.

Zelda's heart sank.

She was shoved down onto the bedroll. She was the new blonde. Activities back here would've been fully obscured when all those containers of coke had been stacked on the pallets. She would be only partly obscured now, obscured from the waist down, thanks to the empty pallets.

Right behind was the bathroom. She could smell the disinfectant.

The rest of the men came on. Six in all, and two pilots.

She waited, needing to see how things would unfold. She didn't have a plan yet—there were too many unknowns. She needed to stay open.

The door slammed shut. Voices from the cockpit. They were moving.

The plane taxied and took off, engines droning loudly.

She settled down on the pad behind the wooden pallets. When she sat straight up, she could just see them over the pallets, but she found when she stretched out on her side, she could get a good view of all of them through the gap between the stacks. That was where she put herself.

She swallowed, ears popping as they gained altitude, wishing she'd taken her chances running back in town. Wishing she had tennis shoes on. Wishing she'd gotten those files. Wishing she hadn't given up Randall's name like a despicable coward.

She watched them and studied them, trying to get the old mind-set back, before Agent Randall, before Friar Hovde, before she'd crumbled. She needed to survive this flight.

Thankfully, the food was more interesting than she was for the moment. Calamari tacos, corn tamales, and something else. She was surprised they weren't making her suck them off while they ate, but they were all apparently waiting for the curly-haired leader, and the curly-haired leader was into the food. He'd heard that the fried calamari was supposed to be the best in the land, but they all agreed that it wasn't.

The teen looked on hungrily. There was more than enough to go around—why weren't they letting him have any? Was he just some innocent kid they'd pulled into the gang? Even so, they should feed the kid. Assholes.

They'd apparently gotten the memo that she didn't speak Spanish, or maybe they meant to kill her at the end of the flight, because they were discussing Brujos. They didn't like him and didn't respect him, and the leader worried about his fitness as a long-term partner for El Gorrion. At one point one of the men called the leader Guz. Short for Guzman, maybe.

They liked that she was Mikos's whore—*la puta de Mikos*—and they seemed to know who Mikos was, but considered him a snot. They felt his fast rise was luck.

There was one thing they could agree on.

They laughed about the blonde and relived the kill, as very bad men typically did.

"¿Vieron la cara de Brujos?" one of them said. *Did you see Brujos's face?* When they killed her, they meant. They all laughed about that and agreed that the blonde had cried too much on the way up. They began to exchange kill stories, casually, the way people might discuss pet antics. *You should see this trick my dog does.* Except that men, women, and children were dying. *You should've seen...*

The stories seemed to center on things they'd done recently in a village called Buena Vista. Zelda was glad they couldn't see her face—keeping the disgust away took energy, and she needed energy for handling this. She should've taken the run. The odds of surviving a run into the jungle while getting shot at were far better; but no, she'd choked. Dax had been right to try to talk her out of this thing. She had no business in the field.

The old Zelda would never have made these errors. She would've put things together faster. She'd been in the South American network, and she'd had a keen sense for trouble. You had to if you were in the field during the regional civil wars. Valencia had been the worst—the war had ravaged the tiny country for years, a raging bonfire of mythical proportions. There hadn't been a good side. It was one of those conflicts where the minute you decided who was least bad, they did something horrific.

These days, the regional situation was more like glowing coals with occasional flare-ups. It didn't help that the men roaming the countryside across Valencia had only killing and terrorizing on their résumés. The men on the plane were murderers and terrorists. Fighters like them had been banding together in different factions and flavors for years. Some guerrilla factions were political and anti-drug; others were political, but funded through drugs. Some were more about kidnapping and coups. Some were simply gangs of thugs, thriving on the coca trade; others were more sophisticated, such as organized crime families with anti-government roots and international networks. Even the oil-rig pirates could be traced back to the wars. And then there were the paramilitary groups with their own varieties of hate, politics, and violence.

El Gorrion was of the quasi-political, drug-thug variety of guerrilla. He'd come up fast and hard since the sweep of arrests some ten years back, and his people were strong and battle-hardened. She had no illusions about fighting five of them, plus a teenage kid and two pilots. She'd need luck to win.

They spoke more about Buena Vista, which means *beautiful view* in Spanish.

The leader, Guz, was slowing his eating. It was about time. They'd make her go up, or Guz would come back.

Guz's right-hand man, a guy with a small black moustache and a bandana, was back on the Buena Vista village takeover. They argued about the division of the new cropland. An overseer would be brought in. That was pretty standard guerrilla practice in order to force the farmers to grow coca. It was the most lucrative crop; yes, but most farmers would grow the legit crop if given a chance—it wouldn't pay as much, and there were logistical and start-up obstacles, but they wouldn't have to deal with guys like these. They argued about one of the farmers. Guz thought he would be trouble, but his right-hand man felt confident he'd stay in line.

"*Que Kabakas te castigue*," one of the farmers said, and they all laughed about that.

Que Kabakas te castigue.

For a second, she forgot to breathe. *Que Kabakas te castigue.* Loosely translated, it meant *I hope Kabakas will punish you.* The saying had been popular during the war; a curse. People were still saying that? Energy surged through her, a wild energy sparkling with magic and anger and longing. For a second, she wasn't trapped on a plane clad in ridiculous maid lingerie in the midst of ruthless killer-rapists—she was back in the field, confident and fierce and in control again. Back in the field hunting Kabakas.

Kabakas was a near-mythical assassin who'd burst out of nowhere at the height of the Valencian Civil War, though *assassin* was barely even accurate; Kabakas had been more like a super-mercenary, capable of taking on armies single-handedly. He'd become famous across Valencia in a matter of months, the subject of tales epic and tall. One story had it that he'd go into a killing trance that made it so bullets couldn't touch him. Another said that he could use his mind to throw off people's aim, or even to explode weapons in fighters' hands. Some said that he would pre-tie his limbs before battle to prevent blood loss so that he could be shot multiple times and still fight. He killed with knives and barong blades more often than with guns. Well, that one was true. She'd seen the gruesome aftermath of his attacks with her own eyes.

Yeah, she'd known all about Kabakas—he'd been a white whale for her back when she was based in South America. It wasn't just the bounty on his head, though you could buy a small island with it. He was the ultimate prize. The Holy Grail and Rambo rolled into one. Maybe a little bit of an obsession.

Kabakas had started out as something of a benevolent mercenary; threatened villages would often recruit him to attack their attackers, although, sometimes different factions of fighters would pay him a lot of money to destroy various enemies.

The really serious Kabakas hunters agreed he'd been trained by the Moros of the Philippines, and most believed he'd come out of the Balkans in the late 1990s—a teen mercenary with brown skin, jet-black hair, and the uncanny ability to put a blade in a man's right eye from a hundred feet away. Similar stories came out of Algeria, and later along the Israeli/Lebanese border. The sheer old-school strangeness of throwing a blade and always hitting the eye had spooked a lot of fighters, and myths began to swirl around him. Zelda's thinking—and she was not alone in this—was that his ideas for the Kabakas persona had been formed in these conflicts when he was just a mercenary. He'd brought the persona to Valencia at the height of the war. At this point he'd taken up the mask, a blood-red mask with silver stars painted on it.

He charged a lot for his services, but he would do freebies—that was a known fact. Fighting on the side of the really downtrodden. Not often, but he did it.

The CIA's interest in Kabakas had been pragmatic. The fear was that he'd create a guerrilla faction of his own, seize power, and threaten the oil industry. The bounty on his head had come from the Valencian vice president himself, whose grudge seemed personal, but everybody in Valencian politics hated and feared Kabakas. His popularity made him dangerous. People thought he was something special.

And then he'd carried out the infamous Yacon fields massacre. She and the other hunters would spend hours over pitchers of Pilsen in tiny torchlit cafés, armed to the teeth, arguing about what had turned Kabakas so dark so fast, or if he'd always been dark. She'd seen the aftermath herself: all those people with blades through their eyes, bloody faces, and frozen expressions. Chilling.

Even after the Yacon fields massacre, Kabakas masks were sold in most street-corner stalls; even fake barong swords. Props for the fantasies of Valencian males, but still deadly. People still wanted to believe.

The best intelligence had it that Kabakas had died in a fire nine years back. A Kabakas hunter considered one of the best had tracked him to a small town called Vasquez, only to see him run into a burning house that exploded seconds later. She knew the man; he was good. Smart. Trustworthy.

What's more, Kabakas's activity had ceased at that point—further proof that he'd perished there.

Considering the Yacon fields massacre, she should've been overjoyed about Kabakas's death. But losing him as a quarry had been...strange. She still thought about him and dreamed about him, too.

There was one known photo of Kabakas in existence, taken from the phone of one of the dead. The photo caught the killer in whirling motion—masked face, body, and barong swords a blur—everything a blur except for a large hand clad in a black leather glove. At the height of the hunt, Zelda had the image blown up and she'd hung it above her desk. She'd stare at that huge, muscular form and that leather-wrapped hand for hours, trying to get into his head. Wondering what it was like to have that kind of nerve, that insane level of ability, and no mercy whatsoever. Unapologetic might and darkness.

She looked around at her esteemed fellow passengers. The beauty inside the human spirit. So much bullshit.

She kept her arms behind her back—even though she'd long since worked free of the tie.

Total submission or total domination.

What would Kabakas do?

She banished the thought. Fuck Kabakas. The old Zelda could handle these guys. She could return to that mind-set.

The leader had a .357 in a shoulder holster. If he came back alone, maybe she could take it off him.

She sucked in a breath, reminding herself that the sexy

maid outfit was a power outfit; it endowed her with a massive element of surprise.

Twenty minutes into the flight, Guz stood. He took a swig of beer and adjusted his cock, eyeing her through the crates. "*Te estoy viendo,*" he taunted. *I see you.* The guys laughed.

At that moment, something kicked in. The decision made.

She scurried backward, hiding in the corner, hands clasped behind her back. An old trick, pulling back—like pulling a line, inciting the predator to stalk toward you, luring him away from his pack.

Could she do it?

Hell, she *was* doing it. She watched herself position Guz like an out-of-body experience.

Boot on metal. One step. Another.

He arrived and stood over her, enjoying her fear.

"*Estás lista para mí?*" he asked. *You ready for me?*

She whimpered as he unzipped his pants and took out his cock.

He went on, more for the benefit of his companions, of course. "*Tú sabes la palabra* mamar?"

She gave him bewilderment and fear. It wasn't hard—she really fucking felt it, and he was enjoying it. They were connected now; what he didn't understand was that she was stoking that connection to control him. She scooted back, drawing him deeper behind the pallets, out of sight.

He finally caught up. He reached down and grabbed her hair and stood her on her knees, shoving her face into his cock. "*Mámamela,*" he said, making a sucking sound.

And just like that, she had his gun.

She pulled his pants to his knees and jerked the fabric forward, making him fall on his ass.

She took off the safety and aimed, relieving him of the blade in his ankle sheath before he could gather his wits. Hesitation would kill her now.

"Stay down. Down!" she screamed when he lifted his head. "Down!"

Guz complied. The men up front stood and stared.

She slid his knife into her garter. With trembling fingers, she crouched behind him. She'd positioned him well; they'd have to shoot through him to get to her. What's more, a lot of electrical was behind her.

Weapons came up.

"*No disparen!*" Guz yelled. He instructed a man named Aguilo to talk to her.

"You cannot shoot in the plane," one of the guards said. That would be Aguilo, then. An English speaker. Good. "The plane." Aguilo made a crashing sound.

That wasn't exactly true. You could shoot through the skin of the plane a few times and it could still fly. A good crew could plug it up, but it was risky as hell. And if you shot out the electrical or the fuel, you were screwed.

But they didn't need to know she knew that. Or that she could understand their Spanish.

"I'll shoot if he moves," she growled. "Tell him to put his head down and *keep* it down."

Aguilo repeated her instructions in Spanish. He got it right. Good.

Guz lowered his head. He lay crosswise on the pallets a few feet in front of her, head turned toward the group.

"Look at me," she said. She nodded to the English

speaker. "Eyes?"

"*Ojos*," he said.

"*Ojos* on me," she said to Guz, pointing with two fingers to his eyes and then hers. She didn't want him coordinating with his men. A good fighter could do that without a word.

Guz was obeying. For now.

Time. She needed to be tracking time. They were going to Valencia, probably the southeast. She calculated the flight time—four more hours. They would land around dawn.

Back when she was a confident, competitive, high-performing agent, she would've gotten off on the thrill of holding the plane for four hours; it would've been about feeling the men, adjusting to their emotions, keeping the rein on them from minute to minute, stoking their fear.

She'd lost so much of herself the night with Friar Hovde. His end-of-the-world cult had operations in several countries, and destructive plans involving missile theft. She'd posed as a follower, working with Agent Randall, who'd climbed into Hovde's inner circle. Hovde had caught her with files and quickly realized he had a mole. He'd brought her to the basement of an outbuilding, tied her up, and gotten the name out of her. It had taken a few hours, but he'd gotten it in the end. And Agent Randall had paid the price. The agency had moved on Hovde soon after, but it was too late for Randall.

She'd gone on cases after that, but it was luck that she hadn't gotten herself or anybody else killed. Shame and guilt tended to erode your sense of self-preservation, your awareness. The minute she thought of it all she could feel her very awareness contract to a small tube.

She needed to not think about it now.

Focus.

"I saw what happened to your last girl," she announced. "I know that's what will happen to me." Best for them to believe she had nothing to lose, that she'd crash the plane.

"No," said Aguilo, the English-speaking guard. "We'll let you go."

Right. "Lies." She took a breath. It was lucky, her getting the gun. If they could underestimate her language skills as well as her fighting skills, she might do this.

"Let him go," Aguilo tried.

"No!" she screamed. "If he moves, I'm shooting him, and then all of you!"

"Mantenla tranquila," Guz said. *Keep her calm.*

"Okay," Aguilo said.

"Put your guns in the aisle," she said. "All of you!"

Nobody complied.

She pointed the gun at Guz's face, letting him see the determination, finger on the trigger, hand shaking for effect. You never held a gun with your finger on the trigger; that was Firearms 101. But she kept her finger on the trigger, enjoying the fear in Guz's eyes. "I kill you first." He'd know the word for kill.

"Háganlo!" Guz commanded.

A few weapons went into the aisle. She heard the telltale sounds of chambers being emptied. It was a start.

Guz spoke in Spanish, calmly. He was looking at her, but addressing his men, telling them to keep her focused on getting off the plane. They'd bide their time, and they'd take her when they landed. She'd be done for once they landed. She had no chance. A voice from the cockpit over the crackly radio. The pilot assured them he'd already radioed ahead and told them of the situation.

They'd be headed to a private jungle airstrip. Somebody like El Gorrion would have a few of them, and every drug-running guerrilla airstrip worth its salt had an armed contingent sitting around. They probably didn't even have to call in extra guys.

Except that she didn't intend to let them land there. They'd have a change of travel plans toward the end. Yeah, she might die today, but she'd go out fighting.

She assessed the five men and pointed at the man with the bushiest beard. "Tell the man with the big beard to tie everyone up. Hands behind the back." Aguilo repeated her instructions, and the man with the beard complied after urging from Guz.

She watched, waiting.

"Tell the man with the big beard to bring the guns to me. One by one. And he should hold them by their noses." She pointed to the barrel.

The mistake a novice would make would be to have the teen play gofer, but the teen was the one with the least to lose here, and the most likely to be impulsive.

The guard translated, including her calling the barrel the nose. They all exchanged glances. That had been on purpose. Best that they think her a novice—it was one of her few advantages.

Yeah, what she'd done, it wasn't a novice move, but they could tell themselves she got lucky. A man with his pants down, a sidearm. It could happen. And the lingerie, fucking with their minds like an optical illusion, preventing them from taking her seriously as a warrior.

The bearded man set the guns near her. Three Smith & Wessons. She beckoned him to push them nearer, and he did, gently, not wanting to upset her. Good. He'd been a good choice.

An extra jacket hung on a hook near the front. She longed to have the bearded man bring that to her, too, so that she could wrap up in it. She couldn't.

The shoes were a problem, though, the way the heels had caught in the walkway. But she couldn't let them see her scars or missing toes. The puncture behind her ankle-bone was visible enough, but that looked like an accident unless you saw the rest. They'd figure out what she was, and she'd lose the advantage of the outfit.

She requested warm, dry socks and a Tuff-Tie, waving the gun, finger on the trigger.

Aguilo translated, and the bearded man brought her the stuff. Quickly and discreetly she pulled off the heels and shoved on the socks. Then she pointed at Guz. "Tie him!" The bearded man regarded her wildly; he didn't want to tie Guz.

"Tie him!" she barked.

The leader angled his wrists as the bearded man fit the tie around—loosely. Like a flash she was up; she smashed Guz's wrists together with her stocking foot and yanked the cord tight, and then she was down. It had been a risky move—it gave away some of her expertise, and exposed her to gunfire, but she couldn't have Guz getting free.

"Tighten the rest like that." She gave him a wild look, and he did as she said. Their bonds might not hold, but it was a start.

Now the wait. The landing would be a bitch. She didn't

know how to fly this sort of plane, so she'd need at least one pilot. She couldn't recognize one airstrip from the next. All she could do was to wait until they were in descent and force them to any airstrip but the one they wanted.

She sat back against the wall just far enough away from the leader that he couldn't get to her easily. If it came to that, she'd have to shoot him somewhere non-vital and hope she wouldn't hit something critical on the plane. She worked out a few angles in her mind.

He was looking away again. Fine. She took the opportunity to check which of the guns were loaded.

She might not be fit to be an agent anymore, but she remembered what to do. She just needed a lot of luck now. And to not think about what she'd done to Randall.

"*Ojos*," she said.

Guz looked back at her, full of oily hate.

She put one of the guns in her garter belt. Another in the center of her bra. "Now I have enough guns to kill all of you twice," she announced to the plane. "I'll shoot everything. I don't care."

Nobody said anything.

She raised her voice. "Translate it. Tell them what I said."

"She's a crazy fucking bitch with those guns," Aguilo said in Spanish.

Yeah, that worked

CHAPTER SIX

Hugo pulled the chest down from the secret compartment above the farmhouse kitchen ceiling and banged it onto the rough wood kitchen table.

The dust pattern and the scratches on the padlock told him that the boy had been into it.

He gave the boy an annoyed look. The boy gave him back a steady look, turning one of Hugo's lessons back on him. *Don't cower unless you have a reason. Don't fall to your knees until they cut you off at the shins.*

Hugo lifted out a heavy bundle and set it on the table. The bandolier of throwing blades. He pulled out a blade. Newly sharpened. Again he gave the boy a look. Again the boy returned defiance.

The boy was almost untouchable now, that was how high he was riding on his fucking tide of excitement.

Hugo had spent time in a dozen different countries thanks to his parents' jobs as domestic servants of a Bolivian oil executive, and every place had their own version of the hero and sidekick. Batman and Robin, Tintin and

Snowy, Asterix and Obelix, Lucky Luke et Jolly Jumper. Valencia itself had Pedro and Paco. No doubt that was what was in the boy's mind. Maybe that was why he accepted life with a harsh and unfeeling recluse, stranded upon a windy mountaintop. Maybe that was why he so diligently played guard dog and groundskeeper when the pain of the burns drove his master into an opium stupor. For the chance to be Kabakas's sidekick. Why not?

The boy had come up in a band of ultraviolent guerrillas. Serving violent men was what he knew. He was five or six years old when Hugo had grabbed him. The boy would remember.

The boy reached out and touched a blade. Hugo grabbed his wrist. "*No es para ti,*" he said. *Not for you.* The boy could never be Kabakas or serve Kabakas. He shouldn't want that. Nobody should want that.

Hugo pointed at the Uzi. The boy sighed.

"*Tú llevaras esa.*" *You'll carry that.*

The boy said nothing. He'd grown up around Uzis. The Uzi was a bore.

"*Entiendes?*" *Understand?* Hugo demanded, watching as the boy's hope dwindled.

Hope was Hugo's least favorite emotion.

The boy walked off. Hugo pulled out the red mask and ran a finger over the paint. Red with silver stars, modeled after something he'd found in a little junk shop in Prague. He'd been aimless that year, having destroyed the oil executive who'd employed and ruined his family. That had been the extent of his life plan—fight and destroy.

Finding the mask had changed something for him—he'd gotten it in his head to do something for the country of his birth, his parents' native home. Doing something to help Valencia was why he'd become Kabakas, and why he'd allowed Kabakas to die.

Most of the Kabakas masks sold by *mercado* vendors were plastic, unlike this one, which had iron plating on the inside and rubber strips designed to hug the cheekbones and nose.

The boy returned from the other room wearing just such a mask in a child's size. He also had his small backpack with Sinawali sticks in the pockets, taking the place of the barongs.

Hugo frowned and held out his hand. The boy removed the flimsy mask from his face. Hugo snatched it and turned it over, bent it this way and that, disgusted. "Have I taught you nothing?" he hissed. He cast it aside and shoved his own mask into the boy's hands. *"Cuál es la diferencia?"*

The boy ran his fingers over the inside of the mask. He'd probably been in the chest while Hugo went on his business trips to the city. Playacting. Maybe even sleeping with the stuff.

"Say more," he demanded.

The boy pointed to Hugo's reinforced mask. "Strength."

True enough. Hugo's mask wouldn't protect against a direct shot to the face, but it could deflect some of the cheap shot out there and had. Wearing an unreinforced mask from a *vendedor de mercado* would be suicide. "Say more," Hugo demanded.

"Imagen y substancia," the boy said.

"Inglés," Hugo said.

"The thin mask, it is all image and no substance. Kabakas is a great warrior of both image and substance."

"Not great. Kabakas is nothing special. He practices hard, so that he is a little better than everybody else, and he doesn't let emotion into his mind."

The boy said nothing. He wanted Kabakas to be something more than a cold-blooded killer. They all had.

Hugo said, "It is the belief that bullets can't hurt him that has his opponents shooting wildly. It's the terror. Kabakas doesn't vanquish his opponents. Kabakas's opponents vanquish themselves."

Undaunted, the boy picked up the Uzi and checked it over with quick, efficient motions. His heart would be thundering. Something you never wanted in the killing business.

"Kabakas is no different from a successful farmer or businessman," Hugo said. "It's about projecting yourself as somebody to respect, to do serious business with. Do you understand?"

The boy frowned. He didn't give a fuck about his flower business now that the Kabakas stuff was out.

The battles Hugo fought were won in the first moment, not the last. He won the moment an enemy understood what he was; the kill was just the outcome. Things worked the same way with women. It was not the last moment, the fucking, that made a woman his. It was in the first moment that a woman fell.

Defiantly, the boy fingered the bandolier. God, he was practically feral. Hugo had really fucked up with him. He could put back entire battalions, but he couldn't get this small boy to behave. He had picked up an old math textbook and he'd been trying to teach him from it, but the boy refused to do the lessons by the book. Hugo himself barely understood it. The boy was growing up as an animal. He needed schooling. The boy liked reading, but nothing else interested him.

Except, of course, Kabakas.

They packed up the things they'd need, and the boy made them a simple meal of beans, rice, and plantains. The beans were undercooked; the rice and plantains burnt. Café Moderno usually packed them off with meals to heat. No more of that, now.

He really should've killed El Gorrion when he'd had the chance. It had just served no practical purpose at the time, and Hugo was a practical man.

Even now he didn't need to kill El Gorrion; he just needed his men to stay off the mountain. It was El Gorrion's men that Hugo needed to terrorize.

Hugo's contact had provided him an acceptable target: a plane expected at dawn in a jungle airfield near the Papas Sud River. He would take out men, money, and a plane in one painful swipe. He'd put the fear in them so deep that they wouldn't even look at the mountain again.

After that, he and the boy would eat in Bumcara.

They headed out five hours early, leaving time for washed-out roads. They stopped at a *mercadillo* and Hugo ran his finger along the thick, leaf-shaped blade of one of the barong swords on display. He could sharpen it. Make it work. He hefted one. It felt heavy and good in his hand—too good. He'd sworn off this, and he didn't want it to feel good. He tried to feel bad about what he was going to do, but he felt only anger. Saw only the old man, dead on the ground. He tightened his hand around the grip.

Espadas de Kabakas, the vendor said approvingly.

Not quite. The blades were much too long. Did people think they were that long? The real ones had been created to his specifications by a famous blacksmith in Mindanao. Unfortunately, those swords were at the bottom of the Azolla River where he'd thrown them soon after the fire.

He tightened his hand around the curved-bone hilt; he'd wrap cord around the grip for better handling. "I'll take all six," he said. He'd never attacked with more than two swords, but the *mercado* swords could break.

They drove for hours, then ditched the Jeep two miles out from the airstrip and went the rest of the way on foot in the dark. It was part of the ritual, to walk and visualize the fight. They had long training sessions on the walking and the visualizing. Partway in, they stopped and made the fire.

Hugo pulled off his green T-shirt and the boy rubbed salve over the seared flesh of his side and back. The scar tissue was fragile and could rip open with a lot of exertion. There would be some exertion coming up.

He and the boy started the visualization together—*anting-anting*, his Moro teachers had called it. They would do it before archery practice, before arms firing. There was nothing exotic about it; armies the world over—from the Russians to the Israeli Special Forces—had their soldiers perform visualizations before battle, though they would not call them visualizations. Even the Marines did it with their songs and their call-and-response chants. Hugo had picked up something from every godforsaken outpost that the oil executive had dragged his family to.

Hugo stared into the fire and imagined killing. In his mind, he pre-killed the guards around the airstrip. He pre-killed their hangers-on. And then he'd take out the plane in a fiery explosion. One soldier would be left alive to carry the message back, to let the fighters know of Kabakas's displeasure. There would be doubt at first, considering Kabakas was dead. But not enough to overcome the fear.

Buena Vista would be safe.

They began the trance, staring into the flames. He led the boy through it, as he'd done a few times before. He'd given the boy a child's version, to help build his concentration. "Perfect concentration on the small and the large," he said. "The movement of the flame below the night sky."

The boy did not concentrate well. Always distracted by his phone, often missing the larger context of things. It worried Hugo.

Hugo became one with the flame, one with the present moment, stilling all thoughts, minute after minute, hour after hour.

Beware, you are not a god, his old Moro teacher would sometimes say. No, he wasn't a god; he was the devil.

El Gorrion's men would see that.

CHAPTER SEVEN

Somewhere over Nicaragua

One of them wanted to take a piss. Aguilo translated, "He must use the bathroom."

Of course they had to try that one.

"Nope," she said.

An hour later, she made the bearded one bring her food. She wasn't hungry, but she needed the ballast. She'd lost her chops as a spy, but the information was still rattling around.

He set it down, but didn't leave.

"Back," she said to him.

He glanced at Guz. She pointed the gun at him. "Don't look at him, look at me! Get back! Translate that! In Spanish!"

Aguilo said nothing.

The bearded man stayed put.

Testing her. Her pulse drummed in her throat.

Fuck.

There was an emperor's-new-clothes aspect to what she was doing. What did she really have? Nothing much beyond her willingness to crash the plane. And she didn't really want to do that.

If they so much as sensed that, she was finished.

She took a deep breath and began to count. "*Uno.*"

The plane droned on. The man didn't move.

She reached down into her heart, into the crazy depths of her fear, and let that show in her eyes, her voice. "*Dos.*"

The bearded man stepped back. She tried to hide her surprise.

They rode in silence.

Maybe she was a little crazy. She calculated how long she'd gone without sleep. The night with Liza was zero sleep. Coming up on thirty-six hours, then. The tension of the takeover had drained her, too, and the drone of the engine was lulling her senses.

The guys struck up a conversation in Spanish about the horrifying things they'd do to her when it was over. What they'd fuck her with. Yeah, that woke her up.

"No talking!" she said.

They shut up.

"Bring me all of the Cokes," she said.

The bearded man brought her five bottles, setting them where he'd set the guns. As if she were some sort of wild animal.

"*Las abro?*" he pantomimed opening a bottle.

"No." She shook her head. She just didn't want the other guys to have them. She'd need them later when she started nodding off.

It came faster than she wanted.

She called the bearded man back. She held up a finger, and then pointed at one of the bottles. "*Uno.*"

He opened one, handed it to her, and shrank back. She took a swig and smacked her lips as though she didn't have a care in the world.

A good front was half the game.

She sometimes wore beautiful clothes to her meetings with Dax, as if she might be heading out on a date afterward. It was important to her that Dax thought she was doing all right, and that he didn't know about how she felt inside, or about her Friar Hovde nightmares. She'd worked with Dax long enough to know how to fool him; you input false variables—and they had to be convincing false variables, surface ripples connected to nothing. It was all about surface ripples with Dax. Or the beating of a butterfly's wings in Tanzania and how that would affect things a world away. You never wanted Dax's laser beam of a brain focused on you.

The guys were talking again. They discussed how much time had passed – three hours. That was about what she'd figured.

"Hey," she barked.

They kept on, pushing it. She could feel Guz assessing her. He didn't tell them to shut up. She'd known this was coming—the moment they would start testing her for real, seeing how far they could push her.

"No talking!"

The one kept on, talked about what they'd do to her. This conversation was scarier than the last, something she hadn't thought possible.

Her pulse raced as she shifted herself into the position she'd worked out in her mind, giving her the angle by which she could graze the leader's kneecap and the bullet would sail right past and into the side of the plane, well below one of the windows. It was in the general direction of the fuel tanks, but safely away. And near the guys too, an extra bonus. Risky, but there was no choice anymore—she needed to reestablish her willingness to take them all down.

She discreetly stuffed a bit of cardboard in each ear. The blast was going to be loud as a motherfucker.

Another started talking, expressly against her rules.

It was time. She let her voice go hysterical. "Stop it!"

He kept on. She jerked up the gun, aimed, and shot. The deafening blast ripped through the little plane. The leader cried out. A flurry of papers whipped around. The roar of the engine filled the air. Men were up, shouting.

"I'll shoot again!"

"*No! Para!*" Guz held his knee. She'd nicked him just as she'd meant to, and pierced the side of the aircraft.

"No more talking!" Aguilo ordered. "No more talking, no more shooting, okay?"

It was official: she was crazy enough to shoot up the plane and shoot at the leader. The guys were already working on the hole. Through his expression, Guz calmed them and showed them he was okay.

Good.

Still, Zelda kept her eyes wild. Her ear canals squeezed with pain. "I'll kill you all!"

"No more talking, okay?" Aguilo said.

They blocked the hole with part of a cardboard box and duct tape. She looked on, shaking like a tree. Thank goodness she'd ditched the heels.

She sat and drank another cola, imagining her exit strategy. She'd need the leader as a hostage. She'd keep the lingerie on no matter where they landed, even if it was a major airfield. People would see her exposed like that, and even though she'd be the one holding a gun to a man's head, she'd seem like the victim. Maybe she'd even rip off the apron. It would be a fucking Escher painting where the stairs lead up onto themselves.

It might be enough to get her out.

She felt the hope rise inside her body, followed by the guilt. It was how it always happened, the good feeling trumped by the sickening guilt of the Friar Hovde incident. Liza had made so much of Zelda's passion for justice, but deep down, Zelda knew if there was real justice, she'd be dead and Agent Randall would still be alive, drinking his shots of Jägermeister and customizing his scopes.

The plane droned on. It was louder now, but the patch looked like it would hold. She pulled the cardboard out of her ears when they weren't watching. Later she peed in a bucket off to the side.

She was tracking time, but even if she hadn't been, she'd know they were near just from the restlessness of her captives.

She directed all five of them to lie on the floor on the far right side, including the leader. She made the bearded man put bags and T-shirts over their heads, a task he completed with an ugly look that she felt almost physically, like bacteria in her chest. She tightened the ties, then she got the co-pilot out, and he got the same treatment.

She yanked the ties tight. They would suspect that she was something more than *la puta de Mikos* at this point. It couldn't be helped.

She hustled Guz up to the front. She took the copilot's

seat, forcing the leader to crouch at her side.

The pilot eyed her nervously, but he worked the controls smoothly and surely. They were in descent. She could see the runway in the growing light. It looked like so many other airstrips around, lush green surrounded by foliage. A few figures in camo. Her welcoming party. A hangar and a row of Quonset huts opposite, a boulder at the corner.

"*Súbelo otra vez*," she said.

The pilot looked at her wildly.

"*Súbelo otra vez*," she hissed, gesturing upward with the gun. "Up in the air. *Ahora!*"

He pointed at the fuel gauge. "*Gasolina!*"

"*No me importa.*" She demanded to know where a different landing strip might be.

He looked down at the leader between them.

She told him to land it elsewhere, or she'd kill them all.

Guz told him to do it and the plane nosed back up. And up.

She'd use the boulder to recognize it if he tried to trick her and fly back there.

She was really doing it. She scanned the dark horizon. She was pulling it off.

A fugitive feeling of triumph appeared in her heart, fragile tendrils of hope. For a second she felt good, but then there it was: the tide of guilt: washing the hope away. Randall's body on the linoleum floor, dead eyes that would never see his children again, see life again. She could get free of these men, but she could never be free of those five seconds of cowardice that trumped everything she was, everything she ever could be.

Totally and completely unforgivable.

Motion at her right. Shit! Guz was getting the bag off his head. She lunged. The pilot banked the plane, throwing her off balance.

Before she could even get in a shot, Guz was twisting the gun from her fingers. She fought him, but he had the arm strength and the hand strength. Strength enough to take it.

Pain exploded in her skull as he smashed her head onto his knee. The plane circled and righted as he held her head to his shin, grip like iron.

"You'll be begging for death by the time I'm done with you," he hissed, roughly ridding her of the rest of her weapons and binding her wrists viciously tight.

He dragged her back to where the guys were and cut one free. They began to free each other. She lay facedown on the metal strip with three boots on her back and her hands tied. Probably six guns on her head.

Guz spoke in Spanish. "I'll deal with her on the ground."

She swallowed as they descended, heart racing. She believed Guz, of course. She'd be begging for death. She'd embarrassed him, and there would be no end to his retaliation.

She whimpered, and somebody gagged her.

Her eyes clouded with tears. She lay there trying to enjoy the way it felt to breathe and have a body that wasn't in too much pain. Soon, she'd give anything to have this feeling. She just prayed he wouldn't start on her feet.

The plane circled. The touchdown was bouncy. The plane taxied and slowed, then did a U-turn and rolled back down, probably to the line of Quonset huts.

She closed her eyes.

The door opened and the cabin filled with the scent of diesel tinged with rich, moist jungle air. She strained against the boot on her back, catching a glimpse out the door. The dirt runway was dark, but the sky was pale yellow and gray, echoing with birdcalls. Dawn in the jungle. Across the way stood a pair of airplane hangars covered with camo net. That would be where they'd store, fix, and fuel the planes.

She could hear a Jeep or two. Guys coming out from the sides.

Aguilo, the translator, grabbed her upper arm and yanked her up, then pulled her down the stairs.

Maybe a dozen soldiers were there to greet them—some in camo, some in civvies.

She lost her footing when they hit the ground. He dragged her the rest of the way, then threw her headfirst into a Jeep, crunching her neck. Without missing a beat, he yanked her up and bound her roughly but effectively to a handhold atop the door. It would be a hard knot to loosen, even with her teeth.

Another guard stood on the outside of the Jeep, weapon trained on her. He watched calmly as she tried to pull apart her wrists, yanking and twisting, feeling the slim nylon rope cut into her wrists. Yeah, he'd seen it before.

The soldiers cleared out the plane, pulling out the pallets and garbage. The leader had the suitcases. He set them in the front of the Jeep, then called over Aguilo and gave him a cloth. *"Véndale los ojos."*

Aguilo came back around and tied the rough fabric around her head, cutting off her sight.

Fear and desperation burned through her. *Fuck.* The

plane had been hers to lose, and she'd lost it.

Spectacularly. God, they'd all make her pay.

She felt spun out, like her senses were everywhere around that field, and she couldn't feel her face. But there was something else now: a kind of peace—like things would finally even out.

No. Stop thinking like that.

She focused on the activity around her—shouts, engines, doors, winches. A waft of diesel, a large motor humming at a different octave—that would be the plane moving. They'd be driving it under the camo scrim at the edge of the strip. She focused on the jungle chatter beyond the guerrillas. Monkeys and birds echoed under the lush canopy.

She turned her head to wipe a bit of sweat from her cheek. Men were laughing nearby. She couldn't hear their words, but they were in the tone of those awful stories they liked to tell. There would be awful stories about her after today.

She sucked in a breath, centering herself. And then she heard a sound she didn't recognize—a *swish-swish-swish*, like something flying through the air, followed by a strange yell—a shout of pain, but worse, somehow. Eerie and high-pitched. Another cry sounded farther away.

Alarm-filled shouts followed. Grunts and groans filled the air. She stayed as low behind the door as the bonds would permit as the world exploded into gunfire.

Frantically, she rubbed her face on her shoulder, trying to dislodge the blindfold as the battle raged on and on. It seemed endless. Eventually she got it shoved up onto her forehead like a headband. She peeked over the seat. She spotted some of El Gorrion's men behind a nearby truck;

more crouched at the corner of a nearby outbuilding. But most were corpses on the runway. The one closest to her was splayed on his back, a knife in his eye. It looked like all of the dead were knife kills. Blades through the right eye.

No way.

Suddenly, everything quieted—even the animals and birds. Everything but the labored breathing that told her somebody was behind the Jeep, frightened out of his mind. *Aguilo.*

Clearly, Aguilo thought this was Kabakas.

But Kabakas was dead. The agent who'd witnessed his death was reliable—she knew him personally. Kabakas's activity had ceased afterward.

No, this had to be an impostor. Somebody had good aim, that's all. It had been twelve years since Kabakas burst onto the scene—you could get those skills with twelve years of practice. Maybe. And there were guns now with automatic aim, almost like video games. It could be that, rigged for blades. Somebody hiding in the jungle, just shooting like that.

She took advantage of the distraction to work on the ropes in earnest, wrists slick with blood. When that didn't work, she leaned over the side of the Jeep and started going at the knot in the door handle with her teeth, right through the gag. It put her in the line of fire, but there was no other way. If she could get free, she could break to the jungle.

"*Ahí! Ahí!*" She recognized Guz's voice. He was pointing at the trees. *There, there!*

She worked faster.

More gunfire. The men were giving their attacker everything. Smoke billowed. The Jeep was pocked now and again.

She worked away, tearing at the rope. When she felt as if her bottom teeth might fall right out, she twisted around and tried to go at it with her fingers, numb as they were. Fruitlessly she toiled. She felt like she was making headway and hauled back around to go at it with her teeth. And paused.

The gunfire had stopped.

The panting grew louder. Aguilo, frightened out of his mind.

She glanced up. Bodies were everywhere. And then she saw him—a huge beast of a man in a Kabakas mask strolling casually and openly across the field toward the truck where one group had taken refuge.

More shots. Still he walked—or more like stalked—right into the gunfire. He wore fatigues, leathers, black boots, pockets, and packs, all battered and battle-worn. He had the bandolier. Blades gleamed between the fingers of his massive leather-gloved hands.

She couldn't believe somebody was out there impersonating Kabakas. You impersonated comedians. Politicians. You didn't impersonate Kabakas. Because he was fucking Kabakas. And he was dead.

Or was he?

One man broke off and ran toward the jungle. In the very next moment, a blade was sailing across the space, flashing in the light. It hit home, and the man went down. Another Kabakas thing—taking the neck when he couldn't get the eye, right through the cervical vertebrae.

More men started running. One by one, he dropped them as though it was the easiest thing in the world. His massive, leather-clad hand dwarfed the blades he threw. He was all dark confidence. Nerves of steel. No mercy, no apologies. Never a fuck-up. Never a break in his excellence. She watched him move, body torqueing, pure economy, fingers hugged by the leather, shining where it gripped tightest.

A silver barong had appeared in his left hand, the essential Kabakas accessory. It seemed to glide alongside him as he closed the distance with a confident stride, brown skin gleaming with sweat, muscles surging over his forearms and disappearing into his gloves. The man pulsed with power.

Surely it couldn't be him after all these years, but her heart pounded all the same. It was like seeing your favorite rock star.

She shouldn't think of him like that, considering the Yacon fields massacre, but she had a special compartment for pre-Yacon fields Kabakas. The Kabakas from the photo. Her white whale.

Another barong appeared. His pack, she noted, contained multiple barong swords. The multiple swords suggested he was a fake. Kabakas always carried just two barongs—never more.

A shot tore the air. Dirt sprayed around his feet. He just kept going as though he believed himself impervious to bullets, another Kabakas thing. Another shot blasted out, and Kabakas, almost lazily, tossed the barong into the far-off jungle.

Another mistake—Kabakas never tossed a barong sword. The barong was not at all a tossing weapon.

And then a body tumbled down from the trees. With a

sword through his face.

She stiffened, transfixed.

Kabakas never did that; yet the brutality, the outrageousness, that felt very Kabakas.

No. No way.

Feverishly she worked at the knots as gunfire raged, as men cried out.

Concentrate, focus.

Things grew silent. When she looked up again, everyone was dead except for Aguilo behind her and Guz, who cowered behind an overturned truck.

Motion from the side. A small, dark figure strolled out from the jungle wall, assault rifle in hand. He, too, wore a blood-red mask, but he was small. Just a child.

The Kabakas impostor ignored the boy; he was going for Guz, clutching the curved hilt of the barong. His hand gripped and pulsed with power inside that glove.

Guz scrambled out from behind and took off toward the Jeep—toward *her*.

No!

He'd draw the Kabakas impostor's attention toward her. She redoubled her efforts to get free.

Guz slowed enough to twist around and shoot wildly behind him as he ran.

Calm and sure as the moon, the Kabakas impostor strode on, right into the gunfire. With a flick of the wrist, he threw a knife, and Guz was down. Pierced in the knee.

Wailing in pain, Guz rolled over, leveling his pistol at his masked attacker.

He was between her and Kabakas now.

She stiffened as Guz shot, once and then again at nearly point-blank range.

The man acting as Kabakas reached over his shoulder into his pack and drew out a barong sword. Now he had two. He began to swing them in a figure eight, Sinawali style, as he strolled toward the leader.

He *wouldn't.*

Except, he would.

He swung them quickly, expertly. It was something to behold, the way the silver ends shone in a figure-eight blur that sometimes shifted into more of an X pattern.

Guz shot at him, and the Kabakas impostor just kept walking. Guz shot again.

Clang.

Zelda felt the breath go out of her. Using the blades to block bullets. A Kabakas hallmark. It wasn't magical; if you angled blades just so, and if you were good at gauging directions and trajectories, you did have roving plates of armor.

Still, it took practice, not to mention guts.

He might not be Kabakas, but this attacker was nothing short of magnificent.

Guz scrambled backward and got in a wild shot.

And the attacker kept going. He understood what Kabakas always had: the closer he got, the more frightened Guz would become and the worse his aim would become, erasing the advantage of point-blank proximity.

The strange attacker was close enough now for her to see the calm in his eyes through his mask. There was something almost mountainous about him: hard, ancient, immovable.

Whoever he was, she knew one true thing about him: he was completely in the zone, beyond confidence, a mindless unity with everything that was happening around him. It broke her heart to recognize it, to remember it.

A desperate yearning for everything she'd lost crashed over her. She worked at the knots.

She could hear Aguilo panting behind the Jeep. Kabakas always killed everybody but one. The messenger. It was why Aguilo was hiding. He wanted to be the last one.

Kabakas had never utilized a female messenger. In fact, he'd slaughtered scores of women at the Yacon fields.

She had to get away. She formed a plan: she'd kill Aguilo herself and force this guy to use her. He'd use her if she forced his hand.

She sat right up on the side of the Jeep, smashing her wrist. She barely felt it in her fury to get free; she went at the knot with her fingers behind her back. It made her big and made her a target, but it was the only way.

Guz had thrown away his gun. He scrambled back as the barong blades flashed. It was like a lawnmower coming at him, tipped the wrong way. Maybe ten more feet before contact.

Kabakas spoke. The breeze had kicked up and she couldn't hear, but she made out the words *Buena Vista* as he advanced. Buena Vista, the town the men had been laughing about.

One side of the knot loosened. *She was getting it!*

Guz was weeping, apologizing. The man didn't stop coming.

The battle trance. The imperviousness to guns. Of course this fighter would have access to all that myth, too.

Furiously she worked at the knot.

He was nearly on top of Guz now, with no sign of letting up. Things were going to get bloody.

She braced for it.

And then there it was: the sickening *thwap-thwap* as he severed the man's ankles, boots and all.

Guz cried out as the attacker lit into him with the two barongs, not missing a beat with his pattern as he moved the chops up to his knees, then his hands, the powerful blades became a kind of mill.

Guz's cries sounded inhuman.

Cleaving the extremities first in a kill calibrated to be as bloody as possible and also to keep the man screaming as long as possible.

This kill would be the one for show, the one designed to be memorable. Kabakas had often singled out leaders for this special treatment.

Running out of time!

She went at the knot with her teeth again, ignoring Guz's cries.

Her heart fell when they ended abruptly. The head.

Out of time.

Bird screeched through the dusk. It felt like they were screeching through her belly.

She looked up to see the fighter standing over Guz's bloody, mangled form.

Movement. The masked boy was advancing on her Jeep from the other side. He had an assault rifle and a revolver, and with a gesture, he had a weeping Aguilo marching out to stand before the attacker. To see the body of his boss.

"*Por favor.*" Aguilo raised his hands and begged to be the messenger. He angled his head at her. "*La puta de Mikos. Ella no es más que una puta gringa. Ella no sabe español.*"

An American whore who doesn't even know Spanish.

Zelda grunted her protest through her gag and shook her head, not that the attacker even noticed her.

Nobody will listen to her; nobody will believe her, Aguilo told him.

Aguilo was right.

The sidekick seemed to concur; he began to address Aguilo in rapid Spanish. "You go and tell everybody that Kabakas will hunt anybody who attacks Buena Vista or any village on the slope of the Verde Sirca. He will chop them up until their screams reach hell itself. Whoever wants to challenge this village and those farms, Kabakas will hunt them when they are sleeping. This is now the kingdom of Kabakas." The boy looked to the attacker as he spoke. The attacker's gaze seemed to darken through the mask. Was he displeased? Well, the kid was definitely off-roading. Kabakas never made speeches, and certainly not one sounding straight out of a fantasy tale. It was Kabakas's style to make a simple statement—*Buena Vista is mine.* Kabakas had a possessive thing going with those he protected.

He would never have a kid speak for him, that was not a Kabakas thing.

"Even an army will not protect anyone from Kabakas. Surrounded by an army of forty men, Kabakas doesn't care."

She worked harder at loosening the knot, watching the man watch the boy. She was getting it. She'd get out of this, dammit! She wouldn't give up.

It was then that the attacker turned his masked face to her.

His deep brown eyes met hers, invaded hers. She felt electrified by the darkness, the fury of his gaze, and its endlessness. His eyes were beautiful and terrifying, shining from the kill, or maybe pain or fury. Her heart hammered out of her chest, but she refused to look away or to freak out. She had the deep sense that she knew this man; that she always had.

She glanced down at those hands. He was near enough now that she saw a sunfire insignia on one of the barong swords, a small mark near the hilt.

The sunfire insignia. He was using street-corner *mercado* swords!

That decided it. This was not Kabakas. No way.

Kabakas's swords had the *ouroboros*, an image of a snake swallowing its tail, the insignia of a blacksmith in Mindanao. The CIA kept that detail under wraps.

She stared him down as she tried to work herself free, using everything she had to picture the knot in her mind.

God, attacking a guerrilla contingent with toys? She didn't know whether to be impressed or disgusted.

"We will take on any army, any day. Do you understand?" the kid continued. "You will carry this message."

There had been twenty fighters at most. Aguilo would remember it as forty.

Still the man looked at her. Her heart pounded. She didn't know what to do with this eerie recognition of him, this connection.

Fuck you, she thought. *You're not Kabakas.*

The boy was on the other side. He yanked open the door on the driver's side and pulled a rifle and three revolvers out of the Jeep, then a lug wrench. He grunted and stepped back, casually spinning the weapon, eying her. He shot a querying look at his master, who watched her still.

The stars on the mask seemed to glitter. Probably also fake.

The man advanced on her, street-corner barongs shining with blood.

He was coming for her. She sat up, pulsing with anger, aliveness, that strange energy from when she'd heard his name on the plane.

This couldn't be how it ended.

Time slowed as the barong blade came down on her. In that moment, she wondered if she'd died on that plane, if this was her mind's weird way of replacing the death.

The blade banged down onto the bar atop the door, severing the rope the held her in place.

She tumbled back into the Jeep seat. Quickly, she scrambled over the door, thinking to run, but the attacker grabbed her hair and forced her to the side—in protection, domination, or ownership, she didn't know, but all her fight came back suddenly and she rammed against his legs, wishing her hands were free so that she could hit him and loosen his grip somehow.

"Go!" he bellowed, glowering at Aguilo.

Aguilo jumped into the driver's side and sped away.

The kid looked up at Kabakas questioningly.

Kabakas stared back at him. The two seemed to be communicating.

Fingers tightened on her scalp. Her heart pounded as she struggled, but it was like struggling against a boulder.

The engine droned away, under the jungle canopy. She could've handled Aguilo unarmed. He'd been stripped of his weapons; she could've taken him out with her feet as he drove.

The fighter looked down. Brown eyes speared into her core.

He had the same hair as his sidekick—short, dark, but it was those eyes that got her, seeing so much, containing so much. He seemed near, yet far. Drugged. In a trance. Something.

His voice, when he spoke, was a gravelly baritone. "Do you cook?"

Accented English. Valencian...but not quite.

"Do you cook?"

"Yes," she said, blood racing.

"Did you graduate from high school?"

"Yes," she said.

"Twenty-one times six. What is that?" he asked.

She gaped at him. "One hundred and twenty-six."

He shoved her to the ground and walked off. "*La puta viene con nosotros.*" The w*hore comes with us.*

Zelda stiffened. Had she heard that right?

The boy aimed his Uzi at her, eyes filled with disgust. "*No la necesitamos.*"

The man halted in his stride. Slowly he turned. The boy stiffened, slim limbs taut with fright.

Zelda's blood raced as the man pulled off his mask, as his wild and stormy gaze zoomed into the boy. He had those high Valencian cheekbones, gleaming with sweat, eyes sharp, dark hair sweaty and tousled. His features were large, like the rest of him, not smooth or polished, but jagged and proud, as though chiseled in stone, all crude power and beauty. "*Cómo?*"

The kid stiffened even more.

He addressed the child in Spanish, "Free her hands and

help her find something to wear. Her outfit disgusts me." Then he turned to her, eyes dark and expressive. "You run, you die." A simple statement. He hardly needed to emphasize his willingness to carry out the threat.

He didn't mean to kill her. She wouldn't be tortured by El Gorrion's men. Relief and gratitude washed over her.

The boy whipped off his mask, a small gesture of defiance.

"Nothing bloody," the attacker added. He picked up a rag from the ground and began to polish a barong.

The boy gestured with his gun. "Up."

So the boy spoke English, too.

Kabakas was from Valencia. Kabakas reportedly spoke English. But Kabakas would never show his face. Unless he meant to kill her.

The jungle chatter had started back up.

The kid had shoved a baseball cap over his head. He holstered his gun and stormed over to her. His brown cheeks had a rosy glow—from exertion or maybe anger; he clearly didn't want her there. She guessed his age at eleven or twelve. So young, yet he moved like an old soldier. His dark hair was slightly shaggy, like his companion's. She got the feeling that these two cut their own hair. They seemed somehow wild.

The kid produced a blade, seemingly out of nowhere, and sliced the rope that bound her hands as the man looked on.

"Thank you," she said. "Both of you. Thank you so much."

A dark look from the kid was her only reply. The fighter remained unreadable.

The kid pointed her in the direction that the man had pointed. She went along, feeling him behind her with that Uzi. He could handle the weapon; that much was clear. She had the element of surprise back, but she had time now. The attacker wanted to know if she cooked. If she knew math. Did he have a job in a drug lab for her?

What if she'd said no, that she couldn't cook? What if she'd done the math problem wrong? Would he have killed her, then?

She inspected her wrists as they went. She'd gouged the side of her arm—that was where the blood had been coming from. It had stopped bleeding.

The boy walked loosely, like a warrior, giving no more thought to the corpses around them than a hiker might give to trees in a forest. He was heading for a hut, faithfully following the direction of faux Kabakas's eyes. He turned and gave her a dark look, an unspoken command to stay. He ducked in and came out with a mechanic's jumpsuit. It was dark blue and stained with grease, but it wasn't bloody—and it wasn't a negligee. Zelda pulled the thing on over the maid's outfit. It was a hundred degrees, but she didn't care. With shaking hands, she buttoned it up.

"Thanks," she said.

The boy had slung his rifle over his back; he had his revolver out now, spinning it on his finger like an old West gunslinger.

"Move."

They reached the fighter, who had completed the task of polishing his swords. He shoved them in his pack. He turned his eyes toward her stocking feet, and then he glared at the boy. A shadow crossed the boy's face. He turned and made a beeline for a group of dead fighters and yanked the boots off one of them and returned. They were too big for her by a mile and smelled bad, but she took them happily.

The boy smirked. He was young, hard, and angry, and he had the kind of emptiness in his eyes that she'd seen in child soldiers and war orphans.

"Put them on," the fighter growled.

She donned the dead man's boots. Whoever these two were, they were giving her clothes to wear, and that was a good sign. She was safe for now.

The fighter pointed to the suitcase some yards away. The boy retrieved it. The fighter then tipped his head and the boy handed it to her. He had perfected the art of commanding the child with minimal effort.

He might not be Kabakas, but he was smart and powerful and dangerous all the same.

The suitcase was heavy, but she bore it without showing it.

"You will cook for us and you will teach the boy his math. Do you understand?"

A cook? A tutor?

"Do you understand? Do you agree?"

"Okay, yes," she said.

The fighter turned and walked into the jungle.

"*Vamos*," the boy said, motioning with the revolver for her to walk in front of him.

She went, mind spinning.

You wheel cook for us. Poot them on. Definitely a Valencian accent, but slightly British, or the kind of British accent you would hear in India in terms of music. One of the Associates, Macmillan, would be able to give her his entire linguistic history from just that sentence.

"En inglés," the fighter commanded. "You will speak to her in English only. Only and always English."

The boy said nothing.

She carried the suitcase in front of the boy and behind this fighter who styled himself as Kabakas. On they trudged, farther and deeper. She caught the vanilla and honey scent of the *Prosthechea fragrans* and looked around in the dim morning light until she spotted a profusion of the cream-colored orchids covering the trunk and branches of some of the older, larger trees. Gratefully she sucked in a breath, sweet and thick with life.

The boy's revolver glinted in the gloom as he spun it. Was he the dark attacker's son? Though he seemed to obey the attacker more as a subordinate to a military commander than a child. A dog to a master.

So much about this fighter said *impostor.*

Yet he *felt* like Kabakas to her.

It was impossible. But what if?

What if?

The possibility felt like a tide of magic inside her.

But no. He'd let her see his face and live.

Sweat poured off her skin. She rolled up her sleeves, loosened the buttons. People didn't realize how heavy a suitcase full of money could be, but she carried it gratefully.

The jungle became darker the deeper they walked. The attacker lit a torch and continued on. Where were they going? Did these two have some sort of a compound nearby? The too-big boots were giving her blisters, but she trod on.

She thought about the tanker standoff. Had anything

new happened? She needed to contact Dax ASAP and let him know the files were not forthcoming, but maybe they could work on the disgruntled guard. And her sister was home free.

The mission was only half a failure.

In maybe two miles, they reached a Jeep. The boy stuffed the rifle and Kabakas's weapons into a pair of duffel bags and then he took the driver's seat; the fighter took the passenger seat. The kid was driving? He was young to drive.

The fighter motioned. "In," he said to her.

She swung the suitcase into the backseat, keeping her expression a blank slate, and settled herself next to it. The fighter was already in the front. He twisted in his seat, nodding at her left arm. "No drugs. Understand?"

Her left arm—that's where they'd put the track marks tattoo. The long sleeves of the jumpsuit covered it now, but even in the heat of battle, he'd seen it, remembered it.

"I'm not on drugs," she said in English, maintaining her cover as Liza, the prostitute who spoke no Spanish. Convenient that Aguilo had made that possible. "I quit. No drugs."

He eyed her. "Lie to me, and you die," he said. "Disobey me, and you die. Run, and you die. Do you understand, *señorita?*"

Her blood raced. The Kabakas impostor was literally taking her *captive?*

"Do you understand?"

Would he expect sex, too? Of course he would. She'd been presented as a prostitute. She'd ditch him before that happened, of course. She'd get to a phone and call Dax for an extraction.

But every time she imagined leaving, a sparkly little question still played in the corner of her mind: *What if?*

Everything about him said *impostor*—his weaponry, the boy, and the carelessness of letting her see his face.

But there was something about him...

What if?

"Answer me."

"I'm not on drugs," she repeated. "I said I wasn't, and I mean it."

He turned in his seat. *"Dale la caja,"* he said to the boy. *Give her the box?* What did it mean? It sounded ominous.

The boy passed back a small box. She opened the top; it was loaded with gauze and bandages. Ready for wounds.

"Thank you," she said quietly.

CHAPTER EIGHT

The headlamps bore into the dim world underneath the thick jungle cover as the boy navigated around masses of vines and fallen trees. Hugo glanced again at the rearview mirror. The American whore had finished bandaging her wrist.

She rode in silence, swaying slightly as the Jeep bounced, eyes fixed upon the surroundings. At times the light illuminated the smooth curves of her cheekbones and her intelligent eyes, and Hugo found that he liked those times.

Hugo forced his eyes from her, teeth clenched in disgust—at himself. He should not focus on her. He should not obsess about her injury—though it did look deep. He should not have shown her his face. He should not have taken her.

It was the killing trance. The trance sometimes moved him to act in deeply primal ways that went beyond fighting. Like taking the woman. He'd known he would take her before he'd asked the questions. It was something in the way she'd held his gaze, and the spirit of her as she'd struggled, like drowning life coming up for air. It was something in the way she had refused to subside in the wake of his power, as though she were forged of a pure metal. That too had struck him.

And so he'd taken her.

He adjusted the side mirror to center her within it. She was inspecting the trees.

Contrary to myth, he did not kill the innocent, but he never took them. Except for the boy.

He told himself he would kill her if he had to. She would've died if he'd sent her off with the messenger—El Gorrion's violent tastes were well known. She would've died even faster left in the jungle. A kinder, faster death, but death all the same. If he had to kill her, he would do it fast. If he couldn't trust her, he would have no choice but to kill her.

He forced himself to note the false and garish green of her eyes, to picture the obscene clothes under the coveralls, the track marks on her arm, but it was no use. She was beautiful—not in the regular way of the women he had down in Bumcara, but in a deep, elemental way. She had the kind of beauty that made beauty irrelevant.

He shifted uncomfortably in his seat. Over the years, bands of scars—contractures, they were called—had tightened across his shoulder and side. The contractures made wild movement painful. Some of the scar tissue would be torn now—the sting was bad, and it would be hell tonight. But his discomfort went deeper than his skin. Even violent animals had souls that could be torn.

He concentrated on the trail ahead, bracing an arm on the door as the boy navigated.

True, she spoke no Spanish. And as an American

whore, she would perhaps be unaware of Kabakas, but it was a risk. He could accept the risk for himself, but not for the boy.

La puta de Mikos. He grabbed a water bottle and tipped it onto his head, letting a little trickle down his front, letting the water seep through and cool the sting, aware of her eyes on him now. He now possessed a stinging flank, a bruised rib, and an American whore.

He wiped the water from his eyes with the back of his hand and checked the mirror.

Her gaze was back on the jungle. He didn't get the sense that she was looking to run; she seemed...interested, engaged. Those marks on her arm said differently. Drug addicts always had tunnel vision, focused on their next fix.

If she tried to rob him in any way or threatened to expose him, he would kill her. If she threatened the boy, that would make it easy.

"You know *llapingachos?*" he barked.

She nodded. "Yes."

Of course she'd say yes. They'd find out soon enough.

They drove on in silence, out of the jungle and into the daylight, up onto the more- traveled road back to Bumcara.

An hour later, they hit pavement. The boy pulled his phone out, waiting to pick up a signal as he drove.

Hugo's belly growled. "What other foods can you prepare?"

"All kinds," she replied.

He found the answer...unconvincing. Could this American prostitute not cook after all? "What foods? Do you have a specialty?"

"I can cook whatever you like as long as I have a recipe."

He frowned. Most every woman in his experience knew how to cook without a recipe—at least the common dishes. He caught the boy's eye. Even the boy looked skeptical.

"I'm a fabulous cook," she said. "If we could get recipes."

"Fine," he said wearily.

"What sort of foods do you like?" she asked.

"Tell her," he commanded the boy. *"En inglés."* The boy could practice English with her. Learn some new words. His English vocabulary was not so large.

The boy began to list meals. *Arepas, cuy, seco de chivo,* bean soup. The menu of Café Moderno.

He shifted again, wishing he could shed his skin like a snake and grow it anew.

She pointed at the boy's phone. "I could look for recipes on there."

"No Internet for you."

She fell silent.

A whore and a drug addict. What had he done?

"Is there a bookstore we could stop at?" she asked after a while. "To find a cookbook?"

He twisted around, though it pained his flank. "Does this look like Disney World to you? Perhaps Mickey Mouse has a cookbook for you."

She kept her face blank, taking his measure with her eyes. Her gaze was more than a tickle; he felt it in his belly. "You were in America?" she asked.

"Questions like that, *señorita,*" he growled, "that is how you die."

She pursed her lips and looked away. He found he wanted her to look back at him.

"You want to live? Then you will cook and you will

teach the boy. You will serve in whatever way I see fit."

She turned back to him, heat hidden in her gaze. He liked the heat of her.

"What's your name?" he asked.

"Liza."

"Liza what?"

"Liza Pierce."

"From where?"

"Miami. Most recently."

"*La puta de Mikos*," he said, echoing what the man had called her. "Was Mikos on the plane?" She could be trouble if he'd killed her pimp, her lover.

"He wasn't on the plane," she said softly.

He waited. He required more than that. "What were you doing on the plane? You were traveling to be with El Gorrion? And you changed your mind? That's why they tied you?"

"There was a card game." She looked away. "I was with Mikos. We were together, but..."

"Your Mikos gambled you. He sold you."

Her silence said yes.

"Say more," he demanded.

She sighed and looked away, putting on a blank face. What did she want to cover? "He lost me to the Brujos Cartel. I was supposed to go to Mexico for a few days, but Brujos put me on the plane..." She shrugged.

"A gift for El Gorrion?"

Another shrug.

Aside from her wrists, she seemed unscathed. Had they been saving her for El Gorrion? She kept her blank face, but surely she had been frightened. "You want to go back home? Is that what you want?"

She seemed to hesitate. Then, "Of course. Yes."

"You will stay with us awhile, and we will see about it."

She regarded him with surprise. "Really?"

He raised his brows. He was not in the habit of answering twice.

"Great," she said. "Thank you. Really."

He nodded. Best to give her something to hope for.

He would have her investigated. He'd gotten to where he was by knowing his enemies. A woman like this, surely she had vulnerable people she needed to protect. A pet or two, perhaps for leverage. He would make her understand that if she caused trouble for him, he'd kill not only her, but also her people and her pets. Americans were obsessed with their pets.

Miami. Of course.

Miami was expensive, dangerous, and flashy. He'd felt assaulted when he'd lived there. In Miami, there was no night and no silence. He didn't know how people could stand it, but the people themselves were flashy, expensive, and dangerous, as if the city had bred its own kind. Including Liza with her flashy blonde hair and outlandish green eyes. The intelligence in her eyes was real, but the green was false. He did not like the green.

He watched a drop of sweat roll down the side of her forehead, down past the outer edge of her eye with its lush, dark lashes, and over the swell of her cheekbone. His mouth went dry watching it.

Another drip followed the same track, glinting in the sun. This second drip moved faster. He imagined swiping his thumb over it. Her skin would be warm and slick with sweat.

The drips had to tickle, but she made no effort to wipe them away. She sat there in a hot jumpsuit in the blistering midmorning heat without complaint. Keeping her thoughts to herself with that blank face. Not stupid, this one.

He swallowed as another drip of sweat ran down the middle of her forehead, tracing the straight, proud line of her nose until it slid down the side and over her nostril. A woman sweating, face perfectly blank, swaying gently in the back of a Jeep. A man could be lost in just this.

He tore his gaze away. Perhaps she was thinking about her next fix. Most of the whores around the drug trade were addicted to coca and the many perversions of coca that Americans enjoyed devising. Perhaps she imagined Valencia as a paradise.

She'd find out differently.

"Give her your hat," he said to the boy.

The boy frowned. He liked his baseball cap, but they were nearing Bumcara now. It would not do to parade her bright and memorable hair through Bumcara.

He grabbed it off the boy's head. "Now it is hers to keep." He extended it back toward Liza.

"I don't need a cap," she said.

His blood raced hot as she watched him, defying him. He could still remember the way her hair had felt between his fingers as he'd held her to him, keeping her out of the line of sight of that dog of a messenger he'd sent back to El Gorrion. He would like to feel her hair again. "Did I not command it?"

She reached out and took the cap and she pressed it

over her head, expression blank. Too blank.

"You're not in America now, you're in Valencia. You are part of my household, and it is *not* a democracy." He turned back around.

"You commanded him to give it to me, not for me to take it and put it on."

Next to him, the boy went still, but Hugo had no doubt that his eyes twinkled at the small uprising.

"You will wear the cap until we are home," he said.

She smiled at the boy as she fit the cap over her head. "What's your name?"

"Paolo," he said.

"Hi, Paolo," she said. "It's nice to meet you. My name is Liza." She waited expectantly for the boy to reply.

Hugo gave him a threatening glare.

"Hello, Liza," the boy said tonelessly. "My name is Paolo."

"What is *his* name?" She pointed at Hugo.

The boy pretended to concentrate on his driving.

"Hugo," Hugo said.

"How old are you, Paolo?" she asked.

The boy looked at him again, uncertain.

"How many years..." She held up her fingers, then pointed at him. "How many years do you have?" She pointed at herself. "I am thirty-eight years old."

Hugo studied the road. She was well preserved for a thirty-eight-year-old cocaine whore.

She touched her chest. "Thirty-eight. How old are you, Paolo?" She waited.

Hugo sighed. "He understands the question. He does not know the answer."

She furrowed her brows. She had pretty brows, dark and thick. She should've left her hair dark. "Do *you* know?"

He shrugged. "Fourteen, maybe."

"When is your birthday?" she asked Paolo.

The boy looked at him. "He doesn't have one," Hugo said.

"What?" She gave him an incredulous look.

"He doesn't have one," Hugo repeated icily.

"Everyone has a birthday."

"Not everyone," he said.

She asked Paolo a few more questions, staying away from the personal. His stomach rumbled. Hours until home. Possibly hours more until she prepared their meal.

They took side roads through Bumcara and stopped at a roadside restaurant. It had the advantage of a shady group of outdoor tables, one of which would provide quick access to their vehicle and escape routes around the back. He twisted and shifted—his flank killed. He wished they had more salve, but the boy had used it all on the way in.

He permitted himself a beer to wash down the ibuprofen; it took the edge off the pain. He would have the boy bring him opium before bed; that would give him a few hours of peace. He drained his beer and began on his *churrasco*. The boy and Liza had *pollo asado*. The boy finally got service. He began surfing the Web, scrolling his phone with one hand and eating with the other.

"You can make this, right?" He nodded at his *churrasco*. "This would be acceptable."

"Let's find a recipe." She inclined her head toward the boy's phone.

"It's only a grilled steak," he said. "This is rice. An avocado. You can find out the recipe from looking at it, can you not?"

She gazed at him straight on. "I like a recipe. I like to do things right."

"The ingredients are there to see."

"To make it the best as possible," she said, "with the right seasonings, I need a recipe."

"The seasoning is *chimichurri* sauce," he said.

She asked the boy to look up three recipes for *chimichurri*.

"Three?" Hugo pressed. "You need three?"

"Yes," she said, still with that blank face. "I want it to be right."

Americans. They needed help with everything. Everything was Mickey Mouse. Shiny. It disgusted him. "Get her three recipes. And three for *llapingachos* stuffed with cheese as well."

They named off more meals. Hugo decided she would make *lomo saltado* for dinner.

The boy furrowed his little brow, punching away at the tiny screen, which shone with the liquid colors of his game, Hugo noticed.

"Now!"

The boy complied, and then passed the phone to her. The boy retrieved a pencil from the Jeep. She copied the recipe onto the back of the wax-paper wrapper. When enough time had passed, Hugo snatched away the phone. "No Internet unless I'm present."

He couldn't have her communicating with the outside world. His eyes fell to the bandage on her wrist. He needed to get a look under there. She was his to care for now.

She dashed a drip of sweat off her forehead with the back of her hand. "I might want to contact a friend to say I'm all right. Could I do that?"

"We'll see," he said as he emailed her name and everything else he had on her—Miami, Mikos, all of it—to his private investigator in Bogotá.

His beautiful mother had been a wonderful cook, and she'd never needed recipes. "Do you know how to make anything without the aid of a recipe?"

"No." She looked him in the eye as she said it, unashamed.

"Not even a peanut butter sandwich?"

Her blank expression lit briefly with a flare of emotion—incredulousness, annoyance. Whatever it was, he liked it. "You want peanut butter sandwiches?" she asked.

"*Ni loco.*" He turned to the traffic speeding by on the dusty street, watching out the corner of his eye as the boy looked up recipes. "No."

Okay, then.

She insisted that they examine three recipes for each dish and create a shopping list. Was she hoping to contact somebody?

They sent the boy down the street to a small market with the list.

"He's not yours, then?"

"No," Hugo said simply.

"A relative?"

He shook his head.

"Orphan?"

"Probably."

"What do you do for his birthday? Do you celebrate the

day you brought him home?"

"I see no reason to celebrate that day," Hugo said, picturing the boy weeping among the bloody bodies. "Do not teach him that word, *señorita*."

"You don't want him to know the word for *birthday*."

"No."

"I've never heard of a child without a birthday."

"I've never heard of a woman who needs three recipes for one sauce."

She kept her face perfectly blank, but she wasn't fooling him. He could feel her flare hard and hot, like a flame upon a match head, and it made his heart speed. "I did not take you on to teach him Mickey Mouse and birthdays."

"Fine," she said. "No birthdays."

Was that a taunt? "Perhaps you could celebrate that you are alive and not a corpse being torn apart by jaguars or El Gorrion's men. It can still be arranged. I can still bring you back there. Is that what you want?"

"No."

He had the sense that she wanted to tell him more. He found he wanted that, too. He waited. Then, "Objections?"

"No."

He gazed at her hard, but what he marveled at wasn't in the looking, it was the way she felt. The contours of her.

She looked away, eyes full of thoughts. He wanted to know her thoughts. He wanted her face to light again with emotion. He wanted her to sweat some more, too. He wanted everything from her. Everything.

He sat back. "You know science? Did they teach that to you in high school?"

"A bit."

"You will teach that to the boy."

Liza looked down and nodded.

He had the sense of secrets in her. What? Had she not finished school?

Hugo's own schooling had ended when he ran away. Everything he knew he'd learned at the hands of fighting men, and that did not include science and math. He would not allow the boy to be limited in this way.

She patted her brow with a napkin. The sun had risen beyond the tin roof that had once shaded them. She would most certainly be roasting, but she didn't complain.

"The last cook who worked at the house left her uniforms. They will be several sizes too large, but they will be cooler than that."

"Thanks," she said. "So Paolo doesn't go to school?"

"He does not like school."

She took this in. "And school doesn't like him?"

He gave her a longer look now. She was perceptive. More...

But then the boy was back.

They returned to the Jeep and the boy drove on glumly, having lost reception and gained a governess sure to disturb his life of reading outer space adventure tales and practicing archery and shooting. Hugo addressed him in Spanish. "You will treat her with respect and obey her in everything, or you will forfeit the phone and all books. Do you understand? I will crush the phone under my boot and rip up your books."

The boy didn't answer.

"Do you understand?"

The boy nodded insolently.

They headed into the foothills, fully at the mercy of the blistering sun now. The boy took to telling him a science fiction tale. Planets, UFOs—*Ovnis* and *extraterrestres*. Hugo nodded. Liza sat in back looking bored; she wouldn't understand the boy's tale, aside from the explosion sound effects. Hugo wondered what she made of those, what she made of him and the boy. The glaring overhead sun made her shining, sweating face look more angular, more sculpted. She really was beautiful, even with the fake hair and eyes.

What had driven her to drugs? She'd said she'd quit. Was it true? It was not an easy thing, quitting. What had inspired her to quit? What was important to her?

She lay down in the back and slept for a few hours, but she woke when they turned off and began the steep climb up the mountainside.

Eventually, they reached Buena Vista. As they motored through the ruined village, Hugo had the strange impulse to cover it up, as though he didn't want her to see it as pitiful.

Her expression was blank as always, but she saw. Somewhere inside, she was reacting. How much of Valencia's struggle did she know about? Did she think of the region only in terms of drug cultivation and drug wars?

"The people will return to this village soon," he assured her. "It will be restored."

She nodded as she took it in—the burnt cars, structures hollowed out by the bomb blast, dark gated shops.

He could see evidence that they'd come and taken the old man's body away to bury. "The danger is over now. The attacks are over."

She nodded. Again, that blaze of intelligence. What was she thinking?

He looked away. Why should he care?

The Jeep whirred as they climbed on past Buena Vista. The sky was pure blue today, and the forest lush. The way up to his home was only two miles as the crow flies, but six miles on the winding trail. He himself had to maintain this path, had to move the rocks when they fell. The way was dangerous and beautiful.

He looked forward to her seeing the grand house come into view.

They'd lived in Bogotá for a year or two when he was a young boy. On a flea market outing with his father, he'd found a postcard of a Buena Vista farming manor. He'd been excited to find an image of the place his mother had come from. The card depicted a Spanish-style farmhouse home perched on a mountaintop that blazed with the reds of the rare *Savinca verde*. He had used up his pesos to purchase it for her, thinking it might remind her of where she'd come from.

She'd hated it. *This is a lie,* she'd told him. *The homes in Buena Vista are not beautiful like that. The people are no better than farm animals. And the flowers are never allowed to bloom.*

Years later, he'd pieced together the story of his mother from conversations he'd overheard at Café Moderno. She'd been a beauty who hated the remote village. She'd wrecked a few marriages and alienated everybody before heading to the big city. Nobody ever heard from her again, not even her heartbroken parents. Years later, her parents—Hugo's grandparents—had tumbled off a cliff. Some said that his grandfather had died trying to save his grandmother. Most, however, seemed to think it was suicide. Hugo imagined his grandparents' tract had bloomed blood red after they'd gone off the cliff.

His mother had never shown up at the funeral. Well, they were living in New Delhi at the time. The villagers had divided the family's tracts among themselves.

They think they are lucky because they are the only ones in the world who can grow the rare savinca, his mother would say, *but the rare savinca is their curse. The flower keeps them stupid, trapped into following the ancient ways.*

But Hugo loved the postcard as a boy. At the time, he'd only known gray cityscapes and violence, so a quiet, rural mountaintop sounded like paradise. He dreamed of going there someday. He believed that beautiful home really was there. He imagined he'd be happy there. Through the worst of his father's violence and his mother's unhappiness, he would cling to his someday life on the mountaintop.

By the time he made it back, war was raging. The war had upset him on a deep level and he'd taken to the killing fields like a duck to water, wild and brutal, battling back the war itself. Never making it to that mountain.

And then came the fire and the explosion that burnt him and took his mother. All meant for him. In those painful, dark days afterward as he lay in the old church, swathed in bandages, unable to think straight, aware of the boy always next to him, he'd imagine the village as a sanctuary. His goal, if he ever recovered, was to find that home—he had enough money to purchase such a property out from under most anybody.

After a few inquiries, he'd learned the home didn't exist.

A figment of the painter's imagination.

There was, however, a lone, crumbling, far-flung estate some miles above Buena Vista, at the upper edge of savinca-growing area, scrubby savincas gone wild.

He'd bought it from the absentee owner and had the home from the postcard built. A massive expense. That was when the rumor of his being American started among the villagers. He allowed it; he preferred they didn't know who he was.

Twenty minutes later, they hit the last bumpy twist in the trail. The red-tile roof and white stucco of the manor came slowly into view. Hugo found himself watching her face in the mirror instead of enjoying the view for himself.

She appeared unimpressed.

Well, this was her home now, whether she liked it or not—until he decided he could trust her enough to let her go, or until he killed her.

He could feel her from across the vehicle. "This mountainside is full of predators, *señorita*." He turned and eyed her straight on. "The most dangerous of which would be me, should you try to run."

A strange light appeared in her eyes—just a flash, and then it was gone. He found he enjoyed this woman and the strange friction between them.

"You understand?"

"I hear you," she said smoothly. Not quite a yes. He had the impulse to pursue her even in this, until he got her assent. What was he doing? He turned, pulse galloping. He forced it to slow.

Up top, the boy shoved the Jeep into park and pulled the emergency brake, and they went in.

He paused in the dining room. "This is where we eat. Dinner is at five. The boy's bedtime is nine." He liked to keep a military-style schedule.

"Okay," she said.

He'd been a fighter long enough to know when people were concealing things. What would it take to break that plaster mask?

He strolled to the bell. "This is how the household will summon you. With this bell." He didn't know what moved him to say such a thing. It was a dinner bell, to be rung for dinner, an old Valencian custom. He rang it.

Clang-clang-clang.

Her outward appearance didn't change, but there it was: that heat, that flare, that something that came alive inside her.

He'd seen dogs react to whistles that no human ear could hear; this woman's emotions were a kind of whistle to him, pitched to his frequency. He found he liked to...push her. And all he could think about, standing there, was how it would feel to take her when she was flared hot like that.

"Put the groceries away. The boy will show you the rest of the home."

CHAPTER NINE

Hugo walked off, undoing the small black scarf from his thick neck as he went. He yanked it off and allowed it to swing from his massive and muscular hand, which looked powerful and even brutal in contrast.

Zelda had built a career on reading people, but she found him impossible to fathom with his stony expression that sometimes seemed so angry. He'd saved her, yes, and then proceeded to take her captive. And this boy he refused to call by name and treated like a dog. What was the deal? And playing Kabakas, getting the details wrong, even the basic ones. But God, the way he felt.

And those hands.

If anybody had ever come to her, telling her they recognized a fugitive by his hands and by the way he made them feel, she would've laughed them out of her sight.

He paused at a large, intricately carved door. "*Muéstrale la casa,*" he began, giving Paolo instruction in Spanish. He didn't think she'd try to run, but they should keep an eye on her all the same. She would have the south bedroom.

Paolo nodded, then turned his angry little face to her.

"Come."

Hugo left the room, slamming the door behind him.

Where was he going?

The windows were covered in fanciful ironwork. Even from across the room, she could see the pale blue sky and the mountaintops awash in burnt sienna and endless shades of green, with shadow below. Once the sun fully set, it would all be shadow.

"Come," Paolo said.

She ignored him and wandered closer to the window. There was a veranda out there, shielded from the wind. She spotted Hugo out beyond, heading down the mountainside past terraced rows of bushy plants. The stiffness with which he moved suggested he'd sustained some sort of injury—possibly during the battle, but it could be old.

There was something so gothic in the harshness of this place, the sheer isolation, like an island prison except high up above sea level. The place was as remote and gothic as Hugo himself.

She longed to follow him, to see what he did.

The manner in which a man fought said a lot about him. But what said just as much was how a man wound down after a kill. Some killers liked to bathe, some fucked, some smoked. A lot of them drank. Some exercised, getting out the adrenaline. She'd always wondered about Kabakas.

Not that Hugo was Kabakas.

And what was he growing down there? She didn't recognize the plants. This was an entirely different climate from the jungle, a kind of microclimate where *araucaria* flourished.

"*Come,*" Paolo said.

She relented, following him around, letting him show her the spartan place. The bathroom. The dining room.

She'd created a Kabakas profile back in the day—a lot of Kabakas hunters had, though they rarely shared them with each other, considering the hot competition for the bounty.

Hers had him as a loner, a rough man who'd perhaps missed critical parts of his socialization. He would've had tragedy in his early life that had affected him deeply—a no-brainer there; you didn't kill like that without being deeply aberrated. She'd never understood why he'd never started his own faction to take back Valencia from the chaos. The fact that he belonged to no faction suggested that he'd grown up outside the country. He would've come from poverty, but why then not fight to erase poverty? And what had happened out at the Yacon fields? What would drive a man to kill every living being in sight? Hugo didn't seem to possess that level of darkness. Or did he?

Paolo would halfheartedly say the English word for the room when he knew it. He knew bedroom and kitchen, but not pantry. "This is called a pantry," she said. "Can you say *pantry?*"

He ignored her.

There was a hatch in the pantry ceiling, edges cleverly concealed in the dark beam work. She looked at the plaster dust pattern on the shelves and floor underneath and concluded that the hatch had been opened recently. Interesting.

"Pantry," she said again.

Finally they arrived in the long, wide room where they'd started. He didn't seem likely to show her the veranda, but she wanted to get out there, so she went.

"No," he said. "Do not go out there."

"This is called a door," she said, playing dumb. "And out here, a veranda."

He gave her a feral glare. "You must not go outside."

"Got it." And out she went, onto a red stone porch overlooking the lush, jagged terrain.

She peered over the stone rail and spotted Hugo near the end of the terraced rows of plants. They were dark and craggy on the bottom with green shoots on top. He slowed near one of the plants, doing something—she couldn't tell what from up here—touching a leaf, maybe. Out with his plants.

She heard Paolo come up behind her. "What are the plants?" she asked.

"You must stay inside."

"The plants." She pointed. "In the field. What are they called?"

"Please," he said.

"What are they called?"

"*Savinca verde*," he said.

A shiver went through her and she turned to him. The rare, beautiful *Savinca verde*. So this was the place where they grew.

She pushed off the rail and followed him in. "Hugo is your father?"

"No," Paolo said in a tone that suggested the very notion was outlandish. He closed and locked the door.

"Your friend?"

He paused and turned. "Yes. My friend." He continued to show her around, walking a bit taller. He clearly idolized the man. Did he believe he was Kabakas, or had the two simply cooked up the Kabakas act? It wasn't exactly something the American prostitute could ask.

Ten, twelve years he'd had to practice the act. It was possible. And Kabakas definitely had a fandom.

She followed him through more rooms with tile floors, white stucco walls, and harsh wooden furniture. Nothing soft, nothing upholstered.

This was not a home built for comfort.

Most windows were adorned with fanciful grates and shutters that stood open to the sides, hooked to the walls, ready to be shut against the chill night air if need be.

She'd never imagined a home for Kabakas; she'd always imagined him dwelling in camps, but if she had imagined a home, it would be hard like this, though not quite as magnificent.

The only rug in the place lay in front of the hearth in what she supposed would be considered the living room, a woven brown rug between two chairs. Did they sit there at night, these two males? It was then her eyes fell on the small, padlocked cabinet in the corner under a decorative sword on the wall. The sword of Moreno was displayed in homes for good luck, or if the inhabitants were superstitious, to ward off demons.

But it was the curio cabinet that interested her. People usually used these cabinets for souvenirs, awards, old coins, ticket stubs, and various other treasures. In later years, you'd find them in market stalls; the larger ones became popular as TV cabinets.

This one was too small for a TV and, anyway, she doubted they had reception up here. Was it possible they used it for its original purpose? Treasures collected over a lifetime? If so, it could hold a lot of clues to this man. She burned to rule him out as Kabakas. She had to know once and for all.

She went to it and ran her hand around the ornate carving. Yeah, she could pick that lock in two seconds flat. "Very pretty." She turned to check Paolo's expression. "What's in it?" She tried to give her question little weight—she didn't want him relating her curiosity to Hugo.

The boy was already shaking his head.

"TV? Television?"

"No."

"What, then?"

"*No sé.* I do not know. Not for you."

She pulled her hand away and smiled. "What is the sword?"

"Moreno. A great warrior," he said. "A story of Valencia."

"What's the story?"

"A story of Valencia," he said again. "Not for you."

Yeah, the boy definitely wanted her gone.

The tour ended in a small side room with nothing but a bed, a table, a dresser, and a window. The window was covered, as they all were, with an ornate grate. A maid's room. She went to the closet and opened the door to a row of gray dresses. Uniforms.

"From your last cook?" she asked.

Paolo grunted.

O-kay.

She pulled one out. It was gray with short sleeves and white buttons that ran all the way down the front between vertical lines of white piping. It was too large for her, as

Hugo had predicted, but wearable. Sensible black shoes sat at the bottom of the closet.

"She cooked? Did she clean and teach, too?" she asked.

He watched her blankly, but he understood perfectly well. This kid was observant, articulate, and definitely intelligent.

"A maid? A governess?" she pointed at the floor. "The woman here?"

"*Sí*," he said, simply. Speaking to her in Spanish. Outside of Hugo's stern purview, it seemed, Paolo was willing to break the rules.

She looked at the dress, wondering if she was trading one dead person's clothes for another's.

"You stay inside." He turned and left, closing the door behind him.

She stripped off her clothes. She didn't know what she hated wearing more—the lingerie or the dead man's jumpsuit.

There was a simple tile bathroom attached to her room. She went in and took a quick shower. Afterward, she pulled off the bandage and inspected the wound on the back of her wrist. It was deeper than she'd realized—quite the gash. She'd really messed it up trying to free herself from the Jeep; in truth, it needed stitches. There was probably a sewing kit around, but sewing a wound with regular thread sucked—you reopened it trying to get the thread out. Hugo might have something more appropriate, like fishing line, but keeping her cover as Liza was critical now. Liza the prostitute would not sit around stitching herself up.

She found an unopened toothbrush. She sat down on

the toilet seat with the towel tucked around her, feeling utterly exhausted now that she was clean and alone. She stared at the toothbrush. The last thing she wanted to do was to scrub the hell out of her wound with a toothbrush and then figure out how to make a meal. She bowed her head on the cool sink, wishing she could just curl up on her couch with her cat. She'd put her face on his soft fur and maybe even cry.

She'd been so frightened. So, so frightened.

Handle it! She stood, ripped open the toothbrush, got out the soap, and started in on her wrist. She scrubbed and scrubbed, biting back the pain, just powering through it. She worked at the wound steadily, getting out the grit and paint flecks, pissed at herself for even imagining falling apart. Imagining falling apart was the first step toward falling apart.

She was alive, unscathed.

When she finished, she refolded and retaped the bandages Hugo had given her in the Jeep, reusing them the best she could, then she searched the chest of drawers for underwear. It was mostly blankets and towels, but she found a small, strappy T-shirt that would have to do for a bra, as well as cotton granny panties and stockings, too. Good.

She pulled on the austere gray uniform and tucked the recipe in the pocket.

What had happened to the former cook or maid?

A scraping sound came from the direction of the kitchen. The scrape of a chair, maybe, followed by a few knocks. That would be the pantry. There had been a small table at the side of it—just right for Paolo to climb up on. Was he putting away the weapons? The hatch was just large enough for those duffel bags. What else was up there? She hadn't seen any phones or communication equipment whatsoever on her tour with Paolo, and he'd clearly lost his signal partway up the mountain. That was bad; she had to find a way to get word to Dax, dammit—before the morning.

She waited until the sounds ceased, and then wandered out.

"Hello?" she called, warning Paolo of her approach.

She followed the sound of Paolo's soft footsteps across the place. The click of a door told her he'd gone out. She moved into the kitchen. Empty. She drew the recipe from her pocket and set it out on the tile counter.

Back at the roadside stand outside Bumcara during those precious few moments when she held that phone, she'd considered trying to get a quick email out, but it was far too risky, what with them both hovering over her, seeming ready to snatch away the phone. Finally Hugo had. He'd checked the screen.

Once she set the meat to marinating, she set out again, creeping through the home, looking for anything she could communicate on, preferably a satellite phone.

She'd ask how they liked their steak cooked if they caught her.

Quietly she moved through the little dining room just outside the kitchen to the large, long living room that overlooked the veranda and even what seemed to be Hugo's bedroom.

Nothing.

She'd seen what looked like a steerable microwave antenna down in the ruined village. There'd be a wrecked satellite phone in there somewhere; they wouldn't have left the antenna if the satellite phone were operational. She could probably get it working, but it would be a bitch to get down there—it was just over five miles away, and not an easy five miles, either—more like a steep and treacherously curvy five miles.

She'd run it tonight if she had to, but it would be slow going with the altitude and her general exhaustion. She'd need a flashlight and a gun.

She took a survey of the herbs and spices in the kitchen, anything she could use as a soporific, and came up empty.

Her mind went to the hatch above the pantry where she suspected the weapons were. If she wanted to hide a satellite phone, that was where it would be.

Door. Footsteps. Paolo came in and grabbed a Coke, then left.

She flattened out the recipe. The dinner needed to be decent. She wasn't stupid—she'd put it all together when they went through the ruined village: this man and this boy depended on resources there to eat—that was why she was alive.

Maybe the only reason.

All men moved on their stomachs. Peaceful men and the killers alike.

She'd never learned to cook Valencian food—she'd spent most of her time in Colombia, Ecuador, and Costa Amarrilla, but the street fare they'd had today had given her an idea of the similarities and differences in the flavorings. She'd had *lomo saltado* before—in Peru, maybe. It was thinly cut steak cooked with onion, tomato, and French fries, of all things. Rice on the side. She started water for the rice.

So much had become clear when she'd seen the ruined little village. El Gorrion had attempted to annex Buena Vista for its surrounding cropland—a lot of the gangs were in expansion mode thanks to the CIA herbicide program; even Roundup-resistant coca wasn't growing well in the heavily sprayed areas. The scene was a classic example of the first phase of a takeover—the gangs sweep in, kill a few people, do superficial damage, and drive the people out. The farmers get ultimatums: switch crops or lose the land.

And Hugo had retaliated.

Kabakas or not, Hugo was a seasoned killer, likely out of the Valencian conflict. The plan might not have worked if the village had been on a transit route, but it was out of the way, a bit of a bother, logistics-wise, to begin with. She could see somebody like El Gorrion dithering over whether to bother with it in the first place. It was high enough up that you could get the rare frost, even. And Hugo had been very convincing...to put it mildly.

She chopped the potatoes.

What if he really was Kabakas? Maybe he'd thrown away his weapons, gained a kid. Maybe he'd sworn off violence. Then the bad guys destroy the village. Little do they know that Kabakas loves that village. They've pushed him too far and he once again takes up the barong blades. It was like a trope straight out of an old western. Her skin tingled. That sparkly good feeling filled her. That old good feeling from before. The feeling of the hunt.

Fucking Kabakas.

What if?

She grabbed an onion and cut out the core, began chopping, thinking about the way Hugo's gloves strained and hugged his massive hands out on the field like a second skin, flexing and stretching, black as night, the leather taut and shiny over his massive knuckles. She'd used to really stare at those gloves in the photo.

A lot.

Stop it. She pushed the onions aside and cut the meat, then seasoned it with salt and pepper. *He's not a rock star,* a colleague had once said. *Not a rock star.*

She went at the bell pepper, then the hot pepper. Kabakas had gone dark at the end. A psychopath. He was dead, and it was good that he was dead.

Zelda turned the meat and spiced the other side. She didn't cook, but she was a scientist, and cooking was nothing but chemistry, complete with a recipe for a formula. She assembled the spices according to the consensus of the three recipes. You always double-sourced where possible, and ideally, you triple-sourced. That was Intelligence 101.

You will not teach the boy the word for birthday.

Who didn't let a child have a birthday? Show him he was worth celebrating?

She had to stop letting him push her buttons. She needed to rule him out as Kabakas and get the hell out.

But what if he was Kabakas?

"You'll cross that bridge when and if you come to it," she mumbled to herself.

"Cross what bridge?"

She spun around and there he was, leaning against the wall in all his dark glory. His unshaven cheeks glinted in the firelight and his shirt was soaked through with sweat, pasted to his muscular form.

"Nothing," she whispered, wiping her hands on her

apron—not because they were dirty but because they were trembling. Because here he was. And Kabakas or not, Hugo did something to her.

He had that elemental beauty that really strong and brutal men could sometimes get; even his harshness was a type of beauty.

He pushed off the wall and came toward her.

She pressed her hands into her apron pockets but stood her ground. She would not be intimidated by a Kabakas impostor.

He stopped in front of her, gaze sweeping over her body. His midnight-black hair was technically short enough to stay within the category of short hair, but it was thick and a tiny bit choppy. The effect was barbaric and ever so slightly arresting.

A shiver ran through her. "What?"

He grasped her arm, drawing her hand from her apron pocket, lifting it in his massive paw. She forgot to breathe as he cradled it. His hands were warm, wrists like small tree trunks jutting out from frayed shirt cuffs. His touch felt electric.

What was he doing? Did he mean to kiss her hand?

Back when she was active in the field, she always knew what to do, how to handle a man. She'd certainly never been bewildered by one.

He didn't kiss it; he simply cradled it in his rough palm. Eventually, it dawned on her that it was her wound he was interested in. Sure enough, he began to work at the tape around the bandage.

"Hey." She tried to pull away, but he tightened his grip around her fingers and continued to peel back the tape, scowling, which caused the crease between his eyes to become downright gouge-like.

"It's fine."

"I will be the judge of that," he said, keeping hold of her as though she were an unruly child.

She gaped at him. He would treat her like a child, now?

Yes. Yes, he would.

She watched, stunned, as he peeled the tape up, little by little.

He would treat her as he wished because she was his captive. She sucked in a breath. It was insane.

She studied his dark brows and his inky lashes, which emphasized the sharp beauty of his eyes. His face had a hard, jagged quality, especially in the harsh cut of his cheekbones. The furrow between his eyes seemed to deepen. Anger? Concern? Annoyance?

He grunted as the bandage came up. Air rushed in around against the pink of the wound, cooling her tender skin. She felt exposed to the world.

"See? It's fine," she whispered hoarsely. "It's nothing." The last thing she wanted was for him to get it into his head that she needed stitches.

He kept her fingers wrapped in his and tipped his head to get a better view, cheek stubble gleaming darkly. Her heart raced as he pressed a thick, callused finger to the pink skin around the wound.

"This. Does it hurt?" he rumbled out. *Does eet hurt?*

She swallowed. "It's fine. It's clean. I cleaned it."

He raised his deep brown eyes to hers. They had just a hint of gold in them, like root beer. "Does it *hurt?*"

"Not much."

"*How* much?"

"Don't worry about it."

"I'll worry about it if I wish to." He waited for her answer, expressionless as a boulder. She amended his eye color to *root beer in the sunshine.* "We do not have the luxury of a hospital on every corner," he added.

"It doesn't hurt. But if it gets infected, hey, Mickey Mouse can come and pick me up in a helicopter, right?" She bit her lip, thinking that was pretty funny, but he didn't seem to, or, if he did, he showed no sign of it, other than the slight tightening of his warm grip on her arm. "Look, I washed it out with soapy water. We're good."

His thick lips twisted slightly. Yeah, he could see as well as she did that it needed stitches. He let go and went to a cabinet, pulling down bandages, boxes, and bottles. She spotted an irrigation bottle.

"Come," he said, standing at the counter sink, holding out a hand.

"I'm fine."

He frowned, hand outstretched.

"Really, I'm good."

He raised his inky brows. "It was not a request. You will come over here. You will give me your arm. You will stand here quietly as I wash it properly."

She felt her lips part in shock, felt heat invade her face.

"It is best."

Suck it up, she told herself. *He just wants to wash it.* She forced herself to put one foot in front of the other, senses tingling.

When she got to him, he took her hand once again, held it gently. She was close to him now—close enough that she could feel his breath on her ear as he growled, low and slow, "Was that so hard?"

She had the weird sense that he was enjoying this.

"Was it?" he pursued.

"Somewhat." She meant it humorously, but it was the truth. It was hard because he bewildered her exhausted mind, and because he *felt* the way she'd always imagined Kabakas would feel, and that was a mindfuck. Ever since the Friar Hovde incident, she hated people fussing over her and caring for her.

When he didn't do anything for a long time, she looked up into those sharp brown eyes and she had the crazy sense that he understood. It felt raw and scary. Like falling.

He went to work, rather expertly irrigating the wound over the sink. She stood there, fully given over to his strange, rough brand of care.

"You're delaying dinner," she said.

"Then you'll cook faster."

She bit her lip, praying for him not to get it in his head to stitch her up, much as she needed it. Of course he'd be good at it. Medievally meticulous, the way he'd been with the knives on the field. He was a man into control and precision.

Hugo patted her skin dry.

"Thank you." She pulled her arm, but he didn't let go— he kept hold, studying the wound.

"This will require a stitch," he said. "Perhaps two or three."

"No," she said.

"It is not a matter of debate. The cut is deep."

Her eyes fell to the box of *vendas de mariposa*—butterfly

bandages—which he'd pulled down with the stuff. "Those bandages—they'll keep the skin together. One of those would be perfect. That's all I need. Please..."

Again he twisted his lips. It meant something when they twisted like that; hesitation, maybe.

"Please, Hugo," she added softly, using his name, aware that she was pulling him, that she *could* pull him, affect him. It was a little bit of a thrill, like walking a bloodthirsty bear on the end of a fragile silken cord.

"Do you remember what I said? This is not a democracy." He released her and grabbed an ice cube from the freezer. "You will hold this to the flesh." He pressed the ice to her wound.

She complied, full of disbelief and awe at the way he was steamrolling her with his one-pointed confidence. She'd had that confidence once, before Friar Hovde. It was a revelation, seeing it in him, being near him. That fuck-it-all confidence. God, it was beautiful.

It was only when you'd lost your confidence that you came to see its beauty, like a long-lost lover who will never again have you.

He taped plastic over the rough counter and wiped down the surface with rubbing alcohol. He then snapped on latex gloves and doused them with the alcohol, rubbing his hands together to spread it around. He watched her eyes as he held his hands still, hovering them, allowing the bacteria to dry and die.

"Seriously, Hugo—"

"*Shhh*," he said.

Shhh? Nobody said *shhh* to her. Treated her like this. Ordered her. She was the co-leader of the fucking Associates.

He torched the needle with a lighter, then rubbed it down with alcohol and threaded it with green fishing line. His technique was good; he was even doing the sterile area. He sterilized his forceps, then he took the ice from her and placed her arm down on the less sterile side of the setup, holding it in place, angled just so. And she found herself thinking about those black leather gloves.

"You can look away if you like."

Right. You couldn't pay her enough to look away from his hand and his beautiful confidence and his utter commitment.

She watched him position the needle at the end of the forceps, felt the pierce when it broke the skin, felt it sink. He worked with steady force, pushing and then pulling with the forceps. His technique was excellent, and little by little she let herself relax into his hold, even into the pain. She found she trusted him. This was a man who committed fully on the battlefield and here, now, he was utterly invested in caring for her.

No—it was more than that. His touch nourished her. And with a lurch in her heart she realized that, aside from the occasional handshake, she'd barely been touched since the Friar Hovde case. And she certainly hadn't been handled like this. Cared for.

Her eyes felt warm. Tearing up.

What the fuck?

She blinked. She would *not* let him see her crying. He'd think it was the pain. She shouldn't care, but she did. She was just exhausted, that was all. And she'd been so frightened.

His grip tightened on her arm as he drew the needle through. Gentle. Efficient. Ruthless.

He made a quick, professional knot and then straightened up and looked into her eyes. He was silent for a long time. "It will be all right, *señorita*."

She nodded, flooded with feeling.

"Two more, okay?"

She nodded again.

He repeated the process, completing another perfect stitch. A fighter like this, he'd probably done it on himself dozens of times.

Protecting his investment, that's all, she told herself.

Finally he let her go. "Was that so bad?" he asked, tearing the wrapper from a bandage. He pressed it on carefully, exerting just the right tension for the wound. A pro. But that had never been in question.

"Thank you," she said, moving away, as if to get back the distance.

"*De nada*," he whispered, voice trancelike. "It is nothing."

There was so much between them now. Too much. It was the thin skin of her. She was overwrought. Fragile. And she had miles to go before sleep.

With a grunt he brushed past her, as if he, too, needed distance. He pulled open the refrigerator and grabbed a beer and tipped it into his mouth. She watched him swallow, his Adam's apple bobbing as the cool liquid moved down his throat.

Hugo had seen his village threatened. He'd killed dozens of men, possibly been injured himself. They'd both traveled far today.

She turned the meat again, just to have something to do. When she next looked up, he was surveying the mess she'd created. Frowning.

"How *is* dinner coming?"

"Great. It's going to be great." No time like the present to start selling it. She heated up the griddle. "Did you need anything else?"

He walked out and came back a few minutes later with a math textbook written in Spanish, decades old, a product of pre–Fortunato Valencia. Pre-dictator, pre–drug-war Valencia. "This is the boy's book."

The boy. She pressed her lips together. *The boy.* He could be so weirdly protective and caring, like with the stitches, and then *the boy.*

He was holding the textbook out for her. He wanted her to come to him. He wanted her...to take it? Inspect it? What did he want?

She set the meat cooking and went to him, wiping her hands on a rag. She took the book and looked through it.

"Do you know this?"

"It's written in Spanish," she said.

"But the numbers are not. And the boy can translate. Do you know it?"

"Yes," she said. High school math. What she didn't remember she'd figure out; she'd always enjoyed math. Unlike Liza, she'd been a very good student. Knowledge in math would have to be one of the Liza characteristics she'd break.

"You will go through this book with him each night. You may ignore the parts in the front of the book; he must memorize the drills. He is on fractions."

"This book is pretty old."

"So? Math has not evolved in the past century, has it? It is my understanding that math is quite ancient." He flipped to the drill section in the back. "You will keep him doing these until he remembers them correctly. Do you understand? He will eventually memorize every answer."

"Memorization..." she said. No wonder Paolo hated math.

He watched her closely. "Do you understand?"

"Well..." She stifled the urge to argue the point, suggest a better method. God, what was she doing? This wasn't a child-rearing conference. Paolo could endure being drilled from a 1970s textbook.

"He'll do the drills. Memorize them." She was conscious of him watching her face. He seemed to like to press her, to push through her compliance until he found her resistance.

She enjoyed it, too. Her belly heated.

"*Problema?*" he grated.

She handed back the book, ignoring the strange excitement vibrating between them. It was as if, in their friction, another element emerged, the way fire sprang from flint on rough. "Nope."

He turned the worn, colorful book in his massive, meaty hand, rough and dark and capable of too many things. "If you have an objection, you will voice it."

"Well..." She shrugged. "Drills aren't how you teach."

"It is how the school taught him addition and multiplication. It is how you will teach him fractions."

"Even if I know a better way?"

"Yes."

She pressed her lips together. *No educational debates,* she told herself. *No, no, no.*

A light in his eyes. "The boy will learn the drills."

The boy. The drills. "Why do you always call him *the boy*? He has a name."

He drew near to her, bullying her with his size. "The boy and I understand each other perfectly."

She gazed into the fire of brown eyes. What the fuck was she doing? Liza wouldn't sit there arguing; she would be frightened of this man. Her gaze fell to his vicious and beautiful brown hand gripping the book, dwarfing it. "Right. Fine." She turned and grabbed the spatula, shoved at the meat. Then she started the oil heating for the fries. When she turned back he was still watching her. She lifted her bandaged hand. "Thanks for this."

He grunted and left. She watched him move, powerful thighs limned in khaki pants. She went back to the meal, vibrating from his care, his presence.

She slid the steak around in the pan, feeling off balance. A nap and a good meal—that was what she needed. And to get a message to Dax.

She flipped the steak with a neat flick, added in the grilled veggies and tomato, and adjusted the flame. This was an expensive European stove and convection oven. The place, however spare, was top shelf. It must have taken massive funds to get this built way high in the middle of nowhere; clearly, Hugo was loaded.

Kabakas was loaded. But then, many people were.

She moved around the veggies and paused when the door leading to the back banged shut. She was getting to know the sounds of the house and this sound told her she was alone; Paolo had gone out while Hugo had been fussing over her wound.

The hatch above the pantry. It was time. Quickly she went in there and climbed up on the table, pressing on the panel with her fingertips. It lifted easily. She shoved it aside and pulled herself up into the small attic, happy she'd kept up the workouts.

Her heart fell as her eyes adjusted to the light; there as nothing that looked like communications equipment. Just an arsenal of exotic weaponry—knives, throwing stars, swords, sticks, training mitts. Fighters were notorious hoarders when it came to weapons. A duffel bag held a selection of guns, but there was no communications equipment. She found the duffel from that day, blades newly cleaned. The barong swords with the street corner mark. Fakes.

She'd personally debriefed two witnesses back in the day, and they'd both drawn versions of the *ouroboros*, the blacksmith's stamp near the hilt of the swords. The blacksmith they'd traced it to claimed to know nothing of Kabakas. He'd suggested his dead father had forged the swords. Total bullshit; the man was clearly frightened. She dug further and touched a bit of leather.

The gloves.

Before she could think better of it, she put one on her hand and brought her knuckles to her nose, breathing in, eyes closed, then slid the backs of the fingers along her cheek. Okay, she was entering crazy territory now. She pulled it off and inspected the stitching. Could this be one of the gloves she'd stared at all those years? That she'd dreamed about?

She stuffed it back, then pocketed a .9 mm and a flashlight. Then she heard footsteps. A voice. Paolo, looking for her. *Fuck!* He was in the kitchen.

She closed her eyes, willing him not to come back into the pantry and see the opening.

The steps receded. Looking for her elsewhere. Stealthy as a cat, she jumped down and replaced the panel, then stashed the gun behind a box of soap. She stole out, just in time to keep the fries from burning.

Paolo was back, a dog trailing after him.

"Do you want to help with dinner?" she asked. "We could practice our math."

"Where were you?"

"Rooting for quixotic rumblas," she said brightly. He wouldn't know what she was saying, and he wouldn't ask—the less interaction with her the better, that seemed to be Paolo's attitude. "Would you like to help while we drill?" she asked, hoping he'd get out.

He grabbed a banana and left.

She went back into the pantry and relocated the gun and the flashlight, then inspected the area for signs of disturbance. Hugo, the quintessential predator, would detect the slightest sign of disturbance. It made her nervous as hell, being out of practice like she was.

She went back and tasted a pepper. A little overdone, but not horrible. She drained the rice and plated everything up, feeling a swell of pride at how beautifully it all looked. She slipped out and cut a few of the wild Wiñay Wayna orchids she'd seen growing along the side of the place…and took the opportunity to stash the flashlight and the gun. Once Hugo and Paolo were asleep, it was marathon time. Back inside she put the flowers in water and set them out on the dinner table atop a bright napkin. The makeshift centerpiece really brightened the place up. It was also a message to Hugo: she could slip out, but she would not run. He could trust her.

Back in the kitchen, she set to hunting in the drawers for the proper silverware.

Again she felt him before she saw him.

Don't look, don't look. She needed to stay in the character of Liza. It had always amazed Zelda, the way Liza would just allow things to unfold around her. The clouds could be dark for hours yet the rain would always surprise her. But then she'd open her mouth and let a raindrop splash on her tongue. Liza had always been about fun.

Zelda rolled forks and knives in colorful napkins. A festive presentation. Very Liza.

He grunted and only then did she turn to face him, hard-cut cheekbones shadowed under midnight black hair. "We are hungry."

"Luckily for you, dinner's ready," she said. "We just need to bring all this stuff out..."

He turned and left just as she'd been about to ask him to take one of the plates to the table.

Well, what did she expect? She was the servant here.

She smoothed her apron, tucked the rolls of silverware into the pockets, and brought plates and the steak platter out to the little table. Where were they? Two empty straight-backed chairs stood waiting. Two empty places. As cook, she wouldn't be eating with them. It was for the best—the less contact, the better. She set down the plates and silverware and went back for more.

They were there the next time she went out, and they'd

changed clothes. There was something quaint and old fashioned about that. Everything was out there now, and she
stood by, eyes averted, looking anywhere but Hugo. "Do
you want anything to drink?"

Paolo frowned as he began to unfurl his silverware.
"Cola."

Hugo glared at the boy. "*Cómo se dice?*"

"May I have a cola, please?"

"Yes, you may, Paolo," she said.

"*Una cerveza,*" Hugo grunted. "Beer." He seemed tired.
Hopefully the lord and master would sleep tight.

She brought the beverages and lingered. They'd started
eating. What was the verdict? Did they like it?

Hugo looked up at her. "Yes?"

She thrust her hands in her apron. "Anything else?"

Hugo eyed her, shadows dancing across his rough face.
"We will ring the bell if there is. The boy will take his
evening math drill after dinner."

"Very good," she said, and left.

In the kitchen she slid what was left of the meal onto a
plate and ate next to the small corner hearth. It was
strange, just sitting and eating. She always ate in front of
the computer or in transit. The clink of her fork against the
plate seemed loud. Her chewing sounded cow-like. The
food tasted pretty good, though. Did they like it? She found
she wanted badly for them to like it. She wanted to add
something nice to this hard-edged existence of theirs. This
man and this boy, rough and alone.

Never name the farm animals—that was something
Thorne, one of their Associates, liked to say. Developing a
relationship made a target too hard to kill or take in when

the time came. And what if this was really Kabakas?

She had to find out. She couldn't leave without finding out.

She took a deep breath and exhaled, leaning back on the tile surround, feeling like it was the first time she'd breathed all day. Fresh, sweet night air flowed through the fanciful ironwork that covered the kitchen window.

Past bedtime in Europe. Asia waking up. It was usually this time of night that she checked up on the Association's capers. So many cataclysmic events to prevent, and so many dangerous criminals to apprehend. Not being able to check on things made the outside world seem unreal, full of stories belonging to somebody else, to some other planet. Even the pirates and the violence they threatened seemed remote.

But it wasn't remote for the hundreds of thousands of people along that coast. Most wouldn't die, but the pollution would threaten their livelihoods. She wondered if the press had gotten wind of the standoff yet. The press would make it worse.

After eating, she worked on cleaning up the kitchen. They'd need breakfast next. What did they eat for breakfast? She wandered into the dining room, but they were gone.

And they'd finished every last scrap of food.

CHAPTER TEN

El Gorrion sat at Ruiz's desk in the greenhouse lab, waiting, tapping a pencil on the wood surface, harder, harder, harder. He wanted to break something. Smash a window. Kill somebody.

Killing Aguilo had been a start. The man's body now swung from a pole at the center of the compound. If only he could've killed Aguilo *before* the coward had brought thirty men out to the airfield to see the bodies of his fiercest fighters dead on the field, killed by one man. Tales of Kabakas would have been damaging enough, but seeing his kill firsthand and hearing Aguilo's account of it guaranteed he'd lose far too many men to desertion if he pushed them up the mountainside.

He'd vowed he would be back in the village, but he simply couldn't lose that many men. He liked to keep his promises, but he was not stupid.

Kabakas.

No, it could not be Kabakas.

Yet that level of mastery over the blade was a rare thing.

But if this was Kabakas, where had he been all this time? Why return now, after all these years?

He'd thought he'd gotten rid of the problem. With his own two eyes he'd watched Kabakas enter the burning building. He'd waited until the man was deep inside before setting off the incendiary devices.

Yet the way Aguilo had described the attack had the ring of those old tales, and every single one of those men Aguilo had brought out there to see the aftermath had heard that same ring—blades coming out of nowhere. A man unafraid of the bullet. The hacked limbs at the end. Enrico Guzman, El Gorrion's best lieutenant, chopped to bits.

And they'd spread the tale throughout El Gorrion's ranks.

El Gorrion didn't like being made a fool. To be made to look like a man who said one thing and did another. It burned him.

He was not a flashy man. He was a clean-cut man, modest in everything. Except for his sense of honor and pride.

Buena Vista would be made to suffer; that was the beginning and the end. He could not keep his word without losing an unacceptable amount of men, and for that Buena Vista would pay a steep price. And he'd find this man—Kabakas or not. He'd find him and he, too, would pay.

The leaders he'd served back when he was coming up had been so pathetically frightened of Kabakas—even shrinking from him. Not El Gorrion.

El Gorrion was a man of integrity who never ran from the enemy. It was his policy to bring the fight to the enemy, no matter what.

At the height of the war, Kabakas had been difficult to find. El Gorrion had done the second best thing and attacked his name and his reputation by carrying out the Yacon fields massacre. It had been one of his most brilliant moves, part massacre and part clever staging, complete with blades they'd collected from other Kabakas attacks, shoved through the eyes of women and children. His idea had been to erode Kabakas's folk-hero status while drawing him out. A man's name and reputation were the most valuable possessions he could ever have. He'd paid a credible man a lot of money to tell the story as he'd crafted it, painting Kabakas as both a killer and a coward. This man was known and trusted, and widely believed. He'd later gone off a cliff.

Pity.

El Gorrion had planned another attack when he'd gotten intelligence on the identity of Kabakas. Or rather, one of the CIA men hunting Kabakas had gotten the intelligence, and El Gorrion's surveillance had picked it up. The intelligence led to Kabakas's mother via a money trail. Far easier to go after Kabakas's mother. He spread word of a threat against her on a specific day, and he had only to hide and wait.

The muscled fighter who'd rushed in wearing dark glasses and a hat was none other than Kabakas—El Gorrion knew it for a fact. You knew these things when you got to a certain level. Like angels or devils, recognizing each other among mortals. And yes, it was chaos, but nobody could have gotten out alive.

What was more, Kabakas was never heard from after that—further proof that Kabakas had died back there.

This could not be him.

Ruiz's ATV sounded out on the trail. Finally.

The greenhouse lab stood hidden in the depths of the jungle a few miles east of the compound and a safe distance up the hill from a processing lab, because Ruiz didn't want his activities near any of El Gorrion's facilities. There was no chance of discovery in the vast wild basin, but Ruiz didn't want to *feel* connected to drugs. He wanted to lie to himself, as if that would protect his self-respect. It was just the opposite—it was by being truly who you were that you gained self-respect.

El Gorrion did not trust a man who lied to himself, but he needed Ruiz. Ruiz was one of El Gorrion's best defenses against the CIA spraying program. Ruiz had led the effort to splice Roundup-resistant coca plants with one another, creating a strain of drug-resistant crops more valuable than diamonds.

He needed every advantage in the battle against the CIA, which was an all-out war these days, with the constant loss of planes, fields, men, and processing labs.

Ruiz had a new project now: an herbicide that destroyed specific crops, suffocating them utterly and driving the farmers to sell the land or simply give up. It broke down a few months later, leaving the soil healthier than ever and ready for a coca crop. By altering the formula, Ruiz would enable him to take over thousands of acres of cropland. El Gorrion could even take out his rival's conventional coca crop, then turn around and grow his own special strain. Such was Ruiz's DNA trickery. Basin blight, they called it. Ruiz was still perfecting it.

Ruiz had been petitioning to test a new faster-acting

version. He'd get his chance.

Did Kabakas imagine he would drive El Gorrion off and that would be that? El Gorrion would destroy his precious mountain and everything on it.

Finally, the door opened. A man looking to be in his fifties, with thick glasses and a flowered shirt under a white lab coat, entered.

Ruiz.

"I have an assignment for you," El Gorrion said. "You wanted to test the new formula. You will test it in Buena Vista."

Ruiz narrowed his eyes, tipping his head ever so slightly. "That would take out the *Savinca verde* bushes. We discussed this. You said you wanted them for cover. That you would plant among them."

"Yes, but now I want them destroyed."

Ruiz stared into the middle distance, careful to avoid El Gorrion's face. "They would go extinct, those bushes. Perhaps if we poisoned the people instead..."

El Gorrion raised his brows.

Ruiz shrank back.

"You asked me for a crop on which to monitor the fast-acting pellets," El Gorrion said softly and carefully, so that he would understand the gravity. "I have now provided it."

"Forgive me. It will do."

"You will drop the pellets as soon as possible, monitor the soils, and do your study there."

"It is a small village; if I suddenly appear—"

A good botanist did not a good strategist make. "Who will they call for help once the plants begin to fail?"

"The university."

"Do you not have a post at the university—"

"During the summers…"

"Figure it out," El Gorrion said. "I want it done tonight."

Ruiz nodded vigorously. He didn't like it, but he would do it, perhaps even justify it in the name of science. Ruiz justified a lot in the name of science. He was not a man of honor.

Once the villagers were ruined and without hope, El Gorrion would offer a reward for information leading to Kabakas. The villagers would have nothing by then. They would sell their connection to Kabakas.

"I'll need something quiet. The glider," Ruiz said.

CHAPTER ELEVEN

It took Zelda an hour to get the kitchen spotless. She splashed her face in the sink afterward, trying to beat back exhaustion. She'd have to make the journey down the mountainside once the household was asleep, and she wasn't looking forward to it.

She pulled off her apron and wandered toward the *thwup–thwup* noises outside. She opened the veranda door and slipped out. There they were—the two of them in the moonlight practicing archery, aiming for a distant tree— and hitting it. Consistently. *Thwup. Thwup.*

Hugo's thick, black hair gleamed, and his chiseled features shone with intensity as he drew back on the bowstring, strong and steady, corded forearms taut.

She could see his body straighten as he became aware of her presence, but his aim stayed true.

Thwup.

He hit his mark. Paolo went next. He, too, hit his mark.

She watched for a long time. They didn't speak at all, these two males. It was as if they communed through this restful art.

She found herself drawn to where they practiced, soft footprints in the cool night. She wanted badly to stand alongside them, to breathe with them, to shoot with them, just the three of them in a time-out from the deception. She had always loved the truth and simplicity of archery.

He'd seemed so tired at dinner. If he was actually Kabakas, he'd been out of it for years. Coming out of retirement, just like her.

He'd be about thirty-nine. Just a year older than she was.

"What do you like for breakfast?" she asked between shots. She'd already found coffee, thankfully. That was always her breakfast. "I saw some eggs, and I thought to make coffee, but I wondered how much."

"The boy and I will both take two mugs and scrambled eggs. You are ready to give the boy his drill now?"

"He looks like he's having a nice time out here," she said. *And he'd been to a massacre and all. Always tiring for a boy.*

Hugo lowered his bow and turned to her. "I wasn't aware I'd asked for your opinion on his nightly schedule."

Paolo's smirk faded as Hugo turned to him. "Finish here and meet her at the table."

Paolo collected the arrows from the tree while Hugo looked on. "We practice each night after dinner. After, the drills." He led her into the house and stationed her at the dining room table with the book.

She turned to the pages of drills featuring the addition, subtraction, and multiplication of fractions. There were little pencil check marks by each one—the ones Paolo had presumably passed.

Her gaze drifted to the cabinet. She really had to get in

there.

He stabbed the book with a meaty finger. "This is where he stalled."

Thees ees where he stalled.

Hugo or Kabakas or whoever he was had a beautiful accent, with a small lilt at the end of certain words, just a tiny extra sound. *Stalled-a.* Macmillan would be able to explain it.

Hugo showed her how he used a paper to cover up the answers. She found it hard to concentrate as he turned the pages—or at least, to concentrate on the world beyond Hugo's hands, so thick with strength and gravity, knuckles just a shade darker than the rest.

She found herself imagining how the pads of his fingers would feel if he were to draw them across her cheek or slide his knuckles along her jawline.

Again, she pictured him on the landing strip, the wild confidence of him—a dark, destructive angel who saw only the kill. She might not have this man's identity nailed down, but she felt like she knew things about him. Like the depth of his conviction in a fight, the way he could lose himself. It was how he'd be as a lover, too, she thought with a start. He'd leave human convention behind and fuck on a primal level. Like an animal.

She looked at his hands and imagined them holding her down, gaze gone wild, lost in passion.

Zelda didn't do passion. She hadn't much done it before the Friar Hovde case, and she definitely didn't do passion now. She barely even tolerated kindness.

"You see?"

He was speaking to her.

"You see?" he asked again.

She shook that train of thought out of her head. "Of course I see." It was fucking high school math. And she was losing her center, mooning over a killer's hands. That's all he was, a killer.

She swallowed as he drew a finger horizontally across a page, forcing it to arch and flip, and then he smoothed it flat. His fingers and hands were extensively scarred—not exactly defensive wounds, but they weren't paper cuts, either His hands had the harsh beauty of the rest of him. The rest of him she'd seen, anyway.

He was saying something. She nodded as if she'd been listening.

Jesus. Maybe she needed to forget the Kabakas bit, get down the hill tonight, and radio for an extraction. Stop the madness!

"...he likes to read in bed, but he must not go until he has produced this column of answers correctly...a *deefeecult* time with these fractions."

"Okay," she said as Paolo arrived and settled glumly in the chair to her right.

Hugo stood, looming over them now, thighs like tree trunks, the bump of his tucked-aside cock just inches from her face. "Begin."

She centered the book between her and Paolo and focused for the first time on the actual quiz. "You don't use scratch paper...at all?" she asked Paolo.

Hugo's voice boomed down from on high. "He does not need the aid of scratch paper."

"It would make things so much easier," she said. "He could memorize some things, but—"

"I do not need the aid of scratch paper," Paolo sneered.

"Okay." She pointed to the first problem, 3/4 + 5/6. He made a few wild guesses. She pointed to the four and the six. "The bottom will be something both can factor into. A larger number."

He made more wild guesses.

"Paolo, look. You have to convert different fractions to the same type of fraction in order to add them. So with six and four—"

"I can do it." He continued guessing until he hit upon the answer. Jesus, he really was memorizing the test.

"Check this out." She began to write the problem out on the back flap.

"I do not need the aid of scratch paper," Paolo said, looking at Hugo.

"What are you doing?" he said. "He can do it the other way. He has done the rest the other way."

"All of them," Paolo said, pointing to the drills with check marks by them.

"Proceed," Hugo said.

She wanted to argue. Learning by rote defeated the whole purpose of math. Apparently Hugo had not been to school, or at least he hadn't gotten past multiplication tables—not if this was how he thought it worked.

Hugo raised his brows.

She pressed her lips together. *Pick your battles,* she told herself. She went on to the next problem, feeling like she was in a pedagogical fun house.

Twenty minutes later, Paolo had gotten three of the ten correct from sheer guessing and had committed them to memory. It was completely insane. Hugo had taken to reading at the other end of the table. Paolo sometimes glanced nervously at Hugo when he couldn't get an answer. Her heart went out to the boy with his fierce little body and big, soulful eyes and his intense desire to please this man.

The fourth. This would take hours.

She recalled the outer-space story Paolo had related to Hugo in the car. There had been a code involved, interplanetary communications.

She sat back, allowing herself to be completely Liza for a moment, the picture of leisure. "I can do any fraction problem instantly with my secret code," she said casually. "There is a code. I will never divulge it. Never." She inspected her nails. "Do the next problem. You will not get it without the code."

She felt Paolo's eyes on her. "There is not a code," he said.

She shrugged. "Show me a problem. Any from the book. I have a code inside my head. So I can crack it."

She could feel Hugo's attention on her, too. "You will teach him what is in the book," Hugo said. "This is not story time."

Paolo watched her now. "I do not believe you."

She smiled. The kid wanted the code. If only he understood the principles behind working with fractions, he could do much of it in his head, but Hugo wasn't biting.

And Jesus, what was she doing? She wasn't here to flaunt his rules. She needed to get them to bed and get down the mountainside.

She sighed a Liza sigh. Slowly and carelessly she pulled the book back, allowing the paper to shift and the answers to show. Paolo's eyes lit on them. Such a Liza thing to do.

She sat back up and they went on.

Paolo, it turned out, was a decent cheater, pretending to struggle, getting just enough wrong. She didn't feel bad; it was idiotic that he'd be taught this way.

Hugo walked around to their end and clamped his hands onto the back of Paolo's chair, an ominous mountain of a man—clueless, stubborn, and totally in charge.

Clueless, stubborn, and totally in charge was one of Zelda's least favorite combinations, and it should most certainly *not* be turning her on.

No, it was his primal love for Paolo she was responding to. Much as he might deny it, he loved that boy, and here he was, fighting for his education—an education that he'd never had. She wondered how many schools Paolo had been kicked out of.

Paolo "guessed" the last one without pretending to stumble.

"Very good," Hugo said. "You see?"

Zelda nodded. It was a lot of fractions to have remembered. Was he using a mnemonic device?

Paolo stood, said good night to Hugo in a ridiculously formal way, and walked off.

Hugo's booming voice startled her. "Wait."

Paolo froze and turned.

"Did you forget something?"

Paolo looked bewildered, his expression ashen. The boy was overtired. What had he forgotten?

Hugo turned and pulled out Paolo's chair.

"What's going on?" she asked.

"The boy forgot his manners. Now he must start a new lesson."

No way.

Paolo was already slinking to the table. Hugo stared at her expectantly.

"You're using math as a *punishment?*"

"You wish him to do two more drills?" Hugo said.

"Well, this'll show him how to love math," she grit out sarcastically, so low that a normal man might not hear. But Hugo was no normal man. He was a hunter, a killer, a man about three klicks up from a caveman.

"Loving math was never the intention," he growled. "The boy must exercise perfect concentration on things small and large. He remembered his drills tonight, but he lost the larger context."

She sat. She was Liza, and Liza would play along.

She turned the page, covered the answers with the paper, and began again. "Next."

She glanced over at Hugo. His eyes didn't have the usual quartz-like intensity, as though the life and the light were out of him. It was like he was consumed with something. Such a fucking tyrant.

Glumly, Paolo cast around for the answers, avoiding her eyes, wishing her gone, no doubt.

The larger context.

The child needed sleep; that was the larger context. The larger context was that might did not make right. And principles mattered. And she told herself that if this were Kabakas, she'd have to bring him in. No one got to massacre whoever he wanted to; certainly not dozens of women and children. She sat up, filled with confidence and conviction. And then, she stilled. This feeling. She hadn't felt this way since...*before* Friar Hovde.

As soon as she turned the spotlight on the good feeling,

it was gone, and she was back tied up in that dark basement, and all the pain and shame and blood and terror flooded her senses. She curled her toes as Paolo toiled away at his quiz.

The toes were where Friar Hovde had begun cutting. God, she'd screamed so much toward the end. Blowing Randall's cover was unforgivable. That was the worst thing to happen down there—letting Friar Hovde know that one of his trusted elders was a CIA agent. But screaming for Friar Hovde had been devastating in a different way, too, because it had been a kind of intimacy. You never wanted to open your heart to your torturer like that, even if you were opening it in fear. Like a bear in a cage, she went over the old pathways of thought, worn flat from compulsive tracing. Something about being with this man had allowed her to break free for a second.

She looked at Hugo, feeling so strange. She felt…different around him.

"What?" he growled.

"Next," she murmured.

Hugo rose and left, moving in and out while they finished the lesson. She could always feel when he neared, somehow, as if he changed the ions in the very air, like a thunderstorm. Through a combination of cheating and sheer willpower, Paolo managed to complete his quiz, and some twenty minutes later, he stood and bid them both good night, doing it the proper way this time, eyes still not quite meeting hers. "Good night, Liza."

"Good night, Paolo," she said.

"Good night, Hugo," Paolo said.

"Good night," Hugo said. Which, in her mind, she

amended to *Good night, PAOLO.*

Paolo walked off.

She turned to Hugo. "Good night." She half expected that twist of his lips, but his expression remained stony, The skin beneath his eyes was shadowed, as if he'd been rubbing them. "It's been such a day," she said softly.

He seemed to focus on her now. "Yes."

"Good night," she said. "*Gracias.*" Her sister knew a few words in Spanish.

He nodded. "Go to bed. Stay there until the bell."

"Right." *The bell.* It was all she could do not to start laughing out of the sheer insanity of it all. She headed off to her room, pausing in the doorway to draw a square of wax paper from her apron pocket. She unfolded it and swiped her finger through the dollop of lard she'd enclosed inside it, and applied it to the door hinges, swinging the heavy paneled thing to work in the lubricant.

She shut and locked the door. With nothing else to do but wait, she turned back the covers and slipped into the cool, smooth sheets.

She was oh, so tired.

Back in New York, she'd always bring her phone and computer to bed in order to get the latest reports, often waking up at intervals.

Not tonight.

She gazed up at the moon and guessed it to be a few minutes before ten. Ten at night in Valencia would be three in the morning in Algiers and ten in the morning in Bangkok.

She wondered how Dax was faring alone. Not well, she imagined. They needed each other. She needed Dax's foresight, and Dax needed her understanding of the field. He couldn't tell when Associates were getting dangerously overworked. He didn't know how to put them into teams. He couldn't recognize a high-performance agent like she could. She was the one who'd recognized the use they could make of the linguist Peter Maxwell, hunting him and verifying his story before sending in Rio for an extraction.

And Dax had serious blind spots. The loftier capabilities of the human heart could mystify him at times. And he was ignorant of his own heart in many ways. Like when he'd lost objectivity with Thorne—he'd been blindsided when he realized Thorne regarded him as a father. She'd had to talk him down from that. And then there were the demons that drove Dax to his sex addiction. He thought he had a handle on them. Yeah, he had a handle on them. The way you have a handle on the tip of an iceberg. Dax was absolutely brilliant and absolutely fucked up.

She lay in bed with just the night birds and bugs for noise—no horns, no planes, and no random yells out on the street, like in Manhattan. And the near total darkness—the moon was just a glow behind the clouds. She hadn't experienced this level of darkness and silence—not to mention tech silence—since she was out in the desert. Like a fucking sensory deprivation chamber, and she didn't like it. The Friar Hovde nightmares were bad enough back home in a sea of noise and gadgets. She felt more vulnerable to them in the quiet, as though they might get hold of her, and she'd be trapped inside that nightmarish loop of trying desperately to get free from the ropes Friar Hovde had bound her with, trying over and over to kill Friar Hovde and save Agent Randall. Save the man whose death she'd so shamefully ensured.

Trying over and over to kill Friar Hovde.

She never could.

She decided to allow herself one hour of sleep, which had her waking at 11:30. She could do that—sleep at precise intervals and tell time by the moon. Some field skills never left you.

CHAPTER TWELVE

Zelda rose exactly two hours later and changed into the dead man's coveralls. She used a selection of knives she'd nicked from the kitchen to loosen the grate over the window. Minutes later, she was out front retrieving the weapon and the flashlight. She set off, jogging down the mountain road, moving at a slow, controlled pace, slowing to a walk as the way got steep, staying to the inside, sometimes touching the walls of stone, dodging rocks and snakes, catching the eyes of night creatures here and there with her flashlight. It was hard going, but the way back up would be harder.

It took over an hour to travel the five or six miles to the village ruins. She rounded a corner, panting, making her way down the dark, dusty street toward the little store, her best candidate for a com setup—that's where she'd seen the antenna. The abandoned place was even eerier at night. Dogs barked nearby. Wind rustled leaves and papers.

She picked the lock and slipped into the store, stepping carefully over downed racks. Animals had been in the stock—she heard a few scurrying off.

She found what she was looking for in the far back—the satellite phone terminal. Its casing was destroyed, but all in all, it wasn't so bad. She'd seen repeaters down the mountain when they drove in—they'd go to this. She pulled apart the pieces and began to twist wires, wishing she had her glasses instead of Liza's uncomfortable contacts.

After a half hour, she had a signal. It cut in and out, but she got hold of Dax.

"Zelda, thank God," Dax said. "Everything okay?"

"Yeah, but I got relocated before I could get Brujos's files. They pulled me out of there so fast, dammit. Too fast. I'm in Buena Vista—it's on the southern slope of the Verde Sirca, about seventy miles north of Bumcara."

"Wait—you're in Valencia?"

"I got traded down—Brujos's woman freaked. It's fine. I'm safe. Are the pirates still quiet?"

Dax filled her in—they were still sitting tight. Good. She told him about the Brujos guard, Sal, who might be turned. It wasn't as good as having the files in hand, but Dax got right on it. She could picture him at his desk in his condo overlooking Central Park, could see his thumbs flying over his keyboard, sending out instructions to check out Sal's family ASAP. You needed to know about a man's family to know how to turn him.

"What's your immediate situation?" Dax asked. "I could have a team in Bumcara by lunch."

"Hold off."

"We have a team ready—" The line began to crackle, and then it cut out.

Fuck.

A team. It would be Riley the strategist he'd send in,

along with Cole, all smarts and muscle.

She found the break, bared a new length of wire, and re-twisted. The last thing she needed was a helicopter coming down. Ten minutes later, she had Dax again. "You have to leave me here," she said quickly. "I'm on a farm north of Buena Vista. I'm the help. I've got my own thing going."

"You're the what?"

"Maid, governess. Perfectly safe. Dax, listen," she said. "This is probably nothing, but there's a tiny possibility I've found Kabakas."

Even over the shitty connection, she could hear the breath *whoosh* out of him. "*What?*"

She enjoyed his amazement, but something twisted in her stomach. "It's probably nothing—just a skilled impersonator. And really smart how he did it. Effective."

"You've met him?"

"It's probably not him. A lot of things don't add up."

"But some things do."

"I don't know," she said. "I also haven't slept for two days. I just need to rule him out. It'll bug me if I don't rule this guy out before I leave. He *feels* like Kabakas."

"Kabakas brutally massacred dozens of unarmed civilians," Dax said. "Does this guy feel like that? Because if this guy feels like that—"

"Stop. I'm fine. And, there's a way where he *doesn't* feel right. It's hard to explain..." She didn't know how to explain about the moments where he'd felt like Kabakas from *before* the Yacon fields massacre. The Kabakas she'd profiled and hunted and obsessed over. Out there on that field, he'd felt like the shining warrior from that photo above her desk. "I'm in a position to investigate the fuck out of him, but you need to give me time."

"You're not on his fucking staff, are you? I thought you said you were safe—"

"I am safe," she insisted, deciding to leave the whole captive angle out of it. That was just a little too 300 bc for Dax to handle.

"I'm sending somebody. I've got your location."

"Don't you dare," she said, regretting she'd said anything at all now.

"Wait," he said. "Wait."

A sick feeling came over her.

"Who was it that put up that bounty? The Valencian vice president, right? Juarez? Right? He's in the ministry now. He has influence with the delegation. Jesus, if the pirates could deliver Kabakas—"

"No," she whispered.

"Juarez could put pressure on the right people..." Dax named off a string of people, one affecting another and then another, complex horse trades that could end with the pirate situation getting solved. "We could use Kabakas. He would work as a bargaining chip..."

Bargaining chip. A euphemism for giving Hugo up to be tortured and killed. *What had she done?* "It's very likely not him."

"What name is he using? I'll work it from here. We'll take him down and get the proof."

"No," she said. "I'm telling you, the guard will flip. Sal. Sal will flip. I know the sound of a man ready to flip. Check it out. This guy may not be Kabakas—a really smart agent witnessed Kabakas's death nine years ago. I just need to rule him out for myself. It's a personal thing."

"What's his name?"

Her words came low and slow. "Hands off. This is my personal thing."

The silence on the line was loud as hell now because of the question that hung in the air—if Dax moved in on Hugo, would she stand in the way? Would she work against a team?

"Sal is the better angle," she said. "You have people in place down there."

"Both angles are the better angle."

"This is my thing, my call."

"Question," Dax said after a silence. "What does the Bigfoot hunter hunt?"

Heat rode up her neck. "Dax—" she warned.

"Do you know?"

"I'm not playing this with you." She'd heard Dax turn people inside out. He'd never done it to her.

"Most Bigfoot hunters, Loch Ness Monster hunters, they're not hunting a monster at all," he said. "They don't give a fuck about a monster. They're hunting for something *more*. Something more than *this*. Something magical, special. They need to see that there's something more than this body that wrinkles and dies. Something more than poor, starving jamokes in some war-town country. Something more than suffering assholes tied up in basements getting their flesh cut up until they give up a name. A passageway out of the shame, the guilt—"

"How dare you," she hissed. "How dare you, Dax."

"Is he powerful enough to blot out the pain?"

"Don't—"

"Tell me how you feel when you imagine it might be

him. How do you feel inside?"

She took a breath, collecting herself, forcing a casual tone. The worst thing you could do with Dax was to react. "So let me get this straight. Are you suggesting I'm protecting him? Or are you questioning my objectivity in general? Or do I just have some big fucking death wish?"

"I don't know."

She sighed, loudly. "Look, I have a mountain to climb before I sleep, so if we're done here—"

"Do you still have the Friar Hovde nightmares? You try and try to kill him, but you can't."

"How about you jack off on your own time?" she said coolly. "Bottom line, you will not send in a team. Bottom line, we don't commit Associates until I'm convinced of his identity. You're going to give me a week to do this right. More if I need it. You will lay off until then. You will work on Sal. Sal is the hot option." She let the *or else* go unspoken.

"Five days," he said.

"A week. This is social engineering, Dax."

"Fine."

"I need to get back."

"Zelda—"

"Work on Sal. I'll get back to you." She yanked out the wire and sat in the dark, listening to the night animals. It was so like Dax to hook up Kabakas and Friar Hovde. Throw in the pirates and Mickey Mouse, and they'd have a party.

It stung that he'd question her objectivity like that. *Blind spots,* she told herself. And the closer to home, the larger Dax's blind spots were. Still, it stung.

She stood and picked through the debris of the little shop. She'd seen mouthwash near an overturned rack; contact solution was too much to hope for, but she did find saline solution. She took it and left, jogging slowly upward, wishing to hell that she hadn't told him about Kabakas or the Friar Hovde nightmares. But Dax was her partner, her best friend.

God, she'd always been content to let him run the show. It was part of their vision of cells and secrecy—destroy part of the Association, and other parts would still stand.

She was starting to regret that. Allowing herself to be the silent partner. As if she wasn't worthy to be seen as a leader. Dax had never moved against her, but it wasn't out of the question. Nothing was out of the question for Dax. Dax did the hard things that nobody else would do. He was ruthless—ruthless for good causes, yes—but ruthless all the same.

Well, she could be ruthless, too.

She kept on, huffing and puffing, a little bleary. And fuck, she was so tired of all the problems.

She was actually looking forward to sleeping in that barren little room in that simple, austere home in the middle of nowhere. No phones, no buzzers. No need, even, to choose what to wear, because she had four gray uniforms. Just the gray uniform and the *thwup- thwup* of an arrow. A troubled kid and a dark warrior who could very well be Kabakas.

The mountainside was rich with scent, more so going back up, because her progress was slow. She could smell every layer of soil and decomposition. Decomposition had been a specialty, of course, as a forensic botanist.

At one point, she thought she heard a light crank and flap overhead—something mechanical—a glider. She looked up and saw nothing. Probably nothing. Overtired, overwrought people often fell into sensory hallucinations. It had been a fuck of a day...or two.

Tell me how you feel when you imagine it might be Kabakas. How do you feel inside?

Better—that's how she felt when she thought he might be Kabakas. She felt better in a strange way.

CHAPTER THIRTEEN

She reached the house sweaty and out of breath. She slipped in her bedroom window, stripped off the smelly jumpsuit, and collapsed on her bed. She didn't even get under the covers; she just lay there. This was all she wanted. Just to close her eyes. Just to stop.

Just to sleep.

But like so many times she was overtired, sleep didn't come. She gazed out at the night sky, thinking about Hugo. She needed to find proof that he wasn't Kabakas, and then she needed to get the hell out. She could quiz Paolo. Interview the villagers. Hugo himself could tell her. She could coldfuck it out of him. She'd done it to dozens of targets over the years; why not Hugo? He already thought she was a prostitute.

But coldfucking Hugo…it might not be so easy. The point of coldfucking was that you had to stay cold and remote. Hugo, had her nearly in tears just putting a few stitches in her arm— and it hadn't been about the pain.

Never mind. She was in the man's home. Evidence was

everywhere in a man's home—if you opened your eyes. There would be something—receipts, records. Her mind went back to the cabinet. That was her best bet.

She sat up. Screw sleep. She had to know.

She splashed water over her face and body, toweled off, and pulled on the crisp maid's uniform. Moments later, she was prowling through the darkness, bare feet on cool tiles, flashlight and picking tools in her apron pockets. She slipped through the main rooms, feeling her way along at times—slowly, so as not to knock into anything. Not that there was much to knock into, being that the place was so barren.

She made it to the living room and stopped.

The light from a fire beyond flashed on the fanciful ironwork covering the far windows. A fire—not surprising on a cool night such as this. It smelled good. But then another scent came to her; something slightly flowery, there then gone, so faint that she wondered if she'd imagined it. She crept farther.

One door was closed, but another was open. The origin of the fire—and the flowery smell.

Lavender, but not just lavender. Opium.

She stilled. She hadn't had to drug him after all—he'd done it for her.

It was then that she heard it—a soft grunt of effort. Very male, very distressed. She crept nearer. Foolish, maybe, but she had to see. She slipped nearer and kept going until she stood in the doorway.

And froze.

There he was—Hugo with his shirt off, bent forward in a chair, elbows on his knees, looking almost defeated. His thick, muscular form was lit by the ambient glow of the flames.

But it wasn't his posture or his mountainous physique that froze her.

It was his burns—deep, extensive burns up and down his side and his back, from hip to shoulder. Mottled, disfiguring wounds of a man who'd gone through fire. Scar tissue pulled tight around what looked like skin grafts.

She swallowed.

He sucked in a ragged breath. She couldn't hear it, but she could see it. His pain was very nearly visible. All day he'd seemed the ultimate opponent, aware of her every mood, but he'd lost himself fully to his pain now. She'd seen it in agents before—you hold out, then you collapse. God, the way he'd been moving today—twisting, rolling, fighting—it had to have stretched and torn that fragile skin. He was in agony, this man. The agony you cut with opium.

She eyed a small glass jar—that would be the source of the lavender scent. Some sort of concoction; the Valencians were great ones for concoctions. Some parts of his side and back were shiny, but some weren't. He hadn't reached all of the spots. Had that been the grunt of distress? Was he trying to reach all of the painful spots, and couldn't?

She remembered the way his eyes had looked after dinner—flat—and it came to her now that this was the look of pain. Yet he'd still been out there doing archery with Paolo and overseeing his lessons. Because he loved that kid in his fucked-up way.

He couldn't call him by name, but he loved him.

His voice boomed. "I told you to stay in your room."

She jumped. "I-I needed to get a glass of water."

The fire crackled as Hugo's massive shoulders rose and fell. An injured bull, wall-to-wall muscle, and wall-to-wall agony. Her gaze fell to the belt around the waist of his khakis, which seemed to expand fitfully with his labored breaths.

"Sorry," she said.

"Come here."

She hesitated, then went, heart pounding. Because it was the middle of the night in the middle of nowhere. Because she'd been up for days. Because nothing was neutral between them. Because the sight of this frightening, maddening man in distress did something to her.

Because Kabakas had supposedly perished in a fire nine years ago.

She stopped a few feet away from him, just beyond the sphere of light cast by the flames.

He stared into the hearth as he spoke. "What are you doing?" He was deeply affected by the drug—she could tell by the roughness of his words. She fought the impulse to move closer, to rest her hand on his hair, to comfort him. "Answer! What are you doing?"

She had the crazy sensation that he was speaking from a primitive part of himself, as though the question was meant existentially. Here they were in the middle of nowhere, everything so strange, almost like a dream.

"I don't know," she said, speaking from deep inside herself. "I don't know what I'm doing." It was the truth. She'd been so lost since Friar Hovde.

"You shouldn't be here," he whispered thickly.

"You're burned," she said.

He turned his head and raised his eyes to hers, those

eyes that crackled with intensity. He looked wild. He *was* wild, this man tried to shape the world around him through brute force—forcing Paolo to his lessons. Sewing her up whether she liked it or not. Putting down a guerrilla contingent. Pulling a village back from the dead. *They will come back, they will rebuild.*

He looked at the world as a dark god, bending it to his will. He'd even tried to walk through fire.

But it was his humanity that struck her now. The brutal level of pain he had to be enduring.

"You missed a spot." She stepped softly to his side and took up the little jar of salve.

He watched her every movement with pinprick pupils, a wild animal in the night.

"You're okay," she whispered, dipping two fingers into the cool salve. Gently she slicked it onto the pinkest, most inflamed-looking skin.

Much to her surprise, he allowed it. Maybe the pain outweighed everything else. He turned back to the fire, breath ragged, as she stroked the salve across his tormented flesh.

She'd thought of Kabakas as many things over the years, but never as a suffering being. Never as an old friend. So human, so compelling.

So fucking beautiful.

CHAPTER FOURTEEN

He stifled a sob as Liza's fingers glided across his ruined flesh—not because of the pain; it was the relief of it that got him. The good things sometimes tormented him.

The firelight behind her made the edges of her bright hair glow in a circle around her head. Like a fucking halo.

Hugo lowered his head more deeply into the shadows. He wanted to continue watching her, but this was the position that felt best, elbows on his thighs, burns touching nothing, flesh far enough from the fire to have its company but not its heat.

She had come to him.

And he wanted her more than ever. Even now, raging burns and all.

She painted on the salve so carefully, so gently. Her care calmed him as a new wave of pain came up. He pressed his eyes shut. His mind was out of order, his seared skin exposed to her gentle fingers. He wanted her—badly.

"Go, now," he grated.

"I'm not done yet." She kept on. He could feel her goodness like a shining thing, a force—he didn't know why or how, just that her goodness was a force. Her passion was beautiful.

You missed a spot. His heart nearly shattered when she'd said it.

"Go," he said, eyes drifting shut, because he needed to concentrate on the pain; every few moments it would break the surface of his mind like a jagged rock bursting up from the ocean floor, and he would have to begin again, smoothing, allowing, breathing.

Now she was here, helping. Real, yet somehow not real. Like her hair.

That hair was a clue to things not being right. It bothered him suddenly, that bright hair of hers.

Opium sometimes gave him a keen kind of sight into people. Or maybe it just freed his mind to see what was there. What was it about her fake hair?

He found a thread of the thought, but then the brick of rough pain came up through the placid sea of his mind. He closed his eyes and breathed through it; it was all that he could do.

He felt her move around him. "There's another spot you missed." She waited for his reply.

Something about her did not add up. Tentative. That didn't feel right on her, either. But it was more.

"It's only fair, isn't it?" she said, smoothing on more salve. "After how you helped me today?"

He squeezed his eyes shut, broken by her kindness, by the way she cared to notice this in spite of what he was to her: a captor and a prison guard, provoking her in every way he could when he really just wanted to smell her skin. To kiss her. To take her ferociously.

She touched him, light and sure, fingertips gliding. He felt it clear down to his cock.

"Okay?"

"Yes," he breathed.

His mind was a tapestry of thoughts, threads switching and flowing as she moved her fingers over him. The salve helped greatly, but it was her goodness—her passion—that cut through the pain.

She felt like life.

The village sometimes felt like life to him. There had been times when he would go down there during festivals—purely by accident—but once there, he'd feel a strange excitement, as though he were enjoying himself through them. His kinspeople who did not know they were kin.

She blew on his burns, cooling him.

He was reminded suddenly of the way the boy had cried the day he'd found him in the killing fields, crying alone among the bloody corpses. One battalion had attacked another—killing everyone. He'd taken out the attackers. When it was over, he'd been stunned to discover this boy—like a miracle—alive among the dead.

The boy's cries had sounded as loud as jet blasts. When Hugo had picked him up, the boy had stopped crying.

Some might guess that Hugo had taken the boy, but it was the boy who had taken Hugo. Hugo would protect the boy with everything.

He sighed as she spread the salve onto his skin, cooling the heat, lulling him. "How long?" she whispered. "How long have you had these burns?"

"Nine years," he breathed.

She seemed like an angel. *I don't know what I'm doing,*

she'd said. It was as if she had hit at some deep truth in him, because he didn't know what he was doing, either. He only knew he wanted to take her, to ravish every cool, soft part of her.

He should never have taken this woman from the airfield. He should never have let her see his face. He'd doomed her with that lapse in judgment. She was more a prisoner now than his own mother had ever been as a maid to the Bolivian oilman.

This prostitute, alone in a strange land. Trapped on the mountaintop, miles from civilization, surrounded on all sides by treacherous terrain, a captive of a killer. A woman without choices, being so gentle, and all he could think of was throwing her against a wall and taking her.

Her touch was gone.

A soft *clink* as she set the small glass tub upon the table.

"Will you be okay?" she asked.

He wanted to let her know that it was always worse after exertion and he would be much better tomorrow. He wanted to tell her how in the months after the fire he'd learned how to handle pain. So yes, he would be okay. Yet not. He imagined telling her what it had been like inside that burning home, how he couldn't see anything. How it had felt to hear his mother cry out and not be able to get to her. How it felt to know it was him they had been trying to kill. His own mother's blood was on his hands. Same with those families in the Yacon fields. He hadn't wielded the blades, but he'd inspired the blades.

"Hugo?"

He wanted to tell her about the months after the fire, laid up in a hospital, an unknown patient, alone, and how grateful he'd been. He wanted to tell her how bloody he sometimes felt, as though his very soul were stained a deep savinca red. He wanted to tell her what it was like to walk in the Yacon fields among the dead, knowing those people had been killed in his name. He wanted to make her see that attacking El Gorrion was only about *llapingachos* because the hole in his soul could not take any more tearing.

He'd never revealed these things to anybody, but he wanted to tell Liza all of it, as if telling her would act as salve to his heart.

He could feel another round of pain starting, breaking the calm.

"Can I do anything else? Do you need some water?"

Don't go, he thought, looking up. She stood there in the too-large gray uniform with her arms slightly bent, hands hovering near her hips as though she didn't know what to do with them.

As if in slow motion, he watched himself take her hand, and then he yanked her to him. She gasped as he buried his nose in her belly.

"Please," he whispered. He hadn't meant to scare her; he'd just needed to touch her. And then he looked up and met her eyes—those intelligent eyes so full of truth... with the false color covering them. Her hair, too. Falsehood wrapped in falsehood. *Wrong, wrong, wrong.* The opium sight always showed him when something was wrong.

"Why do you keep your hair like that?" he rasped.

Alarm flashed in her eyes. "What?"

"Your eyes. Your hair. Why?"

She lifted the hand he hadn't captured up to her head. It wasn't the question he'd meant, but that was the thread he

174 | CAROLYN CRANE

had now. Best not to work against the opium instincts.

She regarded him with that blank mask. *No!* He'd caught on to something—he knew it.

"Why?" He squeezed her hand.

"Some people think it looks good."

His stomach felt funny. Why was she in his home? Who was she? *What* was she?

He let go of her hand and stood, shaking with need, forgetting all about his pain; there was only the familiarity of her. The mystery of her. The need to get inside her—mind and body.

"Hugo…"

He pushed her to the wall next to the fire, staring down into her green eyes, which looked all the more strange in the room's glow. They kept him from seeing into her. He reached up and grabbed the back of her hair, so false. Something was off.

She was panting.

He tightened his fist and jerked her head back to better look at her eyes.

He held her there. Then he kissed her.

She sucked in a breath—he felt it inside his mouth. She was a whore and she thought he would fuck her now, and he would. It was bad, yes, but he was bad.

And her lips were soft and sweet.

Pain sizzled across his skin as he pressed her to the wall, pushing in with his hips, feeling her soft belly with his cock as he kissed her salty neck. She was warm and pliant and gasping.

"Hugo."

"No?" He pulled back and began to undo her buttons. He

told himself that he needed to let her say no if she wanted
to say no.

She was trembling. "Your burns."

"I do not feel them, *corazón*," he whispered, hands too
clumsy on her buttons.

She set her hands on his shoulders, just above the burns.
She gasped, trembled with aliveness, as if she'd never been
with a man before. It made him want her like fire.

The buttons did not work. Frustrated, he began to pull
up her skirt, only slowing as he made contact with her
warm thighs. He ran his palms over her skin there. It only
made him need more of her.

And then something happened. She stopped trembling.
She stopped gasping. She seemed to change.

"Fuck me," she whispered, smooth and cool as glass. "Do
it, baby."

He slowed. The hair, the eyes, and now the talk, so
smooth and cool. Why was she hiding?

"What are you waiting for?" She reached down to his
belt buckle and began to undo it.

He grabbed her wrists and pressed her arms to her belly,
backed her harder to the wall, forcing her to be still so that
he could think. His burns raged, his cock strained against
her belly. He had her trapped, yet she was hiding right in
front him.

"W-what?"

"*Shhhh,*" he said as her skirt fell back down.

"Don't you want to fuck?"

He took her wrists in one hand and clapped his palm
over her mouth. Yes, he wanted to fuck, but he wanted to
fuck the trembling, gasping, living Liza. Not this one.

There was something wrong here. What?

She watched him warily, breathing through her nose, now. He removed his hand and kissed her tenderly. He didn't usually kiss like that, but instinct moved him that way now, and a hunter always paid attention to instinct.

He kissed her lips and her neck and her cheek, and then he slid his whiskered cheek against her silken cheekbone, gently now.

And that was when he felt the lurch in her. A trapped bird in her chest.

He remembered the kitchen. She'd almost cried—not when he'd put the needle in, but after. He'd imagined it to be a delayed reaction, but now he knew: it was the gentle way he'd touched her.

She was at home with hard men, cold men. Men who paid her, maybe even hurt her. She was steel for such men. But tenderness melted her. Made her alive.

He liked her alive.

He slid a hand down the side of her neck, watching her eyes.

"What are you doing?" she asked.

He kissed her in answer. Finally he could see into her, in spite of the false green eyes and all the rest. She'd been hurt, maybe badly—how had he not seen that?

She felt so deeply familiar.

Her wounds were not fresh; they felt worn. Those sorts of wounds he understood well thanks to years of fists and boots and his father cursing God above. Liza was a drug whore—of course bad things had happened to her. Very bad things, he now realized.

"Don't you want me?" she asked.

"Yes," he grated out. He let her wrists go and grazed his knuckles over her cheek. "I do," he said. Like a fever he wanted her.

She pushed her hips against his and his breath hitched. God, yes, he wanted her.

"Please," she said. He believed her now. *Do it, baby* had been a lie, but this *please* was not.

He slid up her skirt again, but differently this time. Slowly, making it about her. His hands slid along the warm, smooth flesh of her thighs. He let her feel his desire for her, let her hear the beautiful slide of her skin, down and up, down and up. The sound filled the space around them. Just the sound and feel of her skin under his skin was more erotic than anything he'd ever done with all the women he'd ever fucked.

And then, slowly, he slid one hand around her hips and gripped her bare ass under the panties. Her breath sped. The other hand he slid between her legs, touching her over her panties, almost chastely.

She gasped.

He took the gasp in a kiss. She was his again.

He began to make lazy circles on the damp cotton between her legs. Slow and lazy.

She pulled away. "It's okay, you can just fuck me."

"I know," he said, continuing the circles, watching her eyes.

"Hugo."

He kissed her again as he slid his fingers under the elastic now, into the warm, wet folds of her core.

"You don't have to," she said into the kiss.

You don't have to be good to me, she meant. *You don't have to make me come.*

He kissed her neck as he fondled her. He felt her body move with every lengthening stroke. "I'll do what I want."

"Hugo..." Her whisper sounded thick. He stoked up the pleasure, sliding his fingers relentlessly, invading her, finding the rhythm that seemed to match her undulations. "Hugo." Her voice sounded far away.

"*Shhhh,*" he said.

She gasped as he pushed his fingers inside her now, thumb stroking her taut nub. He would not take her; he would make her feel good. It was all he wanted now—just that.

He stroked her to a rhythm that matched her soft breath. He could always feel when a woman's body became his, control switching over, pleasure building.

Mercilessly he drew his rough fingers through her tender folds. She felt like molten silk, and his touch was a tide, pulling her out to sea.

CHAPTER FIFTEEN

She tried not to rock along, but he was pulling her apart. Killing her with tenderness.

Feeling too much of her.

She pushed at his bare chest. "Not like this," she said.

He stilled. "Not like what?"

Not gentle, she thought. *Not kind.*

She let out a sound of frustration and he started up again, seeming able to read her body. When had anybody ever touched her like this? He nuzzled her again, that heavy slide of whisker on her cheek as he stroked her. "It's okay, *corazón*," he whispered.

And it was his words that broke her, made her shatter to pieces there in his hand.

He held her as she came, slowing his motions, whispering endearments in Spanish that she should not understand.

Corazón, he called her. Heart.

He kissed her one last time, on the cheek. He drew away slowly, as if to make sure she could still stand upright, as if he knew he'd torn her apart with kindness. Then he returned to his seat, leaving her standing there, boneless in the firelight, flames dancing on the ceiling.

She straightened her dress, heart thundering. "Nothing more?" she whispered.

"Leave me."

He didn't want to fuck? Not even for her to blow him? She wished he would, just so she could take something back.

Like herself.

"Do not come out again until you hear the bell."

She stared down at this beast of a man who just might be Kabakas, who'd battered her defenses with kindness. It seemed like a dream.

"Go."

She turned and stumbled to her room, exhausted beyond comprehension. She flopped onto her bed, buzzing with his touch. What had just happened?

***

She opened her eyes, stunned at the brilliant sunshine streaming through the window. It was late morning—nine, maybe. How had she slept so deeply?

And then she remembered Hugo making her come with his hand. She still felt him on her body.

And then she remembered the burns.

Nine years ago, her colleague had seen Kabakas walk into a fire—an explosion. If he'd survived, he would have burns. But then, everyone knew the story of the fire. Other people in the world had burns. He said he'd been burned nine years ago. People lied. If he were some sort of Kabakas superfan, that would be what he would say.

I'll send a team, Dax had said. *We'll take him down and get the proof.*

Fuck.

She washed up and put on a fresh uniform and fresh granny panties and headed out to the kitchen, breathing in the scent of coffee. Nobody around.

She wandered through the place and to the back. The sun peeked over the hills, lighting up the rows of the green savinca bushes. She saw Hugo and Paolo, both wearing broad-brimmed hats, heads bent over the bushes. Farmers.

They seemed to be studying the leaves. They went to the next plant and studied that one. Then to the next. Hugo walked behind Paolo, moving stiffly. At one Paolo walked behind Hugo, and Hugo moved normally. Hiding the pain. Not a surprise.

Had the pain at least lessened? And how much of the night did he remember?

She wandered back to the kitchen, stopping by the locked cabinet. She fingered the padlock. Decorative, but strong. She could get in. She should get in. There were pirates holding a tanker. If Dax thought that offering up Kabakas's whereabouts would grease the wheels for an end to the standoff, then it would work. Dax's assumptions on the geopolitical level were always spot-on—she knew that. And the sure thing was always the best—she knew that, too. But turning that Brujos guard, Sal, and getting a bargaining chip through him—she wouldn't have offered it up if she didn't think it would work. She knew the sound of a disgruntled employee. They could offer him a lot.

She ran a thumbnail over the ridged side of the lock. Burns didn't make him Kabakas. A lot of people had burns.

Anyway, her colleague had seen Kabakas die. They'd recovered bodies. They didn't have Kabakas's dental records, true, but her colleague wasn't stupid.

And with that, she returned to the kitchen. She lifted the sturdy silver press pot. Partly full. For her? She poured herself a cup and set to work on the scrambled eggs. She'd put chicken and egg and sliced avocado on the side, a regional favorite.

Eventually, Paolo wandered in.

"Good morning, Paolo," she said.

He mumbled his good morning.

"Do you and Hugo like cinnamon on your plantains?"

He watched her blankly. *Cinnamon* was a big word for him.

"I'll just put it out." She set the chicken roasting. He seemed content to stay. Was he beginning to warm up to her?

"Does Hugo teach you other languages?"

If Paolo understood, he hid it.

She put up a finger. "Spanish." She put up another: "English..." She put up a third finger with a questioning gaze. It would be interesting, for example, if he was teaching Paolo Chinese or something.

He just looked at her. Yeah, he understood. "The code," he finally said. "It allows you to determine any answer?"

"For fractions," she said.

"Say more."

She wiped her hands on her apron, stifling a smile—that was Hugo's line. She covered the potato cakes and grabbed a stack of paper plates she'd spotted the day before. "You have to convert it, just like a code." She cut a paper plate in half, then one half in quarters. She gave him a half and a quarter. "Add this."

He looked up at her.

She pointed at the half, then the quarter. "This plus this."

He frowned, confused. She then cut the half into quarters. "Now?"

"Three quarters."

She smiled. He straightened. That was how she could tell when it clicked, that making the fractions all of a kind, a family, was the key. They went through several more paper plates, doing eighths, thirds. She gave him new plates to cut up and convert. After, she showed him the trick of multiplying crosswise. He practiced while she checked the chicken. He was incredibly smart, this kid.

While he practiced the crosswise trick, she wrote him a note where the common denominators revealed the letters. Like a real code.

He went at it with gusto as she flipped the cakes...which had gotten a bit burnt. She put them under a cloth and started two more.

He wrote her an answer back, watching over her shoulder as she cracked the code, laughing when she got it. He liked writing the code better than cracking it, which was fine with her.

He wrote her a new one: *No cinnamon.* She laughed. This kid was smart as hell. And the drill—he'd ace that fucker now. There was another word for her to decode. Paolo laughed as she slowly worked it out.

She felt Hugo before she saw him. She straightened up, turned and met his eyes. He seemed so huge and cold and unmovable.

But God, the way he'd touched her last night. Her face heated.

He turned his dark eyes to Paolo. "Are you distracting her?"

"We're playing a math game," she said.

Hugo narrowed his eyes.

Paolo scurried away.

Hugo turned to her, searching her face. "Games are not how you are to teach."

"Why? It makes it fun for him. Fun to work with fractions."

"You would disobey my instruction?"

"Well...he understands it now."

"You will teach future lessons from the book." He made his oo's long. *Boook.*

"Why?"

A flash of surprise. "Because you will."

She pressed her lips together.

"Private thoughts, *señorita?*" His eyes glittered. "You are an expert in math instruction?"

"No, but I know this is the way to teach fractions, considering..."

Her words trailed off as he advanced on her, and suddenly she was back in the opium and lavender scented room, being consumed by him and his fingers. "Considering what?"

"That he can solve the problems now."

He eyed her suspiciously. "Do you have other talents I should know about?"

She fought not to show her alarm. This was why you

didn't break character. "I like games, that's all." Liza loved games. She wouldn't have been able to teach math with a game but she loved them. Was he just trying to rattle her?

He was so close now, his breath stirred the hair around her forehead. "You do not teach with games. It is not how you prepare for life."

"So it all has to be hard and harsh and unpleasant?"

He tilted his head and looked at her strangely. "I do not know, *señorita*. Does it?"

Her heart was pounding now. She'd been worried about him busting through her Liza disguise.

She should have been worried about him busting through Zelda.

"Breakfast is getting cold." She pushed past him and went into the kitchen to grab the plates.

CHAPTER SIXTEEN

He stood at the doorway between the kitchen and the dining room, watching her set the table.

In one deft stroke, Liza had done what he never had—made a game with the boy. Drawn him into play.

Had Paolo wanted to play all this time? Hugo had never played as a child—not that he could remember, anyway. He'd learned early on that showing any kind of happiness was the fastest route to punishment at the hands of the man married to his mother. So he'd stuffed down his happiness. You couldn't take away what you couldn't see.

After he'd learned the truth about himself and run off to the islands, he was too old for play, and the fighting men he'd joined up with were the opposite of playful. He'd liked it that way. He'd imagined he'd found his tribe.

He'd assumed that Paolo, coming from blood and hate as he had, would be well past play. He'd imagined that they were connected in at least that way.

And then in came Liza, creating a secret world of fun just big enough for the two of them, weaving a story, winning him over, all in the space of one morning. He'd stood watching with the strangest feeling in his belly.

He'd gotten used to getting what he wanted and taking what he wanted, molding the world around him.

She was changing everything.

She said, "I'll go grab the serving platter."

He slammed a hand on the doorframe before she could slip by, remembering the way she had felt.

He remembered every second of her. Every breath of her. She fascinated him—dangerously so, perhaps—because he still didn't know her. Last night had only underlined that.

"You will obey my instructions in your work with the boy," he said, gripping the wood. "It is important that you obey my instructions."

She bristled. Just that one movement made him go hard. "Fine."

His gaze fell to her lips, parted in surprise. "You disagree?"

"The boy is a real person who needs...more than instruction," she said.

"You don't know what he needs."

"He needs more. He needs *you*, Hugo. God, he idolizes you so much, but you keep your heart as locked up and closed up as that little cabinet," she said. "*See* him, Hugo."

"You think I do not see him? I see him and hear him in ways that you never can." He still heard him crying out on that bloody field. Even now, Hugo was desperate to silence those cries. "You will teach out of the book. The book is superior."

"The facts don't serve at your whim," she bit out.

He leaned in. "But you do."

Her nostrils flared. Her eyes flared. All he could think now was how badly he wanted to drag his lips down the side of her neck and taste her heartbeat. To move inside her.

"Don't you?" he whispered.

"So it seems." She ducked under his arm to grab the platter.

With a casual attitude, he wandered in and took a seat at the head of the table.

She ferried in the dishes, not looking at him. He couldn't have that, couldn't be banished from her sphere. "Liza," he said, and when she looked up, he pointed at a napkin she'd dropped on the way in.

She stared in disbelief. She wasn't cut out to be a domestic—not in any way. God, he wanted her to never leave.

"Did you not agree to housekeeping duties?"

She picked it up with an exaggerated motion, then she did something shocking—she grabbed the sides of her skirt, and curtseyed. An angry, mocking curtsey. His mother used to have to do that— curtsey. But she'd never curtseyed like Liza. It was a fuck-you curtsey.

She came around and set a last dish on the table. "Do you want me to call *the boy*?"

He stared at her levelly. Was she mocking him? "I thought you had decided to call him Paolo."

"So I can call the boy by his real name, but I can't practice math with him in any sensible way? Maybe I need a drill to memorize, too."

He wanted to laugh. How had anyone traded this woman in a card game? He moved toward her as the dead move toward light. "Maybe you *do* need a drill to memorize."

The space between them surged with energy and need. He wanted to kiss her more than he wanted his next breath. He could feel the rise in her spirit. She would meet him. Everything was between them.

Suddenly Paolo was there, taking his seat. He dug into the chicken.

Somehow, Hugo found the will to turn. One step. Two steps. He went to the side table where he'd left his book and brought it to his seat at the table. *One Hundred Years of Solitude.* He'd read it before, but he was a man who enjoyed reading a book over again, letting it speak to him in different moods. "You will place my book here with my coffee at the breakfast table. I read my book at breakfast."

He opened it without looking up, conscious of her curiosity—about the book? Or did she imagine that he should converse with Paolo at the breakfast table? He wanted her to say it, to push just so he could push back. When he was reasonably certain she wouldn't speak up, he flipped a page and fixed her with a glare. "The boy and I have a big day. We'll need lunches prepared to take to the field." He gave her instructions.

She nodded and left.

He stared at the page, still feeling her. Again he went over the night before. The way she'd come to him. The music of her thighs under the slide of his palms. The way she'd gasped and trembled. *How long?* she'd whispered. *How long have you had these burns?*

Nine years, he'd said.

The words swam on the page. She hadn't asked what happened. She had asked, *How long?*

Alarm bells clanged.

What happened? Were you burned? Those were natural first questions to ask when faced with scars such as his. But to ask *how long...* Who asked that?

Somebody who knew about Kabakas asked that.

Somebody who suspected.

He closed the book and picked up his fork, though he was no longer hungry. Nobody could learn his identity. It wasn't simply a matter of protecting himself; he had to protect the boy. He would protect him with everything. The enemies of Kabakas would go after the boy.

He could not allow her to live if she'd guessed about Kabakas. It was too dangerous.

No, she could not know.

He felt the boy's eyes on him. The boy monitored him the way the villagers monitored the weather, sensitive to the minutest shifts in pressure. He dug in, just to put the boy's mind at ease.

Llapingachos. Finally. They were decent, too. They were nothing like Café Moderno's but decent enough. He piled on a bit of chicken.

There was no way she could know, this American prostitute. She could not have known he'd be at the airfield. And even if she had, no hunter could arrange that. It was far too elaborate. Insane, even. Handcuffed, helpless.

No, he was spinning notions from the empty air. This is what came of bringing a woman like this into his home. He'd always confined his sexual liaisons to Bumcara. Here he was, focusing on the help.

Preying on the help.

Like his father.

The realization turned the food in his mouth to cardboard. He could feel the boy's eyes on him, sensing his shift in mood.

"*Bueno*," he grunted, forcing himself to scrape the fork along the plate, gathering up another bite.

The boy resumed eating.

Hugo chewed the food woodenly. Preying on the help. Was he no different from his predator of a father? The Bolivian oilman who'd fucked the maid, cuckolded the husband, ignored his biological child? The oilman who'd destroyed his family's happiness? His mother had been a maid. What choice did she have? What choice did Liza have?

He disgusted himself.

***

He and Paolo spent that day walking the rows on the sunny side of the field with their small scythes, cutting the stems with buds that were ready to go. There was a shape the bud took on when it was just about to unfurl, a certain outward swell, and you had to get them out of the sun and into the citric acid solution, or you were done. They collected them in the large wheeled trays, bundling them in groups of 120, and brought them to the shed to be cooled. Everything with the harvest was in groups of twelve—so much of it followed traditional tales and rituals, and those processes had gotten built into the trade.

His burns pained him, but the window for the harvest was shutting—once the flowers started to bloom, they became worthless to the floral wholesalers, who bought only tight, mature buds with the telltale swell. And he always helped the boy.

There was something strange about the plants, however; the leaves looked shiny. That was not normal.

They came in late and ate dinner silently. He instructed her to stay in her room that night and she did; she seemed as interested in keeping a distance between them as he did. He got through the night with only a small bit of opium.

***

The next day after breakfast, he drove down to the village.

Still deserted. His heart fell.

The villagers needed to be out harvesting their crops. How could he prove to them that the danger was past?

The sunny sides would be popping soon, and then it would be too late. Hugo and the boy could live without doing a harvest, but the villagers could not.

He drove to the spot north of the village square where Paolo always seemed to get cell service. There he contacted his PI, who gave him background on Liza.

Hugo listened, fascinated, as the investigator recounted her history. Her father was in the army, stationed in Japan on the American base at Okinawa. He had married a woman from town. Liza was an only child, though the investigator wanted to dig into that more—there was something strange there. He wondered if a child had been given up. Liza had graduated high school with good grades and had even attended college for a year. There were photos of her as a dancer in Vegas. Later, head shots; Liza the Hollywood actress. According to the investigator, the only role Liza had landed was that of a high-priced escort. There were photos from that period, too—mostly parties. Liza in beautiful dresses and hanging on the arms of various men. Liza on a yacht. Liza always laughing. She had a blog, too. The man forwarded the link to him at the end of the call.

Hugo leaned on the Jeep, reading the blog hungrily. It was about an American soap opera. Liza had many opinions on amnesia, it seemed, and carried on lengthy discussions in the comments. She was kind, this woman, replying to each and every person. A hostess in this little space.

He got into his Jeep and drove up the winding path out onto the mountainside where terraced fields hugged the terrain, a great expanse of brown and green. His nerves always calmed in the fields. He drove to the point where the entire terraced range was visible.

The sight chilled his bones.

The upper-edge field, the slice that got the longest day of sun, was awash in red, a blade in the heart of the village. Months of income lost.

He'd said El Gorrion wasn't coming back, but they hadn't believed him. Why should they? They did not know him. They thought him an American dilettante; a hobbyist reclaiming his South American roots. He had encouraged this image.

Right before harvest was the worst time to scare the farmers from their fields.

He drove to the part of the fields nearest to Julian's tracts. If anybody was trying to save his harvest, it would be Julian. He stopped the vehicle and got out, heading toward the bloody edge, kicking aside the Luquesolama stones left over from the Primer Verde some months back. The ceremonial arrangement of the stones before each harvest was one of the many superstitions his mother had despised. The story went that if the rocks were not sized and arranged in a specific design at specific intervals, the earth below would not welcome the *Savinca verde* crop as its child and would not care for it.

Even the villagers seemed to regard it as superstition, but not quite enough to reject the practice. He had no problem with the superstitions, but he found the villagers' constant celebrations an annoyance because Fernando would shut down Café Moderno.

He strolled down the row. The leaves and swelled buds were shoulder high, shot up from the gnarled, woody bases. The plants were trimmed back to those bases after each harvest, spring and fall. Some of those bases were two centuries old.

Like every farmer, Julian had a specific trimming style passed down through his family. Julian cut deep into the base, creating a triangular shape. Others created a flat top. Others rounded to a circle. Paolo had chosen Julian's style to emulate the first year of his business.

Hugo ran one of the wide, heart-shaped leaves through his fingers, wondering as he sometimes did what the trimming style of his ancestors had been. He turned the leaf. It didn't look right—too shiny. He'd noticed the shine up top, too, though it was more intense here. Shine could indicate a lack of moisture and sun, yet there had been plenty of rain and sun.

Were they sick? Was it emotions? The villagers believed the plants could feel. He, too, believed it at times, and he felt a sudden rush of grief for them. Like a small child, a plant could not run away when there was trouble or fighting. It could only grow, vulnerable in its tiny patch of dirt. An unaccountable thickness filled his throat as he peered across to the red swath at the top side of the slope. Flowers blooming unloved in the fields.

He heard rustling and pulled his scythe from his belt.

A man in a red woven hat approached. He wore a coarse gray shirt and a bright gold chain around his neck—the medal of Caribbo.

"Julian!"

Julian holstered his gun. He wore long pants and a utility belt holding two sizes of scythes and several pairs of gloves.

"*Buenas!*" Hugo said, heading toward the man, hand outstretched.

Julian took his hand. There was something about being the only two men in this place, surrounded by the blooming savinca sweet with death, which made Hugo feel a bond with Julian. He was a leading farmer, passionate about progress. Julian had a son Paolo's age. A good boy, and one of the few who tolerated Paolo.

Julian would be working the field from the protected center. He was wary of El Gorrion's men, but not enough to lose his crop. One man working the fields, though—it wasn't enough.

"Where is everybody?" Hugo asked.

Julian waved a helpless hand toward the village. "You know what happened."

"But it's safe now. They're not coming back."

"They still could," Julian said. "And you know what they do. You saw what they did to Pedro."

"They aren't coming back—'

"You can't know," Julian said.

"El Gorrion's men were attacked," Hugo said. "They aren't coming back."

Julian squinted. "I will risk coming back, yes, but to bring my family back. Hugo..."

"Nobody attacks a village once it falls under the protection of Kabakas," he said.

"We heard the rumors of that, but it seems... farfetched," Julian said, squinting down the mountainside.

Hugo felt so helpless. He could destroy a contingent of guerrilla fighters, but he couldn't coax a few families into a field of flower buds. His hands balled into fists deep inside his pockets as Liza's words rang through his mind. *He is a real person. See him.* She'd meant it about Paolo, but she could've said it of Julian and the villagers. Why should his word have weight? Hugo wasn't a part of the village. He barely interacted with them or treated them as neighbors. How arrogant to assume they would trust him about El Gorrion not coming back, or risk their families on rumors—or on the casual word of an outsider to a shopkeeper. He'd thought it would be enough.

It wasn't.

But now the flowers would bloom unharvested. His heart pounded. Hugo looked Julian in the eye. He needed to give him something more. "The village is under Kabakas's protection," Hugo said. "I give you my word on that."

Julian's dark gaze snapped to his. He could see the question in Julian's eyes. Julian would hardly suspect he was Kabakas, but as a wealthy American, maybe he'd hired Kabakas.

Julian watched him warily. It was a grave thing, to confess to knowing Kabakas. During the war, people had been tortured for knowledge of Kabakas. "El Gorrion said they would be back yesterday. They did not come, did they?"

El Gorrion liked to be known as a man who kept his promises. His image was important to him; if he didn't come when he said he would, there would have to be a good reason.

"They did not," Julian said. Still he had reservations.

"My boy and I are going to come back in an hour," Hugo said. "The maid as well. We'll harvest at the edge, by the road."

Julian eyed him. They both knew that if El Gorrion's men were to return, those harvesting near the road would be slaughtered first.

CHAPTER SEVENTEEN

Back at home, Hugo found Liza chatting brightly with the boy out on the veranda. They were building something out of cardboard. Their chatter ceased as he approached. The boy's wary look pierced his heart.

He stared down at the small structure, recognizing trees and houses. They were building a world. How fitting.

He addressed the boy in Spanish. "Get your harvesting things and collect a set for her, too."

The boy scurried into the shed. Hugo eyed her gray dress. "Do you still have the one-piece?"

"Yes, but it's dirty."

"You'll put it on. You will work in the savinca fields. The stems have prickers."

"We're going into the fields?"

He eyed her. Waited.

"Okay."

He watched her go in to the house, following her movements with his mind. Moments later, her curtains shifted with the pressure of the door opening. He imagined her in there, stripping off her outfit down to her underwear.

His cock hardened. He thought hatefully of his father, the genius oilman, with all of his tables and spreadsheets.

He forced his mind to other concerns. Did she have decent underwear? He hadn't considered the things he'd need for her in order to keep her. The other maids, cooks, and governesses had come with luggage. Did she have decent undergarments or toiletries? He hadn't thought of those things for her, although she hadn't asked.

The boy came out with the gloves, and soon enough she appeared in the dirty one-piece. She'd rolled up the sleeves and the pant legs, making the dark blue garment look almost fashionable. She'd gathered her bright blonde hair into two short braids, tied at the ends with red rubber bands. The braids weren't quite long or heavy enough to hang straight; they curved slightly outward from the straw hat, as if they had lives of their own, a life inside. Like everything about her. The gorgeous American prostitute with her games and her blog and her fashions.

He didn't recall the jumper being so dirty, and he experienced a pang of guilt for making her wear it. Right or wrong, she was his to care for now. He felt a strange twist in his chest at the thought.

"That won't do. Come." He led her into the house and into his bedroom.

She seemed nervous. Remembering the night.

He picked out one of his own work shirts, plus a belt and worn khakis and brought them to her.

She clutched them to her chest, expression blank. "Thank you."

He took a braid in his fingers, remembering the way she'd felt in his hands. "I can trust you out there? Not to try to leave? Not to excite the villagers with tales?"

She watched him without expression. "Yes."

"You do understand that I'll send you home when it is time," he said.

"Yes," she said.

Her assent was a challenge. Her blank face was a challenge. Everything about her...he tightened his fingers around the short braid, wanting badly to pull, to push. "And the way I settled things with my enemies the other day..." He looped the braid around his finger now, allowing it to graze her ear. "I would not treat a friend in such a way. You understand? Never a friend."

The flash in her eyes told him that she understood the veiled threat: best to stay a friend.

And God, he wanted to take her right there, to push her to the wall, to pull her hair. Consume her.

He let go. "Take them to your room and change." He watched her pad off.

The boy was out back with the supplies in the bucket, waiting. "We already cut all the ready buds," he said. "We have at least a day before more grow ready."

"We aren't going to work in our fields..." He paused, thinking to use his name. *We aren't going to work in our fields, Paolo.* It felt strange...and too late, somehow. "We're going down to the village to show them that it's safe," he continued. "We will work there as long as it takes."

The boy nodded. "They worry that El Gorrion will return."

"*Sí.*" Hugo picked out the newest gloves for her. He

turned them inside out and shook them. Not so dirty. Good.

And then she appeared, coming across the porch. In his clothes.

It did something to him. His shirt on her. His pants. *His.*

He swallowed and turned. "Let's go."

Soon they were bumping down the road in the Jeep. Hugo drove. He spoke in Spanish to the boy. "We will stay until their fields are done. I told them our fields are finished. They will not question that."

The boy nodded glumly; worrying, no doubt, that he wouldn't earn enough to afford the game console he had his eye on.

"You will have your game console, do you understand?"

Worry remained on the boy's face. Did he not understand? Hugo would supplement the income he lost by allowing his savincas to bloom.

"I will buy it if you cannot."

This didn't seem to comfort him.

"We want Café Moderno to open again, do we not?" he added.

"Of course." The boy gave him his best fake smile. What was the problem, then? Hugo realized some moments later what it was: the boy thought that if Café Moderno started up again, that they might get rid of Liza. And the boy didn't want Liza to leave.

They parked at the side edge and headed down to Julian's field. Hugo breathed in deep, feeling at home with the plants. But that shiny look—it made him nervous. And the shoots didn't seem as straight and strong as usual. It was so subtle that it was almost a feeling more than anything visual, but it was there.

He slowed at a large, healthy plant and plucked a leaf, inspecting the stem as Liza and the boy watched. Had he noticed the change in the plants? *"No te parece que se ve rara?"* Hugo asked.

The boy was silent.

Hugo looked down into the boy's solemn face and repeated the question.

"Sí."

"You have noticed it?"

"Yes," the boy said.

"How would you characterize it?"

The boy regarded the plant. *"Débil,"* he said. *"Demasiado brillante."*

Hugo nodded. *Weak. Too shiny.* *"Sí."*

"The rains?" the boy guessed.

Hugo shook his head and knelt down, now, fingering the soil. It wasn't dehydration. He could feel her eyes on him. "Is something wrong?" she asked.

"No sé," he said. *I don't know.* She'd only hear the *no,* and think he said no. She didn't need to know anything; she didn't need to matter.

Maybe it was the attack. To his mother, the idea that the flowers had emotions was a sign of how backward the villagers were, but they had a voice, these plants. A gesture. They were so very much alive, stretching up toward the sky. He would do his best to give them what they needed. He was doing his best with the boy. He wished the boy could understand that.

Julian arrived and sent the boy up to help in one of the fields that didn't have help coming. Sending the boy to a safer field farther from the road. The gesture touched Hugo.

Hugo announced that he and Liza would handle the side along the road.

"I will work there with you." Julian sucked down a bottle of water, eyeing the spread. He'd been working since dawn, no doubt. "We'll move inward as a group," he said.

Hugo asked, "Do the leaves look strange to you?"

"*Brillantes,*" Julian said. "It's the roots," he said. "Yours?"

"The same. I didn't inspect the roots..." He hadn't thought of it.

"Come see." Julian led them across two dozen rows to where he'd been working. Buds were bundled onto carts. He turned crosswise up to an especially shiny plant. This one was not well; the leaves angled down. Droopy. Somebody had dug around the root system—Julian, presumably. He knelt and brushed away the dirt.

Hugo knelt beside him, feeling his belly turn. The roots looked white—coated. He brushed away more of the dirt to expose more of the roots. Julian scratched at a root with a fingernail, scraping the waxy white off. "*Está por todos lados. En todas las plantas.*"

They knelt together in silence, linked in the knowledge of how grave this was. All of the plants had it. Coated roots could not take up nutrients or water.

"*Qué es?*" Hugo asked.

Julian shook his head. "*No lo sé.*" He told him that there were other plants where the white coating was starting up the stem, as if it moved upward, slowly suffocating the bush.

Hugo could feel her in the background; he imagined he

could feel her sympathy. She wouldn't understand the conversation, but she would sense the distress.

"No es glifosato," Julian said. That was what the CIA sprayed the fields with, but surely they wouldn't hit the mountain. It was well known that the savincas grew here—national treasures. And anyway, this wasn't the effect. They'd all seen Roundup kills. Julian plucked a leaf and tore it in half. *"Es otra cosa."* *Some other thing.* The leaf was not right. Again he felt that bond with Julian. It was easy with the plants between them.

He became aware of Liza touching a nearby plant. She ran a leaf between two fingers just as he had. "It's beautiful," she said, turning over the leaf to look underneath, understanding nothing of the disaster unfolding before her.

She came and knelt beside him, on the other side of Julian, wondering, he supposed, what they found so fascinating on the ground.

"The plants are sick," Hugo explained.

"I'm sorry. How can you tell?" She seemed genuinely interested. She cared about things like this.

"The leaves are shiny. They shouldn't be like that. And then my friend looked at the roots." He brushed away the dirt around the root. "Something is coating them."

"They shouldn't be that color?" she asked.

"No. They are typically brown." He scraped off some of the wax to show her.

"Oh," she said, running her finger over the coating, back and forth and then up and down.

Julian rose first. Hugo straightened up and extended a hand to Liza. She took it, and he squeezed gently as he pulled her up, her fingers warm and soft inside his hand.

"Let's get on with it," he said, forcing himself to release her. He pulled his gloves over his hands and looked up to find her staring at his hands with the strangest look.

"Something wrong, *señorita?*" he asked.

She shook her head.

He grabbed a wheeled cart and led her back to the edge of the field. He had her put on her gloves and he showed her how to grasp the stems just above the base, cutting evenly. He pointed out the thorns, warning her of the danger they posed to the forearms. He showed her the parts not to touch and how far down to remove the leaves.

He watched her do one. She handled the plant gently, reverently, but with confident movements nevertheless. A natural.

"You've worked in fields?"

"Gardens." She looked up, shading her eyes. "How can you tell?"

"The confidence in the touch. It shows when somebody is used to handling plants or weapons or animals..." *Or women,* he thought, looking up at her.

She swallowed. Was she thinking it, too?

"You'll do this whole row," he continued, "and then up and back. We have this whole field to do." Julian was already half a row ahead.

She cast her gaze over the rows of rows. "You won't get dinner."

"Just do it," he growled. "And when we're all done, you'll make us dinner."

She narrowed her eyes in mock anger.

His heart thundered. He should not love this—not any of it. He forced himself to remember the oilman and turned to his row.

They worked side by side. When he got ahead, he caught her up. He gave her pointers now and then. As she got used to the tool, he taught her the twist motion to make as she cut. She wasn't as fast as he was, but she was thorough and thoughtful. She could be trusted with the plants. And that trust, he found as he worked, went deeper than the harvest.

He didn't quite trust her on the outward things. In some ways, she didn't add up. The way in which she held things back, for instance. It wouldn't shock him entirely if she imagined running. He would catch her, of course. Surely she understood that.

He didn't entirely trust her thoughts or strategies, but he trusted her heart; imagined, even, that he could feel her soul.

He had always drawn something from the plants; or rather, he and the plants had always drawn something from each other. He always felt it when he entered the field, but he most strongly felt it when he became quiet and dwelled with the plants. He and the plants exchanged something as real as rain.

He felt that now working side by side with this woman.

As if the silent labor was a more potent conversation than a smoke screen of speech ever could be. As if he knew her from her soft, sure movements, from the effort she put into assessing the bud's readiness for harvest, from the care with which she handled the stems. She tried hard to avoid the prickers and to make good clean cuts. She concentrated so hard at times that her tongue peeked out of the side of her mouth. It drove him a little mad to see it.

He understood, as they went from row to row, that she hadn't been lying about the drugs—this was not a woman in withdrawal. Though there were times, over the past two days, when he sensed a certain melancholy in her. Shadows under her eyes. The pain that she'd experienced, the hardship. He wanted very much to ask her about it.

Would she answer?

On they worked, filling one cart after another. They made good progress, and he was heartened when a few of the women showed up with water and snacks. His word wasn't good, but his actions spoke.

As they moved inward, he heard others at work. An iPod speaker played Reggaeton.

They worked on.

He stopped, pulled off his gloves, and drew a water bottle from his pack. He handed it to her and watched her drink, watching the undulations in her soft, pale throat, remembering the taste of her skin and her sweat.

"What drove you onto that plane, Liza?"

The motion in her throat ceased as she turned her green eyes to him. She lowered the bottle from her lips and licked. "What do you mean?"

"You quit drugs. Your life was your own. How was it that you became a chip in a card game? Did you owe Mikos money? Was that it?"

"Not exactly."

"What, then?"

She gazed across the bright valley. "Sometimes you sink so deeply into a life, you don't understand that you're trapped until it's too late." She handed the bottle back to him, still not meeting his eyes. "Once it happened, it was dangerous not to go through with it. And I thought I was dealing with Brujos, not El Gorrion. I didn't sign on for El Gorrion. So..." She shrugged.

"So...what?"

She blinked her unnaturally green eyes. "There's not much more to say."

"Why was it too late?" he pressed.

"It does seem..." She paused. He waited in the silence that followed for her to finish the sentence. "It seems extreme, doesn't it?"

"A bit."

She smiled.

He wasn't accustomed to not getting answers. "It was not drugs. What, then?"

He found himself hoping that it would not be love. Love for this Mikos.

Her look was thoughtful. This was a woman looking inward, searching her soul. She would give him the truth. "Maybe I needed to make up for something. Something that I had done. I didn't owe money, but I *owed*."

"What did you have to make up for that would put you in such a position?"

She looked away. "Did you ever do something you wish you could undo? Or really fail somebody?"

"Yes."

Her gaze snapped to his. She wanted more. He found he wanted to give her more; he found he wanted to give her everything. He thought again of that pain he'd sensed in her; it had made him feel connected to her, and it wasn't just the opium; he was feeling it out here in the fresh air and sunshine.

"It's worse, isn't it?" he said. "It's not what is done to you, but what you do to others that can hurt the most."

"Yes," she said.

"You cannot absorb it. You are prevented from that."

The blank mask was gone, and in its place, that blaze of intelligence. "So, what do you do? How did you get back from it?"

"I don't know," he whispered. "I wish I did."

"I think..." She paused. "Guilt makes you small."

His breath stopped. In one utterance, she described what he'd become after the Kabakas impostor had killed so many, after he couldn't save his mother. After the burns.

"Or you make choices from a shrunken heart or a shrunken spirit or something," she added. "Or maybe it just hurts too much to be who you are after that. To be large and happy, you know? That probably sounds weird."

"Not at all," he said.

The moment swelled between them. They stood together in their pain, there among the savincas. It was easy to be with her—as easy as falling. He'd never imagined he could feel so connected to another person. Never imagined he deserved it.

Was this what he denied Paolo?

You keep your heart locked up as tight as that cabinet. Was it true? Out here with this woman surrounded by the plants that fed his soul, he wanted to be a better man.

He pulled the gloves back on, feeling her eyes on him, enjoying them. He took extra care, fitting them to his fingers. He never wanted her eyes off him.

He never wanted her to leave.

"Onward," he said.

CHAPTER EIGHTEEN

Hugo had an almost frightening amount of insight where she was concerned. She'd told him the truth: her existence had been constrained since the Friar Hovde case. She'd come to realize this out in this wild place, cut off from her entire world, like a crazy bit of espionage wrapped in a vacation from herself. She'd answered his questions with her own truth, more or less, but it made her wonder what Liza would say. Liza had stopped short of getting on that plane, but things had obviously gotten pretty bad. Would it have helped Liza if Zelda had stayed in her life and kept bailing her out? Conventional wisdom said no, that it only enabled Liza in her addiction. But sometimes, conventional wisdom sucked. Zelda had missed Liza so much; keeping tabs on her from afar made it almost worse. So many times, she wanted to pick up the phone and call her to see how she was doing and let her know she was there. Now and then, she'd hear about a job opportunity or a really good rehab program and she'd think about getting Liza away from that Miami crowd of hers, setting her up in a clean new life, but how many times had she tried that? But God, she missed her. The good things never seemed very good without Liza to drag her out for a celebration, and the bad things...she could've used a sister after the Friar Hovde thing. Whatever happened, she'd be sticking by Liza's side.

She cut the stems, setting them gently onto the cart. Kids from the village came by with empty carts and took away the full carts. It was exhausting, repetitive work, but an exciting honor on a different level. These were the rare, storied *Savinca verde*. She loved their gnarled bottoms, their finely serrated leaf margins.

Those roots were wrong, though. A plant couldn't survive with coated roots like that. The bushes were already being affected; she didn't see it, but Hugo and the other farmers did, and they would know. Farmers were like field agents in that way—you always trusted the opinion of the guy on the ground.

The men had concluded it wasn't Roundup, and she agreed. Had the CIA switched up the cocktail? But why spray here? These beautiful, legendary plants—the only ones on earth. Who would make a mistake like that?

As a forensic botanist, she'd never had anything to do with the spraying program or herbicides at all, really. Weeds were her friends. So was pollen and mold. As a forensic botanist, she asked the plants questions about crime scenes and listened to their answers. The herbicide guys were all about killing. They'd always struck her a bit like boys pulling the legs off spiders.

When Hugo was distracted with Julian, she knelt and dug into the soil, then scraped a bit of the waxy substance off the root and rubbed it between her fingers. What was it? She smelled it. It just didn't seem natural. She wished she could analyze it. One thing she knew: if it stayed on there, that plant was dead. All of them were.

Hugo was back, sweat dripping from his brow, so morose and dark, worried about the plants. Most of the men had their shirts off, but he didn't. She wondered if the sunshine hurt his burns. Or maybe he didn't like them seeing.

They moved to a new field, working together. He was sure and tender with the plants; sometimes her belly would twist around when she watched him. Sometimes she wanted to go to him. Touch him.

She wanted him not to be Kabakas.

According to her profile, Kabakas had lived many places as a kid, particularly Thailand and the Philippines, which meant that there was no way he could've come from a farming family. Farmers barely took weekend vacations. And the *mercado* swords, the whole thing.

No.

But what if he was? It didn't seem possible that this man, who cared so deeply for these villagers, for the plants, for Paolo—this man who stole her breath every time he came near—it didn't seem possible that this man could be responsible for the massacre in the Yacon fields. It didn't feel right in her gut, and not really in her brain, either. The killing of unarmed innocents required a deep, dark aberration. A mental illness, really.

Could there be two Kabakas's? She'd ruled it out before. Had she been wrong in that? Or did she just not want the Yacon fields killer to be Hugo? Was she losing her objectivity, as Dax had suggested?

Fuck that. She just had to trust. Sometimes a hunter's best tool was quiet.

Above all, she needed to avoid deepening their emotional entanglement. That would help nobody.

She moved to the next bush, clipping carefully.

In college, she'd worked the test gardens, mostly corn. Trying to grow giant hybrids had felt important, but it was really just a game compared to these flowers. People depended on these flowers for their survival, their future. Being out here with Hugo and the rest, pulling for the village to survive, she felt like a part of something larger in a way she hadn't for a very long time.

As soon as they got home, Hugo went to his own field with a flashlight, thinking to check the roots, no doubt. She wanted desperately to go out with him, to continue their connection around the plants. Had this mysterious disease reached so far up the mountain? She wanted to know, too. It didn't look natural, but then, she wasn't exactly a savinca expert. Still, it didn't look natural.

She went to the kitchen and started the rice and beans going, then chopped plantains and potatoes.

She knew from Hugo's expression at the dinner table that the roots he'd checked were coated, too. She wished she could be Zelda the botanist now instead of Liza the drug whore. She and Hugo could dig up a plant and bring it down to the city and locate a microscope to put it under. She'd give anything to know what the substance was made of. It seemed to spread in globules. There were a few basic tests she could do with what was on hand in the kitchen. She could try them if she got the chance. She hated feeling helpless.

Julian had contacted the Universidad de Valencia, and they were sending somebody—one of the region's top botanists had happened to be on-site, and he'd volunteered to go out immediately. That would be good.

A stroke of luck.

After dinner Hugo threw down his napkin and turned to Paolo. "No math tonight, Paolo.

She nearly forgot to breathe as Paolo turned to him, trying his best to maintain his usual stern look.

He'd called him Paolo.

"I understand you did an excellent job out in the field," Hugo continued. "Such work deserves a night off, don't you think?"

She looked away, not wanting to intrude on the moment.

"Thank you," Paolo said.

***

They handled a different field the next day, taking rows three by three, which put her farther away from Hugo, but it made sense for speed now that she'd been trained. The work, when Hugo wasn't around, was monotonous—peaceful, but monotonous. Her whole existence was like another planet; no TVs, no phones, bells, or buzzers, and no world crises to consume her. She felt strangely weightless.

Even the villagers were more connected to technology and the strife of everyday life than she was now, what with their phones and their lives and their constant arguments about whether to risk rebuilding. They had access to the news, and most of them seemed to be on Facebook.

Hugo didn't want her on the Internet, of course.

She should steal a phone and check in...but she found she very much didn't want to. She didn't want to deal with Dax, didn't want him staring into her mind. He needed to work on turning Sal, the Brujos guard. Dax was a genius billionaire with a team of spies at his beck and call. He should be able to turn one guard.

The plants continued to deteriorate at a suspiciously rapid rate. The botanist had come by, according to Julian. He'd dug up a plant and collected some soil for tests.

She wished she could've talked to him and gotten his impressions of the strange substance on the roots. Hugo had said it was climbing the stems on some plants.

She should stay out of it, but she couldn't.

"Science," she declared after dinner that night. Hugo was bent over reports of some sort in front of the fire. She'd just finished cleaning. "Paolo and I are going to do a science project."

He waved them away. It was as if they had a silent pact to keep their distance from each other now—physically, at least.

The sun was going down as she and Paolo set out. "Let's go to your plants. The ones whose buds you've harvested," she said. They could experiment there. She'd put together several agents from the kitchen and laundry—lemon juice, borax. Maybe they could find something that would break up the waxy coating. A shot in the dark. Nevertheless.

She showed Paolo how to make an observation chart. They numbered the plants and decided on characteristics to track: level of wilting, shininess, color, and root coating consistency. "It's how the plants talk," she said. "It's important that we listen closely." They assigned numbers. She sprinkled baking soda around the base of the first, and Paolo watered it to let it soak in. She did nothing to the second, but she put borax around the third.

"Like the *luna de febrero*," Paolo mumbled as she sprinkled the powder at the base of the fifth plant.

"What is? What I'm doing right now?" She looked up. "It's like the February moon?"

"It's a celebration," Paolo said. "Primer Verde. The old people make designs with the stones along the sides of the rows, sometimes large. Sometimes they break them." He pointed to the powder. "Afterward there is a party. Dancing. Food. Hugo does not like to go. He does not like to dance and sing."

"They powder the stone to make designs in the soil?" she asked. "Every February?"

"A tradition." He shrugged. "Silly."

"What's the stone?"

He stood and looked around. "Come." She followed him across the path to the hill. He kicked at a dirty outcrop until something broke off. "Luquesolama, it is called." He knelt down and smashed at the pieces with the bottom of his scythe. She gathered a selection of pieces into her hands, tipping it this way and than in the dying light. She crumbled a bit. The mineral was soft, almost like soapstone. "An old tradition?"

"Very old," Paolo said.

From what she'd gathered over the days in the field, there were three harvests: May, August, and November. They then cut the plants back and let them go dormant for three months. February was when the plants would come out of the dormancy cycle. "The new leaves appear right after?"

"Yes," he said, surprised she'd guessed it. A ritual this old was more science than superstition—she'd bet on it. She didn't recognize the stone, but it could be that it was deeply linked to the savinca. Most people didn't realize how symbiotic plants and rocks were. Plants broke up the stone and dispersed the minerals. Minerals nourished the plants. Had these farmers developed a ritualized way to help it along over the decades? Did this stone add something essential to the savinca? Did it stimulate growth? Support the plant's resistance to maladies? "Collect the stones for me."

"It's not February."

"As an experiment. I'm going to make some solution in the kitchen with these stones. We'll pour it on, and then we will see what they say."

"We can help the village," he said. "Like Hugo."

An hour later, she'd cooked up a solution with a carrier—those roots needed to get good and coated. Paolo poured it as they discussed the chart. "You have to check it every day," she said. "You are a scientist now."

Paolo nodded. Saving the plants was a long shot, but science was method and consistency—that was a good lesson for Paolo.

CHAPTER NINETEEN

She missed the university botanist again the next day. She knew she couldn't talk with him, but she wished she could at least see what he did—that would give her a clue as to what he thought the substance was made of.

She definitely learned more about Hugo, though. He didn't talk about his past, but he had views on everything from Paolo's reading habits to Valencian rebuilding. He was thoughtful. He cared. She could see him as a man who might have gone up against soldiers, but the later, darker Kabakas who'd slaughtered indiscriminately?

It seemed more and more unlikely.

He asked her a lot of questions. She answered as Liza for the most part, hating that she had to. But she could tell he'd found Liza's blog.

She could see from his movements that his pain had lessened, and she hadn't smelled opium for a while. Knowing Hugo, he'd reserve it for extreme occasions.

That morning, she and Paolo had gone out to check the results of the test area; there was only increased wilting and more shine. Nothing was helping. Not even the Luquesolama.

The plants were getting worse; it seemed a race now to pull them in before the buds were worthless.

The villagers were out in force, resolved to complete the harvest no matter what. The older women delivered lunch around noon and the younger women gathered at the tree-shaded picnic table while Hugo ate somewhere else with the men. A few of them spoke English; she asked them about the university botanist but she didn't get anything new.

She spotted a phone in one of the women's bags. She could check in on the situation. Maybe buy more time. And consult on the roots.

They were involved in an argument. She slipped it out, and then made excuses about having to pee. The phone didn't have a lot of charge left, but it had enough. She sped down the hill to the outhouse and went in. It was hot and pungent. There was a crack in the wall and she shoved a pebble into it to widen it enough to see though. Nobody coming. She Googled "Luquesolama" and got nothing. Quickly, she dialed an old CIA colleague, a botanist, and told him about the look of the roots and her theories. Had the spraying program evolved in some way? He didn't think so, but he'd check. He promised to look into the geological makeup of the mountain and the Luquesolama stone.

She got Dax right after that. Dax should've been first.

His voice was full of concern. "Are you okay? What's going on?"

"We've had a situation in the fields," she said.

"A situation?" he asked, thinking, she realized too late, that it was a situation of danger.

"Nothing like that. It's the savinca harvest. These little

villages, you take their crop and the whole thing implodes. And now there's this suspicious blight. I don't think it's the CIA, but who knows? If there were a way to reverse it...I'm running tests, but I can't get equipment without blowing my cover. Supposedly, some researcher from the university is here, but he hasn't come up with anything. It's not natural...it's..."

She paused, listening to herself. Obsessed with the crop. "What's going on with the pirates? Did you turn Sal yet? Is he getting the files?"

"Sal's scared. He might not turn, Zelda."

"He wants to turn—I heard it."

"Not in time. Kabakas is our best bet," he said.

Her heart sank. "I don't have any kind of clarity on that yet."

"No sense at all yet?"

"It's been difficult..."

"*Difficult.*"

"Yes." She hated when he echoed her back. "Difficult."

"You're staying with a man who may be Kabakas, and over a course of several days you've gained no clarity as to his identity whatsoever?"

"Are you questioning me?"

"You're the smartest, most tenacious person I've ever met. So, yes, that's exactly what I'm doing. I'm questioning you."

She forced her voice to sound calm. "This is a situation with innumerable variables, none of which you have any understanding of." *Having never been in the field.* She left that part unsaid.

"Did you crack that cabinet?"

"I haven't gotten the chance." She'd never before lied to Dax, though it wasn't entirely a lie. She hadn't made the chance.

"So you haven't been able to rule him in or rule him out."

"Some evidence says no, and some evidence says yes. We can't use him if we're not sure."

The silence on the line made her nervous.

"You're one of the foremost Kabakas experts in the world," he said finally. "If you can look at the evidence and think there's a possibility he's Kabakas, I think it's safe to say we can help the pirates pass him off to the delegation as Kabakas, don't you?"

"Dax—"

"We don't need Kabakas; we need a solution. If the delegation believes he's Kabakas, that's a solution."

She felt sick. "What if we put him in the mix and it's proven that he isn't Kabakas? What then?"

"He's got *you* baffled."

"Jesus. He has a little boy."

"Everybody is expendable."

Her heart pounded. This was what they did all the time as Associates, sent people into peril and even to their deaths if it would save the many. Sometimes even innocents.

"You need to pull together everything that says Kabakas."

"My week isn't up. You gave me a week."

"Two days won't matter."

"They will to me. I need to know for myself if it's him."

"And what if it's not him?" Dax asked. Meaning, *Will she*

go along with destroying him?

"I need to know," she said. "I'm the one who can sell it. This is what I need."

She could feel his unhappiness through the phone. "The tanker situation won't stay cold forever," he said. "You have until Saturday."

"You don't want to send Associates after Hugo blind. You'll lose men. You will wait for me," she warned.

She traced the edge of the phone after they hung up. They'd need to find a way to handle the long distance bill this poor woman was going to get. That was what she thought about—as if that was the problem.

Would he heed her warning?

She replaced the phone just before the group returned to the fields.

She smiled when she caught sight of Hugo; he seemed to feel her, and he turned and smiled back. Out there in the sunshine and fresh air, it was as if all the lies and secrets were gone, and they were simply working shoulder to shoulder. She was beginning to feel less like an impostor in this life, and the world of Dax and geopolitical concerns seemed farther away.

CHAPTER TWENTY

Usually when confronted with a situation like this, a problem with an agent, Dax would discuss it with Zelda. Her years of experience gave her insights into life in the field that he didn't have. She supplied that for him. Or at least she had in the past.

She wasn't under duress now—that was clear. And she didn't seem frightened, either. They had her working the fields, working as some sort of a maid or governess. Her journey down had sounded trying, but she'd come through intact. Unviolated. He'd gotten that in subtext.

Yet something was happening down there, and she was hiding it.

He wished he could see her eyes. He'd know things from her eyes, but all he had was her voice and it didn't sound normal—it was lower in pitch, smoother. That could indicate a snap. Or relaxation. Sometimes they felt the same.

Relaxation.

He cringed when he thought back through the years he'd known her and realized she'd never taken a vacation—not even a day off. And God, she was working around plants, in nature now. She was a botanist, for fuck's sake. You didn't go into botany without a love for nature, and aside from Association-related excursions here and there, she hadn't been out of the city in...what? Seven years? Eight?

She seemed consumed with the crop, this village. It was part of a cover, yes, but it felt like more. He thought about Brando in *Apocalypse Now*, a soldier who'd gone into the depths of the jungle, leaving war behind. Entering a different reality, lost to everything he'd once worked for and believed in.

Was that happening to Zelda now?

Sometimes when he couldn't work out a problem with his mind, he resorted to the smell of a thing—not literally, but emotionally—how it smelled when he closed his eyes to the thoughts. This really did smell like loss. Like he was losing Zelda in some essential way. Protest as she might, deep down she had a death wish—that incident with Friar Hovde hadn't simply hurt her, it had destroyed her. She'd been riding the edge ever since. And Kabakas, he represented something *ultimate* to her. Did she unconsciously want him to find her out? Did she want him to end it?

A death wish and an ultimate being. It was not a good combination.

Was he losing Zelda to her greatest enemy?

CHAPTER TWENTY-ONE

Some of the leaves had started curling, and people were in a panic. They were right to panic.

The scientist returned that afternoon. Finally.

Dr. Ernesto Ruiz had a friendly face and salt-and-pepper hair. The name sounded familiar to Zelda. He was somebody; he'd written papers.

Ruiz gathered Hugo, Julian, and the other men around the picnic table. Zelda was desperate to join them, but she wasn't a man and she supposedly didn't understand Spanish, dammit. So she watched from afar.

As if he felt her gaze upon him, Hugo glanced at her, eyes like a caress. It made her want to die.

After the talk, Dr. Ruiz walked the fields with Julian and a few of the other men. Hugo stayed behind, and she waylaid him.

"What did he say?"

Hugo watched them disappear down the slope; she knew just from his expression that he didn't like the man. "He is not sure. Phosphorous deficiency, he guesses."

She tried not to act surprised, but she'd seen nothing that would indicate a phosphorous deficiency—not in the color, not in the growth. Phosphorous didn't coat the roots with wax. "Really?"

He took a breath as if to gather his thoughts, and related what Ruiz had said. It sounded reasonable...unless you were a botanist.

"Does he have a cure? A remedy?" she asked.

"He's working on it. We're to monitor the crop and the surrounding area. Even the trees."

She wished she could question him, but it was too much of a stretch for her cover. *Phosphorous.* Why would Ruiz lie?

Hugo was his aloof self on the way back to the house that night. "Try to have dinner on time tonight, *señorita*," he grumbled before heading out. Paolo helped her fix it while they worked on the skills he'd need to pass the nightly drill. Hugo came back in a worse mood.

"The leaves?" she said.

He looked helplessly at the field, not even bothering with a surly answer.

Hugo took his dinner at his desk that night. She'd barely spoken one word to him. She went out to the experiments and crouched in front of the row of plants staked out so carefully with sticks and string. The plants were getting worse. The waxy coating seemed to be thickening and extending upward. Even the plant that had gotten the Luquesolama solution wasn't improving.

The whole thing seemed unnatural. And here was this scientist, lying.

"Phosphorous, my ass. Ruiz, you motherfucker, what are you up to?"

"Ruiz is no good?"

She stood and spun around to find Paolo standing there.

Paolo repeated her words, mimicking her tone. "Phosphorous, my ass. Ruiz, you motherfucker, what are you up to?" He smiled, enjoying that he'd caught her swearing.

She fixed him with a hard gaze. "I was wrong to say that."

CHAPTER TWENTY-TWO

The presence of the Americans had disturbed Dr. Ernesto Ruiz like a low and persistent hum—something buzzing at the back of his head.

He'd made casual inquiries and learned that the farmer, Hugo, was an American businessman—a builder who had moved from Miami seven or eight years ago to become a hobbyist farmer. The woman his new cook. The American builder was apparently helpless with the restaurant gone. It seemed further that the American and his boy had cooks before, but the cooks had always quit. Established farmers were taking bets on how long this one would stay.

That low and persistent buzz changed the next day when he overheard the child informing his friends of what this cook said. *Phosphorous, my ass. Ruiz, you motherfucker, what are you up to?*

According to the child, she was running tests of her own, complete with observation charts.

It was at that point that the hum became an all-out alarm bell.

He was good with children. He gave the boys jobs and joked with them. It took the afternoon to coax the child into describing the tests.

A chill descended over him as he listened, but he forced

a tight smile. "*Bueno. Ella es muy inteligente.*"

The child smiled proudly. Ruiz asked him about how they'd found their maid, and he was suspiciously vague. In the valley, he said.

She'd arrived before he'd had the pellets dropped, so her presence wasn't in reaction to the blight. But she was doing the right tests. She was suspicious of him. And she was no ordinary maid.

He snapped a photo of her and sent it to El Gorrion.

El Gorrion had contacts all over; he'd find out who she was and figure out what to do.

CHAPTER TWENTY-THREE

Hugo stared into the fire while Liza and Paolo played a word game on the floor at the foot of his chair.

Liza had made the game out of bits of cardboard. *Scrabble*, she called it. Good for the boy's spelling, she explained. She'd tried to get Hugo to play, but games in front of a fire, that was too much like a family. Too saccharine-sweet. "It is not for me," he'd said.

"Maybe it is for you," she'd said.

He'd glowered. "Paolo knows not to ask me twice when I've said *no* to something."

She'd eyed him in that way of hers, and then turned away.

They enjoyed each other, these two, with their games and nature experiments. Her expression always lightened when Paolo entered the room. Paolo, too, grew brighter when she was around.

Your heart is locked up as tightly as that little cabinet. She thought it was selfish that he kept it closed. She didn't understand that some things were best left closed. Like the cabinet with its painful memories. Like the bloody heart of the savinca.

Liza laid the small squares out to spell a word. Paolo added her score. *Paolo.* He'd liked being called by his name.

Such a simple thing.

Paolo laughed and set a few squares of cardboard down.

It never ceased to amaze Hugo, the way things could go on as the world crashed. As Kabakas he could destroy entire armies, and now he couldn't stop a simple white substance from killing the savinca. Some of the men had taken to manually scraping the roots of the older, stronger bushes, but the coating would regrow overnight.

He hadn't felt this helpless since the other Kabakas had gone out and slaughtered in his name. Hugo had spent weeks hunting the impostor, determined to make him pay. That had all ended with the fire, and when he'd emerged from months of recuperation, he'd found the war winding down, and rumors that Kabakas had died in a fire. He didn't know how the rumors had started, but the other Kabakas had not struck again, and Hugo felt certain that going back into action as Kabakas would only bring this Dark Kabakas back to life.

He could see over her shoulder, and it frustrated him to watch. She was going too easy on the boy. She put down *tire* and smiled up at Hugo. He frowned and pointed at the *D*.

She gave him a blank look. Letting Paolo win. If he had her letters, oh, the words he'd spell.

On they went, laughing. Their laughter made him feel very alone. She'd accused him of locking everybody out of his dark cabinet, but he did not know how to do anything else. It felt dangerous to open the cabinet. Nearly as dangerous as opening his heart.

She formed the word *vent.*

Hugo cleared his throat. She had an *A* and a *D* in reserve; she could make *advent*. She turned to face him, raised her pretty dark brows in mock annoyance.

He frowned. She shouldn't let Paolo off like that; Paolo needed to be toughened up, not coddled. She turned back to the game, firelight kissing the slope of her forehead and the voluptuous curve of her cheekbone. Her skin would be warm to the touch.

He'd told himself to leave her alone. He was not his father; he would fuck the hotel lobby women in Bumcara if he wanted to fuck. He'd always had that rule, to keep his sexual exploits out of his home.

On they played.

She shifted when it was her turn, intent on the game, tucking her legs anew. At one point she leaned sideways against what she thought was his chair but was, in fact, his leg. He went still, not daring even to breathe, so awash in desire for her he couldn't stand it. It was a gift, just this touch. Who would gamble her away in a card game? Who would do that?

She laid out *corn* on the board when she could've laid out *corner*.

Hugo sighed.

Again she twisted to look up at him. The movement removed her soft weight from his leg and he wanted to cry out.

She narrowed her eyes. "What?"

"You know what."

Her green eyes flashed with humor and happiness. "If you won't play, then please, no commentary."

Was she toying with him? Drawing him into the game with deliberately careless play?

He frowned. "If you're going to do something, do it right, or there is no point..." The sentence died as he saw Paolo stiffen, thinking, perhaps, that he'd put a stop to the game. That was what Paolo thought of him. Right there. He couldn't have it.

He wouldn't have it.

He stood up from the chair, feeling both their eyes on him, and then lowered himself to the floor between them. "Give me some of those letters."

The boy seemed to have forgotten how to breathe.

Liza slid over seven bits of cardboard. She kept a neutral face, savoring it, perhaps, as a victory.

Hugo felt huge and clumsy down there with them. He formed the word *lute*. And just like that, he was playing.

And the game went on.

She laughed a lot. She'd seemed rigid and drawn when he'd first pulled her from that field, but her face had softened in the space of a week. She looked calmer, more beautiful. She'd modified some of the old housekeeper's clothes by hand, with needle and thread she'd found, and this version of the gray dress left her long arms bare. Even the track marks seemed less pronounced.

"Your turn."

She looked up and caught his eye. "I know."

"Need help?"

She smiled and looked down.

Paolo concentrated, switching his letters into different combinations behind the small box that served as a barrier, and sometimes he'd consult the English dictionary. Maybe it was good spelling practice.

Little by little, Hugo relaxed. He was playing with them.

There was no trick to playing, it seemed; no mystery to it other than the participation. Simple participation. You didn't have to laugh or have fun; you simply had to participate.

He stood at one point and placed another log on the fire. He crouched in front of it, stoking the flames to get more warmth into the room on the crisp night, and then he stood and turned.

Paolo curled sleepily on his side with a tiny smile. Liza was brushing a hand over the boy's hair with a look of fondness that shattered Hugo's heart. And his fire blazed and warmed them.

And then she looked up at him and smiled.

And he knew that there had never been a moment when he didn't want a son, a family.

She cocked her head quizzically, sensing his strong emotion. He wanted to tell her that he, too, loved Paolo. He wished she could understand that. He turned back and built the fire higher, as if that might show it.

She set a hand on the boy's arm. "Paolo," she whispered. "Bedtime."

"No," Hugo whispered, drawing near to the boy. He knelt on the other side of him and, gently as he could, he lifted him in his arms, something he hadn't done since Paolo was small.

He grumbled about it being a long day, but seeing Paolo play in front of the fire, being a boy in a way that Hugo never had, it made him want to hold him, to care for him.

It was Paolo he wanted to hold, yes, but maybe, just a little bit, it was Hugo's younger self.

Hugo left, holding his boy to his breaking heart. All these years. It would've been so easy to play with him.

So easy to call him by his name.

CHAPTER TWENTY-FOUR

Rio stepped out of the Aeropuerto Internacional El Dorado in Bogotá into a chaos of taxis and buses. He made his way past harried travelers and hurried businesspeople and on past scammers who wanted to befriend him, most of whom quickly turned away, deciding that they didn't, after all, want to befriend him. The air was cool and rich with the scent of smoked meat and diesel; he drew in a deep breath as he straightened his black jacket and fixed the cuffs of his silk shirt, looking forward to a good, hard hunt with a supposedly lethal opponent at the end. They were all supposed to be lethal, but they never were. Maybe this one was.

The car Dax had arranged for him was right where he said it would be. Rio slipped in and began to reassemble his Smith & Wesson Platinum 500 from the various pieces he'd sent through baggage. He could get firearms in Bogotá; in fact, there was a sniper rifle waiting for him in a little shop in the Bogotá suburbs, but he was sentimental about his weapons. He didn't mind new friends. But he liked to have old friends around him, too. And the 500 was a good friend.

He'd never heard Dax sound so worried. *Find her. Extract her if you sense danger. I prefer Kabakas alive, but I can just as well use him dead. Kill everybody you have to.*

Dax had warned him about Kabakas. Rio had heard of the man, of course, but he wasn't worried. He was more than ready, and he'd worn his best suit.

Kill everybody you have to, Dax had said.

He always did. He slipped in the magazine.

CHAPTER TWENTY-FIVE

Hugo forced himself to sit in the boy's room and watch him sleep.

He'd done that a lot at first, watching him, this small being who'd been robbed of his parents.

A noise out in the great room. He hoped it was her going to bed—the feeling between them was too strong, too big. He was not his father, forcing himself on the help.

It was only when everything was quiet out there that he allowed himself to return. His heart leapt when he saw her, curled up in front of the fire herself, head next to the stupid word game.

Sleeping.

He knelt beside her, sucking in her scent like a burglar inside her house. His heart pounded. He wanted to have her so badly it was very nearly a physical pain.

Then she turned and opened her eyes. Her cheekbone was marred by imprints of the rough jute rug. There was no softness here; it was no place for a woman.

"Isn't it your bedtime, *señorita?*"

She smiled, then. "It meant a lot to him that you played." She turned away and gazed into the fire. Was she thinking about that first night? The night he'd made her come? Did she regret it?

Even in stillness she had an unceasing quality, like a spring-fed stream. He'd felt the depth of her silence out in the field, but he felt it so much more now.

He took his chair. He should direct her to bed, but instead he sat with her at his foot. He enjoyed it perhaps a little too much. Her bright hair flashed in the light, but the part nearest to him was dark. That was the part that he wanted to touch.

"It meant a lot that you played," she said again.

"I never...I never knew," he confessed. *Never knew the boy would want that. Never knew how.*

"But you went ahead and did it," she said, gazing at the flames.

She would make him sound noble. As if he'd noticed that Paolo wanted to play and had indulged him, when really, he'd been pulled by the ear. By her.

Like a starving man, he feasted on the beauty of her stillness and the glow of her skin—this woman who'd done her own terrible things, who could dwell with him in the quiet. He'd never met anybody like her. He found that he loved everything about her.

Could she be happy here? She had been a prostitute in her other life; surely that wasn't a good life. Could he induce her to stay?

The idea stunned him.

No. Somebody light and free and passionate like Liza, she wouldn't choose life with a man who kept himself locked as tightly as that cabinet.

He glanced over at the cabinet itself—all that pain and yearning that was in there. His life was in there. What if he showed what was inside? Wasn't that her accusation—that he was as closed as the cabinet? What if he proved her wrong? Opening it would feel very much like opening himself.

He couldn't believe he was considering it. Then again, the act itself was simple: walk over and open it.

"I want you to see something," he blurted.

She looked up, green, green eyes awash in humorous light. He got up and went to the cabinet, and when he looked back at her, the humor had faded. He himself hardly believed he was doing it. He'd never shown anybody the treasures and tokens he'd collected. Not even Paolo. He pressed up on the bit of molding that secured the key, and drew it out.

She stayed by the fire. Did she not want to see inside? "Come," he said.

She rose tentatively and came to him. Why would she resist? Hadn't she wanted this? Well, it was too late now. When he committed to something he committed with his whole heart.

He unlocked it and drew open the door, revealing the carefully arranged trinkets and medals. Shiny coins. Train tickets. Colorful bottle caps he'd collected as a boy, before he'd learned the truth of who he was. Miniature figurines he'd loved. Colorful stamps, Swiss army knife, Chinese jade carvings, American baseball cards, a Canadian pen with a maple leaf on it.

She stood next to him, now. Even the air between them grew livelier when she came near.

He drew out an American baseball card. "It may not seem exotic to you," he said, "but when I was first in America, these cards seemed so very American with the shiny bits and the bold marks." He tipped it back and forth, letting the hologram coating catch the light as he'd done so often as a boy. "Everything so bright and important." He felt so bare to her, suddenly. A strange feeling, but not altogether bad. He felt as if something inside him shifted. As if the scar tissue covering his heart had softened.

He put it back and drew out the puzzle box. "Have you ever seen one?"

"It's beautiful." She sounded so sad. Why?

He handed it to her. "Try to open it," he coaxed. "I think you cannot."

"Probably not." She seemed hesitant suddenly. Why? Had he made a mistake in showing her?

"A gift. My father chose it," he went on. "He chose it for me, and it meant a lot." He wasn't explaining it well. It had been one of the good moments, when the man who raised him had seemed to care. It had meant the world. "He was a gardener, a handyman."

"Is that where you got your love of plants?"

"No, he hated plants." He should tell her. If he truly wanted to let her in, he would tell her the things that he never told anybody. He wasn't sure if he could; he had never developed that muscle. "Go ahead. See if you can open it."

Fruitlessly, she slid around the pieces. Their hands brushed as he took it from her and slid the panels in the combination that would make the lid spring open. There inside was a lion's head.

"It's beautiful," she said in a faraway tone.

"All of these little treasures I collected."

He felt her keen interest in spite of that strange hesitation. "Go ahead." He forced himself to gesture toward the box, inviting her in further. He stiffened as she touched a Jordanian coin, drew out a bus ticket from Nigeria, a pink jade box, and then a pen with the name of a Bangkok restaurant emblazoned upon it.

"You visited all of these places?"

"Lived in all of these places."

Finally, her fingers lip upon a small, blunt stick with a few crude carvings. The Moro graduation rite wand. It looked like nothing next to the shinier, more colorful treasures, but it was the most important item he owned. He'd struggled long and hard to earn it, spending years perfecting his skills, hands bloody from throwing the blades, from working the patterns. She seemed to sense its importance in the same way in which she sensed just how to touch a plant, the way she sensed what the boy needed. She turned it in her fingers. "Where did you buy this?"

"It was given to me."

She would not meet his eyes. "A gift?"

"In a way," he said.

"From your parents?"

"No." He studied the side of her face, needing her to look at him. "From a teacher on Quoro, on the southern islands of the Philippines. I had left my parents by then." He took it from her and gestured at the box. "I was miserable in all of these places; but this place, it saved my life."

She met his eyes now. "You left your parents..." It was more a statement than a question.

He took a breath and studied the rites stick. "My mother and father served an oil company consultant who traveled the world. A Bolivian man. Very wealthy. My father hated the plants, but not as much as he hated me." He slid his finger up and down the side. "Over and over I would go to him, thinking that this time I'll make him proud, but with every accomplishment, he seemed to hate me more. I remember times he'd take the belt to me for good marks in school. He would beat me for being good. I never understood. But then one day I did—I was not his child. I was the Bolivian's bastard. My mother, she would not have wanted her employer in that way. But she and my father needed those jobs, and sometimes you do what you must..." He had never revealed these things to anybody. "Hurting me, that was how my supposed father punished the oilman."

"Hugo." She set a hand on his arm.

He shrugged. "My biological father, he knew what was happening to me, but he would not stop it. My mother tried to intervene, but she could not guard me, and could not square off against her husband. That home, it was like poisonous soil. You take that poison into your veins, and it forms you."

"That's not how it works."

"Our relocation to Manila made things worse. So much worse. One day I took all of the money that I had saved and my small box of trinkets—these things here—and I stole a boat, thinking to live on an island alone. I went deep into the Sulu Archipelago and arrived on a remote island, wild and quiet. I thought it was uninhabited, but I was wrong. The island people, the Moros, took me in. They were warring with other islands at the time, and I was big and strong and fast. And so angry, Liza, so angry. They trained me. They put me in their army. They were fierce, these fighters, descended from generations of fierce fighters. Even the Americans could not subdue the islands. The Moro fighters were the reason the army switched from .22 to .38 caliber sidearms. Those men taught me everything."

"Your mother must have missed you."

"I don't know."

"She tried to protect you."

"The fights were getting worse. She would've had to choose. It was better that I left."

"I'm sorry."

"*No importa.*" He shrugged. "My so-called father died years later The oilman cast my mother out for a younger and prettier servant. I was rich by then. I found a way to ruin him."

"Oh," she said.

"I set her up in a small house." He put down the stick and picked up the puzzle box again. "Paolo would love this. I could have given it to him, but I kept it locked up instead."

"You could give it to him now."

"What I mean..." He paused. "This remoteness; it is a coward's way to raise a boy. I let him think I don't care."

"He knows you care. He thinks the world of you."

"I will give this to him."

She picked up the Moro wand again, eyes half hidden by dark lashes, but he did not miss the sadness. She set it down. "Thank you for showing me. These things are wonderful."

He heard the lie in her words—she didn't think they were wonderful at all. They'd shared too much stillness for her to lie to him effectively.

She turned and went to the fireplace.

Sometimes his instincts as a killer doubled as instincts as a lover, like the instinct to chase down prey when it darted away. He did that now. He went after her. They'd connected for a moment, and he couldn't stand to lose that. He could not let her go.

He set his hands on her shoulders, feeling torn in two.

He tightened his grip and turned her.

She looked...worried.

She'd seen inside the box, which was more like his heart than she could ever imagine. And she'd come out worried.

"*Corazón*," he said, brushing a knuckle across her cheek. "I won't hurt you." And like the killer that he was, like the taker that he was, he closed his mouth over hers.

He felt her body change between his hands. She seemed to fill with lust, or maybe loathing. Still he kissed her, pressing his tongue to the seam of her lips, forcing her open, desire pulsing through him. "*Entrégate a mí*," he gasped. *Give yourself to me.*

She pulled away, breath coming fast. "Fuck," she breathed.

"What?"

She studied his face. It was strange, the way she looked at him, as if she were seeing him for the first time. "Fuck," she said again. It meant something different the second time; what, he didn't know.

He simply pulled her to him, hands fit over the small of her back and the swell of her ass, molding her to fit him.

She grabbed onto his hair as he took her mouth. His cock was a hot, rigid bar against her heaving belly. He sucked in her tongue, hands exploring her body.

She sighed. Softened. Melted into him like sunshine.

CHAPTER TWENTY-SIX

He was Kabakas. And he was kissing her. *Kabakas.*

He was beautiful and dangerous and wild, and he was kissing her, taking her over, and in that moment she didn't care; she just wanted him. She'd always wanted him. It was no time to lie to herself.

Ever since she'd tacked that blurry photo up on the bulletin board, she'd wanted him.

She pulled away, looking at him again. *Kabakas.* "Fuck, yes," she amended, twisting her fingers in his sooty hair, pulse skittering. Then she kissed him again.

He groaned into her kiss, moving against her.

This is fucked up. A little voice in her head kept chanting it over and over as his huge hungry hands roamed over her hips and ass. *This is fucked up.*

And she'd never been more turned on in her life.

He spoke to her in Spanish. Hot, dirty words.

"Tell me in English." She wanted to be with him on every level.

"I want to strip you bare and devour you." He stood back to undo her buttons. "I want to hold you still and fuck you in every hole."

She opened her mouth to speak. She wanted to tell him *fuck, yes*. She wanted to tell him that he wasn't alone, that she was here with him under the endless night sky. That she'd always been with him. She wanted to tell him that the things inside the cabinet were beautiful. That the Moro wand was amazing. All of these things she'd wondered about for so long. Like treasures he'd kept for her.

"I want to fuck you and devour you with every part of myself," he said. "Every part. And make you come as much as I please."

Nothing mattered, nothing made sense. Loving Kabakas—it was all wrong and all right.

She stiffened. *Love*—where had that come from? What was she doing?

"You never have to say yes when you're thinking no," he said, sensing her stiffness. He still thought she was a prostitute, of course. "I'll be gentle," he whispered into her hair. "If you prefer it," he added.

She closed her eyes as he sucked in a bit of skin from her tender neck, a bright, sharp bite of pleasure, and then he licked her there, and kissed her.

Heat pooled between her legs.

"You have nothing to fear from me."

Except that she did. He touched something raw in her, made her feel out of control. She was so full of guilt and shame, she didn't know if she could survive too much of a breach.

And on a more practical level, if he ever found out who she was, he'd kill her.

He'd have to; he'd see her as a threat to himself and Paolo, and he'd have to kill her. His harsh love for Paolo ran deeper than midnight.

"*Corazón.*" His hands shook as he pulled up her dress, up, up, over her thighs, over her hips.

He seemed to be trying to be extra gentle with her and barely managing it—his touch was bottled thunder, liable to shatter the glass at any moment. It turned her on like nothing else.

"You," she said, tracing the scruff on his chin.

He kissed her forehead, and with a swift, sure movement, he picked her up and carried her to his bedroom. She undid the buttons on his shirt, kissing every newly bared space until he set her down on his bed.

She went up on her knees, then undid his belt buckle and shoved down his pants. His massive cock sprang up, golden brown, skin taut over ropy veins, like a map to somewhere else.

She grabbed him at the root and pulled. He groaned and shoved into her hand. His wild energy intoxicated her, but it also frightened her.

"*Me estás matando,*" he said. *You're killing me.*

She bent over to lick the tip. He shuddered just from that. He was Kabakas. She was driving Kabakas crazy. She took him all the way in, coaxing him into a rhythm that would get him senseless, needing to get back some order, some control. She took him in deeper and deeper, but he grabbed her hair and stopped her.

"What?"

He rolled away and went to a cabinet. He unzipped something and came back with a condom.

She rid herself of the last of her clothes.

He tipped his head down to face her as he stood over

her, rolling it onto himself, eyes wild. It scared her a little, how present he was, how raw everything was.

"Fuck me," she said, feeling frightened, feeling too much.

He pushed her down onto the bed and buried his head in her belly. She touched his hair, senses ablaze. She felt as though he could see all her secrets when he pressed his face to her like that. It felt unbearably intimate.

He touched her breast, fingered her clit, but it was his soft, wet kiss on her belly that destroyed her.

And suddenly it was too much. She grabbed his hair in two fists and yanked his head to hers. He grabbed her wrists. "*Corazón,*" he said with a dark, warning look.

She let go of his hair and he pressed her hands above her head, intense eyes on hers.

She could feel it even more now, that barely restrained thunder under the surface of his skin. His thunder, his passion, his desire to be gentle with her, those treasures he'd collected, this windswept place of his, his love for Paolo, all of these belonged to the same class of things—true things, important things, human things, raw things. The raw things that could break through her walls.

"Guide me," he whispered.

She took his cock and pressed the fat head to her entrance. He pushed in little by little, stretching her, filling her, letting her see the naked desire in his eyes. She felt like she might drown in the truth of his eyes as he entered her.

He pushed all the way in, stretching her.

She gasped; he was so huge inside her, moving and filling her.

"Okay?"

"Please, yes. Please," she said, though she hardly knew what she was asking for. Just *please*. His gentleness scared her. The thundering passion below the surface scared her. But she didn't want a coldfuck.

She didn't want to be alone anymore.

The legendary and semi-mythical Kabakas was the only real thing to her now, and everything else seemed unreal.

Rabbit hole was a term they used a lot in spycraft, mostly for distraction. But she felt like she was coming up against the original meaning, the true *Alice in Wonderland* rabbit hole, a new world just as vital as her own.

He pumped into her slowly, breathing her secrets with his cock. "I'm here," he whispered as he shoved into her, devouring her. She squeezed her pussy as he thrust, trying to make herself feel extra tight, trying to take over. But he wouldn't go on autopilot. He wouldn't get lost. He would stay with her. Keep her there, present and gasping.

"*Corazón*," he groaned. He kissed her all over her face and neck as he fucked her.

He fucked her like he cared. Like he was fucking *her* instead of just fucking. Like a waterfall of dangerous feeling crashing right through her.

CHAPTER TWENTY-SEVEN

Dr. Ruiz's phone rang late that afternoon. El Gorrion's connections in the CIA hadn't even needed to run facial recognition: they knew this woman. The name wasn't Liza. It was Zelda Pierce, a forensic botanist and former field agent.

"Has she said anything to you about the blight?" El Gorrion asked.

"She doesn't speak Spanish," Ruiz said.

"Oh, yes, she does," El Gorrion said. "She was an agent during the war. She was part of the Peru network. And she helped take down the Lopez ring. She was in Ecuador the year after..."

El Gorrion went on, but Ruiz had stopped listening at *botanist*. "A botanist? She could ruin me."

"Stop whining. She is a Kabakas hunter—that is her interest. This woman—she is retired now, but she was one of the leading hunters. Every single one of my contacts mentions this," El Gorrion said. "She is still active, but with her own organization—so that she can hunt Kabakas full time, perhaps. They do not know. This interest in the crop—it is extra. She is using the American farmer to get close to the villagers. She wants them to open up about Kabakas."

"But she is suspicious of me," Ruiz said. "What if she uses her knowledge of the crop to gain the trust of the villagers? If I go down, our work together...it could be harmed." He wouldn't go so far as to suggest that if the blight was linked to him, it could then be traced to El Gorrion. You never threatened El Gorrion.

"She has been there longer than you, no?" El Gorrion said.

"Yes," Ruiz said. "She arrived the day before I dropped the pellets."

"We use her, then," he said. "We will say that she caused the blight. A CIA botanist. It's perfect. Unmask her, and see what happens."

"Why not kill her?" Ruiz said.

"Because I want to see what happens."

"You think she will get a lead on Kabakas? You will follow her?"

"Perhaps. But if the scourge is traced to her, we may get something better—she may get the wrath of Kabakas turned onto her. He killed for that village once. We keep watch on her, and Kabakas may reveal himself."

"The farmer is in love with her," Ruiz said. "That's what the villagers say. He may try to hide her. Protect her."

"An American hobbyist farmer will never protect her from Kabakas," El Gorrion growled. "More likely, she'll kill him and leave. We follow. She'll lead us to Kabakas."

"Could the farmer himself be Kabakas?" Ruiz asked. "There's something about him..."

El Gorrion frowned. "With a Kabakas hunter as a

maid?" He seemed to ponder this. "Well, then, he'll kill her—and we'll have him. One way or another, we'll find Kabakas and attack him where he lives. He won't be so formidable without his mask and his swords."

El Gorrion instructed him to wait until night to unmask her to the village. He would have men in place, watching the road to see who went up to the American's home after that. Only one way in or out. It was the perfect bait for the trap.

When Dr. Ruiz next opened his computer, his mailbox was full of images: a CIA ID badge, commendations, and photos of an awards ceremony. He drove back to the village, ready to call a meeting.

CHAPTER TWENTY-EIGHT

H ugo furrowed his brow at the knock. It was unusual to get visitors at all at the house, but particularly after dark.

It was Julian, wet from the rain. "Dr. Ruiz has called a meeting. He has found the cause of the blight."

Hugo felt a great weight release from his heart. "And a cure?"

"*No sé.* He's gathering the farmers at the *cantina.* That is all I know."

Hugo's heart lifted. Liza had been about to serve dinner; he'd been looking forward to it, thinking they could repeat the night in front of the fire, but this was excellent news, and he was touched that Julian had made the trek up the mountainside in the dark.

"*Un momento.*" He went in and grabbed his jacket and informed Liza, who seemed more surprised than happy. Well, he was happy enough for both of them. All three of them. He drew her to him and kissed her.

"I'll be interested to hear," she said.

Julian played "Color Esperanza" by Diego Torres on the trek down, the perfect music for the cautious hope they both felt. They pulled up in front of the cinder block building that had served as a supply store of sorts. The night air was cool, but the room was lit warmly on the inside, as if it glowed with happiness. The racks and shelves had been pushed to the side and two dozen villagers were gathered around a table; mostly men. People were drinking sodas; a few had beers. A pack of Marlboros got passed around.

Dr. Ruiz looked up, eyes eerie, thanks to the angle of the light. Hugo had never liked him—he'd always seemed condescending toward the villagers—but he might have the cure. He'd seemed to be waiting for them.

There were chairs for maybe half of the people. Julian and Hugo stood.

"It is not good news," Dr. Ruiz said, opening the lid of his laptop. Hugo's heart fell. He could feel Julian deflate beside him. "I will try to do all that I can, but this disease is not natural. It is man-made. A poison that moves rapidly through the soil to attack the root."

The botanist stabbed a few buttons.

Hugo glanced around at the faces. Few looked surprised. They had all suspected there would be no cure. But none had suspected what came next: that this blight was the CIA's new weapon in the war on drugs.

The men protested. They weren't growing drugs. They weren't near the coca fields. Did the CIA believe the *Savinca verde* to be a cover crop? Could they not be made to see?

Dr. Ruiz raised his hands, insisting he didn't know.

Julian and Hugo exchanged helpless glances.

He typed on his laptop. "This woman is a CIA scientist. A CIA botanist. She is the one responsible." He turned the laptop to the group.

Hugo's brain froze, unable to make sense of what he was

seeing: A young, dark-haired Liza, wearing a white lab coat, holding a clipboard. She wore glasses and stood grinning next to an impossibly high stalk of corn. She looked like a scientist. His heart slammed inside his chest. "What is this?" he demanded.

Ruiz flipped to the next image: Liza in camo, still with that dark hair, holding a rifle like she knew how to hold a rifle. Mountains in the background. Afghanistan? Another: Liza kneeling on the ground next to a half-buried skeleton, baggie and tweezers clutched in her latex-gloved hands, sidearm visible. A grainy hotel surveillance shot of Liza in a skirt suit, gun down at her thigh, followed. The images didn't make sense to his mind, but they made sense to his heart. This was her true nature—a hunter, a warrior. She'd fooled him.

Betrayed him.

The photos continued. He felt the men's gazes on him, but he could not look away. Her name was Zelda, not Liza, Ruiz said. CIA.

Hugo gripped the back of the chair in front of him. "I didn't know."

"She's highly trained," Ruiz said.

So was he. Supposedly.

There was a shot of Liza—no, Zelda—in a ceremony with a medal on her suit jacket, dark hair pulled into a ponytail, telltale bulge of a holstered gun right there for the world to see. Lastly, an elementary school picture with two dark-haired little girls. Twins.

The room felt too warm. Too smoky.

Her question about his burns: *How long?* The recognition with which she'd first looked at him. Her strange attitude toward the cabinet. The way she'd picked out the Moro wand. He thought he was revealing his heart to the woman he was falling for.

Instead, he was providing clues to an enemy.

She knew who he was. It was only a matter of time before his enemies moved on him...*and Paolo*. That was the worst part of it—the threat to Paolo.

He gripped the wooden chair back, rage coursing through his fingertips.

Ruiz went on about how she was there to kill the savinca. Sent by the CIA or a rogue, perhaps. Experimenting. The men asked angry questions.

Ruiz knew very little. "She is here to conduct experiments on the plants. There may be something special about the savinca that has attracted them. If I can isolate that element, that reason..." He went on. Hugo was no longer listening.

Killing the plants was...what? A taunt? It made no sense. But too many other things did. The fading track marks. The way her story never felt real. Her eyes, her hair.

Rage clouded the edges of his vision as he thought of Paolo, there alone with her. His enemies would hurt Paolo as a way to hurt him—she would know that, of course.

He turned to Julian. "I have to get back. I have to get Paolo away from her."

"Shall I take him for the night?"

"Please," Hugo said, pulling on his jacket. He would kill her. He would not be merciful.

One of the men spoke up: he'd seen a light bobbing down the side of the mountain six days back, heading downward from the direction of Hugo's home. Another chimed in: he, too, had seen it.

"Perhaps she released an airborne agent," Ruiz said smugly. "Or she seeded the ground. She's here to study, to perform tests at different altitudes, or perhaps studying the half-life of her poison."

The light bobbing down the mountainside—that was the first night. The night she'd come to him in his opium stupor.

The villagers asked Ruiz about a cure, an antidote. Would the spy know it? Could she be forced to reveal it?

"No, the CIA is not in the business of plant rehabilitation," Ruiz said. "That's my job." Ruiz seemed to be setting up teams. They were to monitor things. He would return to his lab and work on a solution with the help of the data the men collected.

"I will make this right," Hugo grated out. "I'll pay for the ruined crops. Any expense to save them, I will pay it."

The men couldn't even look at him. It wouldn't be enough: the savinca plants were dying, and centuries of tradition along with them. Some of the men wanted to go to confront Liza—Zelda—but Hugo shook his head. "I will deal with her," he said, grimly. "I will make this right."

They assumed he was talking about money, programs. They assumed wrong.

She wanted Kabakas.

She would have Kabakas.

He turned to Julian. "Now."

Ruiz waylaid them on the way out to the Jeep. "What will you do?" he asked. "She could be dangerous."

"*Yo me encargaré,*" he said. *I'll handle it.*

Ruiz regarded him with an intensity Hugo did not like.

"What will you do?"

"I'll *handle* it."

Hugo and Julian got into the Jeep and sped back up the mountainside in the dark.

His mind raced. Why poison the crop? How had she obtained the poison? Or had she made it? Had she made a report to the CIA on him yet, or was she collecting evidence first? How much time did he and Paolo have until a team descended?

The CIA would turn him over to the vice president, the man who'd put the bounty on his head so many years ago. The Vice President blamed Hugo for the death of his son at the Yacon fields.

They would kill him, of course, but it wasn't death he feared—it was the sound of Paolo suffering. They would force Hugo to listen. They would also hurt the village he'd tried to help. Could that be the motivation behind poisoning the crops?

His heart twisted as he imagined that night with Liza and Paolo in front of the fire. They'd felt like a family.

How thoroughly and deeply she had fooled him!

No more. She was at the door when he arrived. "What is it?" she asked.

"Hopeless." He brushed past her to find the boy, hoping she hadn't recognized the anger roaring through him.

"What did he say?" she called after him.

He pointed at the dining room table. "The food is not yet out." An accurate observation, but none of them would eat tonight.

He found Paolo in his room with his books. Paolo looked up at him, trustingly. He picked Paolo up and held him tight. He needed to find out what kind of reports she'd made. If she'd circulated photos of him. And then he'd kill her. They would survive this; he and Paolo would survive together, just as they always had. "Rodolfo wants you to sleep over," he whispered roughly. Rodolfo was Julian's boy.

Paolo's face brightened. More fake currency.

Hugo stuffed some of Paolo's favorite things into bag and then, impulsively, he clapped his palms onto both sides of the boy's head and kissed him on the forehead.

The boy looked stunned.

"Hurry," Hugo said gruffly. He guided him out through the home and out to the dark drive. He stood there until Julian's taillights disappeared. Then he turned toward the house.

And met her eyes through the kitchen window.

And he knew that she knew.

He burst in and stormed down the tile hall to the kitchen as though he were carried on a boiling tide of rage. He always visualized the kill before he did it, but he could not visualize this one, not even what he would use.

She'd be ready for him, of course. She might even attack him. He hoped that she would. He would tear her apart.

She stood in the middle of the kitchen as he entered, body erect, arms down at her sides, knives in each hand, no doubt, concealed in the folds of the white apron. Maybe something extra in her apron pocket.

He had underestimated her for the last time.

"What's up?" She searched his face. "What did he say?" If she decided there was no danger, she'd likely turn and bustle at the counter, discreetly ridding herself of the knives.

He said nothing; he simply advanced on her as he had the night of the game, only he was coming in for the kill, fully who he was.

It was then that her face changed. It was nearly imperceptible—a minute relaxation—a shift from the bright, blank expression to what she was. Her true face. This was a woman who saw the world as it was. She was beautiful like this.

"Why?" he rasped, blood racing.

To her credit, she didn't make excuses or try to talk her way out of things; she just raised her knives.

She knew all about him.

He was on her like a flash. He trapped and deflected, taking an unexpected knee to his thigh and an expected cut to his forearm in order to get in close enough to control her arms. She slammed a foot into his knee, wobbling him.

He swore and twisted the weapons from her, and then he spun her around, holding her back against his big body. He held her wrists in one hand, pressed to her breastbone. With the other hand he held her wooden-handled kitchen knife to her jugular.

He could feel her heart beating against his, even through her back. He pulled her in more tightly, and even now he wanted her, this woman who'd burrowed so deeply into his home, his heart.

Her breath sounded ragged. "Hugo—"

"CIA. You hoped to cash in on the vice president's bounty, but why poison the fields?" Angrily, he jerked her closer. "You know who I am, but to *poison the fields?*"

"It wasn't me—it's Ruiz."

"Ruiz is here to help."

"He's not—I swear it."

"And I should believe you?" He wanted to, and he hated himself for it.

"Think how we felt out there—we were united in saving the plants. We shared that. You felt it."

"Like we were united in helping Paolo? You know what they'll do to him, do you not?"

She sagged against his chest, given up to him, and if he weren't gripping the knife in his bleeding arm, it might feel like something else. "I'm sorry. So sorry. You have no reason to believe me. I know that."

He appreciated that she didn't try to get out of it. He held her against his thundering heart.

"I don't know why, but Ruiz is faking things," she continued. "You can't trust him. Take the soil to somebody independent—there's still a chance—"

He squeezed her harder. "Stop it."

"I'm not! It's true. I'm ex-CIA, yes. And yes, I've been investigating you, but I didn't poison the fields. You have to believe me. I could help save them..."

"Killing plants was your specialty in the CIA," he said.

"Killing plants was never my specialty." She tried to jerk from his arms but he wouldn't let her go. "I studied crime scenes. It's true, I hunted you for years, yes, but think how it's been this week, working those fields together."

"Ruiz was called, invited."

"And I wasn't? Invited? You invited me."

"You came and now the plants are dying. Ruiz came after."

"I'm telling you the truth."

He wanted to believe her, but he couldn't think clearly

where she was concerned. Because he loved her—he knew it now. The realization was shards of glass in his soul. He had loved her for that short space. Now he had to kill her. "The CIA knows about me?"

"I'm no longer with the CIA."

"Who?"

"The Associates," she said. "I'm with the Associates."

He swore under his breath. The Associates. "What else?"

"That's it. They know I suspect; that's all, but I have a feeling they'll be showing up either way. You have about thirty-six hours before they come and take you. You'll be traded out. Part of a package to quell a situation—"

"Traded to the vice president."

He felt her body soften. Communication enough.

"You've sent back photos, I presume." He hated the sound in his voice, the weakness.

"I haven't," she said. "I swear it."

The truth. He recognized it with his whole being. Everything between them was instinct now.

So the peaceful life he'd built was over. At least with her dead, they might not find him. They would suspect the American farmer, but he'd be long gone with a new identity, and she wouldn't be around to identify him.

He spun her around, holding her wrists, backing her to the wall before she could knee him, immobilizing her with the full force of his weight, pressing her to the wall. Even if she could move, she was good enough to know she could not fight him.

The understanding between them ran thick and primitive. He held the knife to the place where her pulse thrummed in her neck, heart thundering. The least he could do was to look into her eyes as he killed her.

"Don't trust Ruiz," she gasped, eyes shining with unshed tears. "I have nothing to lose right now, okay? That's what I'm telling you. I'm so sorry...for everything."

Something lurched in him as he studied her eyes. That guilt that chased her; she'd be rid of it now. He hadn't been wrong about her—not in the deepest way. Understanding blazed between them like fire. "Your name. Not even Liza."

"Zelda," she said.

He tightened his grip on the knife. Her skin burned against his knuckles. Her breath was warm on his chin. "Choose. The knife or the gun?"

He waited, knowing she'd take the superior intimacy of the knife. He forced himself to visualize it. He would plunge it in quick and deep.

Their breath moved as one.

"I have no choice."

"I know," she said.

She would die like a warrior, this woman. They were the same in many ways.

He gripped the knife, knuckles white, pressing the tip to her neck, to flesh he couldn't imagine breaking. He hated her and he loved her. He kept it there, as if to show it to himself—this is what you do.

"Say it," she said. "Please."

He stilled, unsure what she meant by that.

"Say my name."

"Zelda." He pressed the flat of the blade harder against her throat, depressing the skin but not slicing it.

He could feel her tremble as he lowered it to the bony

plate at the center of her chest, handle gripped in his fist. He could feel her heartbeat through his knuckles, this woman who'd betrayed him and his boy.

He no longer considered her green eyes to be fake. Those green eyes were the eyes of a spy, a hunter. His pulse roared in his ears as he gazed into them, as he repeated her name. "Zelda."

She gasped in a breath, staring up at him, trembling, so alive.

The air thundered all around, or maybe that was the earthquake ripping apart his heart. Anger and love and churned in him, and something seized him, gripped him, and he found himself bringing his lips down onto hers. He hated her and he kissed her. He kissed her with the knife pressed between them—the knife he would use to kill her. He channeled all of his emotion into that one kiss. He kissed her so hard that he tasted blood.

He pulled back, panting. It wasn't right. Nothing was right.

"Don't stop," she said.

"Knife or gun. You have to choose," he said.

The steady look in her eyes—he'd seen that look hundreds of times on hundreds of battlefields. A warrior, ready for death.

"Your hands," she gasped. "At the end."

He watched her, bewildered. And then he understood. She wanted him to choke her—as she came. "No."

"Your hands. At the end." She grabbed the back of his head and pulled him into a kiss.

Desire surged through him. He'd never wanted anybody more. He flattened her against the wall and kissed her, probing at the seam of her lips with his tongue, knife flat between them.

"Say it again," she said.

"Zelda," he grated out. "Zelda."

He would say it forever, because she was no longer Liza. She was a warrior, his equal, and his enemy.

He kissed the side of her neck and pressed his killer's body into her.

"Yes," she said.

And he was lost.

CHAPTER TWENTY-NINE

Knife in hand, Kabakas twined his fingers between hers. He pressed the back of her hands to the wall, knife between their palms. She was a good enough fighter to understand that even now she couldn't take him, even when he let her touch the knife.

Perversely, it made her want him more.

Is he powerful enough to blot out all the pain? Dax had asked.

Kabakas groaned into their kiss, moving against her, fitting the steel of his cock between her legs. He kissed her neck, face warm and whiskery, as tears streamed from her eyes.

He let her go suddenly and lifted her up and set her on the counter. She gasped as he slipped the knife between the buttonholes of her dress, moving upward toward her neck, and then downward, renting her dress in half. He looked into her eyes as he sliced the center of her bra, slicing through every shred of clothing until she was naked to him.

Then he threw aside the knife.

All notions of Dark Kabakas, blood-red flowers, and geopolitics fell away as he ripped off the last shreds of her dress. There was just this man, now, with an expression she'd never seen on a man before—grave and determined and wild.

He held the sides of her head. He did not tell her not to cry. Instead, he kissed her cheeks, her forehead, kissing away the tears.

She reached down to undo his belt buckle. She didn't have to care about anything anymore. Not pirates commandeering a freighter, not condoms. Not Friar Hovde or Agent Randall.

She felt elemental, like the sun or the wind. She felt free.

"Zelda," he whispered as she grabbed his cock. He muscled her hand away and guided himself to her entrance.

Her belly pulled tight as she felt his fingers there, his cock there.

When she felt him begin to fill her, she let her eyes drift shut.

He stopped. "Look at me," he grated, pulling nearly all the way out. "Look at me, *corazón*."

She opened her eyes to meet the crackly root-beer brightness of his. He thrust into her and filled her, blotting out every thought in her mind.

She grabbed onto his hair with one fist, his shoulder with the other, nails piercing his skin. "More," she said.

He shoved into her again and again, breath ragged in her hair. A man completely undone.

Then he picked her up and held her, sliding her up and down on him on his cock, fingers clawing into her ass. None of it was enough; they could rip each other apart and it wouldn't be enough.

She bit his lip, needing to keep them fused; she tasted

his blood. He walked to the wall, carrying her, and slammed her against it.

The swell of pleasure began to overtake her. Not yet, she thought, but they weren't in charge. The earth and the sun and the wind were in charge and the world itself fucked them as he thrust into her relentlessly.

He growled a refusal, tears shining in his eyes, even though she'd said nothing.

"It's what I choose." He would do it. No other man would have the guts, but Kabakas would.

She couldn't die down in that basement with Friar Hovde. She wasn't brave then, but she was brave now.

Still fucking her, he laid her back down on the counter. He pressed thumbs to her neck, as if to test it out, thrusting into her, staring down into her eyes.

This man, he was so beautiful. Her quarry for so long. "Kabakas," she gasped, feeling the rising swell of pleasure.

With a wild, tortured look carved onto his harsh features, he pressed his thumbs into her windpipe, cutting off speech, breath. She tried to suck in a breath but it wouldn't come. She coughed and fought, instinct taking over at last. He tightened his hold on her as he fucked her and choked her, thrusting on and on. The edges of her vision went hazy as she began to come. The orgasm swept through her like fire, filling her head with stars and shattering her mind. She was plummeting, spinning, dissolving into pure pleasure and darkness—perfectly blameless, perfectly free.

CHAPTER THIRTY

When she came to, he was gathering her up in his arms, whispering her name over and over, *Zelda, Zelda, Zelda.* He held her aloft, flush to his chest, and she could feel him trembling.

The world still spun. She was naked. Her throat hurt like hell.

"What—" she grated out.

"I'll say where and when I kill you." He carried her down the hall and into her bedroom, dropping her onto her bed. He threw the khakis and shirt at her—the ones he'd lent her, still dirty from the fields. She washed them by hand every night, but she hadn't gotten a chance to this night. "Put them on," he said hoarsely.

Would he let her live? He couldn't. He was too smart. Too careful. But she didn't want to die—she didn't.

She pulled on the pants and shirt, buttoning up as he watched.

He pulled the kerchief from his pocket and tied it tightly around her mouth. It smelled of him, tasted of him.

"You will not speak to me," he said, even though she hadn't tried. He pointed to a chair. "Sit."

She moved stiffly off the bed and sat.

His hands trembled as he tied her wrists behind her

back. He secured her to the chair in such a way that if she moved to extract herself it would only make things worse. He knew all the tricks, of course. Knew what she might try. He tied her ankles and stood back. She panted, body abuzz from the blackout, from the orgasm that had thundered through her.

Without a word he left her.

He'd let her live...for *now*.

She'd revealed that the Association barely knew anything. She'd been telling the truth, and he had to know that. With her dead, he could outrun them and outwit them. Protect Paolo.

But only with her dead. What was he doing? He had to kill her. He knew it as well as she did.

Curtains covered the window, preventing her from telling time. It was night, maybe ten, maybe midnight. How long had they fucked? But what did it matter?

She wished he would return. She didn't want to be alone. That would be the hell of death, she thought—the utter aloneness. Her heart ached at the thought of never seeing Liza again. Her parents. Dax. She hadn't said goodbye. There was so much she wanted to say to people.

But that was death. You were rarely ready for it.

***

He was there when she awoke, sitting heavily in a chair across the room, gazing out the window, blade on the table next to him. Had he come to kill her in her sleep?

She didn't have to make a sound; he'd know she was awake. Their eyes met and everything was there between them, terrifyingly clear.

The blade. The betrayal.

The fucking.

It had been the most powerful experience of her life, as if he'd broken through her scars and fucked her clear to her core. She'd wanted to give up everything to him—literally everything—and for a moment she'd felt free.

Finally he spoke. "Eventually, they will come for you, won't they?" Whether he killed her or not, he meant.

With a lurch in her chest, she nodded. His life here was over, no matter what happened with the plants. They would come for her. Could Dax have sent somebody already?

"How long?"

It was Thursday night. She shook her head. Dax had said Saturday. Could she trust it?

"A day? Less?"

She shrugged.

He gazed out the window, lost in misery. Losing his home. The plants were dying—and he blamed her. Yes, she'd lied. She had been a CIA botanist. But the idea she'd hurt the plants—it killed her that he could think it.

She mumbled, asking him to remove the gag. She wanted to tell him to check her experiments; it was possible the plants had reacted to one of the compounds she and Paolo had tried. She wanted to help—he needed to see that.

He ignored her.

She grunted again, and he shook his head. She growled and glared in frustration.

His whisper, when it came out, was hoarse. "I felt like a family."

Her heart stuttered. She'd felt it, too. That brief, happy window. She'd felt happy.

"I felt like a family," he said again. "I thought, this is what a family is, being together. Feeling happy." He looked out the window. "I'll tell Paolo that I sent you away. I don't wish him to think that you left of your own accord. Not for you, but for him. He loves you, I think. It will be better."

From behind the gag she mumbled that Paolo loved him, too, but it came out hopelessly garbled. The gag bit into the sides of her mouth with the just-right amount of pressure. He was an overachieving killer in every way.

"I'll play with him more. Try to be lighter. I know to do that now." He paused, and then dropped his voice to a gruff whisper. "But when I see the hope in his eyes...I do not like it. It makes him vulnerable, that hope. Perhaps it is unfair. The boy is not me." He stared at the window. "The small puzzle box in the cabinet, it was a gift from my father. One of the few times my father was kind. It filled me with hope."

Her heart broke as she imagined him as a child, reaching out, full of need and hope, receiving only loathing in return.

He leaned against the wall in front of her. "I didn't kill his mother—she was dead, a young girl, a child soldier, when I came upon him. I was in my full gear, sent to attack a battalion that had been preying upon the countryside. Somebody had been there first. Rival guerrillas. You know how the war was at its height. The chaos. The bodies, the fires. Paolo was sitting by his dead mother's side, no more than five, crying. He had gotten hold of her revolver. It was too heavy for him. I went to him and took it from him. His cries grew louder, frightened by the mask, I thought, until I realized he was looking at something behind me. Soldiers coming, presumably the ones who'd killed his mother and her troop. They were not happy to see it was me, of course."

Kabakas. She nodded.

"Up until then, I had always killed for money. Or an idea. That day I killed for Paolo." He gazed down at his hands, as though they surprised him still. "I was so full of rage. I wanted to kill every last person who had made him cry. I cut them all down, every one of them. When I turned back to him, he was stretching his arms up to me. I had to keep him. I had no choice. I should have brought him to an agency, but..."

She snorted her dissent. He was being an idiot, and if she had the gag off she'd tell him so. Paolo had a good home with Hugo.

"You are suggesting, perhaps, that he is better off with me? You understand what my enemies will do to him, do you not? Can you imagine?"

She had nothing to say. He was right, of course.

"I should have let him go. Especially after my enemies killed my mother." He went to the window and opened the curtains. "My enemies worked it out that I owned that little pink house in the Bumcara suburb. Marked money, perhaps, traced in some way, I don't know. I learned of the danger, but not in time. They set her home on fire." He paused. She knew what was coming. "I could not save her."

One simple, pain-laced sentence. Those were the burns.

He turned to her. "What Paolo has never understood was that it could have been me who killed his mother. It's not as if I avoided child soldiers out there. Nobody could." He looked back out the window. "I kept him all the same. I couldn't let him go."

In movies, villains often revealed their plans to the person they were about to kill. Sometimes they even forced them to watch their triumphant moment. The final explosion, or whatever. A lot of people considered the convention to be ridiculous.

It wasn't ridiculous.

When afforded the chance to be known by another, if only for a short time, most couldn't pass it up. The yearning to be known was quintessentially human, and spies, fugitives, and killers rarely got the chance. The person you were about to kill made the ultimate confessional.

She should want him to stop, but part of her needed him to keep going. Because he was Kabakas. She didn't know which of them needed the fullness of his confession more—him, to be known, or her, to know him. All these years she'd been so full of questions: Where had he come from? Why hadn't he stepped up to lead when he was at the height of his powers? Why had he turned dark? But Kabakas was giving her something more, something deeper: the love and loss inside him. The true things he wrestled with. The things that drove him.

She'd wanted to know Kabakas. Now she would.

"The way he reached up to me," Hugo continued, "it was as if he chose me." He was silent for some time, seeming content to dwell with her. "Hope." He practically spat out the word. Her pulse pounded when his eyes met hers. "How foolish not to note the fact that of all the shiny things in the cabinet, you selected the Moro rites stick to hold and examine. Or how foolish of you. Did you think I wouldn't notice?" He drew near to her, stood over her. "You needed to take it, didn't you? You had to touch it. It belongs to that class of things...the class of things that call out. A hunter feels it."

His eyes crackled that root-beer brown, jewels set deep set against the harsh angles of his face and the midnight darkness of his hair.

"It was as if we were a family," he whispered again. "It wasn't real, I know that now, but it felt real."

She shook her head. It was all she could do.

He searched her face, as though he couldn't believe her cruelty. "Even the devil doesn't give people heaven before sending them to hell."

CHAPTER THIRTY-ONE

The savinca had once calmed him, but when he walked the rows in the early morning dew, he felt only rage, and a pain that reached deeper than the pain of his burns. She'd said she didn't poison them, but how could he believe her? She was a former CIA botanist. The blight had begun with her arrival. She'd been seen creeping around on the mountainside. Of course she'd try to deflect blame to Ruiz.

He should kill her and get Paolo out. The Association was worse than the CIA. Smaller, smarter, and more dangerous because they answered to no one. Run by a billionaire genius and his shadowy partner.

He came to a savinca bush whose leaves had begun to drop. He fell to his knees before it, scrabbling the soil away to expose the white-coated roots. In a rage he grabbed the base and tore it from the ground, throwing it down the mountainside, wild with pain.

She'd done this.

Still, he couldn't get into the mood to kill her. He'd fucked her like an animal, taken her when she was utterly in his power. He wasn't so unlike his biological father after all.

He'd taken her like an animal and enjoyed it. It was how he liked to fuck.

He walked the rows. He'd have to pull Paolo out of the only real home he'd known. They could no longer farm, not as hunted men. He'd been so careful. And even if Ruiz reversed the blight, even if the fields could be rescued, without him here, the village was vulnerable to El Gorrion.

Unless he killed him. Paolo would be safe with Julian for the time being. He could go out killing. He could kill Zelda and then kill El Gorrion. Kill everybody. It was what he did.

As he made his way down the side of the field, he heard a Jeep in the distance. Who would be coming up the mountain so early?

He sprinted around the side of the house and out of the drive just as Julian pulled up. Paolo got out, looking small, so vulnerable.

Hugo held out a hand. "Come here." Paolo went to him and he settled his arms around the boy's fragile shoulders. Julian watched him grimly.

"I need you to stay with Julian another night," he said.

"Is everything under control?" Julian asked, coming up behind him.

"Yes," Hugo said.

Julian nodded, unable to meet his eyes. Hugo couldn't imagine what was in his mind.

"I promised Liza I'd work on our experiment," Paolo said. "I can't miss a day."

Julian looked apologetic behind him. "He insisted. He would've run up himself. I didn't want him to..."

"You were right to bring him." Hugo knelt in front of him. "She does not mind if you take a break from your studies."

"You can't take a break from the experiment. If I don't chart the results correctly, it means we are not listening to the savinca, and we could miss a clue for how to save them."

He exchanged glances with Julian, his heart so filled with rage he could not speak.

"Plants cannot talk," Julian said.

"Liza says they will. She says they can tell us how to save them if we ask the right questions and listen to the answer."

So cruel to give the boy such hope! It was then, finally, that he felt he could kill her. Hugo spoke through gritted teeth. "Liza cannot talk to the plants, and she cannot save them."

"At least she's trying to!" Paolo screamed. "Don't you even want to try?"

He put his hand on the boy's shoulder, but he shook it off. "I promised Liza! Where is she?"

Hugo moved to prevent him from going in the front door. "Busy. You'll go back with Julian."

"I have to fill in my chart!" Paolo took off running, then, around the house, circling down toward the terraces that way.

Julian cast an alarmed look at him.

"I'll get him." Hugo set off in a jog after Paolo; a fast little runner, that kid. He reached the terraced rows and heard something from the direction of the shed. He took off that way. The shed door was open, but Paolo wasn't inside. He finally found him at the far edge of the bushes he tended, off behind the shed. He and Liza had set up colorful strings and tags marked a row of plants, all dying...except for one. The one circled with yellow string looked nearly normal.

Nearly healthy. The only one on all of the mountain-side.

Hugo went to the boy, who was scribbling in a note-book—filling in a chart.

Paolo turned and beamed up at Hugo. "Nines and tens," he said. "This one whispers a clue for how to save them."

"What did you do?"

"She made a solution from the Luquesolama stone." He put aside the notebook and knelt, scrabbling at the dirt, pulling it away from the roots.

Solution. Such a scientific word, but of course, Zelda was a scientist. He should have noticed.

"Look, Hugo!"

Hugo knelt down next to Paolo. The waxy coating around the root had cracked; in places it was gone. You could see the flecks of it in the dirt. The coating, falling off. "I have to tell her—we have to show her."

"How did you get it to crack?" Hugo asked.

Paolo explained what they'd done. The boy pressed the soil back around the base of the plant and touched one of the shoots up top, bending it, seeming to test its strength, and then he felt the leaves. "She says to grade it with your senses and your heart." He pronounced that plant an eight out of ten. He scrutinized the less thriving ones. "Three, four, four. Zero is dead," he said softly, casting his eyes over the pale green rows hugging the contours of the mountain-side. There weren't any zeroes out there. Yet.

She claimed not to have come for the plants; that she might help save them. Was it possible that she meant it?

"You'll go back with Julian," he said.

"But—"

"You must." He took the notebook. "Liza is busy and cannot see you. I will show her your charts."

He ushered a reluctant Paolo back around the outside of the house to the drive and told Julian to hide him if any strangers appeared. Julian made a comment about the masses of boys roving the hills, how they hid themselves just fine. But if it came to it, Julian would go the extra mile to hide him. Hugo had him wait while he went into the house; he grabbed his emergency cash and went back out and pressed it into Julian's hands. "You can return it if you do not use it, but take it for me."

Hugo waited until they'd driven off, just as he had the previous night. Then he brought the small notebook into the house, walking down the tiled hall perhaps a little faster than normal, hating the way his heart swelled when he knew he'd see her.

He slipped inside the bedroom door and tossed the notebook onto the bed, then he took out his knife. There was only a minute change in her expression as she watched him—a turn inward—steeling herself, perhaps.

"Experiments on the field? Have you not done enough?"

She mumbled as he slid his fingers under the gag and pulled it away from her smooth, warm cheek. He slipped the knife under and cut, slicing the fabric as easily as butter.

She licked her lips, rubbing them together. "I heard him out there. Did he show you the test plants? Was there any improvement?"

"Maybe you didn't put enough poison on one of them."

"One is thriving? Which?"

"The yellow string."

She straightened. "What did he grade it?"

"Eight," Hugo said.

"Did you get a look at the root? Is the coating intact?"

"Cracked."

She smiled. "Hugo! This is good, Hugo—it's the Luquesolama stone."

"That's what you would have us believe?"

"You saw it with your own eyes. There's something in that stone that's beneficial to the plant. Protective. That's why the February Moon ceremony evolved. Paolo told me about it, and things like that, they're not just bullshit. I'm wondering if the *Savinca verde* only grows here because of the mineral composition of the soil. Because of that stone. It's a fertilizer, a booster, a protective agent."

"You would maintain Ruiz did this. Why would Ruiz, a leading scientist, do such a thing?

"I'm telling you, Ruiz was out there lying. He suggested the problem might be phosphorous. It's ridiculous. Nobody with any kind of training would think you have a phosphorous problem out there."

"Why would he lie?"

"I don't know," she said. "But why would I do these experiments with Paolo? Why would I lie when I told you everything else? What do I have to lose?"

He sat on the edge of the bed, head resting on fingertips, thinking it through.

Her voice cracked. "We were out there together working on those bushes. We were caring for them together." She wanted him to look at her, but he could not. "Hugo. We cared for those beautiful plants together." She wanted him to remember how it was when they were happy together. He preferred not to.

"Hugo—"

"If you're telling the truth, it means Ruiz is lying. Looking for a scapegoat."

"To deflect blame. That's my guess."

He went to the window. "But, to poison the savinca..."

"Has he ever been associated with El Gorrion?"

Hugo bit his lip. His thinking had run along those lines, too.

"Has he?" she pressed.

"There were rumors..." He paused. "You know about the Roundup-resistant coca."

"Yes," she said.

"They attribute it to the farmers, but it is said Ruiz helped with the project."

"What do you think?"

It was here that the picture began to form. El Gorrion couldn't fight Kabakas, but he could ensure that the mountainside was no longer farmable. He could destroy Buena Vista from the ground up. El Gorrion never liked to feel defeated. "Many people are connected to El Gorrion," Hugo said. "But to destroy the savinca..."

"I'd imagine that El Gorrion can be very persuasive."

Yes, he imagined he could. "So we make the solution? You think that will cure them?"

"I think it *could*, but too much might kill them. And too little would be useless. There's too much I still don't know. What components did Ruiz use, and how much? What was the concentration?"

"You think he sprayed poison?"

She shook her head. "People would've noticed. I think

he dropped pellets. Something fast-acting…"

"So we can try to save them, but we may kill them."

"Fuck that. We need answers, and then to do it right. If you can get me the answers somehow…"

There it was, that passion. Something in his heart squeezed. "You think the answers are on his computer?"

She narrowed her eyes. "An eminent scientist like that? No, he doesn't spell out that sort of thing on his computer. Too risky. The clues would be in his lab. He would have a secret greenhouse somewhere—he wouldn't want colleagues to see him killing plants; they'd ask too many questions. No, he has an off-site workspace, somewhere he can work in peace. He'd need chemical deliveries. Access to a plane."

She went on, fiery and beautiful and seeming to forget she was tied up. It was all about saving the savinca. He closed his eyes. It felt good to hear her like this, and that good feeling was a poison. Nobody had gotten so close to taking him down.

She went on. "The key is the minimal concentration necessary to offset the herbicide. That's the goal. We might not save the shoots—this crop is gone, but there's still time to save the woody bases, the old part of the plant. They've lasted all those years—they're tough and beautiful, those old bases. I could give you a list of questions. A list of things to look for. If you could find the lab."

He couldn't trust her—he knew that now.

But he could trust her passion for the plants.

He flicked open his knife and walked around her chair. He grabbed her hair, looking into her eyes, filled with such a strange mix of feelings—anger that he was doing this, that he had no choice but to trust her. And beneath it all, excitement. They would take a trip together. "I'll find the lab." He sliced the cord that bound her wrists, heart slamming in his throat. "You find the cure."

She brought her hands together and rubbed her wrists, watching him warily.

"And if you try to run," he continued, "I'll kill you. Understand?"

He'd keep her alive—long enough, at least, to find a cure for the blight. She went to the dresser and pulled out underwear. "How will you find the lab?"

He told her how Ruiz had been emailing the farmers with instructions for monitoring the soil. Forwarding things. He felt that his man in Bogotá could get a location from the IP address—he'd done as much before. He might even be able to determine who paid the bill. "But I have my suspicions. Jungle labs, planes, deliveries. This is El Gorrion's compound you're describing."

He leaned in the doorway with the knife, running his thumbnail over the joinery, the small circle of the hinge that allowed it to snap up. She turned away from him and peeled off her clothes, shy about undressing in front of him without the heat of passion to cover her.

Still he wanted her. He did not want to kill her. But how could he trust her?

"Be quick."

She pulled a maid's dress from the closet and put it on.

"We'll have to cover your hair. Or change it."

"It's not my real hair anyway."

"I know," he said. "And you wore glasses."

"I prefer them," she said.

As did he. "One move out of order, and I'll kill you."

"I got it. I'm with you on this. Okay? I give you my word, Hugo." She spoke with intensity and seemed to want him to believe her. Keeping her word meant something to her. She went into the bathroom, and he followed. She hesitated in front of the toilet. "Really?"

"Hurry up."

He turned and leaned back against the sink, eyes fixed on his blade as she peed. They felt again like a family. It was a feeling he enjoyed.

CHAPTER THIRTY-TWO

It wasn't hard for Rio to get the story in the village. He paid for it, yes, but people would've talked for free; they were outraged at the CIA spy who'd come to poison their crops. A female agent; clearly Zelda. Living in the house up the mountain.

On the way up to the house, Rio passed men inspecting the engine of a broken-down car—a stakeout if he'd ever seen one. The road up was being monitored. Interesting.

He kept going—Zelda could be in danger.

He parked and approached quietly, entering through the back, moving through the dark spaces like a ghost, weapon at the ready, itching for a pop of movement of the wrong kind. He was very much in the mood.

Nothing.

He found food left half prepared in the kitchen. He inspected an onion slice. Old. There were plates and pans on the floor, as though there'd been a struggle.

A rustling from the bedroom.

He slipped across and into the open door of the bedroom, his 500 down at his thigh. Curtains blew in the wind; that was the sound he'd heard. There was a chair, cut ropes on the floor. She'd been tied up, then released. Vehicle gone.

Dax wasn't going to like this.

Further inspection turned up a chest at the back of the pantry, recently pulled down.

He opened it to find knives, guns, blades, boxes of shells, and a few decent rifles. A number of weapons had been removed, no doubt. Had Kabakas piled her into his vehicle and left, meaning to kill her elsewhere? Why not kill her out back, where he had complete and utter privacy? Why not send her over the cliff? And where had they gone?

He made his way back down the mountain, pulling off the road a ways up from the stakeout. He went to the stakeout on foot, sweating in his suit jacket, which made him extra unhappy. The men were smoking and leaning on the car, having abandoned their pretense of inspecting the engine. He came up behind them, silent as the night.

They pulled weapons, but they did it too late. Everybody was always too late. He put a knee through the first man's face. The next man was trouble and they fought hard, taking some pain before he was able to break the man's elbow; he did this with a loud *crack*, at which point they all agreed he could tie them up, and that was the end of it.

"You took so long to react," he told them in Spanish. He

nodded at the one with the broken elbow. "You could've rolled and taken cover there, and I'd be dead."

Of course this wasn't the kind of fighting they were trained for and yes, they were watching the road, but still. He nodded at the youngest. "You got a good shot off. A few inches lower..." He shrugged.

The man with the broken elbow sucked in steady breaths, controlling the pain.

Rio questioned the three of them.

He learned they'd been sent by El Gorrion to watch the *gringa*, the maid. They believed she had become a target of Kabakas.

The American farmer had driven off with the maid, trying to protect her from Kabakas, they said. Some of El Gorrion's men were following them; these three were to stay.

They seemed...inordinately frightened of him, as if they expected him to sprout demon horns.

CHAPTER THIRTY-THREE

He made her drive.

She understood. With her driving, he could keep his attention free, keep his weapon handy. She'd do the same if their positions were reversed.

She was even more his captive now. But it was a relief to be fully herself. She wondered if it was a relief for him, too, to be fully himself.

Even the way they'd fucked was different—more real, more powerful, once their masks were off.

They'd be who they were for each other, if only for the space of this trip. She didn't know what would happen after—she'd destroyed his trust in her. If only she could win it back.

An hour in, they reached the populated valley area, sprawling lushly in the shadow of the this far corner of the Andes, road dotted with cinder block buildings, some painted in bright pastels, many with beautiful ironwork grates over windows and passageways. He directed her to stop at a roadside market and gave her money just before they exited the Jeep.

"Clothes," he said. He had her choose a new outfit. She went for an olive green shirt and jeans. Practical. They bought tamales and waters, too. She paid as he stood by, looking for all the world like the sullen boyfriend—not her jailer and would-be executioner with a gun in his pocket aimed at her heart.

"I'm not going to run," she said when they were back outside. "I'm on board for this mission."

"I think you might try," he said. "You would not survive it, but you might try it."

He was so fierce with her, so angry with her.

The rains had made the road muddy and nearly impassible; the Jeep bogged down over and over.

They got stuck so deeply that Hugo had to get out and push. He didn't say anything, just pulled his black gloves from the duffel bag and went back to push. "Pulse it."

She applied the gas, on and off, on and off. Like snowstorm driving.

The gloves.

He'd brought the gloves. But of course, they were the Kabakas gloves.

The Jeep was out on the fifth go. She stopped it, waited for him to get in.

"Did you hear the sound it made?" he asked, not commenting on her having stayed for him instead of speeding off and leaving him in the muck. How much more would it take to prove herself?

"The sound isn't good," she said thoughtfully.

"Just for amusement's sake, how exactly did you imagine you'd bring me in?"

"I don't know. I could've sedated you," she said.

"With what? You had nothing."

"I'm a botanist," she said. "You had a CIA botanist as your cook."

"Yet you didn't move on me."

"No."

"Why?"

"I wasn't sure it was you."

"How could you not be sure?" he asked. "You were there on the airfield."

"I thought you were dead. Everybody did."

"You thought somebody else could throw like that?" He sounded almost insulted.

"With a decade of practice? Maybe."

He snorted.

"And you were using the cheap swords. And you had Paolo there."

"But afterward—" He fixed her with his gaze. "After the cabinet."

She turned to him. "What happened out on the Yacon fields? Leading up to that, you made sense—the people you worked for, the people you attacked. Not that I'm saying you were a good guy before, but..."

"You have a critique of my performance before Yacon?"

She glanced at the rearview mirror and changed lanes. "That truck has been back there a while."

"I know. Never quite catching up."

"A tail?" she asked. Were they being followed?

He grunted. Nothing to do but go forward at this point.

"You had so much goodwill," she said. "And then the Yacon fields. What happened?"

"You don't have a theory?" His bitter tone hit her in the

gut.

"Tell me."

"Perhaps I woke up one day and decided to be evil."

She waited, desperate for him to say it hadn't been him, in spite of the evidence. Stupid to feel disappointed. "Why?"

"Do I need a reason?" he asked.

"Yes. You'd need a reason."

He said nothing. She looked over at him, found him studying her face. "I used to wonder if it could be an impostor," she said, "but Dark Kabakas was so skilled. You spent a lifetime building those skills; they were just too specific for somebody to develop so fast. The eyewitness was so credible."

"Do you know where he is now?" Hugo asked.

She thought back. "He went to live with relatives in Bumcara after we questioned him."

He was silent for a long time. His words, when they came, sounded strange. "He never made it."

"What do you mean?"

"You weren't the only one looking to question him."

She turned to him. "You were after the survivor?"

"He died soon after. His relatives became quite well off, however. A mysterious windfall."

Something turned upside down in her chest. She knew. She'd always known. "It wasn't you."

His gaze was dark and steady. "No, *corazón*."

"He was paid off. It wasn't you." Hope bubbled in her chest, along with despair; how could she have disbelieved him? "I'm sorry."

He shrugged. "It was convincing. The staging. But if

you'd studied the wounds—"

"The scene was compromised too quickly for any real investigation. So many of the bodies taken away."

"I know," he said.

"An impostor," she said. "I should've known."

His shrug didn't cover his pain. It pained him that she'd thought it after spending that time together. "The scene was convincing."

"I should've known."

He said nothing. She felt like she'd betrayed him a second time.

***

Ten miles farther, they hit another mud patch and this one grabbed the tire and didn't let go, and Hugo and his gloves couldn't push it out no matter how he tried. It didn't help that there was another vehicle in the mud close ahead, so that they had to angle it while pushing. No matter. It was going nowhere. He came around to the side, pulling off his gloves, squinting at the terrain behind them. "And where is the truck now?"

It was a good question. Not many places to turn off.

"Change into your new clothes," he said.

"We're walking?"

"Until we find something better." He shifted the pockets he held his weapons in and took the duffel bag over his shoulder. She grabbed the small pack and slung it over her shoulders. He handed her a cap. "Your hair. Too memorable."

She nodded.

"This is your prostitute look?"

She put her hand to her hair. "My sister's."

"Right. Your twin."

Her heart sank. "They know about her, too?"

"Ruiz had a photo of the two of you as children."

She sighed. If word got back to Brujos and Mikos, Liza was in trouble all over again. She hoped Liza would be careful and stay off the grid like she'd promised.

They walked fast; the sun was setting. It wouldn't do to be on such a rural stretch of road at night.

"I would think a photo of your sister is the least of your problems."

"I didn't want her known. This whole thing, me masquerading as her, it was to get her out of trouble."

His voice was so low that it was a whisper. "It is you who are in trouble, *señorita*."

"I'm more ready for it," she said, wondering again what he planned for her afterward. But she'd meant what she said—she was with him for the space of this operation. She would not go down a liar. She didn't want to go down at all, but certainly not as a liar.

She could feel his gaze on her. "The card game was real, then. The story you told."

She nodded.

"You were willing to go in your sister's place. Take what she had coming."

"She's my twin sister, Hugo. I love her, and I wasn't there for her enough. She's not a bad person, but she got into bad shit."

"The track marks."

"Fake. On me, anyway. She's not really a prostitute. Well, at her level, it's ambiguous...it's a flow of drugs and sex, and if one stops, the other does, so...yes, a prostitute.

But she couldn't have handled Brujos. It would've been the death of her."

He turned to her. "So you took her place. "

"Yes."

"To rescue her."

"And get inside the Brujos cartel."

He looked away, nodded.

It was stupid, but she needed him to believe her, to see that she had some nobility in her. But then, like an old familiar song starting up, she pictured Agent Randall's dead eyes, and the suffocating guilt filled her chest. There was no being noble for her anymore. She'd caved. Caused his death. It could never be undone.

They came to a crossroads at dusk and took the high road. Eventually, a bus came into sight.

He gripped her arm and let her see the gun in his belt. "We'll take that bus. I'll kill you if you run. You understand that."

"I think you made that clear."

"Don't think a busload of witnesses would stop me."

She shook away. "I said I'd stay with you to get the cure. I gave you my word."

He watched her eyes. She felt so far away from him now. And then the bus was there. The driver agreed to take them even though the bus was full. Zelda wasn't sure whether it was the bribe he responded to or the threatening air that Hugo seemed to put on so easily, but they got on and sat in the aisle. It was horribly cramped. Zelda wanted to get off at the first small town, but Hugo insisted they stay on through to the next city. "It's closer to our destination," he said. "And there will be vehicles there—a far better selection."

She hunkered down, utterly exhausted. She'd hardly slept that night in the chair. Had he? His eyes always had that weary look, that slight fold under his inky lashes. She let her eyes drift closed.

Sometime later—a minute, an hour, she didn't know—she was jostled awake by a bump. She lifted her head from his shoulder and smiled drowsily at him, feeling happy to be near him, and then she remembered that they were enemies and she rubbed her eyes, like she was maybe just squinting. Had he guided her head to his shoulder? Kept her from rolling down onto the dirty floor as she slept?

"Almost there," he said softly.

She nodded. Huddled together on the dirty floor in the middle of the crowded bus, she had the crazy feeling that they were in their own world.

She felt as if she'd come back from a cliff. It wasn't that he'd almost killed her—she'd been almost killed a lot of times. It was that she'd given in to death.

It scared her that she'd done it.

The bus bumped along, killing her butt bones as she replayed the night. The feel of the blade to her throat. Like she was already over the cliff. And then he'd crushed his lips onto hers, in defiance of the knife, in defiance of who she was, who he was, a kiss full of gravitational force.

And God, the way he'd dug his fingers into her ass as he held her against him, moved her against him, kissing her, fucking her. Kabakas.

She'd fucked Kabakas.

Heat speared through her as she remembered him inside her. The way he'd felt. And the way he slammed her against the wall.

The strength and emotion of him, like a mountain breaking open. *I'll say when and how I kill you.*

She didn't want to die.

She stood and peered out the windows, holding onto a seatback occupied by three sleepy young men. Students, from the look of them. Dawn, but still dark. A glow up ahead. She stayed standing, shaking out her legs, going up and down on her tippy-toes. As they drew nearer, she could see the lights were strung at the end of a corrugated metal overhang swarming with moths. Small clusters of empty chairs were arranged around plastic tables. The foliage had changed, too. More palms and breadfruit trees. Thicker underbrush. Valencia bordered the Amazon basin on this end. She settled back down.

"Juachez is near," he whispered.

She nodded. Approaching the center of El Gorrion territory, then.

"We'll eat," he said. "We'll sleep."

Again she nodded.

***

They stepped off the bus in the midst of an open-air shopping market near the edge of Juachez.

They paused, forming an island of two as people streamed around them. Hugo adjusted the collar of her shirt; it would look like a fawning motion to anybody else, but he was watching the people, the street, and so was she. She smiled and moved a bit to give them new views. They were already working naturally together, both warriors of a sort.

He dropped his dark gaze to hers, letting a finger slide

along her jaw, trailing shivers. "So easy to forget the beautiful cat is lethal."

"What? I'm helping you. We're working together." But of course, her skills were threats, too.

He hoisted the pack over his shoulder. "Come on." He slung an arm around her shoulders and they set off like lovers exploring a city.

They stopped at a café full of foreigners and headed as one to the just-right table, seating themselves at a dark bench along the wall. They didn't even need to discuss it; when you were hunter and hunted, you saw the sight lines and the exit options.

There were times, being with Hugo in this, that she felt her old confidence.

It felt amazing.

They sat and ordered. Beans, rice, eggs, and vegetables with hot *aji* sauce. The food was plain and good.

He played with her hair as she finished her rice. "We need to dye this. There's a *farmacia* up there. I want you with brown hair."

Her heart beat fast. She told herself he hadn't meant it sexually. "Okay."

He slid his rough fingers to her chin.

"What are you doing?"

"Playing the dutiful boyfriend." He picked up a last morsel of tomato from her plate. "We wouldn't want people to think I'm a dark killer with his prisoner. Open," he whispered.

"You're not a dark killer."

"Open."

"I can feed myself."

"Open, somebody's watching."

"I don't believe you." But still she parted her lips.

He slipped it in, pinning her with his eyes, letting his fingers stay inside her mouth, invading her.

Unruly heat surged through her. She closed her lips over his fingers and sucked in his fingers, running her tongue around them.

His only movement was a quick intake of breath.

She was the one invading him, now. The trust and love and danger built thick between them; they were killer and prisoner, hammer and anvil, alive against each other. It was a dangerous game that they could play forever.

"Zelda," he growled, yanking out his fingers and forcing his attention back onto the crowd. She turned to get a better view, curling her feet under on the bench. He pulled her legs over his lap. He was such a natural partner. He pulled off a shoe and began to massage her foot. She tried to pull away, but he kept her.

"Stop," she said.

"What?"

"It doesn't feel good. Just don't." She grabbed her shoe but he wouldn't let go of her foot. He looked down at it now, running fingers over the angry scars between her toes, the mottled skin where the tips had been cut off. She closed her eyes, flooded with shame.

"What happened?" he asked hoarsely. "Who did this?"

"It was a long time ago."

"Say more." Hugo always wanted more. Always more.

"He's dead."

"You killed him?"

"No. He died, that's all."

"Say more."

She sighed and inspected the side of her shoe, knowing he wouldn't stop pressing. "It happened while I was in the agency. Things don't always go right."

He traced his finger to the last cut, the puncture between the Achilles tendon and the anklebone. He examined it, reading it. "It is good they did not continue with this trajectory. It would've hobbled you."

"Enough." She pulled away her foot. "It's over. Who was watching?"

He looked thoughtful. She prayed he wouldn't press. "It was just a prickle," he said finally.

She narrowed her eyes, playfully, as though he hadn't touched her secret shame. "I'm not prickling." She set her chin on his shoulder, surreptitiously scanning the crowd. "At all."

A trio of impoverished-looking Aussies sat next to them. They ordered a meal to share and gobbled it hungrily.

Hugo asked them for lodging recommendations on the way out.

At a *farmacia* down the way they stopped for bottles of water, new clothes, and brown hair dye. It would have about nine hundred different toxins, but it made sense. There was a display of reading magnifiers with sturdy plastic frames.

"Men's glasses," Hugo said.

"If I can get the right magnification I could ditch the contacts." She put them on and smiled.

"Sturdy," he said. "Good."

When they got out onto the street that she, too, felt the

prickle of being watched.

Zelda didn't believe in intuition. The prickle of being followed had nothing to do with a sixth sense, and everything to do with a wrong pattern of movement, something so subtle that the subconscious picked it up and set off the alarm without the details ever rising to the level of the conscious. Something out the corner of the eye.

She looked up at him. Caught his eye and looked away. They agreed. Followed.

"It doesn't make sense," she said.

"Unless you alerted your people."

Her stomach sank; she felt guilty even though she hadn't alerted anybody. When had guilt become an automatic reflex? "I didn't alert anybody." Shit. Dax wouldn't spook and send somebody to follow her, would he? Override her so completely? Treat her like the enemy?

"Best to split up," she said.

"So you can run?"

She raised an eyebrow. If somebody good was following them, splitting up was the best way to lose them. They walked on the shady side of the street to avoid the merciless sun.

"I haven't *alerted my people.*"

"So you say."

"I gave you my word. I won't let you down."

He took her hand and gripped it. "It's one of yours, it has to be."

"I haven't alerted my people."

He pulled out a gun and let it hang down by his side and sped up, nearly dragging her now. "Keep up."

She practically ran beside him. Maybe she deserved it.

Maybe Hugo understood the state of her feet all too well—
that she'd been tortured and that she'd done what it took to
make the pain stop. Those feet—like a scarlet letter.

His movements changed. He pulled her into a crowd
and *he* seemed to change, to melt. He was good—as good as
she'd ever been. He pulled her into a store, but instead of
going through it—that was the technique she expected, he
grabbed a hat and bounced right out with a threesome,
holding her so high and tight, he was practically carrying
her, allowing then to move as one.

It was nearly mystical, the way he moved. She thought
of the way he'd been in the battle, hearing, seeing, moving
in that fluid way. But it crushed her. He'd taken over; they
were no longer partners. When they turned a corner, he
broke off and pulled her up some steps and into a shadowy
doorway. It was then that he finally put her down.

"Fuck you." She hit him, hard, punched him. He caught
her hands. "I can pull my weight. You could've trusted me."

"Could I?"

The throng streamed past, rushing on their errands, but
all she could feel was her grief and guilt and frustration.

"Let me be a partner," she said. "Hear me. We're united
to get this formula."

He stared grimly out at the street.

"Goddammit!" She needed him to trust her—
desperately. It was stupid, but she needed it. And then,
much to her horror, she began to cry.

He looked at her wildly. "What are you doing?"

She hit him. "Fuck you. You could've trusted me. I'm
with you."

Again he looked at her, differently this time.

"Just watch the goddamn street," she said, hating that he'd seen her tears.

He pulled her to him, looking out over her head at the street. "Stop it," he said.

She sniffled.

"It's okay."

"It's not okay." She wanted desperately for him to trust her. To trust herself. To like herself.

He held her tight, holding her in the circle of his warmth, his musky scent. Was somebody really out there? It didn't make sense, but it didn't have to. They both knew that.

Her heart beat slow and steady. He would be able to regulate even that; the best agents could. It was then that she felt his cock, steel hard. Some things a man couldn't regulate.

His eyes changed; he was flustered. The great Kabakas. She watched herself calculate this new variable. His new vulnerability. Fuck it, she was Zelda Pierce. She ran agents.

She shifted, let him feel her differently. His breath hitched.

A second later she had his gun shoved in his ribs.

"Don't move," she whispered. "You're fast and good, but not this fast."

She couldn't believe she'd actually gotten the upper hand on him. *Kabakas.*

She looked into his eyes. So many bad decisions to make now. "I'm telling you it's not one of my people. I'm telling you to trust me."

His eyes sparked. Again she had that feeling of him as a bear on a silken leash. She had him. If it were her people out there, there would be no better time to pull him in.

"And indeed I'm not that fast," he said, breath warm on her neck. "But I *would* take you along."

"I know."

She thought about what Dax had said about her guilt, her wish to be obliterated.

She felt his contours; not just those of his cock, but also the contours of his strength, his danger, his desire, his unpredictability. He was the superior fighter even now; only a stupid agent wouldn't stay keenly aware of that. The gun merely brought things to fifty-fifty.

And she wanted him even now. Because below it all was their dance, strange and wild. Always escalating in its way.

"Right here," he said. His tone was different. He wasn't talking about death anymore. "Or perhaps we could fuck again. Turnabout is fair play—isn't that what they say?" He lowered his voice to a whisper. "I could take you right now. Against the wall. I'd put you in that corner and press you there. I'd push down your pants and hold you there perfectly still, *señorita*. You could hold the gun and I would move into you so completely that the street would disappear."

He shifted closer. But he didn't go for the gun. He knew not to do that.

"I would take you so completely that even the moon would disappear. You would feel only the brick behind you. And me filling you."

Heat built between her legs. It was turning her on.

It was turning him on.

"Everything would disappear but us," he whispered, whiskers warm against her face.

Everything would disappear. It sounded a little bit like a prayer. For everything to disappear. He wanted the world to disappear.

She wanted it, too.

"Is this how it felt in the kitchen?" He bent down to kiss her, nipping her lip. "To have death and fucking twined together?" He kissed her again. "Is this how it felt?"

"Yes," she whispered.

He kissed down her neck.

Was this a trick? She should never forget she was walking a bear. She shoved the gun harder into his ribs, emphasizing its proximity to his heart. "Here's what's going to happen—you're going to meet me at the hotel."

"I would prefer to have you against this wall," he whispered, "here in the darkness. When you sucked my fingers, I wanted to take you right there in the café. Now, Zelda."

Her name again. He knew what it did to her, for him to say it.

He trailed his lips up the side of her neck. "Do you want me to wear the mask? It's in my pack."

Oh, God, he'd guessed about her Kabakas thing.

He settled a hand onto her hip. It was Kabakas seducing her now. She pulled away. "Don't." She needed him to take her seriously.

He kissed her neck again, lips sucking in the tender skin at her jugular.

"When you're in trouble," she whispered, "any shift is good, isn't it?"

"Not the mask, then?"

She pushed her other hand into his pocket, feeling around. "The mask isn't my thing. The gloves, however..." She regretted it instantly. He'd hear the truth in it.

She pulled out a few bills without looking at them. "We'll split up. We'll meet at the hotel the Aussies recommended. Whoever gets there first checks in under the name Martinez. We'll stay until dark."

A smile played on his lips. "Is that enough money? Perhaps you should count it."

"I'm out of practice, not stupid." She knew how much he had. She saw everything, just as he did.

He smiled wearily.

"I'm going to walk away. You're going to trust me to meet you."

The *or else* was implied. Or else she would shoot. She would draw attention. He had much more to lose out here.

"We will come back together because we're both interested in saving those plants."

"And you contact your people?"

"I give you my word that I won't. I can't make you trust me, Hugo. But I give you my word." She cast a glance over her shoulder as a knot of people approached. "I'll melt in and melt out." She wanted her word to be enough. Desperately. She had the idea that if she could get him to trust her, it would change things somehow.

He had no choice but to let her go.

She pushed away, pocketed the weapon, and headed down the steps, toward the people, melting in, matching up. He was back there somewhere, tracing a parallel path, or maybe the same one, if he felt compelled to watch her. She backtracked and turned, walking all around until she was sure nobody could be following her, and finally arrived at the modern-looking two-story hotel, barely a step up from a youth hostel.

The lobby was bright and barren with a colorful straw mat stretched out across the floor in front of the counter. There was a rudimentary coffee counter and some tables and chairs. She got a private room under the name Martinez, second floor, corner with access to adjoining rooftops. "One other person will be joining me," she said.

"*Quiere dejar una nota?*" The clerk asked.

Yes, a note would be good. She took the offered pen and paper and paused. There was so much she wanted to write. *I came. Trust me. You can fucking trust me. I'm not a horrible person.* In the end she folded the blank paper and slipped it in an envelope.

She'd showed up, that was all the communication she'd need. Even then it wasn't enough. Nothing was ever enough, though. It made her feel so tired.

She went up.

It was a hundred degrees hotter on the second floor, but the room was bright and clean with traditional style artwork and a hand-woven bedspread. She checked it over and then she took out the itchy contacts, put on the glasses, and set to reading the directions for the hair color.

CHAPTER THIRTY-FOUR

El Gorrion examined the text on his phone and frowned. The ex-agent, Zelda, had arrived in Juachez with the American farmer. They had behaved amorously in a café and then they had split up, knowing, perhaps, that they were being followed.

On the run together.

She had seduced the farmer. He was protecting her; that much seemed clear.

The other pieces of the puzzle were far stranger.

A fighter in a business suit had arrived in Buena Vista hours after Hugo and Zelda had left. The fighter queried the villagers and then raced up the mountainside to ransack the American's house. On his way back he'd attacked and completely disabled three of El Gorrion's best men—seasoned fighters. The man in the suit was highly trained, that much was clear, but it was something more than his training that had spooked them.

Could it be Kabakas? He didn't wear the mask or carry

the barong swords, but who else could take down three of his best fighters? He spoke fluent Spanish—a Venezuelan, one thought at first. The other said he spoke with a Mexican accent.

The man wore a red silk shirt and shiny black shoes and he was frightened of nothing. Neatly coiffed; urbane, even. It wasn't how El Gorrion remembered Kabakas. He hadn't seen his face, but the impression he had of the man was rough and hulking.

Once he had the men tied, he'd made a phone call in their presence. The conversation was in English. Even more interesting, he'd used Zelda's name twice. A colleague of some sort, or maybe a rival. Not Kabakas.

But Kabakas was in play, and El Gorrion would find him and end him. And this time he would be ready—he was pulling all of his men in, all of his weaponry—grenades, bazookas, all of the heavy stuff.

He would not be made a fool of again. And his men would not run; he'd see that they couldn't. He demanded honor; from himself and from his men, too.

The woman Zelda had gone to a hotel. His men had lost them in the crowds, but El Gorrion had a network of eyes across the town. Even the hotel clerk was his. Zelda had left a note—blank. A signal of some sort.

His source inside the CIA had told him she had been diligent about hunting Kabakas, driven, a serious hunter. Yes, she was the key, somehow. She knew who Kabakas was, and where he was. Or maybe Kabakas knew who she was. El Gorrion didn't understand the pieces, but he knew they were connected.

He texted back: *Stay on them.*

CHAPTER THIRTY-FIVE

She was still sitting on the bed, reading the instructions to the hair color, when he arrived. Heat built in her core the moment she heard the key in the lock. She moved the weapon closer, just in case she was wrong, in case it wasn't him. She still didn't trust herself. It was like missing an arm, missing that trust.

He walked in. "You're here."

"Of course I am." He threw the duffel bag on the bed next to her, and a chunk of his inky hair shifted to cover his eyes. He looked sleepy, dangerous, a wild animal woken from hibernation. He put out his hand and she returned his weapon. He checked the windows and the view to the street and then he headed into the bathroom. A creak. He wanted to know that the windows would open, that they could leave fast. She'd gone through the exact same ritual.

You're here.

One of their top agents, Macmillan, would be able to make a recording of that voice and show it visually as lines on a computer screen. She imagined the words as hard slashes with a strong, deep base full of unheard complexity—hate and lust and need. Or maybe that was just her.

She headed for the bathroom as soon as he came out. "You can sleep while I do my hair. This is going to take awhile." She pulled the door shut, locked it, and leaned against it. Had he been following her? God, what was wrong with her that she hadn't run? She could have killed him in that shadowy doorway and run off. He'd made it pretty clear he was only keeping her alive as long as he needed her to save the savincas. Didn't she deserve more than that? Was showing him she was worthy so much more important than staying alive?

What the hell was wrong with her?

But she would never kill Hugo; that wasn't in her. And then there were the flowers; they alone could save them. Hugo had the muscle, and she had the science. The *Savinca verde* meant something in this rabbit hole of hers. So did Paolo.

Doing right meant something to her. Justice meant something to her. Nobody could take that away from her.

She stripped down to her bra and panties—no sense in getting her clothes full of dye—and started up with the messy business of combining the little bottles of fluid. She put on the plastic gloves that came with the kit and drew the thick, dark solution through her hair, beginning on the side.

And thought about her priorities. Like survival.

When her hair was full of dye, she leaned out the open window and studied the raucous street below.

Deep inside El Gorrion territory. Not ideal.

Most of the buildings were two- or three-story concrete block structures, shops on the bottom and living quarters above, everything painted in a riot of colors. The Valencians were avid artists, incredible muralists.

Small groups of people congregated at street-level entrances. She traced the scent of fried sausages to a busy stall on the corner. The stall next to that one seemed to be selling fried green plantains.

She memorized every detail as she waited the recommended twenty minutes for the dye to take...and tried not to think of Hugo on the other side of the door. Or what would happen once this mission was done.

Or even once she left the bathroom.

When the twenty minutes were up, she moved to the sink to rinse the dye. A knock at the door. Three raps.

"It'll be a while," she said.

The lock clicked. The door opened.

"Hey!" She spun around to face Hugo. He slammed the door shut behind him, gaze roaming wantonly over her mostly naked body.

Her belly felt melty. "You can't be in here."

He said nothing, chest rising and falling under the dark gray T-shirt.

She motioned to the goopy helmet of dye covering her hair. "I'm not done with this process."

"Zelda," he grated, rattling off some dark and wildly dirty Spanish. Then he yanked her to him and kissed her, whiskers rough on her skin.

"Hugo!" she said, pushing him away, leaving brown smudges on his shirt. "We can't—"

"We have to," he panted.

"Look at me! I'm full of dye. You have to let me rinse it off."

He stood there like a predator. It created a kind of vulnerability that she probably shouldn't like. "You'll do it after."

"That's not how it works," she said.

He reached out a finger and touched her bare belly. Slowly he trailed that lone finger up to the bottom of her bra, taking her mind firmly offline with just one swipe. Then he hooked it under and pulled her to him. "I will rinse it, then." He kissed her neck. "I will handle it from here."

She pushed him away, trembling with arousal. Usually, having goop in her hair would be the most unsexy thing she could imagine, but the way he looked at her told her he didn't agree. "I don't need help."

"Then explain to me beauty salons, *corazón*." He jerked his chin. "In the sink? That's how you rinse it?"

"Hugo!"

He glided his finger down her bare belly, causing her insides to undulate. "You have no choice in the matter, Zelda," he said. "You are my prisoner in this. I take care of what's mine. Turn around."

Her heart beat in her throat. "Seriously?"

"Must I turn you myself? Must I tie you? Are we back to that?"

She studied his hooded eyes. Was he serious?

His tone was strangled. "Face the sink. I have this under control."

She pulled off the gloves and turned to face the sink, the mirror. His head loomed above hers in the mirror, gaze dark, hair unruly. He reached around her to turn on the water, adjusting it to his satisfaction. "Bend over."

She complied, putting her head under the stream. He

stood over her, massaging the water through her hair, bringing incredible precision to the chore. This was the precision he brought to throwing blades. An artist. A killer.

He made her tip her head and stroked a bit over her ear. His fingers were magic, movements strong and deliberate. He was making the process his as he made everything his. As he'd made her his that first night with those slow, languorous motions. Destroyed by pain and opium, and still he'd made her his.

He gathered her hair on top of her head and leaned over to kiss the back of her neck. "I have this..." he kissed her again "...under control." He kissed her again, pressing into her. She could feel the hard log of his cock at her ass, nearly bursting through his jeans.

He didn't seem under control. He seemed out of control, and God, she loved it.

"I have needed to be inside you all day," he said, breath ragged, massaging the dye out of her hair.

"Hugo—"

"Quiet, or I will gag you again. All day I have imagined taking you, making you come over and over and over." Her blood raced as he pushed her head to the other side, working symmetrically. "When you sucked in my fingers, I imagined them inside you."

He turned off the water and pulled her up by her hair.

She opened her eyes to see him behind her in the mirror, holding her wet hair, focused down on her with a level of intensity that felt frighteningly primal.

"And I imagined that I would make you come screaming. After that I would take you." His words came out in gusts. "I can wait no longer." The furrow between his eyes looked deeper, his cheekbones more sharp-cut, more ruth-less somehow. Her killer, her lover.

"Okay," she said stupidly.

He tightened his grip on her hair; she could feel his in-tensity clear through his fingers. His voice lowered, control clearly fraying. "Hold on to the sink. You must hold on." He didn't wait for her to comply; he fit her hands to the sides of the sink himself. The way he thought he had to stabilize her for what he was about to do—even that turned her on.

With trembling fingers he undid he bra. Or maybe that was her trembling. The whole room trembled. She had to remove her hands from the sink to allow him to pull the bra free of her arms. He planted them back on the sink like she was an unruly child who hadn't behaved. "You must not let go."

She gripped the cool porcelain, blood racing, as he pushed off her panties. He reached one hand around her hip, pressing his fingers between her legs, and with the other hand he took hold of a nipple, twisting it roughly.

"Tell me to stop," he said. "Tell me now."

"God, no," she said, moving against him. She wanted nothing more than to touch him back, but he seemed to feel so strongly about her need to grip the sink.

With a grunt he pushed a finger into her wet core, then he stilled and pulled it out. "This is not right." He grabbed her hips, hoisted her up, and turned her, settling her onto the edge of the cool porcelain sink, facing him now. He grunted in approval. "You will watch me as I make you come."

"Yes," she whispered, ready to promise anything.

He pushed her legs apart, looking at her with the expression of a man possessed, then he bent his head to her breast, taking a nipple with his teeth, shooting twin bolts of pain and pleasure clear through her. "Back pocket," he rasped.

"What?"

He rocked against her, biting her, coaxing her.

She slid a hand around to his back pocket and found a condom. "You didn't follow me. You stopped at a store." God, he'd bought condoms instead. Did he trust her now? Had he decided not to kill her? You didn't use condoms with a woman you were planning to kill. "You stopped to buy condoms."

He seemed beyond answering. Beyond anything. He snatched it from her and ripped it open with such force she wondered if it had survived intact. "Take me out."

With shaking hands she pulled his jeans open and shoved them down as he stepped out of them. He pulled off his T-shirt, exposing his muscular torso and the scars up and down him. Profanity tore from his lips as she grabbed him at the root; he pushed away her hands and rolled the condom over himself with clumsy movements, out of his mind.

She helped roll it on as he took hold of her knees. He gazed into her eyes, panting, more animal than man, as he spread her legs further.

And everything went still for a moment.

She felt quivery, spread before him like a sacrifice, wet to the air, juices cooling.

"Put me there," he said to her solemnly. "Put me in."

She took him and fit the fat, wide tip of him to her core. He was so huge and hard against her, she couldn't believe he'd ever fit inside her. He began to enter her, stretching her, filling her. She hissed and clunked her head back on the mirror as he speared her deep, pushing in, claiming her utterly. "Yes," she gasped.

His fingers gripped her knees, like he was channeling his intensity there, trying not to be too rough, but then he began rocking into her, pushing into her deeply, relentlessly, gripping her thighs.

"More." She grabbed onto his hips, holding on for the ride as he fucked her mercilessly, pushing her pleasure up and up.

"Of course I purchased condoms." He thrust into her. "You are mine." He pushed in again. "My prisoner."

In and out he thrust. All her life she'd fucked men without emotion, but Hugo was a different species of man, a man who could penetrate through her scars, finding the nerve endings she'd thought were dead.

"Harder," she gasped.

He shoved into her. She loved how he took her over. Every time she fucked him she felt like she was fucking for the first time.

"Where are you? Come back. Look at me," he growled.

She opened her eyes and he held her gaze as he speared her with his cock. "Don't take your eyes from mine."

She watched him, then, his rugged face, his eyes.

It felt so intimate, the way he took her now, like he was crashing into her mind. Her cheeks heated, her body grew warm. Even the porcelain sink under her thighs felt warm. Still she watched his eyes.

Tell me..." He pushed into her harder. "Tell me how it feels when I am inside."

"Huge."

"And?"

"I'm not a dirty talker."

He scowled. "You'll tell me how it feels."

"Hugo," she protested.

He was fumbling around with something on the sink behind her. What? Nothing was back there but a bar of soap.

She heard the water go on. He fumbled some more and then she felt a slick finger at her asshole, sliding up and down, soaping up her asshole.

She gasped when he stopped and fit a fat fingertip into her asshole.

"What…"

"You know what."

She felt his other hand grip her ass cheek, palm warm and rough and huge. Gently he pulled the globe of flesh aside to make way for his soapy finger. Little by little he pushed it into her ass.

"What am I doing now?"

"Ah…" she breathed "…pushing your finger in my ass…"

He stilled the finger and thrust into her again

"…while you fuck me."

"You see?" But he didn't let up; instead, he shoved it in deeper, like he was fucking her entire body into his finger. "How does it feel when your man does this? Tell me."

"Unbelievable."

"What else?" He pushed in deeper, curling the finger inside her asshole. "Or you get another finger."

She trembled. She wanted another finger. "Like I want to give you everything, and for you to take everything."

He put his lips near her ear, breath hot. "And?"

"And huge. Like I can't take more but I want more."

He changed his angle, bearing down on her. She gripped his thick shoulders, on the verge of madness, and closed her eyes.

"Look at me."

She opened her eyes. The hard look he gave her as he invaded her from both sides was the kind that would start a fight if it went between wolves or men—utterly in your face. He shoved two fingers in, deeper.

"Now?"

God, he was invading her from both sides and invading her gaze, too. It felt like he was unfurling her soul.

He slowed, eyes brown and bright and hard. "Say more."

"Don't stop."

He slipped a third finger in, or maybe it was still the two but it felt like three the way he moved them. She reeled as he pounded her from the front and back. He brought his lips close to hers, words hot and hard. "Say more."

"Like you have me completely. So huge inside of me. Like you're everywhere in me..." She went on, raving, repeating herself. It wasn't the words he cared about—he just wanted to hear her undone. Hugo was a man who took everything from you. It was how he fought and it was definitely how he fucked.

He stopped with the demanding questions and kissed her instead, gently now, filling her, loving her. "Touch your nipples. Make yourself ready for me to bite you there."

Jesus.

"Do it."

She removed her hands from his shoulders and took her

nipples in her fingers. He lowered his gaze as he watched her roll them gently, body rocking with his motion.

"Zelda..." he panted "...Zelda." His eyes were changing, glazing, breath going ragged.

He seemed to be losing control. It was the hottest thing she'd ever experienced—him inside her, out of control. Penetrating her as nobody else could.

"This is what your man does to you now." He shoved his face to her breast, nuzzling his way past her fingers, taking a nipple into his teeth.

Bright, sharp waves of sensation speared through her. He thrust again, firm and hard, cock drilling deep, fingers deep in her asshole, teeth pinching tender flesh.

And right there on the sink she shattered apart.

He groaned and went on, taken over by her pleasure, it seemed, driving her orgasm higher. Then he cried out and slowed, stilled. She felt him pulsing inside her.

Afterward he put her down. "Now the shower, no?"

He disposed of his condom and turned on the water, stripping the rest of his clothing off.

She watched him, raw with exhilaration.

He held his hand under the water. "What do you think?"

When she didn't answer, he looked back at her.

"I think that was like no beauty salon I've ever been to," she said.

He gave her a dark look. "The water, *señorita*."

She stretched her hand into the small stall. "Good."

"Go on, then."

She went in and he came after, crowding her in the tiny, steamy space, washing her everywhere. She took the threadbare cloth from his meaty hands and washed him, soaping up the fur of his taut brown belly, carefully avoiding the mottled pink skin of his burn, spending her time softly swiping around his cock, watching him grow hard again as his eyes bore into her. She made him turn and learned his back, the scars beyond the burn, his mighty shoulders.

They kissed slow under the pounding water. He made her come with his mouth this time, and their fucking was gentle and slow.

He dried her off with a towel afterward and carried her to the bed. He liked to carry her. It was in his nature to protect her. He'd never wanted to kill her any more than she'd wanted to turn him over to Dax.

Dax. Dax could find another way to deal with the pirates. Dax always found another way. The easy way was off the table; now he'd just have to figure out something else.

She nestled the covers over herself and he sat at the end of the bed next to the bumps that her feet made under the sheet and the light blue blanket. He shaped the soft fabric around her foot, *the* foot, as if to create a cocoon around it.

Her heart hammered. She prayed he wouldn't ask about it. She had no excuses, no way to make her capitulation to Friar Hovde seem anything but ignoble.

He worked on the strange cocoon with his beautiful hands. "The idea that, with the right training, most people can endure torture, this is one of the most terrible myths, I think."

She fought back the tears that sprang to her eyes. She'd been ready for anything but this.

"It's why you quit as an agent."

She tried to pull away but he had her ankle.

"Why you quit the field," he continued. "Hunters like you, they do not like to quit."

She shook her head. "Please."

"Few endure torture. That's why you hear about the ones who do," he said.

"Hugo, you don't have to—"

"When I was a young fighter in the Balkans, my unit was issued cyanide pills. Torture endurance kit, they called it. Men used it, too. Most will take death over that shame. Even the possibility of that shame. It is a human fact that people will take death over shame. Evolutionary. Or, what do you call it when—"

"Hardwired," she supplied. That was the word they always used. She was familiar with the studies.

He stretched out beside her, laying his arm over her cocoon of covers. "Most cannot endure torture. It does not make you bad. Simply not a superhuman."

"Don't excuse it. I don't want that."

He got in under the covers, pulling her against his big warm body. "Okay," he said

It was this that broke her. That he'd just be with her.

"Tell me, then," he said.

"I can't."

"Please, Zelda."

She pressed her face to his lightly furred chest. He was doing it again, pushing into her raw center. "I wanted it to stop." She began to cry silent tears. "I felt so scared and alone…"

He stroked her hair, nose pressed into the top of her skull.

"And I talked. I was so scared. This terror I'd never

known I could feel." Was she really revealing this? She didn't know what it was, maybe being in this rabbit hole where nobody could find her. Maybe it was this man who had his own darkness. "Hugo, it hurt. He'd shot me with something that made it hurt extra, and kind of tweaked me out," she sobbed. "I was so fucking scared."

"Of course you were scared."

"It's no excuse for giving a name. That agent died, and I lived. And I hate myself every day for it," she said. "I broke and a man died."

"You did not kill him," he said angrily.

"I talked."

"Have you looked at your feet? A man with a knife can do unspeakable things. Most people—"

"I don't care—a man died because I gave in."

"A man was murdered."

"Because I didn't stick to my training."

"There is no training for torture. Only false comfort."

She shook her head, feeling hopeless.

"Did you not do your best?"

"I don't feel like I did."

"I see how long you held. And the drugs he shot into your veins—you cannot be responsible. You did your best. I've been watching you—your best is what you always give. Except to yourself."

She had nothing to say. She didn't feel like she deserved a lot.

"You are alive. You go forward," he whispered.

"How, Hugo?" she said. "I don't know how to make it right."

"You can't make it right."

She turned to him now. People said a lot of things to comfort her, but never that she couldn't make it right. Just *couldn't*. "Thanks."

"You know that you can't," he said. "You know it's true. You cannot make the past right. You can only make it the best part of you—that horror, that shame. You have already made it the best part of you, I think."

"Like you know what's inside me."

He looked into her with those root-beer-brown eyes, fingers digging deeply into her biceps. "I know your heart. You may be something of an enemy, but I do know your heart."

Wild, dark Hugo. It was too much. She looked away.

He allowed it, allowed her to lay inert in his arms.

Talk could never be enough. Nothing would be enough. Agent Randall had died because she had been weak.

"What happened after?"

She sighed.

"Say more."

Say more. Hugo wanted to head into the darkness alongside her.

It felt like love. He squeezed her to him. So much with him felt like love.

"Friar Hovde raced out of there as soon as I spilled that his right-hand man was an agent. I went crazy trying to get loose, trying to save Agent Randall, but the friar got to him and put a bullet in his brain." She told the story fast; afraid she might not get through it otherwise. Things were unraveling by that time. "Agent Randall was such a good man—one of the best you would ever meet." She could still see his face, eyes staring up from a puddle of blood on the blue-and-white-patterned linoleum. "And then Friar Hovde sped off to his weapons cache—we'd defanged the worst of the weapons, and I suppose he'd guessed that. Fucking traffic stop got him in the end—turned into a high-speed chase, and he crashed." He waited, sensing there was more. He seemed to understand so many things. "I never got the chance to apprehend him or kill him. Or even see him dead. Maybe it wouldn't make a difference, anyway."

"Maybe it would," he said.

She told him about the few cases she'd been on after that, how she'd fumbled things, mind-set blown, lucky to be alive and not kill anybody else. She told him about going behind the desk at the CIA and meeting Dax, founding the Association. She told him everything. She'd never told anybody so much. "You said it was what we do to other people that hurts," she said. "You were so right."

He kissed her head. She thought about his mother.

"I still have these dreams about Hovde," she said.

"What happens?"

She shook her head. Talking about the dreams might give them weight and power.

"Tell me. What does he do?"

"Sometimes I get loose and I take his blade, but I can't find him. He's doing horrible things and it's my fault, but I can't find him to stop him. Sometimes I just can't get loose. Sometimes I get loose and I can't find the blade he used on me, and I need that blade because nothing else will kill him. I need to kill him to end it, but I never can."

He pulled her closer, resting his chin on top of her head. "I wish I could give you that. The chance to kill him. To end it."

"You can't."

The mountains and the sky, the whole world, it was all so huge, but suddenly she wasn't alone in it. She was with Hugo. They were two people together in their darkness in the fading Valencia day.

You have already made it the best part of you, I think.

She pressed her forehead to his chest, felt the strong, steady heartbeat of this killer who trusted her heart. Hugo, the killer who liked to carry her—trying so valiantly to help contain her darkness.

He couldn't. Nobody could. She could never forgive herself—not ever.

CHAPTER THIRTY-SIX

Dax lay facedown on the massage table in one of the private rooms connected to the Valencia Hilton spa, towel slung around his waist. The woman across the room arranged the tools of her trade. The small flashes of skin he'd seen under the bathrobe as she'd come out revealed a lot of tattoos she'd perhaps regret someday, though she looked slightly insane, so maybe not.

He, however, was glad for the harsh lines of her and the madness in her eyes. He had an artistic sensibility for these things.

A knock sounded on the door.

"Come in."

Two fair-haired men came in.

The way they held themselves didn't give them away whatsoever. You would never think they were extensively armed and wildly dangerous.

You would never think this was their first face-to-face meeting with the man who'd controlled their destinies for years.

Aside from rare exceptions, Dax and the Associates had only ever dealt with each other on the phone. But that was far more than they'd dealt with Zelda. Most Associates didn't even know Zelda, aside from having heard her name. She'd always been content to stay behind the scenes for the most part, putting her formidable skills toward tactics and execution.

Dax had been content to allow it. He'd anticipated something like this, though nothing so extreme. He adjusted his towel and sat up. "Give us a moment," he said to the attendant, and she left. He nodded at the first man. "Cole."

"Dax, I presume." Cole offered his hand. Dax shook it, and then he shook Riley's.

People said the nature of things was to evolve. That was wrong. Dax knew better than most that it was the nature of things to unravel. It was the nature of systems to degrade. Entropy ruled.

He and Zelda had created the Associates to have a semi-cellular structure, insulating their agents from the two of them at the top. Everyone was safer that way. But with Zelda offline and possibly working against them, Dax knew he needed to remove that layer between him and the men. Nothing was safe now, and the situation with the tanker was devolving fast. The pirate leader was starting to lose it. People would die if they blew up that tanker.

Lots of them.

Dax would do what it took to stop that from happening, no matter what it cost him. And it was starting to look like it would cost him dearly—it would cost him Zelda, the truest friend he'd ever known.

Well, the agents would be loyal to him—they'd always dealt with him; Zelda was just a name to most of them.

"You've found your rooms?"

They nodded.

"I've set it up to look like we're there for the week." Two local women would be making a nice bit of change for the job of occupying the room and ordering enough food for three men and themselves. Unmaking the beds. Playing the TV.

"We just spoke with Rio," Riley said. "He says they're in Juachez, in *la pensión* El Refugio. They're on their way to the El Gorrion compound."

Dax nodded. "Still no word on why?"

Riley shook his head.

Dax squinted at the colorful wallpaper. Vines and bamboo. There wasn't much he didn't understand, but these moves of Zelda's had him mystified.

"El Gorrion is amassing men at his compound." Riley said.

"He's waiting for Kabakas," Dax said. "You've never seen a fighter like Kabakas. He had some very esoteric training, to say the least."

"We could take Kabakas while he's focused on taking the compound." Riley, ever the strategist. "We come in from the rear while he's focused on El Gorrion's people."

"You're not hearing me." Dax leaned down and drew a tablet from the satchel at the foot of the bed. He went up on his elbows and pulled up some photos and handed it up to Riley. "Here's the airstrip after Kabakas attacked it. With nothing but blades." It was a lot of carnage. "And that was him out of practice," Dax added.

"But if he's distracted…"

"No. I do not know the nature of the mission or why she's allied with Kabakas, but if he wants to strike at El

Gorrion, we have to let him. We use Kabakas to strike at El Gorrion. We then use Zelda to strike at Kabakas."

Riley squinted, waiting for an explanation.

Zelda would never forgive him. Dax had known this day would come, but he hadn't imagined it would arrive quite this fast.

She'd be pulling him off that table if she were there. She was always the one to wipe the lipstick from his jaw or bandage his bleeding back and find him a new shirt, to warn him against stranger sex. *Don't go down to the lobby, Dax. Don't go to the park tonight, Dax. Don't lie down on that table, Dax.*

It was just him and his fighters now. They were the best men you could get, but they'd never look through him the way Zelda always had. Her pain gave a level of insight other people couldn't touch.

Riley's gaze was piercing. He was as fierce a student as a leader, and ruthless.

"Zelda will feed him enough tranquilizer to put down an elephant," Dax explained. "She just won't know it."

"How will you get her to do that?"

"People aren't that complicated," Dax said. He'd handle her the way he handled everybody, the way he handled the fucking world—without apology. "Settle into your rooms. Meet me in an hour on the helipad up top." He stretched back out to demonstrate that the meet was over. He'd feel more evened out in an hour.

Did they wonder how it felt to betray his longtime partner?

The men left, and the woman was back. She resumed her place on the chair and continued filing her nails to points. Dax waited for her to blot everything out. He could hear Zelda's voice, the way she'd talk to him at times like this. *Oh, my poor Greek boy. How much fucking will it take to erase this one?*

CHAPTER THIRTY-SEVEN

Hugo woke first. He was stunned that he'd slept at all. She lay in his arms, still out. Quietly, slowly, he bent his head to her neck to take in her scent.

He'd believed her when she'd told him about her sister; it was then he'd begun to trust her. And she could have driven off when he'd pushed that Jeep out of the mud. He'd gone back there to push knowing, in part, that she could try. Needing her not to.

Impossible to kill her. He'd put off killing her in service to the plants, but he'd just been lying to himself—he couldn't kill her. He'd realized it sitting on the dirty rubber floor mat of the bus to Juachez. She'd slept, head on his shoulder. He'd held her all through that trip—lightly, so that his touch wouldn't wake her. It was then that he knew he wouldn't kill her, that he would protect her always.

And then she'd turned up in the hotel room. It had been a risk not to follow her, but something had driven him to take it. He'd needed that certainty, he supposed.

But the way she had opened herself to him, told him her secret. He didn't know what would happen now; he knew only that she was his, and that he would protect her always. He wanted to wake her up and tell her that. What would she say?

She stirred. His pulse stepped up a notch, thinking of her sliding her naked body against the cool sheets, imagining sliding aside the covers, touching her, enjoying her.

She'd trusted him enough to tell him her hardest secrets, and what had he given her? He'd been barely human with her, fucking her like an animal.

He wanted to do it again—and not gently, either.

He extracted himself and went to the window, pushing aside the curtains. Nearly time. He dressed quietly. The gloves tumbled from his pack and he scooped them up from the floor, cock growing hard as steel as he thought of the way she'd looked at them. The mask didn't turn her on, but the gloves—she'd admitted it there in the doorway.

He put them on. And went to her, lowering himself to the bed.

With a gloved finger he touched her arm, the bare skin just above the sheet edge, then trailed that finger down, dragging the sheet with him, down over her hip, over her naked body, baring her to the glove.

She turned and mumbled as he slid his hand up her legs, caressing her thighs.

She opened her eyes and hitched in a breath to see him over her, touching her with the battle-roughened gloves.

The rough, hard gloves on her tender belly, her nipples, it seemed wrong—these were the gloves he wore for killing, but he and Zelda were wrong in so much. She wanted the gloves. He would give her the gloves.

"This is what your man does now," he said to her. "He

fucks you with the gloves."

The gloves cut off sensation from his hands, but the look in her eyes as she realized what he was doing got him hard as granite. He trailed his fingers down her belly and touched her between her legs.

She gasped as he stroked her. He could see her pulse banging madly in her throat. He brought his gloved hand to her lips. "Lick yourself off Kabakas's gloves," he said. She took the leather into her mouth.

"Good." He stood and, still wearing the gloves, pulled open the fly of his cargo pants and shoved them down a ways, letting his cock spring out over her. He threw a condom onto her belly. "Put it on me," he growled.

She didn't put it on. She turned onto her side and rose up, took hold of his cock, and licked the gleaming drop off the tip.

He grabbed her hair and she hissed out a jagged breath as she closed her mouth around the tip, playing her tongue around the head. He pushed into her in frustration, but then he realized what she needed; he took her hair roughly in his gloved hands and shoved into her, fucking her face, making her feel him, making her feel the leather.

She took him deep; he could feel the back of her throat. She gagged once and he pushed in harder. They were somewhere new together, completely wrong and complete-ly right.

"Touch yourself," he said. "Spread your knees and touch yourself so that I can see." It wasn't something he could actually see—the logistics weren't there—but he knew she would like it. They were working in imagination now, the Kabakas who saw all, took all. He'd never imagined fucking as Kabakas. He would prefer not to act the part of Kabakas in this; Kabakas was a creature of death, but the line between them had grown dangerously thin, and her pleasure was his, and her mouth was like hot velvet. He couldn't last...couldn't last...

"Enough!" He pulled out of her mouth and pointed to the condom. She unwrapped it and put it on as he caressed her shoulders with leather-clad fingers. Then he pushed her down and climbed over her, catching up her wrists in one gloved hand, so that she'd feel the leather in a hard way. With the other hand, he caressed her cheek, her neck, her lips, just a little bit of a threat. He couldn't believe how beautiful she was, how utterly on the verge.

"Open," he whispered.

She opened and let him push in a gloved finger.

"How does it taste?"

"Like madness," she said when he took it out and swept his hand over her breasts, her belly. "Like pure and utter..." She trailed off, shuddering with arousal as he touched her.

CHAPTER THIRTY-EIGHT

"Like pure and utter what?" he asked her. Because he wanted to know. He wanted her inside and out.

"Everything, too...just...*uh*..." She loved him touching her with the gloves, taking her with those gloves. She'd always had a thing about them. Especially when she made herself think about the photo she'd marveled at forever. God, Kabakas taking her with those gloves.

So why was it starting to get old?

He put his mouth to her ear, licking the tender shell of it, making it hot with his breath, making her feel him. She liked the gloves, yes.

"Wait," she breathed.

He stilled. "What is it, *señorita*?"

"Take them off."

He pulled away. "What?"

"The gloves."

He knelt over her with a humorous glint in his eyes. "After all this?"

"I want Hugo, not Kabakas."

The humor went out of his eyes.

There'd been a time when she might have described the

expression that crossed his face as stony, unreadable. Now she knew what it was: gratitude. Affection. It swelled her heart.

She reached up and settled her hands on his chest. "I want you to touch me," she said. "Only you."

With a wild force he started yanking off the gloves, tugging feverishly at the fingers like they wouldn't come off fast enough. He threw them aside and settled his hands on her belly.

Just that sent a jolt of pleasure through her. "Like this?"

"Yes," she whispered, feeling lost in his gaze, lost in his hard, jagged beauty.

He slid his hands all over her, covering every inch of her skin, as though he knew she needed that. And then he stretched his big, ruined body over hers and covered her.

"Like this?"

"Yes."

He was a storm, taking her. He touched her in all of her pain and all of her truth. Being touched by Hugo—this, for her, was the ultimate kink.

He kissed her, and just when she thought she couldn't stand the wait any longer, he settled between her legs and guided himself into her, spearing her. "This is what your man does to you now," he whispered.

She loved how he said that, how caveman it was. "Say it again."

He grunted, not one to take commands; instead he fucked her harder, riding them both into oblivion.

***

Darkness fell.

He rolled off the bed and went to the window to peer

out through the small gap between the colorful curtain panels. The scene felt...unnatural. Or was he merely on edge being so deep in El Gorrion's territory?

A rustling sound. The bed. She appeared next to him, clad in just those glasses. He preferred her in glasses and brown hair—far more so than the plumage of bright blonde and crystal green eyes. Her everyday self took his breath away.

"What?" she asked.

"Perhaps nothing." He guided her to stand in front of him and look out the gap.

"We've been found," she said.

He settled his hands on her shoulders, his chin grazing her hair, peering out with her. "Say more."

"The man at one o'clock. The man at eleven o'clock. The one at the bus stop. They're too well placed. It's not natural. The sight lines..."

"Too perfect."

She said nothing. His *señorita*, so silent and lethal. He never wanted to lose this feeling of having a partner. It felt good—too good, maybe. He didn't know how they fit on the outside; but they fit on the inside.

"I'm thinking about the Aussies," she said. "Maybe using them as decoys. The woman is my size, blonde. The man isn't big enough, but if we bulked him up, if they moved fast. We need to find them and hire them."

"Find them without asking around," he added. "This is too much El Gorrion's territory."

They ended up finding them through a process of deduction and a helpful German drug addict. Hugo and Zelda went to their room and made the deal; they would pay them well to dress in their clothes, switch luggage, and sneak down the street. The beleaguered travelers didn't ask a lot of questions—they didn't want the deal to go away. It would be safe enough for them; El Gorrion's men would be angry when they found out, but they would not attack *turistas*. They would gain nothing but trouble from that.

"If they ask what we look like, or any other questions, you tell them everything," Hugo said. "Tell them what they want to know, and they won't hurt you." He was so tired of all of the death. He didn't want any more people to die.

Back in the room, Hugo and Zelda shoved their weapons and essentials into the Aussies' ragged neon-colored packs. He disguised the swords by wrapping them with a sweatshirt, then he nestled them in.

She stilled his hand as he began to wrap the masks. "Let me see." He handed her the heavy one, the metal-lined one. She put it up to her face. "What do you think?"

He grabbed her wrist, forcing her to lower it.

"What?"

"I hate seeing it on you as much as I hated seeing it on Paolo."

"Why?"

He didn't know how to explain it—how he found his taste for being Kabakas waning. "Don't wear it unless we need it." He let her go.

"What I wouldn't have given to hold your mask way back when. This metal backing would distribute a blow," she said. "Even resist a bullet."

"Certain calibers at certain angles," he said, fingering the cheaper mask, the mercadillo version. "Bullet-resistant, not bulletproof. Do not be casual out there. If we must wear these, you must not be casual."

"Wait." She grabbed his mask before he could stop her. "This is the kind they sell at the markets. This is just thin plastic." She looked up. "This is a bullshit one. We need to trade—you can't wear the bullshit one."

"I only need...a bullshit one."

"You'd be the one out there, front and center."

"Fear is my armor," he said.

She snorted. "You need more armor than fear. You've taken blows to the face. It's documented. It was because of this mask that you survived."

He twisted her hair in a finger, voice low. "Your knowledge of my exploits—I do not always enjoy it."

She turned the metal-reinforced one over. "This one is too small. I don't understand..." Inwardly he sighed, knowing he couldn't prevent what was coming—this was a woman who solved puzzles for a living. She looked up when she got it. "You modified your good mask to fit Paolo the day you guys went out to the airfield. You let Paolo have all of the protection."

He twisted her hair another loop. "Paolo's vulnerability was a greater danger to me than bullets, just as it will be with you." She tried to pull away but he kept her hair, not wanting to let her go.

"You need to wear the reinforced one," she said. "You're the one exposed."

"Too small now. I cut the edges down. It would not look right. It would not work."

She said nothing. She of all people could understand the effect of the mask. El Gorrion's men would know, deep down, if it was too small. She was so far inside his secret world it seemed a kind of madness. He never wanted her to leave.

"Hey." She slapped his wrist. "Stop pulling my hair."

He let go. *"Discúlpame."* Forgive me.

"You went out there on the airstrip in this flimsy thing."

"It would seem so."

She sniffed her angry sniff.

"Do not question my choices as Kabakas," he said.

She was silent for a long time. He didn't like it, this unhappy silence of hers. He wanted to shake the words out of her. Finally she spoke. "You said before that Paolo was better off without you." Here she paused. "You are so full of shit."

Her words stilled him. He loved her. Maybe he always had. "If anything happens to me, you will see that Paolo is cared for. You will get the formula to Julian."

She began to protest.

He spoke over her. "You will see that Paolo is cared for and that the crops are put right."

Her gaze was solemn. "Nothing will happen, because I have your back. That's what this is."

He studied her face. "For this mission?"

"For always."

He clapped his hand onto the back of her head and pulled her to him, pressing his lips to her forehead. "And I have yours, *corazón.*" His heart thundered. He'd never had a partner before. He wanted to tell her how much it meant, but he couldn't find the words. And it was time.

They slipped into the Aussies' room and gave them directions. The two of them took off. Hugo and Zelda watched from the Aussies' window, watched as the travelers posing as them moved stealthily down the street toward the alley, following the route Hugo had drawn for them. It was how he and Zelda would've gone.

He rested a hand on her shoulder.

"Ack," Zelda said when the two veered into an alley. "Nothing like a violent turn into an alley to say I'm *furtive*."

The man at the bus stop got up.

"Nevertheless, off they go," he said, mouth close enough to her ear to kiss it. The man in the doorway folded up his newspaper and pushed away from the wall. He too disappeared down the street, shadowing the Aussies. Good.

Zelda and Hugo climbed out of the window and onto the roof wearing the other couple's clothes and backpacks, heavy with weaponry. Hugo felt his scars tear as they dropped onto the next rooftop. He hadn't brought the salve, but he did have something for infection. It would be enough.

They stole across and climbed down into an alley, heading toward the office building district, looking for a good vehicle to take. His man in Bogotá had come through with more information—the connection Ruiz had used for e-mailing Julian was near a small town southeast of their location. It was paid for by El Gorrion's shell company. He'd narrowed down coordinates. The greenhouse they sought would be somewhere around El Gorrion's compound.

They decided on a small rusty Volvo. Zelda slipped right in and started hotwiring it. With her glasses, brown hair, and simple skirt, she looked like she belonged in a library or lab, but here she was, yanking out wires with the quick, confident movements of a predator. She was his woman in full flower, and they were stronger together.

The knowledge that they were stronger together sat with him hard, but it also sat with him easy.

***

They drove until they hit the point where they'd be noticed, and then they hid the Volvo on the side of the road behind a decaying guard post, a relic of the war. He threw brush onto it. From there they headed up through the jungle, loosely following the dirt road that led to the El Gorrion compound. It was perhaps two miles up. They arrived at midnight.

The barbed-wire perimeter was clear of trees but not of soldiers. There were so many of them. Fighters everywhere. El Gorrion was building up. Expecting trouble.

He and Zelda melted back as more men rolled by, eight to a Jeep.

A vegetable truck idled off to the side, just outside the first security entrance, the driver's face lit by his phone. "El Gorrion's," Hugo said. "No vegetables. They'll fill it with product."

He snuck up and dragged the man out of the cab and into the dark jungle, where they questioned him. The man talked easily. Hugo didn't have to touch him, and he talked. He gave them a greenhouse, a mile over. You had to go back down the main road and up a little-used trail. Hugo carried him into an abandoned shed and Zelda tied and gagged him.

"It'll take hours for him to work out of those bindings," she said. "Maybe a day."

He wouldn't have to ask about her knots. She'd been in the CIA. He could trust her knots.

"What?" she asked, noting his expression.

"Nothing," he said, wondering if the trust was on his face, or maybe the love. He took the man's hat, phone, keys, and sunglasses.

"I miss this," she said as they stole back to the truck. "This mission feeling. The energy."

Hugo drove them back down to the main road and turned onto the less-traveled dirt road, heading up into a different part of the jungle.

They were heading to an area that was near El Gorrion's compound, but not on it. Smart of El Gorrion to keep operations away from his main compound, so that one attack couldn't take him all the way down.

This was deeper, darker jungle; the tree trunks here were tall and thin, seeking light at the top of the thick ceiling of foliage. They pulled the truck off to the side and covered it best they could. Hugo pulled on his gloves and arranged his bandolier.

"What do you make of the buildup?" she asked.

"He thinks Kabakas is coming."

"And so he is."

He raised his eyes to her. "I want to save the savinca, not kill more men. Kabakas is a harsh, blunt weapon. Like a bomb when a knife would do."

"Kabakas saved me on that airfield."

He flexed his hands in the gloves, black leather dully lit in the moonlight, enjoying the strength of her gaze. He reached up and drew a leather-clad finger down the pale skin of her cheek. She still liked the gloves. She just liked his hands better.

"Will you wear the mask?" she asked.

"Handling a few obstacles," he said, sliding two fingers

along her jawline, "I think the mask is not so much need-ed." He dropped his hand. This was not so good for con-centration. "I'll put it on if I need to. You'll stay behind."

"They're expecting a sidekick now."

"I don't care."

"Don't shield me." He recognized the hitch in her voice—she got that when she felt emotion. "Trust me as a partner."

He trusted her as he'd never trusted anyone. Didn't she see it? He grabbed her hair and let her feel it that way. Him and the gloves, the way she sometimes liked. "I trust you as more than a partner." It was a revolution inside him, that trust. A seismic shift. A new North Pole.

They continued on foot, staying just outside the ATV tracks with the aid of a flashlight on low. The driver had said there was a processing lab in the area and some out-buildings a mile beyond it. He used the Spanish term for crop science. That would be the greenhouse—it fit all the criteria: near the compound but not on it, accessible for deliveries, but not on a road.

Chemical scents grew stronger as they moved deeper into the midnight-black jungle. He played the dim beam on the decaying foliage, showing her where to walk. The thick canopy made it a good place for an open-air lab for coca processing, but the canopy would soon thin; the chemical waste from even the smallest processing lab was devastat-ing to life of all kinds.

Hugo's blood heated as he thought about the savinca bushes, trapped in the poisoned soil, just as he had been trapped as a boy, nowhere to run, veins filling with anger and fear.

Soon he felt the presence of others. A sense that they weren't alone. Deeper in, he heard the muffled sounds of men walking quietly.

He touched her sleeve and placed a finger upon his lips. She nodded.

He never knew who tripped the wire—her, him; it didn't matter. He heard the snap and pushed her away just as a mass of boulders crashed down from above.

Hugo put on the mask. Shouts rang out. "Don the mask and stay down."

He rushed out onto the ATV path and walked into the gunfire, which quickly ceased as the trio of guards caught sight of him strolling toward them in the moonlight.

They lowered their weapons, stilled.

Hugo pulled out a barong.

Finally, one turned and ran. The other two followed.

He allowed it. With his ears he followed their retreat.

He'd pushed them back without killing. It gave him hope, the ease of it. He did not need them dead.

A rustle in the bushes next to a chemical drum. Somebody hiding.

He stalked toward it, blades poised. He peered over and saw a young boy cowering in the darkness, dirt on his cheek, something that was probably dried blood on his clothes. Maybe twelve, this one.

The boy stared up at him, clutching a rifle, eyes wide—as though Hugo were death itself. It made Hugo feel so tired. He'd felt like a good man for a moment, repelling without killing, but this one saw what he was.

He spoke to the boy as if in a dream. "If you run now, Kabakas cannot see you."

The boy stared.

"Go!"

The boy ran off.

Hugo made another circuit through the area. She strolled up next to him. "Kabakas kills without mercy, allowing only the messenger to escape."

A line from one of the songs. He'd hated those songs, but he understood her meaning; they might think him an impostor. They might come back—with others.

"El Gorrion will kill them for abandoning their posts," Hugo said. "They will not be so eager to report this. Still, we should hurry."

Get the intel and go.

They switched on flashlights and moved through, keeping the ATV trail in sight. Sometime later, they reached the greenhouse, set back in a small clearing. Unguarded.

They had some time here; El Gorrion would be expecting Kabakas to attack the compound or the lab they'd passed; not an out-of-the-way jungle greenhouse.

The ramshackle facility was constructed of cinder block and corrugated metal, with the jungle pushing at the seams. Panels of chicken wire glass stretched over the top.

He kept watch over the surroundings as she picked the lock.

She was taking too long. "Stand back." He burst open the door with a kick and strolled into the dark, cool space. It smelled of bright, angular chemicals and soft, wet soil.

She followed behind him, playing her flashlight beam on four rows of plants of different kinds, evenly spaced apart on wide planks that were supported by sawhorses.

Her stride changed in this space, she became more confident; jaunty, even, as she inspected the rows.

"Gotcha, motherfucker." She stopped in front of one of them. "This is what he's testing on." She slid a leaf through two fingers. "Watching how they die."

He loved how disgusted she sounded. They shared this passion for the plants.

"And this one, dead." She poked the bent-over stem of another plant.

Her anger was as gorgeous as her passion. He moved to her; he'd never wanted her more. It was thrilling and not entirely comfortable. "This is the way you were when I would not call Paolo by name," he rumbled into her ear from somewhere deep in his heart. "Battling on the side of the weak."

"I'm definitely in a battling mood right now." She read a note scribbled on a small pad near one of the plants.

He moved her hair to one side and slid a finger down the back of her neck. "A battling mood renders you especially beautiful, *corazón*."

Even from behind her he could sense her smile—he saw it in the shape of her cheek, heard it in her voice. "I'm not going to be able to concentrate if you stand there saying stuff like that."

"I think you will," he said. "This is your habitat, is it not?"

She sniffed and moved to the next plant. There were notes next to each one.

How could her fellow agents not have forgiven her? How could they not believe in her? Could they not feel her heart? He kissed the back of her neck.

"Ruiz made notes by each plant. Dates, a number—

probably the formula used, the range of intensity. High to low." On she went. He wasn't listening—he couldn't hear over the banging of his pulse in his ears and the realization that he loved her.

He loved her.

She turned to him, always sensing him. Did she sense his love? Did she sense how it made the world new and colorful and dangerous? Her eyes widened as he went to her and slid his hands around her waist—she felt things— they felt each other. The connection disturbed him, yet he wouldn't have it any other way. He jerked her to him with all the violence of the love inside him and devoured her lips, tasting the inside of her mouth, breathing her breath, forcing himself to kiss her more gently than he wished. He would always care for her and protect her, even from himself.

She smiled into the kiss. "What's this for?"

He didn't know what to say to that. He didn't know what to say to her at all, so he pulled away from her and went to the doorway, scanning the jungle beyond with his full senses. Nothing.

So far.

She set to examining a metal shelving unit that held oddly shaped glassware vessels marked with lines and letters, shoved in next to jars and boxes, some with colorful labels; some with the skull and crossbones denoting poison. She shone the flashlight on one label after another. "Likely suspects for the component parts. And let's hope he's as careful as I think he is, and that he has his dirty computer in here. The one he doesn't want people to see." She checked inside cabinets and soon came to a tall metal locker in the corner. Padlocked.

Hugo leaned in the doorway, half his attention on the surrounding jungle, but the liveliest half was on her as she went at the padlock with a pick she had fashioned from paper clips.

"Damn," she said, shoving the clips into her mouth and shaking out her hands. "Let's try that again."

"I think it will never get old," he said, "seeing you in this way."

She smiled. "What way?"

He gestured vaguely, unable to find the words. Perhaps she would take it as her being in a lab, seeing her that way. But really, he was gesturing at the world. At the madness of being in love with her, of no longer being alone. He needed to tell her, but he did not know how. It seemed too big for three words.

She found what she'd wanted—a laptop. She opened it and hit a few buttons, warming up the computer. Then she started pulling jars of solution off the shelves. "The most accessible. The least dust. He tried these last." She smelled one and wrinkled her nose.

"Poison," he observed. "Be careful."

"Doesn't Kabakas have somewhere to be?"

He nodded once. Yes, he'd go out and search the area. He'd do this for her, be her attack dog. "How much time do you need?"

"Maybe ten minutes."

He pulled the mask down over his face. "You'll have it. We won't be able to leave by the trail."

"Roger that," she said.

He slipped out the door and melted out into the jungle,

spinning his awareness out in all directions, moving lightly over the uneven jungle bed. All the years on those islands across the Sulu Archipelago had made him feel comfortable stalking and fighting in this type of terrain, even in the dark, attuned to the sounds, the scatter of small mammals and startled birds, the moist feel of the air, the scent of decay.

Crunches under the vast canopy. He stilled and closed his eyes. Regular human footsteps were heavy and easy to recognize, but a man being quiet could sound like other large animals.

He waited. Nothing.

It had felt good not to kill. He wondered now if it had been foolish. Counting on their fear of El Gorrion.

He went on, thoughts consumed by the boy hiding behind the drum and those wide brown eyes, peering up at him in terror.

People's terror of him had never bothered him before; he'd always taken it as a badge of honor, a type of security, but that boy's terror had felt nearly physical.

It was *her*, he realized. She'd made life feel more precious to him. When he'd looked at the old man dead in his shop in Buena Vista, when he'd bought the street-corner barongs, he'd felt bad for not having empathy. Perhaps he'd been better off without it. She'd made it hurt to be Kabakas.

Crunch.

A human. One. Near the trail, but not on it.

Nearer, now. He melted into the shadows beside a moonlit tree. Somebody was sneaking up the ATV path that led to the greenhouse.

He pulled his blades and moved toward the sound. People spoke about building up a store of goodwill; couldn't he have a store of fear? Of soldiers staying away from him a while longer?

He spotted the man moving along the side of the road, assault rifle at the ready. Was this man playing the hero, checking on the buildings up the road, or had he drawn the short straw?

Mask fixed in place, Hugo stepped out onto the trail. He threw a warning knife, aiming it so that it whizzed by the man's nose and stuck into a nearby tree. "The next hits you in the eye," he said.

"You are not Kabakas." A blast of strobe lighting assaulted Hugo's eyes as gunfire sounded. Hugo reacted instinctively. Even blind and diving for cover he could put a blade in a man's eye.

The shooting ceased as Hugo hit the ground. He rolled and came to a squat, bringing his hand to the stinging pain in his shoulder. Sticky wetness. It was beyond a nick and it stung like hell; his burn scars were torn and searing now, too, thanks to the roll.

But nothing like the other guy, judging from the unholy moan he'd heard so often, that begging kind of moan, not quite a wail.

The sound pierced Hugo to the core. He stood and spotted the guard on all fours on the trail. The strobe from the man's rail mount still flashed, giving the bloody scene an unholy look. As Hugo approached, the man hovered his hand near the blade handle, wanting to pull it out of his eye, yet not. Sometimes they didn't die right away.

Hugo continued slowly toward him.

The moaning had stopped, but even from yards away he

could hear the man's breath, frantic and ragged, more animal than human. Even his posture was animal-like, on hands and knees.

Hugo had chosen the knife through the eye for its effectiveness, for the fear it inspired, but it really was barbaric. How had he become such a fighter?

The man whimpered as Hugo crouched next to him.

"*Hermano*," Hugo said, placing a hand on the man's shoulder.

The man scrambled and fell onto his side. Blood streamed from the wound. "No, no, no..." Hands up defensively.

"Okay, okay, it's okay," Hugo said in Spanish.

The man trembled. He couldn't see anything, but he knew Hugo was there.

Hugo squeezed the man's shoulder.

"*Qué Dios me proteja!*" the man cried, terrified.

Hugo's heart slammed inside his chest. Even his help terrified the soldier, who moaned again, more quietly now, as the strobe flashed on, harsh and cold. The moan twisted painfully inside Hugo, and he reached down, grabbed the blade handle, slipped it from the man's eye, and drew it cleanly across the man's throat. The man jerked, then stilled. Hugo kept his hand on the man's shoulder, feeling the terror, the waning life.

He'd killed dozens like this, and this would be how they all had died—terrified, bewildered. He'd never stayed with them as they died.

"You're okay now," he said softly. A lie. Nothing was okay—not for either of them.

The man had doubted that he was Kabakas. Perhaps

they both had.

Hugo stood and crushed the strobe mount under his boot. The darkness was back. He left the body on the trail. A sign: *Take heed. Kabakas is about.*

He prowled the perimeter, ignoring the sting of the bullet wound and the tearing pain of his burn scars; the feeling of being with that dying man cut deepest. He'd never stayed with them.

The birds had quieted. Even the jungle floor had grown gloomier. How many had he killed like that? Hundreds?

Time was up. He headed back in, glad for the mask that covered his face.

"It's you." She emerged from the shadows and flicked on the flashlight, revolver in her hand. "I heard shots."

"One man. Handled."

She looked beautiful in the ambient glow. "It's nearly cracked. Ruiz is a motherfucker."

"You have the recipe?"

"Almost. We're going to kick this thing." She set the weapon and light on a table. "It's simple. This is a simple, vicious recipe. Not even elegant."

He nodded.

"Take off your mask and stay awhile." She cocked her head. "What's wrong?"

"We'll have company soon. Not now, but soon."

"I'm waiting for something to process. I need fifteen minutes more."

His heart sank. "I'll see that you have it."

His breath hitched as she rounded the table, coming to him, eyes meeting his, even through the mask. If only he had a mask to cover his soul.

Again he saw that fury, as though he was a living thing she needed to save, even as he stood there soaked in death. "You're shot."

"Grazed."

She eyed the wound, Then she pushed up the mask, baring his face. He closed his eyes.

He couldn't stand being bare to her so soon after that kill. Who was he to love this woman? To raise a boy like Paolo? He could still hear the man's terrified last breaths.

"Hey, you." She kissed him.

He received it stiffly. He didn't want her to see him like this or to touch him like this.

She gripped his forearms. "What?"

He shook his head.

"Say more," she said.

"I can't."

"Whatever you did, you had to, okay? Somebody out there was shooting at you. I see the evidence. Don't forget that I'm a trained operative."

"I went to him as he died," he told her. "The sounds he made…"

She listened, steady as sunshine.

"I pulled the blade from his eye and cut his throat. I told myself it was to end his pain, but in truth, it was to end mine."

"Oh, Hugo." She pressed her fingers into his arms, as if to go deeper into him. Best if she didn't. For her, anyway. "You had no choice out there."

He shook his head. He could barely hear her now.

"Don't shut me out."

Too late. It was as if she was speaking through a tube at

the other end of the night, and he was still down there feeling the man's terror.

She pushed him back against the door and took hold of his hand, pulling off his gloves, loosening the fingers as he had. "You were protecting our mission. You were protecting me."

His gaze returned to hers. "I always will." He let her work him like a rag doll.

She pulled off the gloves and tossed them aside. She brought his hand to her mouth and pressed her lips to his palm, kissing him softly there. Then she pressed his hand flat against her pounding heart. "This is how my man feels to me. This is what my man does to me." She gazed up at him. "You make me feel alive again. Because I love you."

She loved him.

Her words were a jolt. He had never imagined the world could become even more dangerous and brilliant than it already was. He gazed down at her, full of unruly love for her. She destroyed him, this woman.

"Everything you are." She kissed him then, trapping his hand between them. "Everything." Right then a bell dinged. "Damn. I have to mix something." She went to a glass vessel.

"You need more time," he said.

"Just a little."

"You'll have it." He lowered the mask and stumbled out. He had the boy and he had the village and he had her, now, and he loved her and he would forever, and by some miracle she loved him, too. He would be this hateful thing for her. He would be whatever she needed.

The jungle was quiet. He walked a pattern that bisected

every possible approach, running the logistics in his mind. He'd been on plenty of fighting forces that needed to move out and mobilize quickly, and that was what he was pondering now: how fast could El Gorrion pull all of those men off the compound, down the road and up to the labs? How ready were they? Would he leave his compound vulnerable?

The one soldier had doubted he was Kabakas. Would that embolden them? Did sparing those few men mean that he would now have to kill many?

Surely he and Zelda would be gone by the time any large group could get to the greenhouse. Moving that many men was never quick. It only meant that they couldn't leave the way they came.

He traversed the area quickly now, playing the guard dog. He thought they were home free when thirteen minutes were up. That was when he heard the engine, gunning for the greenhouse. A Jeep.

He doubled back toward the trail.

He heard the shouts when they discovered their fallen comrade. Four or five of them, it sounded like.

He moved forward and watched through the trees as they pulled the body onto the back. They would leave now. And he'd get Zelda out of there. Guns came off backs. Voices raised.

The driver shoved the Jeep into gear, but they didn't turn or head back down. They continued on up, speeding toward the greenhouse.

Toward *her*.

Everything in him sprang to attention as he sprinted madly after the vehicle, using everything. They were moving fast, but he was faster. He put a blade in the tire. The vehicle jerked. One of the men twisted around, caught sight of him, and shouted. The driver gunned it.

Damn.

They pulled away, speeding around a curve. Hugo crashed through the woods and threw, hitting the driver in the jugular. The Jeep smashed into a tree and the soldiers scrambled out and took cover behind the vehicle. The soldiers, the vehicle, him stalking. Like the airfield in miniature.

Hugo was out in the open, coming for them, an invitation soldiers never seemed to resist.

Soon a soldier raised his head over the edge of the Jeep to shoot and Hugo took him in the eye.

You always needed an eye to shoot.

Silence. Another came up to shoot and he took him, then two came up and he took them both.

He didn't wait for them to die. He ran the half mile up to the greenhouse. She was ready.

"We take the long way," he said. "Hurry."

"You had trouble," she said, following him out.

"I don't know why they didn't wait for backup," he said. "Brave. Stupid."

They took off into the deep foliage. They used his swords to cut through the worst of the undergrowth. More vehicles were coming up the mountainside—you could hear them in the distance. Why hadn't the men in the Jeep waited for their people?

Shouts rang out.

"We're leaving a massive trail," she breathed.

Nothing to be done. They zigzagged through a clearing

and made a loop. It would confuse them. After an hour of hard going, they hit another ATV trail, yards down. They stole an actual ATV, and then a Jeep, probably El Gorrion's. It wasn't long until they found the main road.

"Home free," she said.

CHAPTER THIRTY-NINE

Hugo drove. The sting of the wound was worsening, but he knew the roads.

Some miles beyond El Gorrion's compound, they passed a row of stalls set up to the side of an overlook—a cliff edge enclosed by railings. It was the sort of place tourists liked to photograph themselves in front of, the great green valley sprawling below the wild peaks of the Andes.

"Jelly Belly jelly beans!" she exclaimed, pointing at one of the stands. "We *have* to stop! It's my successful mission treat. Please, Hugo. I always have to have Jelly Bellies at a time like this. Let me buy some for you. If they have a good assortment, I'll show you how to make a blueberry muffin in your mouth. That's the absolute best kind."

"The savinca," he said.

"Five minutes won't make a difference. It's bad luck not to stop."

So few things would drive him to such a frivolous stop. He hurt, but that didn't mean she had to. He found a place to pull over and they walked back toward the overlook together, passing the few vehicles that were parked along the side. No people, though. Hiking, perhaps. "Strange, I think, that they should have such a candy for sale here."

She took his hand and pulled him along, smiling. "It's a good sign that they have such a candy for sale."

They paused at the railing together. She insisted on checking his wound. He allowed it. She could do nothing, but he enjoyed the feel of her care.

Back at the lab, her tests had come out beautifully, she told him. She'd worked out a formula, like a recipe—the amount of crushed Luquesolama stone to put in a gallon of water. He'd teased her, of course—*you need a recipe for everything,* he'd said.

She'd just smiled. She loved him.

He wanted to say it back to her, but more than that, he wanted to show her, to make it feel real to her. He would not have her imagine that he was saying it merely because she had.

They passed the outlook. A few of the stands stood unattended. Where were the *vendedores?* They would not leave their stands like this. But then, he looked over at her and he felt warmed by her smile and the way her dark hair glowed in the sunshine and the knowledge that the *Savinca verde* would now be saved. She drew him to the Jelly Belly stand with its many rows of plastic boxes, each with different colors of jelly beans. So many flavors. She pointed at a box with just two blue ones in it and asked the woman there if she had more blueberry ones in her perfect Spanish.

"Only two left," the old woman told her.

Zelda nodded. "I'll take both of those..." She went on to select two dozen candies. The woman collected them into a paper sack. Zelda insisted on paying.

They headed back to the scenic overlook, Zelda rooting in the bag as they walked. Hugo steered her around the potholes. She knew he would do that, and he did.

She picked out two blue ones and a yellow for him. "This is how you make a blueberry muffin taste. Put the yellow in your mouth first, then the two blues." She held them out. "It's the best ever."

"There were only two left. They are for you."

"I want you to have them. Please."

"If this is your favorite..."

"That's why I need you to have it," she said. "If you don't taste it, how can we discuss how delicious it is later on? Come on—you'll love it."

He could not resist her. He ate the yellow first, as instructed, then the blues.

She popped reds and browns into her mouth. "Chocolate-covered cherry," she said, chewing. "Second-best taste."

"*Americans,*" he teased.

She watched his face as he ate the muffin combination, wanting him to react.

"Strange and sweet," he said. But then, everything was strange and sweet when she was around.

"Did it taste like a blueberry muffin?" she asked.

He pulled her close and breathed in the scent of her hair. "I will tell you when I eat a blueberry muffin."

She rolled her eyes and pushed him away and leaned over the rail, gazing out over the valley. "It's beautiful, the way the shadow and light go in streaks. It makes this crazy feeling in my heart to look at it."

It was how he felt, looking at her.

They stood in silence for a moment. "The one on the

airfield—when you take them down with the barongs like that," she began, "is it him you're killing? Your father, I mean? The one who beat you?"

"Sometimes."

"Does it help?" she asked.

"Sometimes," he said, trying to conceal the weariness in his voice. He tightened his arms around her. He had the impulse, suddenly, to lay his head on her shoulder and rest his eyes. He hadn't realized how weary he was. He fought it.

"Does it bother you if I ask questions like that?"

"It's not the questions that bother me."

She rested her arms over his. "If we can follow up the solution with a good fertilizer, next year could be even better for the savincas." She turned to him with her back on the rail.

He held her shoulders, feeling a sudden sense of vertigo. "Don't fall," he said.

"You won't let me."

He kissed her, then, and he realized that he was happy. Simply happy. It was astonishing, this feeling. But the dizziness—the dizziness was not right.

She fished more jelly beans from the paper sack. "Oranges are good, too."

He gripped the rail, caging her, squinting out over the valley. What was happening?

The sweet cherry scent of the candies she chewed wafted up to him. "Running the Associates, I know we make a difference out there, but it's all felt so theoretical for so long," she said. "But with Buena Vista...if we can start treating the soil, we can bring those livelihoods back. There's this other situation out there, this tanker crisis the

Association is concerned about. It's bad but there's always another solution, you know? There has to be. If not the one that I offered..." She seemed to be talking to herself, about solutions, finding ways to solve things. One door opening when another closed. He wasn't listening. Deep breaths made the dizziness better.

The sack crinkled. She had another candy for him. "Cherry. Open up."

"No, thank you."

"Come on." She tugged on his lip and he opened and she put another candy in, and then closed his jaw and kissed him. What this how normal people acted? Silly like this?

"You like?"

He took her hand. He'd never imagined that he could have this. Somebody who saw what he was and still loved him—not just a part of him, but *all* of him. He loved her, too. He needed to get his balance back, to tell her, to show her. "Zelda—" Alarm shot through him as the world became fuzzy.

"Hugo, what is it?"

"Drugged..." He grabbed onto the rail. He was losing his balance. *The candies.*

She clutched his shoulders. Urgent, animated words came from her lips but he felt consumed by the dizziness. She seemed surprised and angry and so far away. Who was she speaking to? Him?

He went to his knees. She was trying to pull him up, voice raised. He could no longer focus.

He felt several pairs of hands on him—experienced hands—fighters' hands—guiding his fall.

His limbs felt heavy, trapped in taffy. Zelda's voice—

arguing? Giving orders? He turned toward the sound, trying to focus on her face.

She'd said she loved him.

And she'd fed him drugged candies.

His heart broke as darkness closed in.

CHAPTER FORTY

"No!" Zelda screamed and kicked and twisted as two Associates half dragged, half carried Hugo away by the arms. "No!"

Hugo tried to shake them off, but they'd given him something powerful.

"Let me go!" She fought to get out of Riley's grip and get to Hugo. Riley's fingertips dug into her arms. "Be careful! He's shot in the shoulder!"

"They can see that," Riley said. "They'll take care."

Hugo.

God, the way Hugo had looked at her at the end. He thought she'd drugged him. Well, she had. Probably injected right into the middle of the jelly beans. She felt like her heart was being ripped apart.

God, how did they know?

She tried to rip out of Riley's arms, limbs fueled with rage.

Dax appeared in front of her as they shut Hugo into a nearby van.

"Don't do this!"

"I'm sorry," Dax said.

"You can't," she said, knowing full well he could. Hugo's brown shoe lay on the dusty road. "His shoe, you mother-fucker," she said hoarsely.

Dax went over, grabbed the shoe, and threw it into the van. Still Riley held her. He was one of Dax's most power-ful attack dogs.

"I won't have it," she growled when Dax came back.

"No choice," Dax said. "The standoff has to end."

The van sped off. She had the impulse to collapse in tears. *Fuck that,* she thought.

"I gave you a plan. A good plan."

"The Sal angle is a no-go."

"Motherfucker." She jerked Riley's arms off her, or maybe he let her go—and went for Dax, pushing him clear up to the side of the SUV behind them, full of wild energy. "You will fucking call them back."

"And let multitudes of people die? How would you feel if we took the time we needed to turn Sal and send him after the files and the situation went hot? How would you feel about that?"

She jerked him harder against the vehicle. "My plan would've worked."

"This plan is better, faster, surer."

"Except a good man goes down."

"You suspected he was Kabakas. You wouldn't be wrong about that."

She glared, pulse racing. "He didn't do the Yacon fields massacre. He's one of the good guys."

"In *that* war?" Dax shook his head.

She drove her fist into his belly, connecting with soft flesh. He doubled over, holding his belly. He hadn't even hardened for it.

"He's one of the good guys." She caught Riley's haunted look. She had maybe one more strike before he stopped her. "Call them back."

"I won't do that."

Riley stood by, fierce and strong. Dax was the perceived leader now. They'd at least spoken with Dax; they didn't even know her. Yeah, Dax had been too happy to let her be the silent partner and she'd gladly taken it, more effects of the shame. Had he always anticipated a rift?

Of course. Dax anticipated everything.

She sucked in her breath, trying to get her head clear.

"Only two blues and one yellow," she said. "How did you know I wouldn't eat them myself?"

"Because they're your favorites."

"All the more reason for me to eat them."

Dax shook his head. "Rio saw you together. He watched you. He told us that you'd give your favorites over to Kabakas, that you'd want him to have the best."

She went for him again, but this time Riley stopped her.

Her pulse drummed. They knew how she felt about Kabakas. It meant that they would be expecting her to do anything to free him—ready for her to go all-out.

"I wish I could do better for you."

"Fuck you," she hissed. "Act on it, then. Grow a conscience for once!"

He gave her one of those dark Dax looks. Weary resolve.

She surged at him again, but Riley had her. "How many

people did you have to fuck to blot this one out?"

Dax brushed off his sleeve. "Three so far."

She twisted out of Riley's grip and lifted her hands to show she was done. She had to be smart now. She went to the overlook where she and Hugo had stood minutes ago. No matter how she escalated her efforts, she'd be matched by Riley and Dax until she, too was being bound or drugged in the back of their vehicle. That would not help Hugo. She sucked in a breath, trying to calm her rage, trying not to think about what the enemies of Kabakas would do to Hugo. She'd told Hugo that she had his back and now it was happening all over again—her, letting a good man down.

She leaned over, gripping the bar, letting her forehead touch the metal, warm from the sun.

The fact that she hadn't known, couldn't have known, was drowned out by an oceanic surge of old shame and guilt.

Dax came up next to her. "Is El Gorrion still alive?"

"Why wouldn't he be?" she snapped.

"Would've been best if Hugo had killed El Gorrion. Surely you agree."

"Hugo's one of the good guys."

Dax gave her a look. It didn't matter to Dax.

She looked away, disgusted.

"Do you know how most partnerships die?" he asked.

"Betrayal?"

"I deserve that, of course," he said. "But no. It's the things that attract the partners to each other that break them apart. You liked me because I see what nobody else can see. And because I have the balls to do what needs to be done, even if it's repugnant."

She'd said that, of course.

"I liked your tenaciousness," Dax continued. "Your passion for justice. It's what we have in common."

"We have nothing in common."

"What did you say at the beginning when I told you not to go after your sister?" Casually, he flicked a bit of brown hair from his eyes. Just another day at the office for Dax. "You said that everybody is expendable, even you. That what we do is bigger than one person."

"Don't you dare."

"It's what you said, Zelda, and the fact that you don't agree now is irrelevant."

She waited for him to give her some sort of "live by the sword, die by the sword" rationale with Hugo. She thought that if he did that, she really would kill him. But Dax was too smart for that. Too smooth.

She took a measured breath and forced aside the messy spiral of guilt, the shame, the rage. She'd told Hugo she had his back, and she meant it. She'd do what it took to get Hugo back. Whatever it took. She knew how the Associates worked. She could figure out how to defeat them.

She took another breath and loosened her grip on the rail, purely for Dax's benefit, letting the pink go back into her knuckles, even though she felt like ripping the thing from its concrete footings and casting it to the rocks below.

Dax would put Hugo at one of the hotels he owned. The Embajador, probably. It was perfect for holding dangerous people—a few of the rooms featured soundproofing and hookups of the structural kind. Hugo would have to pull the whole hotel down to get loose. They'd arrange a transfer.

They'd expect her to try something. She guessed that Dax would put Riley in charge of her until the transfer of Hugo to the vice president was complete. Nobody got away from Riley.

Cole came up from the other way. He didn't like this— she could tell from his dead expression and from the way he chewed his gum. None of them would like this, but they were loyal, these men. Dax had saved a lot of them.

Cole nodded at her. She nodded back. People were tense.

"The metal canister in the Jeep. We need it to save the *Savinca verde* fields up around Buena Vista," she said. "El Gorrion poisoned the savinca. There's a notebook next to it with a formula and instructions. Somebody needs to take it to this farmer there—Julian." She made Dax put Cole on it and she gave him elaborate instructions. He'd handle it. He took off with one of the guys.

Dax left with another Associate, dust kicking up behind the shiny black vehicle.

She felt Riley come up behind her. "Let's go."

She spun, going for his weapon. In a swift, simple movement he caught her hand in a lock. She'd have to break it in three places to get out. She would've been more of a match for him in her agent days.

"Please," Riley said. "I know you had to try, but..." He would let her break her own hand. And in a way she wanted to break it. She wanted to die when she thought what Hugo must think.

"Fuck," she said.

"I'm sorry, I really am," he said as he whipped out handcuffs.

"Don't."

"Just until this is over." He slapped them around her wrists in front of her.

She wrenched away from him and he caught her by the shoulders. "Save us both the trouble—"

A gunshot sounded, shoving him into her. He tightened his hands on her as if for support. With the second shot he was down.

"Riley!" She knelt and grabbed his gun but they were surrounded suddenly by men in battle fatigues, half with assault rifles pointed at her, half at Riley.

She let go of Riley's gun just as El Gorrion appeared.

Even if she hadn't seen the photos, she'd know him from his aura. El Gorrion was a thickset, clean-cut man with a neatly trimmed beard—he'd look like an office worker on holiday if it weren't for the cold eyes and the camouflage baseball cap that matched his green jacket.

"Where is he? Where is Kabakas?"

"Fuck off."

He grabbed her by the hair. She went for his trachea, then his balls. A blinding pain on the back of her skull made the world burst like a fireball and darken completely.

CHAPTER FORTY-ONE

He was in some sort of hotel room, shackled to a wall by chains that went to a wrist cuff that would be near impossible to break free from.

Hugo didn't know how he'd woken up; he could feel the sedative still working in him. A powerful sedative. The candies. They'd patched up his shoulder at one point. No doubt it had started bleeding again when they dragged him away.

He feigned sleep, fighting to keep real sleep from coming over him by pushing his fingernails into his own flesh. The pain was nothing compared to the fire of confusion raging inside him. It had been her idea to stop, and yes, she had fed him the drugged candies, picking out specific ones and insisting that he eat them. *You will love this.* And yes, these were her people.

Yes, even as every fact around him screamed that she had betrayed him, but still he couldn't believe it. He trusted her passion. He trusted her heart.

Men moved in and out of the room—he tracked them with his eyes closed. There was always at least one keeping watch over him at all times. He could tell by the chat between them that they were setting up a meet of some sort. He'd be handed off—to the vice president, no doubt.

He identified the man in charge by his tone of voice—Dax, people called him. Dax spent time on the phone, negotiating. One trade was to lead to another. Earlier this Dax had sent a team to the mountain, to Hugo's home—to find *proof and provenance*, he'd said. Proof that he was Kabakas, no doubt. They'd pull it together, no problem; these were the famous and feared Associates. He thought about the savinca. Were they doing anything to get the recipe to his people?

He felt Dax draw near at one point, but not near enough that he could take him out with his legs, assuming his legs could still function. Bedsprings creaked, telling him that Dax had settled onto a nearby bed. Silent for a while. Watching him. Alone in the room as far as Hugo could tell. If only he would come near.

"You know what we do," Dax whispered suddenly. "You know how it is."

Hugo's heart thundered. Was he talking to him? Did Dax know he was awake? No, he couldn't know. Hugo stayed still, regulating his breathing to mimic sleep. He had the element of surprise; he wasn't about to lose it.

He knew only one thing: Zelda wouldn't have wanted this. She would stop it if she could. So where was she?

Hugo felt the fire flow into his limbs.

CHAPTER FORTY-TWO

She awoke in a dim, cavernous space, tied upright to a bench of some sort, head lolling to the side, throbbing with pain from the blow.

From the scent on the air and the sounds outside, she guessed she was in El Gorrion's compound. Her wrists were bound behind her to two cool metal poles—slender and squarish with notches in them. Her legs were tied straight out in front of her on a padded bench; ropes cut into her thighs and calves, even through her jeans. She could make out a corrugated metal roof in the dim light. A shed? A garage? She shifted around, realizing that she was on a modified weightlifting machine. Which meant it was very unbreakable.

Not good.

She sensed other people around, possibly behind her, so she stayed quiet as a mouse as she went to work wriggling her hands and wrists. Not a lot of wriggle room, but sometimes if you wriggled enough...

Voices behind her. Three men, maybe four or five, some distance away. Then footsteps, light on the dirt ground. Her heart sunk.

"*Ella está despierta,*" he said. *She's awake.*

The footsteps continued and she found herself face to face with El Gorrion.

She gazed up at the shaft of light coming down from a skylight, working her hands.

He addressed her in Spanish. "You know how to find Kabakas. It's all we need. All we want. Tell us, and you'll be on your way. We know now that he is the farmer, Hugo Martinez. Tell us where he went."

"*Nunca,*" she hissed.

He knelt beside her.

No way would she send El Gorrion's men to the hotel. The Associates would have Hugo chained up—he'd be a sitting duck, especially if they had him in a room alone. And El Gorrion's men would have the element of surprise over the Associates. Good agents could die.

He moved to the end of the bench—near her feet. Horror speared through her. He couldn't know—he couldn't. He began to untie her boot, watching her face.

He knew.

She swallowed, fighting to keep her expression neutral, trying to keep her pulse from racing. Not that it would matter.

El Gorrion focused on her intensely, almost clinically, as he loosened the laces, just as Friar Hovde had. He continued on, seeming fascinated with her lack of reaction. Or maybe he saw some reaction. Surely he saw the pulse banging away inside her throat.

"What should we do now, do you think?" He loosened the leather, pulling apart the sides, freeing the tongue. He pulled off the boot with sickening gentleness.

No jerking, she told herself, *no sounds.* She would give him nothing, and most certainly not the intimacy of her fear. She'd broken down with the Friar, screamed and begged. Never again.

She swallowed as he yanked her sock off. Her foot was bare and vulnerable to him at the end of the bench, now. And she so wanted to scream.

Instead she worked furiously at the knots binding her wrists. Tying bad knots wasn't a mistake El Gorrion's men would make, but she went for it anyway, just to have something to focus on. She couldn't do this again, she *couldn't.*

Stop thinking like that.

He began untying the other boot, watching her in that eerie way, like a vampire, almost, feeding on her fear. She'd gotten the sense that Friar Hovde had no interior life, and El Gorrion seemed like that, too. He spoke to her in Spanish. He'd learned everything about her, apparently. "It's a known fact that people who crumble under pressure once are ten times more likely to crumble again. Did you know that?"

"If that's what you need to believe, go for it," she said with a lightness she didn't feel.

His knuckle grazed her stocking foot as he worked, sending a sickening shock through her. Even the brush of the sock set her nerves going. How would she handle the blade?

He continued on with those gentle movements.

The gentleness was horrible in just the same way that it was horrible to extend kindness to a man you were sending to his death. It was something about the contrast—the lavish last meal followed by the electric chair. This killer's light caress before the cutting. Removing the boot so gently.

Her heart pounded.

He had access to the report, like a treasure map to her weakness, her cowardice, her frailty. He knew everything.

Nothing bad has happened yet, she told herself, but it was a lie. Something bad *had* happened. Something bad would happen now. Finally El Gorrion had both of her boots off. Even in the socks, her feet felt naked. The air was warm and humid, but it felt cold on her feet.

The socks would be next.

Would he start where the Friar had left off? Threatening to sever her Achilles heel, the thick, fat tendon that connected her heel to her calf? Or would he clip off the tips of three toes as the Friar had? Would he take an entire toe?

She told herself it didn't matter. Torture was a kind of odyssey you entered into. Once in, degrees meant nothing. Soft and hard and painful and less painful—it was all part of the same hell.

She closed her eyes. There was one thing he wouldn't know about—the injection to enhance the pain that Friar Hovde had given her. She'd never told anybody about it. Except Hugo.

Her throat felt thick, thinking about Hugo. Where was he now? How many hours had passed?

"It's harder for them to hold up a second time," El Gorrion continued, pulling off a sock. The cotton grazed her ankle as he pulled. It tickled her foot. "The pain has created neural pathways. As has the fear. As has the relief from cooperation. You know how to make it stop. You know it's within your power at any given time."

With that, he tossed aside the sock. He started on the other.

"You disagree?" he pressed when she didn't answer.

He would get nothing from her.

She had Hugo's back—her view of him felt so pure, suddenly. And she had the Association's back—they were still her people. She would go down trusting the things that she knew in her heart.

CHAPTER FORTY-THREE

Hugo wanted to kill this asshole Dax. He had the wild feeling that if Zelda were with him, she would feel just as enraged.

She would come if she could. In his mind he replayed her voice—that angry pitch, that volume. Enraged. Surprised. She was not complicit in this. What had they done to her?

He had to get free.

Another phone call. Dax stood, paced as he spoke. Through the haze of the sedative, Hugo spotted the outline of keys in the man's pocket. If only Dax would pass near enough, he would attack him and take them. But Dax, this was not a stupid man; he was a ruthless man.

Dax would not draw close enough for an attack. Even if he did, he'd make a poor hostage because his ruthlessness would extend to himself—a man like this would kill himself just to neutralize his value. Hugo had met men like Dax at the farthest reaches of jungles and deserts and battlefields. So extreme as to be barely human.

Hugo shut his eyes as another male entered—with coffee, from the smell of it. Dax thanked him. They spoke on about the exchange. Transport. Transfers. Wrappers crunched. The scent of spiced meat and warm bread reached Hugo's nose.

Another came—this one full of energy. "We've lost contact with Riley."

"What?" Dax said.

"GPS shows him still at the overlook. I've sent Kendrick out to investigate."

"That can't be right," Dax said. "He wouldn't have kept her there."

Her?

"What if he lost control of her?" the first one said. "If she was able to surprise him and disable him—"

"We'd know about it by now," Dax said.

Lost control of her? Disable him? Hugo pulled at his bonds, ready to rip them from the wall, rip his hands from his wrists.

She wasn't in on it. He'd always known it. He had to get to her.

"Zelda can't overpower Riley. I don't care what kind of advantage...she's out of practice and this is *Riley*." Dax sounded upset.

They didn't know what had happened, but Hugo had a good idea: El Gorrion had arrived. He'd taken out the Associates' men, and he probably had Zelda now. The whole picture came together suddenly—El Gorrion had connected Zelda to Kabakas. They'd been tracking them through Bumcara. The buildup around the compound was about Kabakas. El Gorrion was looking to square off against Kabakas, somehow.

And if he was right...if El Gorrion thought Zelda knew who he was, where he was...

Another man came in. "Riley's down. Shot, beaten up pretty bad. His vest saved him."

Ice filled Hugo's veins.

A flurry of activity followed—arguments, calls to people on the ground, calls into traffic surveillance.

Hugo slit open his eyes, knowing the focus was firmly off him. His heart pounded—he had to get to her. He wanted to shout and rage, but that would not help her.

CHAPTER FORTY-FOUR

The jowly sides of El Gorrion's thick neck vibrated slightly as he sat himself down on the stool he'd placed at the end of the bench Zelda was tied to.

He arranged a set of scalpels on the cracked red padding on either side of her feet, like a workman arranging his tools. This was part of it, of course, the anticipation. He held each item up, as if to inspect it, but it was really about showing her. Lastly he picked up a small switchblade.

He addressed her in Spanish. "The great Valencian muralist Sima once said, 'steal only what belongs to you.' Have you heard of him?"

Ah, the mindfuck portion. The torturer making himself the agreeable friend.

"He was speaking of subject matter. When you see something that belongs to you, you must make it your own. A rock on the hillside. An old man's expression. Half the key to art is finding what belongs to you."

Her blood raced as he flicked open a blade.

"The answer to my question—where is Kabakas—is trapped inside of you. It is this that belongs to me. You can give it to me, or I will cut it from you. I will not stop cutting until I have it. Do you understand? I will cut as the sculptor cuts the truth from the stone." He tilted his head and looked into her eyes with his flat, cold gaze. "No?"

She would give him nothing.

She cringed as he laid his hand over the top of her right foot with an air of ownership.

"I am man of honor. I will take only the answer. I would not rape you and degrade you as others might, for example. That is not mine. Personally, I believe rape dishonors a man as well as a woman. Don't you agree?"

Yeah, this was the game. He gets her to agree to small easy things as a way to break her for the big things.

She wouldn't even give him that.

"Okay, then." He took hold of her toes and, with his eyes on hers, he pressed the point of the blade to the tender sole of her right foot, letting her feel it.

A sick, panicky feeling filled her chest as the bite of the slice came, then he drew the blade along the bottom of her foot. The blood drops tickled. The tickle made the pain worse.

He paused, but the bite continued. "Must we go on? You understand that I would let you go, given useful information. I would not have to kill you. I am a man of honor, and I have little to fear from the *policía.*"

"You'll get nothing."

"I'll get everything," he said.

He began another cut. She focused on Hugo, a strong rock in the cold sea. She told herself she had Hugo's back, and he had hers. That was their pact.

The cut went deeper. The pain took her over inside, the shrieking feeling of it, and she could no longer hold onto

Hugo; she was back in the farmhouse with the crazy Friar.

"Kabakas is coming," she gasped, trying to keep herself focused on him. "He may make it in time to save me, or he'll come after. Maybe days or weeks after, but he will come, and he will *destroy* you." She clenched her teeth, working at her bonds. She didn't know if she believed it, but it felt good to say. "You're already dead," she gritted out.

"He would save you? He would save the one who hunted him?"

"Yes," she whispered. Yes, she'd hunted Hugo. Yes, she'd unwittingly fed him the drugged Jelly Bellies. Yes, Dax had played her perfectly. But she'd given her word and she'd meant it. Surely he knew.

She had Hugo's back. She loved him.

El Gorrion paused midway in his cutting. He'd been making parallel slices and it messed her up that he'd stopped like that, because it would be worse when he started again at the midpoint. She'd been bearing the pain in swaths.

El Gorrion clicked his tongue twice inside his mouth. *Click, click.* "Nobody will save you."

CHAPTER FORTY-FIVE

Men passed in and out. A team was dispatched. The room emptied. Dax paced, upset, barking orders. Dax wanted to save her; that was clear.

But he wouldn't. He couldn't.

And soon enough, a distracted Dax, alone for the moment, passed just a bit too close to Hugo's unconscious form. Hugo shot out his legs and pulled him down onto the carpeted floor with a thud. Dax shouted in surprise, but the room was clearly soundproofed.

Hugo flipped him around—he'd trained this a million times, dominating and manipulating a man with his legs alone. He quickly had Dax where he wanted him, head and arms pinned between his thighs. He squeezed the man's neck like a vise, creating a triangle with his knee and thigh, cutting off his blood supply. When he felt Dax go limp, he pulled him closer and ripped at his pocket with his teeth, extracting the keys. Not three minutes later he was free and Dax was chained up.

Hugo grabbed every firearm he could find. His dexterity was shot to hell. How would he throw like this? He could barely check to see if the weapons were loaded.

Dax began to rouse. "Where are you going?" he asked casually.

"To do what you can't." His senses were muffled. It wasn't good.

Dax gazed at him, watching him with those penetrating eyes. "You think El Gorrion has her, don't you?"

Hugo said nothing.

"You think he has your Zelda."

"You don't get to say her name," Hugo said. "You don't even see her right."

"I see everybody right. Even you."

He wanted to kick the man's face in, but he wouldn't waste the time. A few of the fighters had left coffees in the room and Hugo slammed them, one after another. He needed the caffeine—it was as if the world was swathed in haze.

"You can't save her," Dax said. "It won't work, what you're going to do."

Hugo slammed another coffee. Too late he felt the presence of other men; he spun around to find a gun barrel pressed against his forehead.

CHAPTER FORTY-SIX

The bottoms of her feet were ribbons. Her pulse was a frenzy of panic, waiting for him to cut again as blood dripped down her heel from the last cut.

El Gorrion put down the blade. Keeping her off balance. He shifted on his stool and pulled something from a pocket of his green fatigue pants.

She'd recognize the implement anywhere—clippers used on the nails of very large dogs, the kind that Friar Hovde had used on her toes.

She felt like throwing up. "Been there, done that," she said, not caring that he wouldn't understand her. He placed the cool end on one of her undamaged toes. She closed her eyes. The pain of what he'd already done spiraled into sharp shapes.

Her eyes flew open and she stared at him, aghast.

She'd only remembered her capitulation; she hadn't remembered the intensity of it. The wild pain. It really was extreme, what she'd endured from the Friar. A man cutting on her? After injecting her with drugs that enhanced her fear? And then the way he'd begun to saw at her Achilles heel? She'd lasted hours in that basement with him. How had she lasted that long? She could barely handle it now and it was only minutes in—and she hadn't been shot full of drugs. How had she endured that night? How could anybody have?

Something dark passed behind El Gorrion's eyes, sensing a trick, perhaps. This was no trick, though.

All these years she'd seen only her failure, hated herself for talking, but God, through the blood, the drugs, the endless hours at the mercy of that psycho Friar, she'd lasted a long time. A very long time.

The realization was more powerful than any cut El Gorrion could make.

She'd lasted as long as she could.

She'd done her best, and she'd do her best now. It was all anybody could do.

She looked into the eyes of this horrible man with his doughy neck and his empty soul and her heart filled with gratitude.

Simple, pure gratitude.

All these years she had never given herself credit for how painful and terrifying it was to be helpless at the hands of a psycho with a table full of terrifying tools.

She'd felt so worthless for so long, so full of shame for talking. The self-hatred was like poison in her veins. But she'd done her best. It was a hard thing and she'd done her best.

Tears streamed down her cheeks. The tears had nothing to do with fear or pain and everything to do with forgiving herself.

"Thank you," she whispered, weeping, now, with the

relief of it.

"Ready to tell me?"

She emitted a breathy laugh, incredulous. "Fuck you," she said. "I was thinking about something else."

CHAPTER FORTY-SEVEN

Hugo rode shotgun, hanging onto the side rail as they sped up the dark jungle trail that led to the back of El Gorrion's compound. He sucked in the humid night air, hoping it would wake him. The Jeep bounced violently, and now and then a branch whipped his face. He barely felt any of it. All he could feel was a sick twist of his heart at the thought of Zelda in the clutches of that madman.

He needed to get to her.

Her eyes got a certain tight look when she was worried or frightened. She would look like that and he wouldn't be by her side. She'd be alone, bravely enduring whatever El Gorrion would do to her.

He found it unbearable.

He had to get to her—whatever it took. In this case, it had taken a promise to Dax that he'd turn himself in to the vice president when it was over. He would let the vice president do what he would. Better him than Zelda.

The killer in the tailored suit drove—Rio, he was called. Rio hadn't introduced himself as a killer, but Hugo had gotten it right away from his gravity. You reached a certain body count in a certain way, and it gave you dark gravity that regular fighters didn't have. Rio drove expertly and relentlessly and Hugo knew that was how he would kill.

Dax rode in back with Riley, the agent El Gorrion's men had taken down. The one who was supposed to have kept Zelda with him. Hugo wanted to hit him, but he hadn't, because the main thing was to get to Zelda. Riley was bloody and injured and pissed as hell and somebody up there would pay, and that would have to be enough.

Four other guys followed behind in a different vehicle. Eight men they had.

The Associates had taken him down easily after he had chained Dax up. Drugged like he'd been, Hugo could fight one man, but not several who were all pointing guns at him. You needed lightning reflexes and a wide awareness to take on several armed men at once, and the sedative in the candies had taken those things from him.

When they'd finally had him subdued, Hugo had told them where he thought Zelda would be, told them about the buildup, which they seemed to know about. They knew, too, that they couldn't take the compound with a handful of fighters—not keeping Zelda alive, anyway. It was Riley who had come up with the plan to infiltrate the compound in concert with Kabakas.

Kabakas would spread fear and take out soldiers. El Gorrion's men would focus on that, allowing the Associates to hit from the sides and back. With Kabakas sowing fear and chaos, they could take the compound.

Dax made Hugo give his word to turn himself in when it was done—he had made it ironclad and formal. Dax was no fighter, but he was as dangerous as any of them in the way he worked you.

They stowed the vehicles and went the rest of the way on foot. Hugo had seen the back way to get in while he and Zelda had been out there earlier. It was harder to find the back trail at night, but not impossible. Hugo had always felt at home in the wilderness.

The small group took down the perimeter guards one by one and stripped them of their weapons and uniforms. El Gorrion liked the uniforms because he saw himself as a general. The uniforms made an infiltration attack easier.

Hugo would go in with the mask and blades.

Hugo preferred to attack on neutral territory; men would give up neutral territory. This was their home base, which was almost as dangerous as putting an enemy against a wall. It would not go easy for him, but nothing would go easy for him ever again.

The only important thing was to get to Zelda. She had changed him deeply and forever—he understood that now. She was his heart, and the idea of her frightened and in pain destroyed him, and it reached into his soul and destroyed that, too.

In addition to the guards' uniforms, the Associates took the guards' radios and used them well, giving reports in Spanish of Kabakas being spotted on different sides of the compound, stoking panic. A few of them could throw knives. Not as well as Hugo could, but knives coming from multiple directions would add to the panic. The one direction they wouldn't come from was the road out. They would funnel them out.

It was a decent plan.

He and Rio split off from the group at the edge. Rio

stayed silent as they slipped through the underbrush. At a stop-off in the shadows, Rio offered Hugo a sidearm. It was a white platinum Smith & Wesson—a custom job, from the looks of it. "Slides in and out of your boot like butter and the action is beautiful," Rio said.

"I like blades," Hugo said.

Rio tipped his head as if to remind him that he was drugged and sluggish. "It's one of my favorites, this one." He pressed it into Hugo's palm, the grip first. "And you're going after Zelda."

Hugo took it also because a man like Rio had intuition, and you wanted to heed that when possible. Also, it was more than a weapon; it was a gesture, and Hugo respected a man who spoke like that. It came to Hugo that if he got cut down, Rio could probably do something for Zelda out there.

"Thank you," he said, slipping it into his boot.

The idea was that he and Rio would work as a team at the center, spearing through to get Zelda. Rio would be his invisible partner. Rio could pretend to hold him prisoner if it came to it, and they could do something that way.

CHAPTER FORTY-EIGHT

Another cut, and then a space of rest. Zelda felt the blood run fast now. She looked away, lightheaded, thinking about savinca flowers, the wild red streak of blooms across the green fields outside Hugo's home. Cole would get that formula to Julian. Those two men would get along well, actually. Those beautiful flowers would be saved.

God, she'd had so much beauty in these past days—spending time with her sister, being able to help her. Feeling like a family with Hugo and Paolo. Loving Hugo. She loved him—she really did. Maybe he didn't love her back, but her love wasn't conditional. She loved him, and it felt amazing, like something good inside her heart. Being with Hugo made her feel like her old self. Better, really.

She felt the blood and thought about the *Savinca verde*.

"Perhaps we should proceed to the main event." El Gorrion picked up the blade.

He touched her just behind the anklebone, cold and sharp on the fleshy indent he meant to slice into.

"When I sever this muscle, it will pull up into your leg most painfully."

He waited, watching her.

She furrowed her brow, feeling strangely removed from the situation, maybe because she'd lived it over and over in her dreams so many times, and that made it seem less dire. She'd lived through the worst of it already. She was ready.

CHAPTER FORTY-NINE

Hugo and Rio headed in the side. Rio cut apart a section of barbed wire with practiced efficiency, then Hugo held the chain link fence, and Rio clipped that. They tossed the tools and stole in.

El Gorrion's men were milling around inside, a group of them talking some hundred yards away near a hut. Noisy trucks passed back and forth with men hanging out the back. The compound was arranged like an army base, with crude roads on a grid between metal huts, and lights strung up on poles. Lots of light. Lots of shadow. Vehicles were parked all around—perhaps intentionally; they'd make good cover. Some distance behind the first group were maybe a hundred men around an outbuilding, and more beyond that.

If this was how many waited on the side of the compound, it meant that there were a lot more men than they'd imagined.

It meant they'd take longer getting to Zelda.

The soldiers hadn't noticed the two of them yet, but they would soon. That was the plan.

It was time. Hugo caught Rio's eye.

Rio nodded. *I have your back*—that was what the nod

said. Hugo trusted Rio—he was the kind of dangerous man you wanted with you in a fight. But there was something else there in the killer's eyes, a certain calm that Hugo didn't like. This would be a hard fight—there were too many men—but Rio seemed calm, even indifferent. Some indifference was critical in a fight—worrying about getting hit was the fastest way to get hit—but Rio struck him as too indifferent. Too dark.

Rio caught his eyes and something passed between them, a kind of understanding.

Rio nodded and moved off, disappearing into the shadows. It was time. Hugo lowered his mask, pulled a pair of blades from his bandolier, and threw.

Cries went up and a man staggered. The field erupted in a deafening chaos of gunfire.

He began his trek toward the mass of men. Into the shooting.

Many scattered. Many didn't. Those who didn't kept shooting.

This was bad.

Hugo kept on as they shot, heart pounding, throwing as fast as he could, hitting the worst-seeming threats. He could hear gunfire from the side—Rio, taking out the men. Some of them fell, more of them broke off and ran. Still some stayed and shot, most taking cover behind vehicles and huts. It was a battle of nerves as more appeared and shot. They were shooting wild, frightened. Why weren't they running? Had El Gorrion threatened them? Their families?

He was hit in the left thigh, like a punch to the leg. He forced himself to keep walking through the lightning burn of it, to keep throwing blades. He could feel the blood warm on his leg, spreading. It hurt like hell, and every time he put his weight on that leg, he wasn't sure it wouldn't collapse under him like a house of cards. But he kept on—image was important. He felt the zing of a bullet at his ear. A nick.

More blood. More warmth.

Then the assault weaponry started. The Associates, coming from behind. That sent a lot of men running. Everything was blood and confusion suddenly.

The focus was off Hugo. He took off at a run for the center of the compound where they believed she was being held, leg blaring with pain, blood running down his neck. Legions more men appeared and he had to stop and fight again. Tossing, walking, bleeding. He began to feel faint. The drugs. Maybe the blood loss.

The pattern of the fallen told him that Rio had stayed with him, but there were so many men, too many. Could they do enough damage to get to her?

Men kept appearing. He was tiring, losing blood.

CHAPTER FIFTY

She took a breath, centering herself. She could trust herself to handle things. To do her best.

Shouts and gunfire sounded in the near distance. El Gorrion waved lazily, dispatching one of the men to investigate. Then he turned to her. "You think this is funny?"

"No," she said simply.

He turned her ankle, positioned it. Then he inspected his implements, taking his time, trying to unnerve her.

More gunfire. Were the men celebrating? She felt sick. The shooting grew in volume, intensity.

El Gorrion rose, moving toward the door.

A respite. String together enough of them and you had a life. Zelda took another deep breath.

There were more shouts and shots. Not a celebration; the place was under attack.

Could it be?

From the door, El Gorrion gave her a sly glance. "It works also if he comes to us."

Her blood raced.

El Gorrion and his three men flattened themselves on either side of the door. She worked furiously at the bonds, with renewed effort, now. Hugo needed her. And Jesus, if Hugo looked in, he'd see only her. He'd come in. it was like the nightmare, her not getting free. She could sense when he was near.

"It's a trap!" she screamed.

El Gorrion grinned. She felt sick.

"Don't come in!"

The door darkened and Hugo bounded in, staggering, mask off, neck and shirt bloody. *Hugo.* He'd fought his way to her.

She cried out as El Gorrion's men closed around him. They struggled, kicked, and finally took him down. It didn't seem possible, but they had him. He'd been drugged not so long ago, of course.

He faced her, cheek to the ground, a boot on his head. Five men holding him down. He'd been wounded—in the thigh.

"Hugo," she whispered.

El Gorrion strolled across the place and stopped between them. She cried out in frustration as he blocked her from looking into Hugo's eyes. She needed him. She always had.

"Is this Kabakas?" he asked.

"I'm Kabakas," Hugo said.

El Gorrion crowed in rapid Spanish. "And here he is. As I had always said, Kabakas is nothing but flash. You remove the mask, the sword...." He toed Hugo's neck. "He is nothing but a fairy tale."

A new man came in with a pair of swords—the souvenir kind. "Thank you," El Gorrion said, taking them and swinging them in the pattern that Hugo typically did. "I could never get a man in the eye with a blade as you could, but I made a rather fair facsimile out in the Yacon fields. You leave only one man alive. It is convenient—it meant I had only one person to plant, to pay. I found a man with exceptional storytelling talent."

Her heart jumped into her throat. It was just as Hugo had told her—the Yacon fields massacre was a setup. Hugo gazed at El Gorrion grimly, listening, seeming to wait. For what?

El Gorrion was Dark Kabakas. She worked furiously at her bonds.

El Gorrion smiled an oily smile. "Heroic Kabakas did not seem so heroic after that." He strolled a few steps, going on about what he'd done, and once again she had the connection with Hugo.

"I love you," Hugo said.

He loved her.

"Hugo," she whispered. The love felt like an old friend, like it had always been there. Hugo had always been there, and she was happy to be with him now. She never wanted to be away from him. "Hugo," she said. The name contained everything.

And then somebody kicked him. The kick stung worse than any cut El Gorrion had made. She could endure her own injuries, but not Hugo's. It frightened her deeply, the power their connection gave to El Gorrion. But at the same time, she found strength in that connection. It was bright and beautiful and it stretched forever.

"I love you, Hugo," she said. She felt like they were somewhere forever together. But oh, he was bleeding badly—the whole side of his head.

Soldiers began crowding in the door, lining up around the sides. She yanked at the ropes. El Gorrion was going to chop Hugo with the blades.

But then El Gorrion turned to her with a grin on his jowly face, and she realized she was wrong. He'd chop her first.

She took a breath and eyed Hugo. She wouldn't scream; she'd live and die in his eyes.

Hugo eyed her back. She'd learned to read Hugo in these past days, and the calm she saw now baffled her, but she let herself fall into it, trusting him.

El Gorrion advanced, slow steps, or maybe it was the adrenaline kicking in, slowing things. It seemed slow motion when some of the soldiers standing around the edges of the dim space began to cry out and fall. What was going on?

There were shouts and shots. The men all around seemed to be fighting amongst themselves. Suddenly Hugo surged to his feet. He took a soldier on his right with a blade and the other with a gun.

El Gorrion spun on him, and Hugo lunged. The movement was pure animal, knocking him to the ground.

Shots came from somewhere else. Had one of the soldiers turned?

The place erupted into mayhem.

The barongs flew. There was a crack as Hugo hit El Gorrion in the face.

Suddenly somebody was behind her, untying her hands.

"Rio!" She rubbed her wrists as he cut her legs free. She could hear him swear as he saw her feet. "I'm getting you out of here," he said.

"No, we have to help Hugo. Give me something."

"Some of these guys coming in are ours," he said, pulling her off the bench. He pushed it over to create a shield. And started shooting.

Her mouth fell open. "You're *coordinating* with Hugo."

"Long story."

Everything was confusion in the place, but there was Hugo, fighting like a bloody Phoenix. Chaos was his element. He took people down.

El Gorrion's soldiers were already scattering.

And then they were gone and everything was quiet. El Gorrion lay on the ground, cowering at the end of Hugo's blade. Riley and Cole and Kendrick and a few other guys were there in the El Gorrion greens. They took over for Hugo, who cast his blades aside and headed for her like a man on fire.

She stood. She didn't care about her feet. She didn't feel anything except the pull of Hugo, long legs eating up the distance between them.

"You were working together," she said to nobody in particular.

"*Corazón.*" Hugo wrapped his arms around her, lifting her up into his arms. "*Corazón, corazón, corazón,*" he whispered.

"I'm okay," she said, because he needed to know that first and foremost. She linked her arms around his neck. "I'm okay."

He pulled her violently against his body. The way he clutched her to him was harsh and good, like him.

Over his shoulder she saw a soldier who looked a lot like Dax join the men who were standing over El Gorrion.

It *was* Dax. He gave her a look. She met his eyes over Hugo's shoulder, feeling none of the old friendship.

Dax went to stand over El Gorrion. "We've got plans for you," Dax said. "I find it exceedingly interesting that El Gorrion..." he looked up at her "...was Kabakas all along."

She understood instantly. Dax would be delivering El Gorrion to the vice president. El Gorrion had confessed to acting as Kabakas. Delivering him would end the standoff.

She just took it in. It would take more than that to repair things.

Riley yanked El Gorrion up and somebody spun him around and cuffed him.

Hugo swiped a small blade from the bench—the blade El Gorrion had used to cut her—and handed it to her. "Take the blade, *corazón*.

"What?"

"Do it."

She took it. Hugo spun with her in his arms and headed over to where they had El Gorrion handcuffed. She felt the energy vibrating through him. "He's hers," Hugo growled to the group as he stopped, still holding her aloft, face to face now with El Gorrion.

Dax's dark eyes flashed from the side. "We need him. We're going to use him."

"Only if she doesn't want him." Hugo kissed her cheek. "He's yours, *corazón*. Finish him."

The blade felt electric in her hands. El Gorrion shrank against the wall. "Finish him. Finish the nightmares. He cut you with the blade. You'll finish it."

Kendrick held him in place. She thought he might slide to the ground if Kendrick wasn't holding him.

"She shouldn't kill him," Riley said.

"No, let her," Dax said "Let her do it. Kabakas is just as useful dead."

She looked into the man's eyes. He was Friar Hovde, right down the blade. Right down to the way he'd tied her. He'd killed so many without mercy. They could turn him over dead as well as alive. In the dream she'd wanted to stab Friar Hovde. She was always sure everything would be repaired if only she could find him and kill him.

She held onto Hugo's neck with one hand, the other she gripped the blade, caught between waking and dreaming.

Hugo lowered his voice. "He waits for you, *corazón*. If you want him."

"No." She lowered it and turned to look into Hugo's beautiful eyes. "It's not about him. It's not about any of them." She tossed it.

She became aware of a helicopter sound. Strafing the ground. Their ride home. It was done.

Riley and Kendrick led El Gorrion away.

Hugo held her close. She thought he might never put her down, and that was okay. "Did it help?" he asked. "To have his life in your hands?"

"Not really," she said.

"It didn't help a little bit?"

She smiled. "A little bit."

He kissed her forehead. "Let's go home."

EPILOGUE: FOUR MONTHS LATER

Buena Vista

Zelda ran a finger over the edge of the SUV's rear door panel. You could hardly see the seam; no clue that it was false; nothing even rattled when you thumped it.

Same with the side panels; nobody would guess a veritable arsenal was hidden in the vehicle.

Riley, Rio, Angel, and Cole would be traveling through some very hot territory—best they came off like tourists for as long as possible. The Association was in deep pursuit of a vicious organ-peddling ring—a group with lots of firepower and deep political connections throughout North and South America. Exactly the kind of case she and Dax had created the Association for.

Sometimes she couldn't swallow past the lump in her throat when she thought about what had happened between her and Dax and the other Associates. She understood Dax's choices on a theoretical level, but in her heart, she felt betrayed.

And she knew Cole, Rio, Riley, and the rest had just been taking orders from the person they'd always taken orders from. It stung, nevertheless.

The pirate standoff had been resolved, thanks to the offering of El Gorrion. Zelda had been tremendously relieved when she'd heard. Justice was as important to her as ever. Innocent lives were still important, and for her and Hugo, opening up the remote mountainside home as a staging ground for this operation against the organ ring was a no-brainer. It had been a busy week with the group of them resting up and carefully focusing on strategies, logistics, and supplies instead of what had happened out there in El Gorrion territory. They'd even done some training together out on the windswept grounds, much to Paolo's delight. It had felt good; a baby step back into Association business. Her first. And the respect had run thick between them all.

And in truth, it had been a nice break. She and Hugo and Paolo had spent a long, hot summer cutting back the plants and treating the soil. Grueling work, but it had repaired something deep in her soul, dealing with living things again, and working side by side with people who knew the plants as well as their own hands. She'd had more interesting botany conversations and arguments over the past few months than she'd had in years. And it had been amazing to see Hugo develop relationships with the people here, and the way they accepted him—especially when they found out who his mother and grandparents were.

She found the welding seam. Yeah, almost imperceptible. This, too, called to her. She ran her finger over the beginning and end of it; the metal was still cool from the night air.

Footsteps. She turned to see Riley coming out of the house with a duffel bag. He wore one of the brightly woven shirts they'd gotten at the Bumcara market. He nodded at the back panel. "You like that?"

Yeah, she liked it. "Can't even tell."

He stowed the bag and turned. "Thanks," he said. "For letting us rest and regroup. Run things out of here. I know you're still conflicted."

"Only about some things."

"Like my part in it? Keeping you from going after him?"

"I can't fault you for being loyal," she said. "Anyway, doing the wrong things for the right reasons, that's pretty much the mission statement for the whole Association, isn't it?"

He leaned back against the truck and folded his arms. "You can't extend that understanding to Dax?"

She gazed out over the valley as Hugo came out with Rio, who looked cool and crisp and dangerous as ever, even disguised as a *turista*. "It's not about understanding, it's about trust. Dax is still my best friend and I *am* coming back; it just has to be different after this. It's painful still."

"He's not doing well," Rio said. "He needs you back as a friend. Thorne thinks he's imploding."

"Dax is tougher than he seems," she said as the others came out and stuffed bags into the vehicle. "And I won't dishonor our friendship with a false reconciliation. He would hate that. And look, we've got you losers basing out of this place, right? That's a step."

Rio eyed her, relieved to finally be talking about it, she guessed. "We okay?"

"After you tried to kill the man I love?" she asked playfully.

Rio's smile was evil and beautiful. "I *didn't* kill him,

though, did I?"

Hugo's lip quirked.

Rio caught it, said nothing. They looked so different, Rio smooth and polished, Hugo with his hard, rough gravity. But they had dark things in common, these two assassins. They had entire underground rivers in common.

"Boys." Angel came up and shoved a box into the backseat. "Here's what's killing me—that fucking décor in there. I have one word for you—upholstery." She narrowed her eyes. "Maybe I should stay. Help you fix up the place."

Hugo gave the Association's resident safecracker/interior designer a dirty look. She and Hugo were ready for some alone time, and everybody knew it.

Angel snorted. "Fine. Maybe I come back here when we're done with this job. It disturbs me that it would even be like that." She opened the driver's side door. "You guys ready?"

Zelda took Hugo's hand. It felt so natural to be with him. Partners. Lovers.

Angel and Cole argued about who would drive as Liza walked out with Paolo. She and Paolo were getting dropped off at the big waterpark in Guayaquil. Liza was doing great these days—she was a natural with Paolo and she'd really pitched in on the harvest. She was thinking about staying in Buena Vista after the trip the two of them were planning to visit their parents in Okinawa.

Zelda watched Hugo roughhouse with Paolo. They were so much more physical now.

She and Hugo had talked a lot about the future. She wanted to get back into the field, maybe even freelance with the Association, but Hugo was into working the literal fields and raising Paolo. They would make it work. She could base out of Buena Vista as easily as New York. She needed the distance now.

The group of them piled into the vehicle, all except Liza, who came up and kissed Zelda on the cheek. She was back to blonde, but she had blue eyes now. "Don't do anything I wouldn't do."

Zelda narrowed her eyes.

Hugo wrapped his arms around her as Liza spun around and headed toward the SUV. Hugo had that energy she'd come to recognize, like a wild bear. She trembled with anticipation.

"And light on the junk food for Paolo, or you'll be sorry," Zelda called as Liza shut the door.

The vehicle pulled out, disappeared down the mountainside, leaving them in blissful peace and quiet.

Kind of.

When even the sound of the SUV faded into the wind, Hugo lifted her up.

"Hugo!"

He carried her into the house. His legs were all but healed now. "I am sorry, *corazón*, I cannot wait." He brought her clear through the house and out to the veranda, setting her on a slate-topped table in the sun and the wind.

"Out here?"

He didn't answer, just began tearing at her clothes.

She pushed him off. "Hold up." She slipped off and stood in front of him, unbuttoning her shirt little by little, stoking his frenzy.

She glanced out over his shoulder as she undressed,

looking out at the newly harvested field. Really it was partly harvested. There was a row on the far edge where they let the savincas bloom. She and Hugo had decided on it together, to let that farthest row of flowers bloom wild and free.

"I love you," he rasped.

She gazed into his brown eyes. "Do you think that's going to get me to take off my shirt faster?"

He came to her then and started on her pants, feverishly.

"I love you more," she whispered.

"Do you think that's going to make me not rip your clothes?"

She snorted. Everything was so different now. She understood that no amount of penance could erase the death she had caused. Her painful guilt and shame would always be with her, but that time with El Gorrion had freed her from some of the worst of it, ironically. She saw now that the guilt and shame were only small facets of her. There were other facets of her, like her love for Hugo and Liza and Paolo. And the way she was rediscovering her passion for growing things, her passion for spycraft, for justice.

It felt strange and beautiful to feel whole after feeling reduced for so long.

Hugo set her back onto the stone table and fumbled with her bra, a sexy front-clasp number. He swore in Spanish, having lost his characteristic dexterity. She let him struggle; it was just stoking up his frenzy. "Don't you dare wreck it," she commanded.

"I cannot wait, *corazón*." He tugged the bra downward over her breasts, an animal needing to get in. She loved him like this. He nuzzled and kissed her breasts, tender and rough and whiskery out there in the sunshine.

"Yes," she whispered, holding onto him tightly.

She loved this man more than anything in the world. And beyond him, at the far edge of the terraced fields, the savincas bloomed in all their wild, blood-red glory.

Thank you for reading *Behind the Mask*. I hope you enjoyed your time with Hugo and Zelda and Paolo as much as I did!

Visit me at www.authorcarolyncrane.com to learn more about my books or to get on my new release alerts list. Are you as huge of a social media addict as I am? I'm @CarolynCrane on twitter and facebook.com/AuthorCarolynCrane on Facebook. Come say hi! My email addy: carolyn@authorcarolyncrane.com.

About Carolyn Crane

Lucky for Carolyn Crane, romance novels have given her a safe outlet though which to work out her not at all insane fascination with tortured killers, dangerous secret agents, and kinky bank robbers. Today she is a RITA® Award-winning author of romantic suspense, urban fantasy, and other steamy tales adventure; she's been published by Random House, Samhain, and now her own indie self. She is married to her best friend, and they live in Minnesota with their two adoring cats. Her dirty-writing alter ego is NYT bestselling author Annika Martin.

Acknowledgments

I want to deeply and profusely thank my critique partners – Joanna Chambers, Carolyn Jewel, Jeffe Kennedy, Mark Powell, Katie Reus, and Skye Warren - for their smart, generous feedback and ideas, and for reading this book when it was in various states of chaos. You guys are so amazing—I would be lost without you. Deb Nemeth did the beautiful developmental edit and copy edit, and Carrie Smoot seriously delivered with the proofreading! Author Penny Watson (who also happens to be a trained botanist) spent tons of time helping me brainstorm the botany aspects of this book—her expertise really made this plot pop. Marcela of http://thebookaholiccat.blogspot.com acted as my Spanish language and Latin American culture virtual assistant, helping me to bring this beautiful setting to life (any Spanish mistakes in the final edition will be mine and not hers). Kisses to my Facebook page gang, and a special shout out to Facebook pals Dena Howard Embree, Debi Murray, Kacy Flowers, Debbie Oxier, Prue Dwyer, Robin Driscoll, and Natalie Bookloverslife for the idea for using Jelly Bellies this past winter! It worked really great, guys!! BookBeautiful perfectly captured the mood of Hugo on this lovely cover, and this amazing formatting job was done by bbebooksthailand.com. Gratitude and kisses to you all!

Also by Carolyn Crane

Romantic Suspense
Against the Dark (Book #1 of the Associates)
Off the Edge (Book #2 of the Associates)
Into the Shadows (Book #3 of the Associates)
Behind the Mask (Book #4 of the Associates)

Urban Fantasy
Mind Games (Book #1 of the Disillusionists)
Double Cross (Book #2 of the Disillusionists)
Kitten-tiger and the Monk, a Disillusionists novella (2.5)
Head Rush (Book #3 of the Disillusionists)
Devil's Luck, a Disillusionists novella (3.5)

~ Thank you for reading the Associates. ~